The *Wedding* Season

Bestselling Australian Author

Ally Blake & Cara Colter

MILLS & BOON

THE WEDDING SEASON © 2022 by Harlequin Books S.A.

THE WEDDING FAVOUR
© 2022 by Ally Blake
Australian Copyright 2022
New Zealand Copyright 2022

First Published 2022
First Australian Paperback Edition 2022
ISBN 978 1 867 25728 8

BAHAMAS ESCAPE WITH THE BEST MAN
© 2022 by Cara Colter
Australian Copyright 2022
New Zealand Copyright 2022

First Published 2022
First Australian Paperback Edition 2022
ISBN 978 1 867 25728 8

Published by
Mills & Boon
An imprint of Harlequin Enterprises (Australia) Pty Limited
(ABN 47 001 180 918), a subsidiary of HarperCollins
Publishers Australia Pty Limited (ABN 36 009 913 517)
Level 13, 201 Elizabeth Street
SYDNEY NSW 2000
AUSTRALIA

Printed and bound in Australia by McPherson's Printing Group

CONTENTS

The Wedding Favour

Ally Blake

Also by Ally Blake

Crazy About Her Impossible Boss
Brooding Rebel to Baby Daddy
Dream Vacation, Surprise Baby
The Millionaire's Melbourne Proposal

Discover more at
millsandboon.com.au.

Australian author **Ally Blake** loves reading and strong coffee, porch swings and dappled sunshine, beautiful notebooks and soft, dark pencils. Her inquisitive, rumbustious, spectacular children are her exquisite delight. And she adores writing love stories so much she'd write them even if nobody read them. No wonder, then, having sold over four million copies of her romance novels worldwide, Ally is living her bliss. Find out more about Ally's books at allyblake.com.

My books are not the books they are without
my wonderful writerly friends: those suppliers of
laughter, bastions of empathy and lighters of creative
fires. This story owes so much to Kali Anthony,
for her boundless love of romance and dazzling
"glitter bomb" lightbulb moment, and to
Amy Andrews for her spit-take-worthy
NSFW insights and invaluable word sprints.
I am so grateful for you both.

PROLOGUE

THE FIRST TIME Emerson Adler's heart broke she was ten years old.

Well, ten years and one day to be exact. Her actual birthday had been wondrous—her dad surprising her, and her mum, for that matter, with a caramel-coloured fluffball in the shape of a cocker spaniel.

The bigger surprise had come the morning after, when her dad had roused her from her sleep before the sun was even up, tweaked her on the nose, called her his favourite girl, and said, "Life ebbs and flows, kiddo. When it feels hard, remember it'll be okay. It always gets better."

Then he'd kissed her hair and walked out the front door. Never to return.

Emerson's mum had coped by turning her naturally cheerful nature up to eleven, starting a mini-orchard in their small back yard as a symbol of "growth", hugging her daughter a hundred times a day, and adoring Pumpkin, the puppy she'd had no say in taking on.

Throwing in the occasional telling words of wisdom of her own, such as, "Take care when falling in love, as things that fall often end up broken." As if quips and dauntless sunshine might make her daughter bomb-proof to the shock she herself had endured.

Unfortunately, as it turned out, that first heart-break had created some kind of crack in the space-time continuum, making young Emerson a conduit for heartache.

So many heartaches that she—like a prisoner scrap-ing tallies in the walls of her cell—had kept count. Of the big ones, especially. The ones that took some-thing from her. That changed the course of her life. Though in lieu of fingernails on concrete she'd used a pen with a pom-pom on the end, and a dedicated notebook with a sparkly cartoon cactus on the cover.

Heartache Number One: ten years old.

Dad left. Obviously.

Heartache Number Two: eleven years old.

Mrs Abernathy, the teacher who gave her extra stars on her homework and seemed to know when her mum was not feeling quite as sunny as usual, had also upped and left! Retired, they said, but how could she be sure?

Heartache Number Three: twelve years old.

Kailey Deluca, best friend, turned up on the first day of high school with a new haircut, new earring holes, new boobs, new clothes…and new friends. Totally awful.

And so the Heartache List had gone on.

That was its name, scrawled in big black bubble writing on the front page, begun in reaction to:

Heartache Number Four: fourteen years old.

A devastating, unrequited high school crush which had soon morphed into a detailed, annotated roadmap penned in a special notebook, ruling and shaping Emerson's decisions in the hopes she might one day figure out how to make sure she never broke her heart again.

And then…

Heartache Number Eight: twenty-five years old.

Her beautiful mum passed away, after a breathlessly quick battle with cancer.

After that there would be no *Heartache Number Nine.* For surely it would be the end of her.

This story starts nearly two decades on from that seminal heartache.

The Heartache List, with its spiky cactus cover and pages filled with detailed ramblings and deeply felt promises, has long since gone.

Emerson no longer has need to keep track of heartbreaks, for hers is a meticulously curated life, vigilant in its setting of boundaries. She enjoys a small crew of trusted friends. Work at Pitch Perfect, her very own bespoke recruitment firm, is immensely satisfying. Her life is no longer fettered by the assumption that it all may be whipped out from under her at any moment.

For she knows that everything comes to an end eventually. Opportunities, employment, favourite restaurants, favourite lipsticks, relationships. The trick, she has discovered, is in the accepting and the moving on.

It is a warm spring day on the glorious Mornington Peninsula of southern Victoria, and a wedding has taken place. The bride, Camille, is Emerson's very best friend in the entire world, and the groom, Phillip, is an utterly lovely guy who would not dare break his bride's heart—due, in no small part, to the fact he'd have Emerson to deal with.

Dusk is settling over the gorgeous reception marquee perched at the edge of a forest a short drive in from the coast. Birds flutter and chatter as they fill the sky, following the last rays of the sun. And the air tastes like the first lick of spring after a long, cool, coastal winter. It brings with it the scent of impending change.

While inside the marquee, Emerson has no clue that her comprehensively fortified heart is about to be put to the ultimate test…

CHAPTER ONE

THE TIDE OF anticipation rippling through the crowd was palpable, voices ascending, glasses clinking, dresses shimmering in the buttery light of a marquee strung with enough fairy lights to bring a plane safely home on a cloudy night.

All the single ladies—along with a handful of convivial and unattached guys—stood in a loose group at the edge of the dance floor, shifting from foot to foot, jostling for position, eyes sharp on the deviously grinning bride who stood alone beneath a spotlight waving her lavish bouquet back and forth like some kind of lure.

Emerson Adler alone remained immune to the collective fervour.

As Maid of Honour, Emerson felt duty-bound to at least *appear* as if she was taking part. Though the bride was hardly what one might call traditional. Emerson's place card read "Best Woman/Sister/Wife" and her dress—as chosen by the bride—was less pastel eighties prom, more backless glittery bronze *va-va-voom* Vegas hostess. The bride was nothing if not extra.

Speaking of the bride… Camille planted her bare feet, backside wiggling dramatically as she readied to make the toss, and the rowdy crowd held its collective breath. Then a *whoop* split the evening air as the bouquet arced high in a tumble of white roses, orchids, moonflowers, and faux pearls.

The group surged up and to the left—like a rugby scrum, only better dressed. While Emerson and her glass of warm bubbly took a deft step to the right.

The bouquet landed atop a shelf of groping hands, then bounced—once, twice—leaving those in the bullseye in an entangled heap on the parquetry floor. Finally, like a whale breaching the surface of a stormy sea, Bernadette, sweet younger cousin to the bride, leapt to her feet, brandishing the bunch as if it were Excalibur.

Congratulations ensued before the competitors moved off to reclaim their partners, their drinks, their chairs. While Emerson sighed in contentment, happy that she'd navigated that whole affair with subtle aplomb.

Or so she thought, till she caught the bride's gaze across the crowded room.

Camille, being Camille, grinned broadly as she waggled a *naughty, naughty* finger Emerson's way, clearly finding Emerson's mini-rebellion hilarious.

Emerson offered a sly shrug, lifted her bubbly in salute, downed the lot in one gulp, placed the empty glass on the tray of a wandering waiter, found a gap in the crowd, and took it.

Camille's bark of laughter was loud enough that it could be heard above the band, who'd just heralded their return to the stage with a clash of cymbals and blurt of a trumpet.

"Dance with me, Emmy!" one of Phillip's groomsmen begged as she slipped by.

Emerson took his hand, spun deftly beneath his arm, and let go, before disappearing into the throng, stopping only when she reached her desired destination—the empty, moody, dimly lit, back corner bar, half hidden behind a screen of stripped willow.

Catching the eye of the bartender, Emerson motioned to the fresh tray of glasses filled with golden bubbles. Chewing on a toothpick and drying wine glasses by hand, he lifted his chin the barest amount in confirmation. Not a chatty one. Perfect.

While the soft strains of moody, forties jazz filled the marquee like smoke, bringing the slow dancers to the floor, Emerson plonked her clutch bag on the bar, leaned her back against warm wood, and took a moment to herself for the first time in what felt like days.

Without busy work keeping her occupied, it wasn't long before she noticed the uncomfortable feeling that had grown in her belly, incrementally, as the day had gone on. Not hunger. She'd had the fish, and the chocolate mousse. More as if her innards were being pickled in something bittersweet. More as if she felt a little...downhearted.

It made no sense, for the wedding had gone off without a hitch, the ceremony whimsical, the after-party decadent and joyful.

So why these…*feelings*?

If the Heartache List had taught her anything, it was that *feelings* were messy and perilous. Far better to keep them squished deep down inside where they might shrivel up and die due to acute lack of oxygen.

And yet, as she watched the crowd on the dance floor part, right as Phillip swept Camille into his arms and twirled her about, before hauling her close and slow dancing as if they were the only people in the room, and her two favourite humans move on to the next stage of their lives in real time, a stage that would no longer include her, Emerson dropped her hand to her belly and the—dare she even think it—*ache* therein.

"Then again," she muttered, "maybe it was the fish."

Shaking off the feeling as best she could, Emerson rolled her shoulders, closed her eyes, and drank deeply, the bubbles biting winningly at the inside of her throat on the way down. She nudged a high heel off one foot, releasing a small sound of relief as she stretched her toes, twirled her ankle and—

"Emmy?"

The voice calling her name, invading her moment of sanctuary, was a masculine one, deep, rumbling, and lit with the expectation of conversation returned. "Emmy Adler? Of East Kew High? Or, more particularly, the cracked hard plastic chairs outside the guidance counsellor's office?"

Emerson took a small breath before twisting to face the interloper now leaning back against the bar beside her.

Used, as she was, in her work as a professional recruiter of human resources to determining first impressions in a blink, Emerson took mental bullet points: tall, great hair, hell of a jawline, beautiful suit, exceptional tailoring required to contain those mighty shoulders, slow smile tugging at the corners of a wide mouth, rather lovely crinkles at the edges of a pair of magnetic eyes the colour of a coming storm—

All too late a skitter of warning thundered its way down Emerson's back, knocking against the bumps in her spine like a pinball.

The jaw, the shoulders, the stormy eyes, the *cracked hard plastic chairs outside the guidance counsellor's office*—they belonged to none other than Holden Roarke.

Aka *Heartache Number Four.*

Emerson's eyes skewed to the dance floor, seeking Camille—the very person who had bought the sparkly cactus notebook in which the Heartache List had been etched, right after the guy now standing beside her had broken Emmy's teenaged heart.

Holden's voice cut through the fog. "It is Emmy Adler, right? If not, then the words echoing disastrously inside my head must sound like the most dubious line."

Realising that, bar bolting for the exit, there was no

way out of this moment but through, Emerson forced a neutral smile onto her face, then held out a hand, as if this was all cool and normal.

"Holden Roarke," she said, her voice admirably even. "Yes, it is me. Though I go by Emerson. Mostly."

"Emerson," he said, smiling into her eyes, her name sounding like an endearment in that low, slow, velvety dark voice. "Mostly."

Then he took her hand in his. Encompassing, cool, good pressure, she'd have given him a big tick next to the "handshake" box if she was taking him on as a client. Though the shimmer of warmth that shot up her arm as he held her hand was overkill.

But he was not a prospective client. He was a guy who had, at one time, made her cry into her unicorn pillowcase simply because he existed.

Emerson let go first, her hand springing back as a zing sparked from his hand to hers. A zing that seemed to spark in his eyes as well. Though that was more likely from the fairy lights. There really were a lot of them.

Wishing she'd waited a minute before mainlining a glass of champagne, Emerson pushed her near empty glass across the bar.

The bartender, finding within himself a sudden burst of helpfulness, slid a full one her way.

"How long *has* it been?" Holden crooned. Well, he didn't croon exactly, but he had the kind of voice—all warm and deep—that, when combined with the acoustics in their little alcove, made it sound just so.

When Emerson blinked, rather more slowly than was natural, the bartender coughed, his eyebrow flickering, a knowing smile growing around his toothpick.

Emerson narrowed her eyes meaningfully at the guy, then turned her back on him to shoot Holden a quick, bland glance. "How long? Aeons, at least."

"That long?" Holden asked. "And there I was, thinking it had only been ages."

Unfortunately, Emerson's quick glance had somehow stuck, meaning she was forced to bear the full brunt of those stormy blue eyes crinkling in that very particular, effortlessly charming, entirely discombobulating way that had put her under his spell all those years ago.

Aeons. Ages. Once upon a time, when she'd been a dreamy young thing, desperate for some guy to see her oodles of wondrous potential.

Emerson grabbed herself by the metaphorical collar and yanked herself back to the present, only to nearly topple sideways, having forgotten she was wearing only one shoe.

Stomach swooping, she white-knuckled the bar behind her and glanced down at the floor to find no sign of her own missing heel, only a gleaming, Holden-Roarke-sized shoe cocked roguishly out in front.

"Having a good time?" Holden said, his shoe kicking back further, so that the toes faced the ceiling.

"Of course," she said through gritted teeth as she swept her bare toes behind her.

"Big fan of weddings?"

"A fan of *this* wedding," she managed as she sank a little lower, her toes searching a little farther.

"Mmm. I'd put good money behind the bet you have no plans to star in one of your own anytime soon."

Now manically searching for her shoe so she could extricate herself as quickly as possible, Emerson muttered, "Now, *that's* a dubious line."

After a beat, Holden burst into laughter, the sound deeply relaxed and entirely unselfconscious. "I wouldn't dare. If I *did* dare, I'd hope I had better material."

Emerson's foot stopped mid-search as she realised what she'd just intimated.

Of course, it hadn't been a line. Even at sixteen he'd smiled with ease, made eye contact and held it, listened when people spoke. At fourteen she'd mistaken it to mean something other than what it was, and had been proven mortifyingly wrong.

She would not be making that same mistake twice.

"I'd hope so too," she said, holding eye contact to show just how undaunted she was. "Or you'd be the kind of guy who'd follow up with a little, *Hey, aren't you the Maid of* Dis*honour?*"

Holden's smile was broad. And when he turned his body towards her he blocked some of the light. "Then I'd come at you with a little side-eye and a dare—fifty points for a kiss with a stranger in the cloakroom, a hundred for landing the bride's garter, twenty-five points for getting Aunty Verna sloshed."

"Poor Aunty Verna. Seems a tad low."

"Turns out it's not that hard."

His smile grew, yet again, and she felt her mouth kick into a quick smile of its own, despite itself. Damn those eyes, with their lovely crinkles. And zillion lashes. How could she have forgotten about all those lashes?

"How many points for making a bridesmaid blush?"

Emerson blinked her eyes back into focus as she felt heat creep into her cheeks. "Now, that's definitely a line."

This time when his smile flashed, she glimpsed canines. "Not at all. A purely academic exercise, as we stand here together, a part of the festivities and yet not. Outliers in arms."

Before Emerson could unpack all that, the bartender piped up with, "If blush is a euphemism for what I think it is, two hundred and fifty points, at the very least."

As one, Emerson and Holden turned to face the bar.

Emerson asked, "That much?"

"I've done a lot of weddings. And a lot of bridesmaids." With that the bartender moseyed off to serve someone at the other end of the bar.

"That, ladies and gentlemen, is a line," said Holden.

"And from such an unexpected source." Out of the corner of her eye, Emerson saw Holden slowly lift a fist, knuckles out. What choice did she have but to bump it back?

A waiter came by, grabbed the tray of bubbly from behind the bar, readying to swish it out into the crowd. It took half a millisecond for Emerson to decide to nab another glass. For her shoe had obviously disappeared into some alternate dimension and she'd just fist-bumped Holden Roarke. Bubbly seemed the only sane choice.

"I've been thinking," said Holden, looking back out into the crowd. "If I was a line guy, you'd know it."

"Would I, now?"

"I wouldn't throw them out there without a care. I'd take my time. Curate them, incessantly. Until I had a small but specific set. Instant classics. World class. Legendary."

He's more playful than I remember, she thought. What she said was, "Settle down, Casanova, I get it. If you *had* taken it upon yourself to hit on me, I might never have recovered."

Her eyes were on his when he smiled—a slow, deliberate lift of the corners of his mouth. A wave of heat swept from her cheeks to her toes.

"What are you doing here, Holden?"

He blinked. "At this very moment? Having an unexpectedly delightful exchange with an old acquaintance. You?"

Emerson didn't let the sudden rough edge to his voice distract her. "I know the guest list back to front and you're not on it."

"Open yourself up to the universe and the universe provides, don't you find?"

Emerson coughed out a laugh. For no, she did not *find*.

Holden leaned in, as if about to bestow upon her

a secret, and she caught his scent—freshly cut grass, bubbling brook, warm male skin.

"My earlier quip, such as it was," he said, "was in reference to the fact I've never seen anyone less interested in a bouquet toss."

Emerson followed the lift of his glass, to see the bouquet in question now waving its way through the crowd, a snake of conga dancers falling in behind.

Oh. Her spare hand moved to her neck. "Was I that obvious?"

"Not at all," he said, gathering his glass back towards the snowy white shirt straining against acres of broad chest. "You were the very picture of discretion. I just happen to have a keen eye for understated insurrection. I'm a bit of an expert, you see. Years of experience given to the cause. It's not often I spot a kindred spirit, then there you were."

There she was. Holden Roarke's kindred spirit. It was all she could do not to burst into laughter.

Holden's eyebrow lifted, slowly, in question. As if it was her turn to say something.

"Yes," she said, her voice a little breathless. "I mean no. It's not my thing. Not even in my top hundred."

"Fighting over a used bunch of flowers?" A pause to give her an extra centimetre of smile. "Or marriage?"

"Both," she shot back.

"And not a moment's hesitation," he said, his voice tinged with awe.

She shrugged, unapologetically.

Holden Roarke's stormy blue gaze followed the

move, landing on her bare shoulder for a beat, before moving to the shift of a dangly diamante earring against her cheek, then sweeping back to her eyes with such a rush, Emerson felt herself sway. And it all happened in a single heartbeat.

It was all too bizarre, standing like a flamingo, under a starfield of romantic fairy lights, with *Zoot Suit Riot* blasting in the background, as she talked marriage with the man who had dashed her teenaged heart into a thousand tiny little pieces.

"Now, what do we have here?" Mr Heartache murmured, placing his drink on the bar before dropping to an easy crouch, reaching under the closest barstool and coming up with her shoe. Just like that.

His gaze dropped to her feet—well, one foot, for the other was tucked away inside the matching four-inch heel. "Yours, I presume?"

At which point Holden Roarke dropped a knee, and held out a hand.

Emerson blinked, the ridiculousness factor having just turned up to eleven. Enough that she actually gave her arm a quick pinch.

Wobbling on her one heel, Emerson snapped her fingers at Holden. "Up. Up, up, up. I can do it myself."

"I have no doubt," he said, his gaze stuck on hers. "Yet here I am, shoe in hand, knee in the dust, willing and able to do you this small favour."

That voice of his—deep, unhurried, and laced with

humour—wound around some delicate, unprotected part of herself she was too flummoxed to keep locked down.

A small favour. Over in a jiffy.

"Fine."

Taking great pains not to feel like freaking Cinderella, Emerson looked away as he slid his hand along the soft, sensitive underpart of her foot, leaving prickles and shimmers in his wake, before his long, strong fingers moved to curl around her ankle. At which point the prickles and shimmers rushed up her calf, the back of her thigh, higher, as if connected directly to nerves, muscles, tendons, the very marrow of her bones.

Five hundred points, she thought, *at the very least, for making a Maid of Honour blush. No euphemism required.*

Then it was over before it began, with Holden shucking the heel neatly into place and gently lowering her foot to the ground. Entirely G-rated. No lingering touches, or signs of fetishism. Just a guy helping a girl he'd once known, out of a jam.

Though when Holden stood, sweeping to his feet with a whoosh, dragging a hand through his hair leaving thick, dark tracks in its wake, he had noticeably more colour in his cheeks. Was it possible the prickles and shimmers weren't hers alone?

Emerson shook her head. She'd lived half her life since Holden Roarke had broken her heart. Had survived several shiny new heartbreaks since. Those collective experiences building up the phenomenal resistance she had today. Yet, standing here beside him, it was if she'd learned nothing at all.

Now that she had both shoes on, it was time to vamoose. "Look, this has been—"

Emerson cut herself off when Holden spun dramatically to face the bar, his fingers tightening on the wood, as if he was thinking about leaping over the thing.

Intrigued, despite herself, she asked, "What's happening right now?"

Holden's jaw twitched. "Did she see me?"

"Did who—?"

A high-pitched voice called from the crowd, "Holden!"

Emerson followed the sound to find Bernadette, bouquet gripped in her hand as she battled her way through the dense crowd now dancing to a wild, fast, jazz rendition of *Dancing Queen*.

"Holden! Where are you?"

"Ah. So that's how you got in. You're here with Bernadette," said Emerson, mad at herself for the sting that brought on.

He shook his head. "We met half an hour ago when she tried to slip her room key into the pocket of my suit pants."

Emerson coughed on her surprise. "Front pocket or back?"

Holden's mouth twitched before he turned her way, his voice low, and intimate, as he asked, "Why? Is one worth more points than the other?"

"Goes without saying. But, actually, don't tell me. I've known Bernie since she was eight." A thought. "Do you still have it? The key?"

"No, I don't have the *key*. I tactfully declined." He sounded abashed. Which was unexpectedly…adorable.

And finally, for the first time since he'd ambled up to her and said her name, she felt the dynamic shift. This she preferred, by far. "I'm not sure you were as clear as you imagine you were. In fact, it seems congratulations might be in order."

Frowning, Holden leaned in a little closer in order to pick up her voice, his upper arm making contact with hers.

"She won the bouquet," she said, eyes flicking between his. Meaning she caught the moment his hunted look dissipated and a glint took its place.

Their arms still touching, Emerson could feel the man's body heat. The rise and fall of his breaths. Their faces were close enough she could make out the swirls of blue and gusts of grey around his deep, dark pupils. Count those glorious lashes, including the one that had fallen to his cheek.

She would *not* lift her hand to sweep that lash away. *She would not.*

Her voice was a little husky as she said, "Don't think, just because I am not into the bouquet-toss-winner-is-next-to-marry thing, you can't be all for it. Truly. More power to you."

Slowly, as if time stretched, Holden's eyes seemed to narrow, even as the eye crinkles returned, deepening deliciously. Till his expression turned wolfish. And very, very grown-up. "Emerson."

"Mm-hmm?"

"You know that small favour I did for you, not too many moments ago?"

"Favour?"

"Helping you with your errant shoe. I'd be hugely grateful if you'd allow me to ask for one in return."

Emerson felt, with every fibre of her being, that she ought to say no. To give him a light, chummy punch on the arm, wish him luck, then go on about her Maid of Honour duties for the rest of the night.

But his words, simple and respectful, hooked her, like a claw in a buttonhole.

"What do you need?"

The man grinned—the move so bright, so joyful, she felt it in the backs of her knees. Then he turned, lifted his arm over her head, and placed it behind her along the bar, so that she found herself tucked against his big, warm, hard body, wondering how the heck she'd ended up there.

Bernadette's big doe eyes lit up as she spotted Emerson, before she slipped through a gap in the crowd and was upon them. "Emmy!"

"Emmy?" Holden murmured.

"She gets to call me whatever she wants. She's special."

"There you are!" said Bernadette.

"How you going, Bernie?" Emerson asked.

"I'm wonderful. Such a gorgeous wedding! And

you look amazing. That dress! *Phwoar.*" Only then did Bernie seem to spot Holden. "Oh, hi! I was looking for you! And there you are too!"

"Here I am too," he said.

Then he shifted, just a fraction. Enough that Emerson felt surrounded by the guy. On all sides. Trapped in a haze of his scent, his warmth, his shelter.

For all that he presented as relaxed, it was suddenly all too clear that it was an act. Calculated misdirection. An ocean of energy pulsed through him, deep, rich, barely contained. Ready for anything.

"Look!" said Bernadette, oblivious, holding out the bouquet and waving it under Holden's nose as if it might put him in her thrall. "I won!"

"We saw. Hell of a leap you have."

On the "we" he lifted the arm he'd positioned behind Emerson, his fingers curling around her elbow on her far side. So aware of him was she, Emerson had been waiting for it. Her body primed for his touch before he'd even moved.

Which was when she heard the alarm bells go off deep inside her, echoing, as if they'd been ringing for some time but she'd only just begun to notice.

Bernadette pointed the bouquet towards Emerson, nearly poking her in the eye with a rose. "Hey, do you know Emmy?"

Holden's hand slid up Emerson's arm to find her shoulder, then the back of her neck. There, his thumb shifted back and forth over the small covered button holding the halter neck of her dress in place as he said, "*Emmy* and I go way back."

Emerson nudged an elbow into his side, his wince evidence she'd hit the mark.

Bernadette's eyes grew wide and she said, "Now it all makes sense." After which she gave Emerson a big, slow almost-wink, then she spun on her heel, gaze dancing over the crowd as she called, "Barry! Barry!"

And then she was gone, the air around them fluttering back to normal, like leaves in the wake of a whirlwind.

"Barry?" Holden asked, removing his hand from the back of her neck, the hairs there lifting, as if reaching for his touch.

"One of Phillip's hundred-odd groomsmen," she said. Then, "A hundred and fifty points, at least." She felt Holden's grin even though they were both still facing the crowd.

"Far more cache than a mere guest," he added, his voice a low burr.

"Oodles."

"So we actually did *her* a favour."

"Gosh, I hope so. If she remembers even half of it, she's going to be mortified."

"No need. Only way to find out if someone you like likes you back is to be a little brave."

Unable to help herself, Emerson glanced at Holden's face, expecting a glint of humour. But his expression, as he looked into her eyes, was keen. Direct. It nudged against some soft, unprotected part of her.

Then the music changed. Slowed. A sigh coming over the crowd as the opening strains of *The Way You Look Tonight* began to fill the space. A spotlight hit a disco ball, which sent shards of warm light scattering over them both.

Feeling warm and a little light in the head, for one moment, a single breath, Emerson opened herself up to it. To the full force of him. To see if, after all this time, she could.

Time seemed to stretch, the sound of the band muffled, and everything at the edges of her vision became a blur. Her breath turned a little slow and viscous, her skin tingly and tight. She may have even felt herself sway towards him, just a smidge.

Turned out, despite excellent inroads into self-actualisation since she'd moved on from the Heartache List, testing it was a form of sadomasochism.

Emerson pulled herself back from the brink, just, and asked, "How did you end up here, Holden?"

He watched her for a few long, drawn-out moments, before a smile tugged at the corners of his eyes. "Ours is not to reason why, young Emerson. Ours is but to enjoy what is, in fact, a damn fine band, pretty good plonk, and excellent company, all on someone else's dime."

Her dad's voice suddenly floated up out of the deepest recesses of her memory. *Loosen up, little one, so you don't snap. It'll be okay.* He would say *It'll be okay* quite a bit, her dad. As if that might make up for any number of disappointments.

Funny that she'd thought of him now, while talking to someone else on her Heartache List. Funny ironic? Or funny cautionary?

Before she could decide, Holden took a distinct step away from the bar. "I've been keeping you. I'm sure, as Maid of Dishonour, you have many duties."

"Many," she agreed, breathing out hard. "Lots. A plethora."

A crease, like a super-dimple, formed at one corner of his mouth, heaven help her.

"It was really good to see you again, Emerson." He nodded, as if surprised by the truth of his own words. "Now I must be off, perhaps even to indulge in my newfound respect for a good pick-up line."

"Or perhaps not," she offered.

He touched the side of his nose in agreement, before dipping an invisible cap, and ambling back out into the fray.

Mere seconds later, Camille burst through the edge of the crowd. So much for finding a quiet corner.

Camille held up her middle finger. "I broke a nail. Help me before I snag."

"On it." Very glad to have a purpose, a distraction, Emerson found an emery board in her clutch bag, then grabbed Camille's outstretched hand and buffed away the ragged corner.

"Whoa. Slow down, honeybun! Everything okay?"

Emerson eased back before she buffed the nail clean away. "Did you know Holden Roarke was here?"

Camille's eyes popped. "What's that, now?"

Emerson waved a hand at the crowd. "Holden Roarke—aka *Heartache Number Four*—is out there. Right now." Possibly trying out dubious lines on unexpecting—and unresisting—guests.

Camille growled, "Phillip."

"Phillip?" Emerson asked.

Camille took her hand back and nibbled on the nail. "Okay, so Phillip banged into the guy a couple of weeks back at some ex-uni networking thing where Holden was the guest speaker. Turns out they went to uni together for a tiny bit before Holden dropped out. Did you know that? That he dropped out? No, unlike the rest of us you don't keep tabs on those who did you wrong. Anyway, apparently he's some app design genius—infamously retired in his early twenties when he sold his first app for zillions, so I guess it's more like he 'dropped up' than 'out'. Everyone at the networking thing was drooling over him from a distance, while Phillip being Phillip walked up and said, 'I'm getting hitched, you should come!' Thankfully—for Phillip's sake—Holden politely refused, so I figured it best to leave it at that rather than stir everything up for you unnecessarily. I had no idea he'd actually come!"

Emerson puffed out a don't-worry-about-it breath, surprised to find her lips were slightly numb. After nursing one glass of champagne all evening, she'd somehow gone through a few in a short burst.

Camille's eyes narrowed as she peered out into the crowd. "I've done enough bride stuff today. I'm now on keep-Holden-Roarke-away-from-my-beloved-Emerson duty."

"We already spoke. And it was fine. I'm a big girl. I handled it."

Camille's eyes skewed back to Emerson's. "Of course you did. You're a brilliant, mature, magical unicorn." Then, "So, what was he like? Smarmy? Flirty? A douche? Ground down by the weight of the world? Still a total hunk, or has the middle-aged spread hit early? Often does with the big guys."

Emerson let go of a sigh before she even felt it coming.

"Really?" Camille said, drawing out the word. "That good, huh? Hey, remember that time I thought I saw Kailey Deluca at a shopping mall, two tiny, screaming children clinging to her knee-high Ugg boots?"

Kailey Deluca, aka *Heartache Number Three*, aka Emerson's best friend in primary school, who'd dumped her on day one of high school.

"If she hadn't turned weird we'd never have found one another, and would not be standing here, together, right now." Camille's hand slid through the crook of Emerson's arm and they leaned towards one another, skulls gently knocking. "Thank you for being my best woman. No one else could possibly have fitted that title. Much less that dress."

Emerson glanced down at her slinky sparkles. "It is quite a dress."

Camille grinned. "Has it worked?"

"In what way?"

"Did you not wonder why I allowed you to look hotter than me on my wedding day? I was hoping some dashing friend of Phillip's would man up and sweep you off your feet, then you'd fall in love and be as deliriously happy as I am. Then we could buy houses side by side and have babies together..." She stopped to take a breath. "Was that too much to ask?"

It seemed Emerson wasn't the only one sensing change in the air. Her heart squeezed—not an ache, but it was close.

She held Camille's face between her hands and gave the cheeks a wiggle. "The night is still young; who knows what it might yet bring? Now, is this a party or is this a party?"

"It's a party!"

With that Emerson downed the last drops of her third—or was it fourth?—bubbly, grabbed Camille by the hand, and together they boogied out onto the dance floor.

Where the rest of the night slid by in a beautiful, ache-free blur.

CHAPTER TWO

Holden's gaze glanced off the minutiae of a wedding done and dusted, cake stand empty bar a few stray crumbs, tablecloths no longer centred, centrepieces pilfered by light-fingered guests.

He righted a chair that had fallen to the ground, as Barry—the groomsman young Bernadette had taken a belated shine to—came out of nowhere to slap Holden on the back for the umpteenth time of the night.

"Last man standing!" said Barry. Then, "It was really good to meet you, mate. Don't be a stranger." When Barry looked ready to move in for what looked to be a teary hug, the remaining groomsmen descended, midway through the umpteenth rendition of *Sweet Caroline* of the night, and dragged Barry out of the marquee's gently flapping exit.

And all was quiet once more.

The noise and light had done an admirable job of drowning out Holden's thoughts, but the moment they could they returned with a flourish, unhappy memories, unprocessed regrets...all of them wrapped up in this damn city.

He had meant it when he'd declined Phillip's generous invitation, for he was back in the country for a limited time and a specific purpose and had every intention of getting the hell out of Dodge the moment he was done. Then the weekend had whipped around, and with it hours of dead time looming before him.

An hour-and-a-half drive to Sorrento—late enough to miss the ceremony, early enough to fill the evening with the perpetual blur of cheerful company, innocuous conversation, blunting distraction—had seemed just the ticket.

It had delivered. Not two minutes had passed all night long without him finding himself cornered.

You're that app guy, right? Heard about you. Are you really retired?

Ostensibly.

As good as it sounds?

People were usually happy with a quick, *Yes*. They didn't want to hear that dreams of sitting on a beach for the rest of time lost their lustre faster than expected. That sitting still in any place for too long made that place feel like any other.

Or perhaps that was just him. The chase the thing that drove him, rather than the spoils.

So-and-So said you live in Sweden/San Francisco/Singapore. Or are you home for good? Some new opportunity we could get in on?

A sage smile, some linguistic prevarication, and flipping the questions their way was the fastest route out of that rabbit hole.

At least the chatter had ably filled the time.

Till the bouquet toss. More specifically, the woman glinting darkly at the edge of the group, blithely refusing to partake.

While everyone else shifted and shuffled, she'd seemed so unruffled. Above it all. No, not *above*. Extrinsic. Enjoying their enjoyment, but not a part of it. As if—despite that dress with its gravity-defying architecture, and magical fabric sparking light in a thousand directions, despite her loveliness even beyond the bewitching dress—she believed herself unseen.

Something had uncoiled inside him then, some flicker of recognition, as she watched the world as if from the other side of the looking glass.

He'd had no intention of approaching her, his plan being to take the path of least resistance. Then someone had called out "Dance with me, Emmy!" as she'd stalked past.

Swap the glossy waves for wild curls, and the tiny bag clutched in her hand for a unicorn backpack, and it was Emmy Adler—his one-time hallway buddy.

How could he not say *hello*? And then, after finding her unexpectedly crisp and zesty, like that first hit of lime in a glass of iced water, how could he not stay? For, surely, she would be the most perfect distraction of all.

A chatter of voices broke into Holden's reverie as the clean-up crew bustled through the marquee entrance hauling trolleys of supplies and packing crates. He lifted a hand to intimate he'd move out of their way.

A glance at his watch showed it was a minute before midnight, and he had a long drive ahead.

Picking his way around the detritus, he made it to the exit when he heard a commotion. He turned to find Emmy, an open magnum of bubbly in one hand, the heels of her shoes dangling from the other, her clutch bag under her chin as she bore down on the cleaners.

"Let me help," she insisted. "Do you have spare gloves?"

A murmur from one of the cleaners was followed by, "I know. Such a great wedding. Though bitter-sweet, you know?"

The cleaner nodded, while also clearly looking for a way out.

Holden worked his way around the maze of tables and chairs. Long drive or no, he wasn't going anywhere till he knew she was okay.

"My very best friend in the whole wide world," Emmy continued, her voice lifting. "My sister by choice if not by blood, just stepped onto a conveyor belt that runs perpendicular to my own."

When she pointed off into the distance her bag dropped to the ground, and she sank to pick it up. The cleaner saw his chance and bolted.

"I didn't expect this. Not today," Emmy muttered from her crouch. Then she lifted her hand—the one holding her shoes, not her bubbly—to her heart. "The ache, right here. I thought I was done with all that. That the List had made me immune."

"The list?" Holden asked.

Emmy looked up, her eyes wide, her mouth a comical "O". Her voice was a stage whisper as she said, "Holden Roarke. There you are again. And how on earth do *you* know about the List?"

Holden held out a hand. She offered up the near empty bottle for him to use as leverage to get her back to her feet.

"You're taller than you used to be," she said, punctuating her accusation with a slow blink of those big bright eyes of hers, a rare, mossy green, fringed by insanely long lashes and tinged with mistrust.

Holden bit his lip to stop himself from laughing. "Only because this time you're completely barefoot. Now, what's this about a list?"

She waved her shoes towards him, nearly blinding him with a heel. "You can't use it against me, if that's your nefarious plan."

Holden held out both hands in surrender. "I have no plans, nefarious, dubious, or otherwise."

"Good. All that matters is that, while my heart might feel a little squidgy right now, I will survive this. The List taught me that. Where is everyone?" She looked around.

"We're it. Camille and Phillip left some time ago."

"Yes, they did." Emmy lifted her bottle in salute, only to find it was empty. She slowly placed it on a table by her side, the way she unwound her fingers from the neck almost ceremonial.

Then she took a step sideways, teetering so that Holden reached out to cup her elbow, to steady her. Soft, smudged, and slanted, she looked up at him.

"Gosh you smell good," she said, breathing deep. Then, "Camille made me wear this dress. So we could have babies together. Then *you* turn up smelling like fresh cut grass. It really isn't fair, considering my insides already feel like a soufflé on the verge of collapse."

Holden tried to keep up, he really did, but it was a lot, what with her leaning against him, smelling rather lovely herself. *Citrus,* he thought, *citrus, and some wholly female concoction she wore on her skin. Or maybe it was her skin. All on its own.*

"Apologies?" he murmured.

"For what?"

"I have no idea." Holden took the opportunity to lean back, so that he might breathe air not filled with her. "While your current lack of a filter is extremely enjoyable, I think the clean-up crew would love to see the back of us. Come on, let's get you home safe. Unless…"

Holden looked around to see if there were any other stray guests. "Unless you came with someone?" He wasn't entirely surprised to find discomfort in that notion.

"Are you kidding? I get a thousand trillion points for *not* bringing a plus one."

"Because…"

"Bringing a *date* to a *wedding* is as indefensible as actively going for the bouquet."

"I hear that," he said. But only because it made getting the heck out of there easier. "Shall we?"

"Shall we what?" she asked, her hazy gaze dropping to his mouth before lifting to his eyes. And his discomfort became…creative and focused.

"Shall we…blow this joint?"

The haze cleared, pushed aside by indignation. The woman was a veritable pot luck of reactions and it was mighty entertaining.

"I'm not 'blowing' anything with you, Holden Roarke," she said, using liberal air quotes. "Or doing you any more 'favours' for that matter. I mean, the guy shrugs his big, manly shoulders, and flashes his fetching eye crinkles, and thinks he can get away with anything."

"Can't believe I'm about to say this… Fetching eye crinkles?"

Emmy blinked.

Holden smiled. "Take care you don't reveal your secret crush. Or your banking password—"

"Kevin Costner," she shot back.

"Crush, or password?"

She ignored him, her pupils growing dense, her expression dreamy. "*Field of Dreams. Bull Durham. Hidden Figures.* Sigh… How about you, Holden Roarke? Ever had a secret crush?"

When her eyes moved back to his they were so dark,

so deep, he felt the ground beneath his feet shift. Just a smidge.

"Crush, sure. Secret, no. Now, Emerson Adler, do you call everyone by both names, or should I feel special?"

Emmy shot him a look.

"Special," he muttered. "Well, that's nice, then. I'm still not giving you my passwords, so don't ask."

Her indignation cracked and she glimmered. There was no other word for it. Her eyes filled with light, and that dress—all those bronze sparkles wrapped about her as if she'd been sewn into the thing—reflected any and all atmospheric light that remained in the semi-darkness.

Holden breathed in. Emmy breathed out. And the night seemed to spin out around them.

Till Holden remembered himself, held out an arm, and gently shepherded her towards the exit.

Stepping over linen napkins, bruised flowers, a dropped fork, they made their way outside, where the forest was dark, the trees tall. And up above, the stars twinkled like sugar spilled across a black velvet rug.

Emmy stopped, looked up, rubbing her bare arms as a breeze swept off the nearby bay. "Don't move," she said, shifting a little closer. "You're warm. Like you have your own personal furnace."

Holden didn't move a muscle.

"I understand why people see stars as pretty," she said, "but they've always felt more poignant to me."

"And why's that?" he asked, tucking his hands into the pockets of his suit as he looked up at the night sky. "I can never tell if they are happy or sad."

"I find the most beautiful things are often both."

After a few quiet moments he glanced down to find her eyes were on him. They were huge, sparkling in the starlight. A curl of dark hair dangled beside one eye. And when she smiled, she appeared completely lucid. "Holden Roarke, aren't you a surprise and a half?"

Right back at you.

Then she frowned, and shook, as if the cold night air had snapped her decision-making faculties back online. "I think it's time to go."

Holden couldn't agree more. "Where are you staying?"

"The Bay Inn with everyone else," she said, pulling her room key out of her bag. "Don't panic. I'm not about to stuff it into your pocket."

The edge of his mouth flickered. "I appreciate it. Come on, I'll drop you off before I head home."

"You're not at the inn?"

"Coming tonight was a…last-minute decision."

Funny. If she'd asked him why, with the forest shifting gently around them, and all that starlight pouring into her big, dark, attentive eyes, he might even have told her.

Instead, her eyes squeezed shut as she let go of the world's biggest yawn. Then she slipped on her shoes, one at a time, and went delving into her tiny bag for her phone as she said, "Thank you, I will accept a lift to my hotel. Though, since I do barely know you, I will send Camille a message to let her know you have me. That sounded wrong. That you're taking me— Nope. That's not right either."

Holden huffed out a ragged laugh.

"Just come here." Emmy grabbed him by the arm and hauled him close. Her cheek hovering near his own, she held up her phone. She frowned so hard he grinned, right as she touched the screen.

While she tapped at her phone, Holden ushered her to his rental sedan. Once he had her settled in the front seat, her eyes drifted closed. As if she was unable to hold them open a single second longer. As if—despite her protestations—she knew him enough to trust he'd do right by her. Which brought on a rush of affection he hadn't seen coming.

Keying the Bay Inn into his GPS, Holden took off down the coast road. Soon the gentle growl of the engine and the repetitive flash of the cat's eyes set the pace for his flickering thoughts.

Dazzling fairy lights above. The hum of the sound system at his back. Emmy, exquisitely still, at the edge of the bouquet toss. That moment, right when he'd started to enjoy her rebellion, for its own sake, when she'd turned, a slow, sensuous, bolshie upward tilt of her lips as she'd lifted her glass in salute to the laughing bride, before disappearing into the crowd.

That moment he'd found himself stuck. Literally

unable to move. Till she'd swept by him. And someone had called her name.

Slowing as the road curved with the coastline, Holden spared a glance sideways. Head tipped towards the glass, her face in the reflection of the window was soft with sleep. The moonlight shimmered over the coppery sparkles on Emmy's dress. Her hands—nails short and painted almost black—lightly clutched her bag, as if even in sleep she was on guard.

Who was this woman? Spectral and defiant as she had been on the dance floor? Wary and witty as she'd been in the bar? Or delightfully candid as she was at the end of what must have been a very long, very emotional day?

Not that he'd get the chance to find out. For he'd drop her at her hotel, drive back to his apartment in the city, attend the event he'd come home to attend, then get on a plane and end up someplace far, far away from here.

CHAPTER THREE

EMERSON SLUNK INTO work early Monday morning.

She'd made it home from the peninsula around lunchtime the day before, only to be met with a load of washing still in the machine, a note under her door from a grumpy neighbour about her mum's lemon tree dropping lemons over the fence, and a "gift" from Pumpkin on the kitchen floor.

Her planned recovery day on the couch listening to true crime podcasts had not eventuated. And it showed.

Strong takeaway coffee in hand, Pumpkin plodding sweetly beside her, the entire place quiet and empty that early in the morning, she—

"Happy Monday, Emerson!"

Emerson flinched and came to a halt, as Freya, her enthusiastic and highly dedicated assistant, appeared out of nowhere looking perky and fresh and wide awake. Pumpkin plonked his backside on the floor with a huff.

Freya crouched to give Pumpkin a little treat from the bag she kept on her person for the days he came into the office, then popped back up like a Jack in the box. Her eyes widened as she said, "Did you know you're still wearing your sunglasses?"

Emerson hitched her handbag on her elbow, the move making her brain hurt, and slowly lifted her hand to her face to find, yes, her Jackie O sunglasses were still perched on the end of her nose.

The thing she'd loved most about the top-floor warehouse conversion for which Pitch Perfect had been paying eye-watering rent for the past couple of years, was the light. The double-storey outer walls were mostly window—lots of tiny panels, ancient and all but impossible to clean—and the soaring ceilings boasted big, new, storm-resistant skylights.

She braced herself before sliding her sunglasses free.

"Whoa," Freya intoned. "You look wrecked. Big weekend?"

Emerson coughed out a laugh, a gentle one that didn't shake her skull too much. Yes, Freya was a natural wonder when it came to keeping Emerson's intricate schedule balanced, but she was also as blunt as a well-used pencil.

"Camille's wedding," Emerson reminded Freya.

"Of course! Saw pics on Insta. Looked amazing."

Freya, talking through the day's schedule, took Pumpkin's lead and gave it a gentle tug, then led the way past the currently uninhabited open-plan desks of the rest of the staff, towards Emerson's office at the very rear of the space.

Leaving Emerson an extra hand to check her email on her phone, only to find her photo gallery open. More precisely, a selfie of her and Holden. Her likeness was frowning, eye make-up smudged, expression bolshie. While she'd caught Holden at the apex of an utterly heartache-inducing smile.

She'd never ended up sending it to Camille, hardly the kind of thing she needed to worry about on her wedding night, but she'd kept it all the same.

"Who's *he*?" said Freya.

Emerson slapped her phone to her chest and gave her assistant a look.

Freya backed up an inch. "Sorry."

"No, you're not."

Freya shot Emerson a grin. "You're right. I'm not. Come on, spill. Who's the guy?"

"He's nobody." Emerson gave her screen a deliberate swipe, before tossing her phone into her bag. "Can you eke me out a little time this morning?"

"Of course," said Freya, hooking the lead over her elbow, lifting her tablet, and hovering her finger over the keyboard. Assistant Extraordinaire Mode: Activated.

"No calls till…ten. I have some work—" aka mainlining coffee and napping with her eyes open "—to catch up on."

"Done." Freya tapped the note into her calendar, before passing the lead to Emerson and angling her way to her own floating desk outside the smoky glass wall of Emerson's office.

Emerson took the opportunity to close her glass door with a soft snick. The moment she was one with her office she breathed easier. With its delicately canted rear wall, aesthetic of cream furnishings, pale wood and caramel leather accents, its aseptic beauty was like a splash of cold water to the face. In the best way.

She picked Pumpkin up, so that he didn't have to navigate the gargantuan rug covering the pale wood floor, and popped him into his bed under her desk. Then sat in the chair behind her desk, kicked off her heels, and let her face sink into her hands.

With half an ear she heard her teams starting to arrive. The Temp Team chatting about their weekends, while readying to shore up employment contracts for the regulars who kept the business ticking over. While the Head Hunters made Monday morning plans to land a whale—the kind of client who could pay someone's yearly salary with one perfect placement.

After filling a spate of high-end corporate positions in the past few months, Pitch Perfect was generating some real buzz. Another one or two and Emerson could relax for a stretch. Or maybe even put in place the expansion dreams she harboured.

That was usually where her mind went, and stayed, when she daydreamed. But that morning her mind kept turning to the wedding.

Phillip attempting to do the dolphin and doing himself a damage instead, the kind that would not have helped his wedding night. Bernadette showing the bouquet to many a wide-eyed male guest. Camille, panda eyes filled with tears, blowing Emerson a kiss before their Mustang rumbled off into the night.

And then there was the veritable slideshow of memorable moments featuring Holden Roarke. His hands on her ankle as he'd helped her with her shoe. His body heat as they'd stood side by side, looking at the stars. The rather large *oomph* sound he'd made as he'd swept her into his arms outside the door to her hotel room, then carried her inside, like *The Bodyguard* poster—

Emerson's eyes popped open. Oh, no. That had happened. And not in some romantic, over-the-threshold movie moment. Not even slightly.

She'd woken in his car. Edit. Holden had had to *wake* her after she'd fallen asleep in his car, the muffled sound in the back of her head the echo of her snoring.

She next remembered leaning. In the lift? Yes, there. And again, in the hall. There had been a cool brush of wallpaper against her shoulder as she slumped against the wall in order to kick off a shoe. Around which time he'd taken her by the hand, slipped an arm beneath her knees, then hoisted her into his arms.

The next bit was a little fuzzy—due to bubbly, or a self-protective brain snap—but she felt sure she'd said something, maybe even something risqué, as his eyes had gone dark, even as he'd laughed—a rough, raw, deep sound that had scraped perilously against her insides.

Then he'd let her slide to the floor, her hand running down his hard chest. His throat bobbing when she'd stayed there, bodily against him. Her nails scraping against expensive cotton as she'd curled her fingers into his shirt.

Yep, that had happened too. And he'd been nothing but a gentleman, extricating himself from her clutches and backing slowly out of the door. Then, finally, his deep voice on the other side of the door, telling her he wasn't leaving till he heard the click of the lock.

"Emerson?"

Emerson opened her eyes to find the room had changed colour, losing the sharp cool of the early hours and filling with the buttery warmth of mid-morning. She felt lost in the loose, soft warmth that came from a dream that wasn't entirely a dream.

Emerson cleared her throat. "Come on in."

Freya hustled into the room, bearing a tall, steaming glass of black coffee and a pretty plate bearing a mix of pastel macaroons.

Emerson felt Pumpkin's tail thump slowly under her desk at the scent of sugar on the air.

Freya said, "I managed to hold back the flood but it's half past ten. Perfect time for Pumpkin to have his outside time while you take your first call. Charming, but insistent this one."

"Right. Thanks. Give me thirty seconds then send it through."

Freya nodded, gathered a soft and sleepy Pumpkin,

then hustled off to sprinkle whatever dark magic she practised to keep Pitch Perfect running like clockwork.

After running her fingers through her hair, Emerson reached out for the sparkly pink paperweight that sat incongruously on her spartan desk.

Before her mum passed a couple of years back—the cancer quick and ferocious, the heartache worse than the rest of them combined—she had collected paperweights, the clear kind with swirls of resin, or glitter, or flowers suspended within. When cleaning out the childhood home her mum had left to her, Emerson had kept just the one, only for it to become a touchstone. A means of infusing her with her mother's chin-up attitude, her determination to rise after every fall.

Giving the subtle dint in the paperweight one last swipe with her thumb, she put it back in place, then pressed the answer button on her speakerphone. "Emerson Adler."

"Emerson," a deep voice intoned. "It's Holden."

Emerson bumped her coffee, sending a splash over her desk. She quickly mopped up the spill with a bunch of tissues.

Then the voice returned, saying, "Holden *Roarke*," as if that might jog her memory.

And it did. She pictured the smile in his eyes as he noted her habit of calling him by both names. Then, for a second, she pictured him querying her about the List. But that couldn't possibly have happened. Meaning, maybe, other memories of the night were false too.

Awash with relief, she said, "Holden." Then, "How on earth did you get my number?"

"You gave it to me."

Her relief dissipated in a flash. "I did?"

"Work, mobile, home, email, social media. You were extremely thorough."

"That does not sound like me at all."

"Bolshie brunette? Sparkly dress? Maid of Dishonour? Before I left you to your beauty sleep, you clicked your fingers in my face till I passed my phone over. Humming a Neil Diamond medley under your breath, rather out of tune, I'm afraid to say. Then you added all your contact details, using the picture of the two of us you'd taken to send to Camille, and—"

"Yep. Okay." The clicking did sound like her. And the picture was real. Emerson slapped her hand across her eyes. "Well, this is mortifying."

His laughter rumbled down the line. "Not at all. It was, all in all, an unexpectedly fun night. Illuminating." Then, "Whoa! All good!"

"Pardon?"

"Sorry. That wasn't for you. Almost had a collision with a Great Dane. I'm in Albert Park. Running."

"Oh," she said, leaning in towards the phone, as if she might hear the slap of his feet on the path, or any kind of stress in his breath.

Then, from nowhere, she remembered him running track in high school. Remembered taking her lunch on the hillside overlooking the oval, slowly eating her warm Vegemite sandwich as she watched his long, loping stride, and the sweat patches growing down the sides of his T-shirt with each lap—

Tossing her coffee-soaked tissue in the bin, Emerson righted herself and said, "Look, I'm glad you called, actually."

"I'm glad you're glad."

"Calm down. I'm *mildly* glad, at most."

"I'll take it," he said, his voice a rough burr that made her insides go all squidgy.

"I need to thank you. For your…consideration. After the wedding."

Carrying me over the threshold, not taking it the wrong way when I clutched at your shirt, or when I gave you goo-goo eyes. The way you stayed until I locked the door.

"I'm sure any of Phillip's friends would have done the same."

"Yes. That's true. He is a collector of good people." Emerson also knew that she'd never felt light-headed talking to any of Phillip's friends. She cleared her throat. "That said, I was feeling a little tender, which, again, is unlike me. I'm not at all sentimental—"

Her eyes slid to the paperweight and away again.

"By the end of the night I wasn't handling the…" Emerson waved her hand, trying to find a word that did not stray too close to anything "heart" or "ache" related. "Anyway, I was not exactly at my best, so, thank you for seeing me through it."

"You're welcome."

Emerson squeezed the bridge of her nose, her neck

feeling warm as she worked herself up to say, "Now, as to the phone number thing. Despite what that might imply, I'm actually not in the market for a…phone number."

After a spell, Holden said, "As it turns out, I'm not in the market for…a phone number, either."

"Great," she said, slumping down in her chair, her eyes rolling towards the ceiling. "That's just…"

"Great?" he offered up.

"Yes. Now, can we please wipe Saturday night from our minds? Pretend none of it ever happened?"

"Mmm. Not sure I can. Your rejection of the bouquet toss might be one of the greatest wedding moments of all time. And then there's the fact you told me I had big, manly shoulders and…what was it? Fetching eye crinkles—"

"Holden," Emerson declared, her fingers now rubbing her temples.

"Yes, Emmy."

She thought about correcting him, but the truth was, the implied intimacy of Holden calling her Emmy was the least of her worries. "Wipe it," she said. "Wipe it from your mind."

Holden laughed, all rough and raw. For a man who wasn't in the market for her *phone number*, he sure did phone call well.

Emerson rocked her chair side to side. "Now, what can I do for you, Holden?" See, she could say his name. Singularly. Not special at all.

"Right. Yes. I have a favour to ask."

"Another favour."

"Mmm?"

"Do me a favour. Protect me from the sweet young woman wielding the evil bouquet," said Emerson, her voice as deep and rough as she could manage.

Holden laughed. Something in the sound making her picture him slowing to a walk, a drip of sweat making a slow trail down the sculpted edge of his jaw.

Then suddenly she remembered what she'd said to Holden when he'd carried her into the hotel room. *Do me a favour. Don't leave, this time, without saying goodbye.*

So very glad this was a phone call not a video call, Emerson let her head fall to her desk. And there she stayed as Holden's voice said, "I'd rather think tucking you up in bed, and wishing you sweet dreams, would put me one favour up."

"You did *not* tuck me into bed." Of that she was nearly absolutely sure.

"Consider that artistic licence. Look. I truly do need a favour, Emmy. I have no problem taking no for an answer. But if you do this one thing for me, then... then we would not be even. Not even close. I would owe you, big time."

Emerson lifted her head and stared at her speakerphone.

Yes, bumping into him had been nowhere near as horrible as she'd imagined it might be. Yes, the ache she'd once felt any time she even thought his name was long gone. But pushing it any further was tempting fate.

Unless…

Unless this was actually an opportunity. A chance to be absolutely sure that the Heartache List had done its job. That, due to the foundation built upon its lessons, no matter what life threw at her she would be okay.

"No promises," she said, "but give me the gist."

"Can do. I need you to be my date on Friday night."

Emerson may have snorted. And coughed. At the same time. Leading to a rather unladylike choking noise.

"Actually, strike that," Holden said. "*Not* a date, a plus one. Not to a wedding, for that would wipe out all the points I'd earned at the last one. The wedding I have now forgotten completely."

He stopped talking. Took a breath. Said, "What I am truly in need of is someone to accompany me to an upcoming dinner. And I was hoping you might be the one."

"A date," Emerson responded, the words flat, as if she didn't like the taste.

"But *not* a date," Holden reiterated, smiling briefly at another runner as he moved off the path and into the speckled shade of a gum tree, pacing so that the lactic acid wouldn't start to itch. "A seat at a table, on which there will be food and drink for you to enjoy. At a place. With great people who love a chance to dress up. And have a laugh. And eat together."

Holden pressed his earbud deeper into his ear and was reminded how it had been the other night, standing danger close, their voices low and intimate, the star-spangled sky hovering silently above. He wiped his hand down the side of his shorts, actually sweating as he waited for her response.

Which was, "So long as that's clear."

They'd spent a grand total of an hour together, at most, during and after the wedding, and yet he could picture, with clarity, Emmy's expression as she deadpanned him. Gaze direct, a slight lift of her right eyebrow, her mouth twisted to the left, a healthy amount of reticence apparent on her lovely face.

"Thought you'd appreciate the delineation," he said. "Considering your aversion to phone numbers."

She laughed at that. Or maybe it was a sigh. Either way, he pictured a squint to those striking, moss-green eyes. Impossibly long lashes creating shadows over elegant cheekbones. A brief flash of teeth, the front two slightly too long, slightly too big, adding whimsy to the list of things about her that he'd found stunning.

Dappled shade fluttering over his face, Holden pressed the bud deeper into his ear again, and looked to the jut of the Melbourne city skyline, a smear of grey on the horizon.

Yes, she was stunning. Empirically. Objectively. And yes, there had been a spark, one which he'd bet quite a bit went both ways. But he was in town for a blink. A fraught blink, at that. So that wasn't what this was about.

He was asking her to accompany him because he knew she'd be able to handle herself with the dinner crowd. And when he was with her, for whatever reason, she drew his focus and kept it. Add her stated lack of interest in his "phone number" and she was perfect. The perfect non-date date.

"Look," he said, "the entire reason I am here, in Melbourne, is to catch up with some people I haven't seen in some time. There is history between us. Complicated history. And I feel that it all might go more smoothly if I bring..." *a distraction, a foil, someone shiny and lovely and bright* "...a friend."

A definite sigh that time. "And you want me for this."

"I do want you. For this," he added belatedly enough he feared he might have shot himself in the foot.

Not quite, as she said, "Surely you could get an easy yes from anyone else."

Pacing no longer cutting it, he waited for a gap, then jogged back out onto the track. "As a single man, of good fortune, 'tis true, I am hugely popular."

"Good grief," she muttered.

"Thing is, Emmy, I trust that you are savvy enough to see this for what it is, a favour done, giving you a favour in hand, should you ever need it. Nothing more."

"Let me get this straight," she said. "You're asking me to join you for some complicated mystery dinner, because you believe I won't mistake a favour date for a *date-date* and what? Accidentally fall in love with you?"

Holden grinned, as he eased around a little old lady out walking her tiny dog. "Not accidentally falling in love with me is absolutely imperative. So, if that's going to be a problem…"

"The man's ego knows no bounds."

"So?"

"Just…give me a minute."

Emmy breathed out hard, and when Holden next swallowed he had the sense memory of lime on the back of his tongue.

He picked up his pace and looked out across the acres of parkland. Parents speed-walked, prams bumped over every tiny crack in the path, shuffle runners shuffled, and bike riders wove.

To think this was the same city in which he'd grown up.

His childhood had not been so green, or nearly so free. Controlled, it had been, by a man who'd taken every chance to assure him that being a smart arse would get him nowhere.

The very best thing about finding himself in a position to retire at such a young age had been the autonomy. He could go anywhere, stay as long as he liked, leave on a whim. He could work hard, or do nothing at all. There was no overriding force holding him to any one place, holding him back.

Which meant waiting on someone to decide his fate was now rare.

"What are you worried about?" he asked when he could no longer hold his tongue.

"I'm not worried."

"Great, because I've seen you in action. You're a force to be reckoned with when…sensical."

"Sensical?"

"The opposite of—"

"Nonsensical," she finished for him, the word dripping with irony.

"Don't get me wrong, when nonsensical you're an absolute delight. But I'd be far too worried that you'd hand over your phone number, and passwords, and your address, and your mother's maiden name and—"

"Yes, thank you. I get it."

"Great. So?"

"I think I'm going to regret this. But fine, I will be your platonic, non-date, favour mandated plus one."

Holden punched the air, scaring a golden retriever. He held out a placating hand in apology to the owner, a young woman in head-to-toe pink, who smiled and tugged on her ponytail.

"I honestly can't believe I've agreed to this." Emmy's voice came through his earbuds, husky and rich, yet grounding somehow. A tether, to some point in the past. Or perhaps it was the affinity he'd felt tug between them, as she'd stood on the outside of the crowd looking in.

"You hungry?" he asked.

"Often."

"I mean now. I'm ravenous all of a sudden. Let's have lunch."

"I can't have lunch with you, Holden."

"Sure, you can." A beat, then, "Not a lunch *date*."

"Holden," she said, her voice the very height of *sensical*.

"Yes, Emmy."

"I'll go to this dinner of yours. As a *favour*. Which you will then owe me. And I will call you on that favour any time I wish, for any reason that I see fit. Unless it's illegal, or impossible, you cannot refuse me. Those are the parameters of the deal."

Parameters, discreet edges, a neat and tidy package of an agreement. Actually, that sounded entirely sensical. Especially considering what had been the perilous lack of parameters the last time he'd spent time with the family.

"Deal," he said, picturing an imaginary shaking of hands. She with her short dark nails. The same ones that had gripped his shirt in her hotel room as she'd looked up at him, her eyes swimming with champagne and invitation.

"Friday," said Emmy, all business.

"Friday," he said, mirroring her tone. "I'll pick you up. Office or home?"

"Home." She gave him an address in Kew, not far from their old school. "I'll need to change."

"Nah," he said. "Don't change a thing."

"Smooth."

"I try."

"Stop trying. With me there is no need. For we are...friendly...and do favours...and have clear parameters. Till Friday." With that she rang off.

Holden punched the air again, a subtle, hip-high

jab, before yanking the bud from his ear and shoving it in his pocket.

His return to Melbourne, for the first time in years, had been far easier than he'd imagined. Old friends were calling. Even the infamously changeable weather had been spectacular. As if wounds really might heal over, after enough time.

But he knew it wasn't that simple. Some wounds were so deep, they never fully healed. The scar tissue became formative, a reminder to stay frosty, and alert.

The dinner party would be his reckoning. Payment for his soft landing.

Whether it was right or wrong to rope in Emmy Adler would be something he'd face once it was all said and done.

CHAPTER FOUR

FRIDAY AFTERNOON, EMERSON slid into the back seat of her ride share, mentally spent after a Women in Business lunch at which she'd hobnobbed and networked like there was no tomorrow.

Freya hopped in after her, brimming with energy and enthusiasm, talking a mile a minute about the contacts they'd made.

When Emerson's phone buzzed and she held up a "just a second" finger, Freya turned to the driver to regale him with her stories. While Emerson's heart bucked when she saw Holden's message.

All good for tonight?

Her thumb hovered over the screen. If she wanted to beg off, bone-deep weariness after a long week was a fair excuse. In the end, she typed:

All good.

Brilliant. Quick question: I'm prepping the contract, for our exchange of favours. Would you prefer it typed out in triplicate? Or should we trust we are as good as our word?

Emerson twisted in her seat, tilting her phone so that Freya—who really couldn't help herself—didn't read over her shoulder as she typed:

I have no clue how trustworthy you are. We met outside the guidance counsellor's office, after all.

Holden's reply:

Pot, meet kettle.

Excuse me. My reasons for being there were innocent and good, bordering on angelic. You?

Fair call. So, written in blood. Got it.

Emerson realised she was smiling. She told her face to calm down. Then looked out of the window, watching the cityscape flicker by, before her gaze went back to her phone. She typed:

Look, as far as I could tell, you didn't steal any money from my purse when you saw me to my room, so let's go with our word.

I thought we were never to speak of that night again.

You are not to speak of it. I am under no such gag order.

Freya glanced at Emerson, and the phone she was cradling close to her chest, curiosity written all over her face. Emerson offered up a beatific smile, and Freya lost interest, leaning forward to ask the driver to take a particular route.

Emerson glanced back at her phone. Holden had written:

If I agree to never speak of the drool you left on my car seat, can we take that as the favour returned? Partially at least.

Negative.

Then I make no promises. See you tonight.

Emerson barked out a laugh, the sound echoing in the confined space.

"You're not going to tell me what that was all about, are you?" Freya asked, curiosity leaching so patently from her skin she vibrated.

"Nope," said Emerson, sliding her phone into her bag.

"I know your phone password."

"Ha! I have no doubt. And yet I know you'd never look at my phone without asking because you are the most wonderful, dedicated, loyal assistant in the whole wide world."

"Also true."

With that, Emerson settled into the car, closed her eyes, and gave in to the rocking sensation as they trundled back to work.

Emmy sat slumped in the red plastic chair in the hallway outside Miss Kemp's office, holding her unicorn backpack to her chest, bouncing the heels of her school shoes against the linoleum floor. A loud squeak had her peeking her head around her bag to find she'd left a mark.

After a quick glance to the front desk to make sure ancient Mrs Carmichael hadn't noticed, she licked her thumb, bent at the waist, and rubbed frantically at the stain.

The door banged—the way it always did before opening—and she sat up so fast her head swam.

The sound of laughter, and a deep, warm voice, wafted out into the hall—neither of which meshed with her experiences with the earnest guidance counsellor her mum insisted she see after she told her mum, at dinner one night, that she hated her dad and always would.

Then, through the doorway, came a boy. A boy she'd never seen before. She'd have remembered those smoky blue eyes. Those shoulders—like a man's shoulders. The way he stood, as if he wasn't hyper-aware of himself every moment of the day.

That might be, she thought, *the most beautiful boy to have ever walked planet earth.*

The guidance counsellor leaned in the doorway,

her face etched with concern, the way it had been on Emerson's first visit. Her voice low, private, and possibly muffled by the fluffy white clouds that had wafted into Emmy's head.

Then the boy started moving Emmy's way.

In slow motion, no less, his shoulder turning first, then hips, then feet. His head moved last, his hair swishing slightly, flicking across his face before landing in the most perfect spot for his face. Then he started to walk, slow, easy, chest out, all constrained power and vitality as he swung his near empty black backpack onto his shoulder.

Then, right when she was staring at him the very most, his eyes met hers.

Her heart stopped. Literally. *Ba-dum, ba-dum, ba-dum*...then nothing.

A smile kicked at the corner of his mouth. "Hey," he said, lifting his chin.

Emmy gulped. Eyes burning from not having blinked since the moment he'd appeared.

Then his smile grew, widening, showing actual teeth, as if he knew exactly why she sat there, unmoving. Dumbstruck. Completely and utterly crushing on him.

"I've warmed her up for you," he said, to her, in a voice that spread through her body like liquid heat.

The tip of his finger touched his brow in salute, and then he was gone.

And the guidance counsellor was calling her name as if she'd been calling it for some time.

"Emmy? *Emerson?*"

★ ★ ★

"Emerson. We're here."

Emerson blinked to find herself in the back of the ride share.

Freya slid out of the car, and Emerson went to follow before staying put.

"Are you free to take me to Kew?" she asked the driver.

He poked something into his machine and said, "You bet."

"Super. Freya, I'm clocking out. I have an…event to prepare for."

"Tonight?" Freya frowned at her trusty tablet. "It's not on the calendar."

"A private event."

"Ooh," said Freya, eyebrows waggling. "Exciting."

"No. Not like that."

"Oh," said Freya, her enthusiasm turning to disappointment on a dime.

"Can I leave it to you to make sure everyone leaves on time so they can enjoy their weekend? Can you remind the temp crew we have a meeting ten a.m. Monday? And—"

"I've got it." Freya tapped at her tablet. "I'm up to the task."

"Yes, you are."

Emerson closed the door, gave the driver her address.

With the memory of the first time she'd laid eyes on Holden Roarke still swimming in her subconscious, she made her way home to get ready for a non-date date with the guy.

Figuring a little extra time to put on a little extra armour couldn't hurt.

Emerson paced the entrance hall of her small, but lovingly refurbished childhood home, stepping from floorboard to floorboard in a repetitive pattern as the seconds slipped away till Holden was due to arrive at her door.

Pumpkin, no doubt picking up on her heightened energy, had found enough latent energy of his own in his dear old legs to leave his big, soft bed, his rheumy eyes following her as she paced.

"I'm not nervous," she said, bending to give her beautiful boy a gentle scruff behind his soft ears.

Pumpkin sniffed out a breath that appeared to be a doggy version of an eye roll.

"I'm not! I can hold up my end in *any* conversation. I spend my days going head-to-head with captains of industry. With entrenched politicians. I'm a boss, don't you know? No room in my life for nerves."

Yet as a shadow appeared at the frosted window in her front door just before a knock sounded, her heart *ba-da-boomed* in her chest.

She turned Pumpkin, gave his tail end a light nudge to send him walking back towards his bed for the evening. Then she grabbed her clutch bag, straightened her shoulders, ran a quick hand over her freshly washed and styled hair, another down the hip of her dress, and opened the door.

Only to have her mouth dry up at the sight of Holden Roarke standing on her porch, hands in pockets, smile hooking the corners of his mouth as his eyes roved over her porch swing, the bougainvillea spilling from her hanging pots, and the vintage brass lamps lit up warmly either side of her door.

It had been a little under a week since the wedding, at which time she'd seen him all dolled up. He'd even swept her off her feet that night, literally. But somehow in the days in between her subconscious had worked overtime to mitigate his impact.

Feeling an echo of that first time she'd seen him leaving the guidance counsellor's office, she swallowed at the sight of those shoulders. Those eyes. That mouth—full and relaxed, with the hint of a crescent in one cheek, as if prepared to smile at any time.

"This is not at all what I expected," said Holden, sounding utterly relaxed. While she vibrated like a freshly plucked guitar.

"Meaning?"

"I imagined something cool, modern, sleek. Scandinavian aesthetic. Slightly intimidating. But this might well be the cutest house I have ever seen."

A mite agitated by the fact he'd described her workplace to a T and feeling more than a mite exposed by having this man at her home, she murmured, "I inherited it. From my mum. I grew up here."

"And you live here still? Aw… I'm adjusting my opinion of you accordingly."

"Super."

With that, Holden's eyes finally moved to her, and the open-mouthed delight dropped from his face. A single blink and he'd taken her measure—the gun-metal-grey silk of her dress, tucked and wrapped about her like a sexy toga, the thigh split, the sweep of her hair, left down. Something dark, rich, and devouring overcame his face as he took her in. *Drank her in*, more like. In a great, heady gulp that left her swaying on her heels.

Beyond the hum of cicadas and distant traffic, she could feel the energy trapped behind his loose, cool façade. Electricity barely contained. The man was permanently lying in wait.

"Emerson Adler," he all but growled. "When you do a guy a favour, you do a guy a favour."

Fine. So she'd wanted to look good. No, she'd wanted to look *smoking.* A little bit of a *screw you* to the guy not asking her to accompany him anywhere, not even on a non-date, back when she was a sweet, gawky, smart, interesting, totally worth-it fourteen-year-old.

"You said your friends dress up for dinner," she murmured.

"And I will, from this day forth, be grateful that I did. Now, your turn."

"To?"

"Compliment me on the effort I put into looking nice for you."

"Oh, this," she said, waving a hand down her side, "is not for you."

"Is that so?"

"The more effort I put into this favour, the more effort I'll expect when I call yours in."

"Right. Well, just so we're clear, this," he said, rocking side to side, flapping his jacket open, looking utterly scrumptious while doing so, "was all for you."

Emerson rolled her eyes. "You're not giving up, are you? Fine, you look very nice."

"I try."

"Stop trying!" She shooed him backwards so that she could lock her door.

Only he ignored her and unexpectedly dropped to a crouch.

"And who is this?" Holden asked, reaching out a hand.

Emerson looked down at her feet to find Pumpkin at the door.

Oh, honey, she thought, her heart squeezing at the sight of her old boy, his whole body slowly shaking side to side as he attempted to wag his tail.

"This," said Emerson, her voice softening, "is Pumpkin. Pumpkin, meet Holden Roarke."

Holden ran a gentle hand over Pumpkin's crown, as if he knew he was fragile. "He's a gorgeous thing. Aren't you, mate?"

That he was, Emerson thought, her breath tightening, just a little. Only when seeing him through the eyes of someone new did she notice that his lustrous caramel fur was a little patchy these days, his gait a little wonky. But he was sweet and loving, and—her vet assured her—doing miraculously well for his age. And as precious to her today as when she'd first held him in her arms.

"Into bed," she said.

Holden's dark and stormy eyes lifted to hers.

"The dog," she deadpanned.

She waggled her fingers between them, motioning for Holden to move, then placed her hand under Pumpkin's chin and said, "Bed time."

With a snuffle the old dog gave her his best sad eyes, before he turned and padded back up the hall.

Emerson stood, only to find herself all but flush against her guest, her hand lifted to steady herself, flashing her back to the hotel room, when she'd gripped his shirt.

When her eyes lifted to his, she was certain he knew exactly where her mind had gone.

"Scoot," she said. "I can't shut the door with you standing in the way."

"You're in an all-fire rush," he said, before turning and ambling onto the porch, the view from behind as good as the view from the front.

She locked up. "The sooner we get there, the sooner it will be over."

"Not sure that's how dinner parties work, but hey, happy to be proven wrong."

"Why?" she said, noting a shift in tone beneath his easy words. "Do you not *want* to go?"

Holden shot her a look, as if he hadn't meant for her to take it that way. Or hadn't expected her to pick up on it. Then he jogged down her front steps and backed down her path, a hand pressed against the stark white of his button-down shirt. "Can it not be that I am simply looking forward to being in your incandescent company for as long as I can?"

He was prevaricating. But by that stage he'd reached a sleek black sedan, different from the one he'd taken to the wedding, she was sure.

He held open the car door, smiling into her eyes as he said, "If you feel the need to fall asleep, again, I'm good with that."

"So kind of you," she gritted out, his deep, warm waves of laughter rolling through her as she closed the door.

By the time Holden pulled up by a guarded gate between a wall of long box hedges, Emerson felt faint from holding her breath so as not to drown in his delicious scent. Some magical mix of chopped wood, sea air, and clean skin.

When he slid down his window, she breathed so deeply of the fresh air she nearly choked on it.

A woman in a security uniform popped her head out of the box. "Mr Roarke! It's been—"

"It has been some while." Holden smiled.

"Saw your name on the guest list. Thought it must have been an error."

"No error," said Holden easily. "Should be down for two. This is my friend Emerson Adler. Emerson, this is Sandra."

The guard leaned down. Saw Emerson. Blinked once. "Well. Ain't it the night for surprises?"

With that, the guard moved back inside her booth, and pressed a button that set big wrought-iron gates to opening.

"Good to see you again, Sandra," said Holden.

To which the guard said, "Good luck."

Curiosity spiking in a dozen different directions, Emerson was still deciding which question to ask first when the house came into view. It was like something out of *The Great Gatsby*, three storeys, with wings, and gables and what looked like a forest sprawled out behind it.

"Holy moly," she whispered, leaning so far forward her hands gripped the dashboard.

"Careful," Holden murmured as he curved onto the huge circular drive, "you're starting to drool. Again."

Emerson shot him a look. The humour lighting the storm-cloud blue of his eyes made the backs of her knees tingle, as if he had a direct line to certain nerve clusters in her body and all he had to do was tug.

"Whose house *is* this?" she asked.

She felt rather than heard the slightest hesitation before he said, "Bettina and Chuck Sanderson."

"As in the *Sanderson Group* Sandersons?"

"The very ones."

While her work put her in the path of influential people with impressive staffing needs, the Sanderson real estate family was a whole other level.

This was not merely a favour any more, or the chance to exorcise her Heartache List demons for good. It was a huge opportunity. Perhaps even the opportunity of a lifetime.

Holden pulled the car to a stop in front of the house, its engine softening to a throaty rumble. "You need a moment?"

"Nope. I'm fine."

"Just so you know, I can practically hear the wheels cranking behind those big green eyes of yours."

Emerson looked to her lap, before shooting him a smile. "Perhaps that's the engine whimpering. You ride the clutch, you know."

A liveried gentleman opened her door right at the perfect moment, so that she could decamp the car, rather than face Holden's burst of laughter.

Only to find she had to twist and contort herself, to navigate the split in her madly dressy dress. If only she'd asked more questions she might have dressed like an enterprising HR guru rather than an awards-show presenter.

"Shall we?" Holden asked, ambling around the front of the car, hand palm-up.

Emerson gripped tighter to her clutch bag.

He noticed, the edge of his mouth kicking up. As if

he was playing with her. Testing her parameters. But he didn't press her.

With a tilt of his head, he motioned for her to join him on the walk up the wide front steps.

As they neared the front door—as wide as it was tall, and taller than her by double—Emerson felt Holden hesitate. Felt the energy coiled inside him expand, felt him lock it down hard, as if in preparation for something big.

And all her wild thoughts of using this night to sell herself to the Sandersons blew away like so much dust.

Holden had asked her to accompany him for a reason. This hulking, self-sufficient, charming genius felt as if he needed someone on his side. Maybe it was time to stop thinking about her own part in this, and give the guy a break.

"Hold up for a second," she said, moving in closer and sliding her hand into the crook of his arm. Ignoring, as best she could, the warmth of his skin seeping through the fabric, the hard strength against her palm. "What's our game plan?"

"Game plan?" he asked, the clouds sweeping from his eyes as he looked down into hers.

"What have you told them about me? Do we have a backstory? Are they aware this is not a date-date? Please tell me you don't expect me to act as if I'm madly in love with you. You're right, I'm good on my feet, but that might be beyond me."

"Might?" he asked, and that smile—the one that spread across his face in a slow, easy, sensuous sweep of warmth and deliciousness—came out to play. "No pretending required. You're you. I'm me. We came together. That simple."

"Okay, then," said Emerson, even while she was becoming more and more sure that it was far more complicated than he'd let on.

She realised then that, for all that he had occupied such an important place in *her* backstory, she knew very little about him. Apparently, he made apps and lived overseas. He definitely smelled great, and was devastatingly good-looking, and knew how to wear a suit. The rest was a puzzle that had been tipped out of the box at her feet.

"Ready?" she asked.

"As I'll ever be." With a deep breath, Holden opened the door without knocking, then waited for Emerson to precede him inside.

She barely had time to take in the soaring ceilings, the sweeping staircase, the vases of hydrangeas covering every surface, the art on the walls, when a handsome silver-haired gentleman in a wheelchair descended upon them, pulling to a stop and opening his arms wide.

"Holden, my boy!"

"Chuck," said Holden, his arm hardening beneath Emerson's hand, before he let her hand fall, and opened his arms just as wide.

Emerson held back, clutching her bag, as Holden Roarke and one of the richest men in Australia indulged in a long hug.

"So, when are you coming out of this ridiculous 'retirement' of yours to come back and work for me?" Chuck asked as Holden pulled away.

Holden laughed as he moved back to Emerson's side, putting her hand back into the crook of his arm. She tucked his arm close, aware that his laughter didn't have the same sense of release as when he laughed at her.

"I like retirement," Holden said. "It's only slightly ridiculous. Gives me the means to be a man of the modern zeitgeist, following my bliss."

Chuck's eyes narrowed, as if he didn't believe the spin. "Don't tell my wife you said that. She's constantly telling me it's time to wind back. Take up painting. Meditate. Can't imagine anything worse."

"I heard that," said an attractive ice blonde who'd ambled up behind him. Bettina Sanderson leaned to place a kiss on her husband's cheek before standing and eyeballing Holden. "Why, hello there, stranger."

"Bettina," Holden returned, his voice lit with a level of affection Emerson wasn't expecting, considering how edgy he'd seemed outside.

"One day," said Bettina, "all that rolling stone rubbish will become tiresome and someone will make you an offer you can't refuse. Mark my words."

Chuck's gaze seemed to take in Emerson for the first time, as if he'd been blinded by the man at her side, surprise flickering behind his eyes before he blinked, his face a mask of amiability.

"Well, well, well," said Chuck. "Bettina mentioned you were bringing a friend."

Holden looked to Emerson, bathing her in a smile that sent goosebumps up and down her arms. "Chuck, Bettina, this is my friend Emerson Adler. Emerson, I give you Chuck and Bettina Sanderson."

Bettina moved out from behind her husband's wheelchair, took Emerson by the hands and looked her over as if trying to commit her to memory. "We are so pleased to meet you, Emerson."

"Likewise, I assure you."

"My turn," said Chuck, rolling his chair towards her.

Emerson readied to shake, only to find herself pulled down into her own warm, solid hug.

"Oh," she said, one hand fluttering against the man's beefy shoulder, the other still gripping her clutch bag. She truly hoped she didn't look as awkward as she felt.

Until she glanced to the side to find Holden being summarily hugged by Bettina, and he hugging her back. Something about the shape of them, the hunched shoulders, the closed eyes, the tight mouths, made her heart thud against her ribs. Made her look away, as if she'd accidentally witnessed something private.

"So, what do you do, Emerson? What's your *bliss*?" said Chuck, gathering her attention, a hand still holding hers.

"My bliss? Much like you, I fear, my bliss is my work. I run my own HR firm, Pitch Perfect. We wield a small, exclusive pool of highly experienced temps, but at our core we consult, source, scout, and place quality applicants into significant positions in corporate, charitable and political environments. And…that sounded like it came straight from our website. I'm so sorry. I was at the Women in Business lunch today and must have said those exact words a hundred times."

Chuck's eyes sharpened, the infamous businessman showing beneath the mask of gracious host. "You're a head hunter."

"I am. And a damned fine one at that."

Chuck chuckled as his wife came back to his side. "We're going to have to watch out for this one."

"Then we shall." Bettina's smile was kind and warm. "You're the last here—let's head in."

Emerson nodded, so starstruck she didn't realise how quiet Holden had been since that moment with Bettina until it was just the two of them, trailing behind their hosts as they made their way through the house.

Emerson slowed with him, lifting an eyebrow in question.

Everything okay?

His response, a flicker below one eye, and a shake of the head.

All good.

But he wasn't. Which was why she slowed further, till they walked side by side.

"Are you really retired? Like, actually?"

"Since I was in my mid-twenties. Though I'm dragged out of it on occasion, usually when finding myself frustrated by the lack of an app that I can't believe is yet to exist, and so have to build it myself."

She shook her head. Unable to imagine what it might feel like not to chase, not to grind, not to keep a sharp, narrow focus on one's life plan. Not to need that kind of control.

"What *have* you dragged me into, Roarke?" she asked, looking up as they passed under yet another chandelier. "Is it Stepford or Virginia Woolf?"

Holden's face broke into a quick, delighted grin, before it faded to a humourless smile. His spare hand ran the back of his neck, pinching hard. "Long story."

"Too long to tell me before dinner?"

"Much."

"I see."

He paused, forcing her to stop. "Emmy, if this is too much, if you'd prefer to leave, I will take you home. No judgement. No questions asked. Favour still owed to you in full."

She looked at him then, really looked at him. This real-life, flesh-and-blood man who needed her.

Before she could second guess herself, she held out her hand. A question flickered behind his eyes, before his long fingers closed around hers. Then they walked shoulder to shoulder, hip to hip, the fabric of his suit creating soft, rhythmic, enthralling friction all down her side.

When he leaned towards her, his mouth near her ear, and murmured, "Why do I get the feeling you've just amped up the kind of favour you plan to ask in return?" it took everything in her power not to shiver.

"Favour is such a small word for what I have in mind for you, Holden."

"Lucky me."

CHAPTER FIVE

HOLDEN'S JACKET HUNG over the back of the gilt dining chair, his shirtsleeves now rolled to his elbows. His right leg shook up and down beneath the table, dissipating the lashings of excess energy he could not hope to contain.

For the laughter, the heads tilted together in deep conversation, the random hands passing food across the table… It was years since he'd been a regular at such gatherings in this house, and yet it was so familiar to him it stung.

When he realised that he was rubbing the heel of his palm over his chest Holden dropped his hand to the table. Stretching out tight fingers. Rolling a tense shoulder till it cracked. He glanced down the table to find Emmy watching him over the top of her glass of wine.

She sat near enough that he could see the curiosity in her eyes. Too far away for his liking.

For, he was discovering, he liked having her close.

When he'd called, asking for her to join him, he hadn't exactly thought it through. It had been instinct, more than anything. An idea that, knowing she'd be there, he'd actually show up.

But the bigger truth was, he liked Emerson Adler. He found her lovely, and surprising, and hugely entertaining. Then there was the way she walked, as if a big band with a heavy bass drum played her into every room. And the way she smelled, like lime and spring time—

Holden blinked and looked deliberately about the table, to the walls, the ostentatious fresco on the ceiling, before finding Emmy's eyes again, unsurprised to find her watching him still.

So he offered up a slow smile. Intimate. Playful. Chancy, considering the company. But everything about the night was precarious; what was one more layer of exposure?

Nice digs, huh? he said with his eyes.

Emmy's glass twirled in response, the stem twisting between her fingers, catching the light which glinted and shifted across her lovely face. Then she lifted a shoulder in a shrug, the shoulder covered in the silken dark hair swept to one side like some forties siren.

Sure. Whatever.

He laughed out loud.

"Holden?"

He flinched. Then turned to Bettina, who sat to his left, at the end of the table. "Sorry. I was a million miles away."

Her chin tilted towards the other end of the table. "Not so very far as that."

His leg started jiggling once again.

"I only hope, now you're back, that you'll stay. For a while at least. All that rushing about isn't good for a person's health." Her gaze went to her husband.

Her comment, for all its sincerity, made his gut curl in on itself, like self-perpetuating quicksand. For there was enough water under that bridge to drown a man in minutes.

They were all there, ostensibly, to celebrate Chuck's seventieth birthday. But this month was ripe with unspoken anniversaries for this family. Five years since the accident that had put Chuck in that wheelchair, since Marnie had run off, Holden too.

And seven years since…since the horror that had tied them inexorably together in the first place.

Bettina looked at him and smiled. As if it had all been forgiven in five minutes. Then she asked, "Have you spoken to my daughter?"

"On occasion," Holden admitted, reaching for his iced water.

Marnie. Bettina and Chuck's daughter, who'd run off to America with the gardener. While still engaged to Holden. She now lived happily ever after in Maine with their two young kids.

"I thought she might be here."

Bettina's smile was soft. "She's always gone her own way, as you well know. But I am glad you two have kept in touch. You were always friends above all else."

A sip of wine, then, "I knew she'd bounce back, she's a tough cookie. But I worried that what we did to you… I worried that whole thing might have given you all the ammunition you needed to go into your cave and stay there."

"What you did to me?" Holden reiterated, honestly stunned to hear her put it that way. "Taking me on, taking me in? Monsters, the lot of you."

She cocked her head. And waited.

"I'm fine," he assured her.

Bettina took his words at face value. Then leaned back in her chair. "I like her."

"Your daughter? I hope so."

Bettina slapped him lightly on the hand. And nodded once again towards Emmy. "I wasn't expecting to. In fact, I was ready to pretend like crazy. But she's wonderful."

"She's all right, I guess, if you can get past the toenail collection and raging kleptomania."

"Don't do that. She's *wonderful*, Holden. Stunning, which is no surprise. But that's only the half of it. She's substantial, and shrewd, with just a touch of wild. The two of you, together? Watch out, world."

Holden's chest grew tight, the muscles contracting as if weary of trying to hold all the parts of him together. "She's just a friend, Bettina. Newly minted. We knew one another for a short time a long time ago, met again at a wedding a week or so ago, and I invited her here in a fit of panic."

Bettina huffed out a small laugh. "You are the only

young man I know who would do such a thing, and still end up with the gem of the ball. I've missed that. Missed you. Not just for Marnie's sake. Or Chuck's. Or Saul's."

Bettina blinked, a shimmer in her eyes that disappeared almost instantly, before she tipped her chin towards the other end of the table. "But since she is merely a friend, as you attest, then you won't mind if young Kris over there makes a play."

Though he knew he was being baited, Holden glanced down the table to find "young Kris" leaning into Emmy, resting his arm across the back of her chair.

A spike of possessiveness, for which he was not prepared or particularly proud, shot down his spine. Until Emmy turned to "young Kris", glanced pointedly at his arm, and watched as it was removed.

Feeling much better about things, Holden turned his back on the scene. "How is Chuck?"

"Retiring."

"You're kidding."

Bettina waved a placating hand. "It's time. I want him with me. By my side. As much as I can have him. I have him ninety-nine per cent convinced."

It was a night for surprises.

"On that note..." Bettina surged to her feet, tapping a spoon against her wine glass, and the conversation fizzled to a halt. "I want to thank you all for coming tonight to help us celebrate our beloved Chuck, on his birthday. Five years ago this very week we imagined this day might not come. And two years before that…" She stopped. Swallowed. "We couldn't imagine much in the way of happiness at all. Yet here we are. With our favourite people, celebrating the good that rises. If you would all be so kind, if you have any booze left in your glasses, I'd ask you all to raise them."

Shuffle of chairs and quick pours, the clink of glass against silverware and a couple of dozen glasses lifted into the air.

"To Chuck," she said.

"And my next seventy years," Chuck added from the other end of the table.

Much laughter followed, amid *hear hears*.

Until Bettina kept her own glass raised. "And to those who could not be with us today. Our beloved Marnie, and her beautiful family, all the way over in Maine. And to our most precious boy, Saul." The shimmer no longer held as it slid over her cheeks in a silvery waterfall. "We love him. We miss him. Oh, that he was here with us still."

"To Saul," said Chuck and the rest of the table followed suit.

After dinner, nobody seemed in any way inclined to leave, moving into the library, the pool room, the halls, despite the hotbed of emotion underpinning the evening, the very air overflowing with the taste of it, the temperature, the weight.

Only half understanding the stories whispered around her, Emerson's smiles and pep had begun to wane. So she made her way around the ground floor in search of her ride home.

Bettina was talking to Kris, the super-chatty guy who'd been hitting on her all through dinner. When she caught Emerson's eye, the older woman waved a hand towards the terrace.

A quick smile of thanks then Emerson made her way outside, but not before noting Bettina grabbing Kris by the elbow and hauling him back.

Emerson made her way down the back stairs, past heavily scented gardenia bushes growing lushly by the garden walls leading down to the lawn, small fountains, tall stone statues. Music and chatter spilled from inside, creating a kind of Renaissance Eden.

The stars were out again that night but the deeper she went into the garden, the less ground the house lights touched, creating patches of velvety darkness. Then she rounded a copse of conifers to find Holden, sitting on a bench, alone, elbows on knees, back hunched, eyes closed.

He seemed to stir at her approach, as if he'd felt a shift in the air, before he opened his eyes and turned to find her. And his eyes… They were savage. Pained. Punished.

And any discomfort she felt at not being in the know fluttered off into the night like ash on the wind.

"Sorry," he said, making to stand. "I only meant to come out for a minute. What time is it?"

"Stay," she said, with a staying hand to match. For he looked far more exhausted than she felt.

Her heels sinking gently into the turf, she sat on the bench beside him, her hands curling around the cool stone.

"So," she said.

"So," he returned.

"I have questions."

He coughed out a rough laugh. "I bet you do. Do you want the long story or the short?"

"The short version is fine."

When she shivered, the cool of the night sending goosebumps down her arms, Holden lifted his jacket from the bench and moved closer to place it over her shoulders. She thanked him with a half-smile. Breathed deep, drinking in the scent of him. She could chastise herself for it later.

Holden went back to leaning forearms on his thighs, one hand rubbing over his chin, his body taut beside hers. "I must have been seventeen the first time I ate at that table, invited over by a new friend I'd made at my last high school. The one I went to after leaving East Kew, in fact. He was this towering, life-is-there-for-the-taking smile of a guy named Saul Sanderson."

We love him. We miss him. Oh, that he was here with us still.

"Chuck and Bettina's son?"

He nodded. "I went to so many dinners here after that. Spent entire school holidays. I'd been shuffling between couches of distant cousins at the time, none of whom particularly wanted me there; in comparison, this place was like a dream."

"You were a teenager. Why were you living with cousins?"

Holden glanced up, as if he'd almost forgotten she was there. Which was half the reason she'd spoken—she wanted him to remember who he was talking to.

He sat up, his hand gripping the concrete beside hers. "I grew up with my dad, though 'dad' might be too warm and fuzzy a term to describe the guy."

"How so?" she asked.

"The girl with all the questions," he said, his voice sounding far away. Then, "My father drank, he fought, he got into trouble, he pretended to look for work, he had a reputation, he owed money, and he took out all of life's frustrations on me."

Emmy thought of Chuck's open arms. Those big hugs that had stirred up all kinds of parental issues for her too. What a lure that must have been.

Emerson looked out into the night. Confronting the uncomfortable fact that when she'd been crushing on Holden Roarke, imagining him a happy, popular, easy-going hunk, she'd never once considered why a guy like that might need to see a guidance counsellor.

"Tell me about Saul," she said.

A muscle worked in his cheek. "We were like brothers. Even when we went to different universities we kept in touch, caught up every holiday. And then I wrote my app. The interest in the thing was insane, from right at the start. The early offers staggering for a twenty-year-old kid. Infamy ensued. Partying, travel, free hotels, more money than I knew what to do with.

I lost touch with pretty much everyone who'd been a part of life in the 'before'. Including Saul."

A shadow passed over his face.

"A couple of years later I was in Amsterdam, prepping to speak at some future symposium, when there was a phone call, deep into the night. Saul was gone. Could I come home?"

"How did it happen?" she asked, her voice soft, yet it carried in the dark of the night.

"Car accident. Wet roads. Late night. Speed. Thankfully no one else was hurt."

That wasn't true. Every person inside that house at dinner had been hurt by what had happened to Saul Sanderson, and despite the festivities, and the birthday cheer, many were clearly hurting still.

"Come home, they said?" she nudged.

"So, I came home," Holden went on. "I was pall bearer. I spoke at the funeral. It was so damned sad. Yet, I seemed to make them feel as if there was still a small connection to their boy. They asked me to stick around afterwards. What could I say?"

"So you stayed."

"I stayed. And, feeling utterly useless in the face of what those good people were all going through, I wrote an app. For Chuck. As if that might somehow make up for my prior absence. And Saul's. It was twisty stuff."

"What was the app?"

"It was called Real Time. Tracked movement in the real estate market, finding patterns in house sales with regards to suburbs, streets, pockets. I'd quietly imagined it a parting gift, before running away to Bermuda. Instead, Chuck convinced me to stay on, ostensibly to teach his staff how to wield it. And then he promoted me, again and again. Even after my father showed up in Chuck's office one day, asking for money, as he was wont to do now that I'd turned out not to be so useless after all. Then there was Marnie."

She'd heard the name bandied about through the night, with both censure and delight, as if she was a polarising character in the Sandersons' story, and yet she hadn't felt the dull pain in her belly as she did when Holden said the name.

"Marnie is Saul's older sister and she did not think it was healthy for Chuck to keep me around. Her bluntness was a relief. Both hurting, and angry, we soon became a thing. Got engaged, really quickly. Chuck and Bettina wholeheartedly approved. But Marnie didn't love me. She was working through her own pain, and I had become the family conduit."

"Holden," Emerson whispered. Or maybe it was an internal thing—the echo of the ache she felt for him, now flowing freely through her.

"She snapped out of it. Started seeing the gardener. Did fall in love. Fell pregnant. And fled. Chuck was devastated. Accused her of spoiling Saul's memory by hurting me. Watching them fall apart was the final straw. I took the blame. Insisted she'd only left after realising I wasn't in love with her. Excruciating. But, at least, it was true."

Holden ran both hands over his face, kept his head tipped down, his hair falling over his forehead. "Then I quit. Announced, in a press release no less, that I was retiring. Moving to a beach somewhere. I knew it would send interest in Chuck's new app through the roof, which it did, as if that might mitigate the mess I'd let unfold. Then I got on a plane and left.

"And while I was in the air, Chuck had a heart attack, fell down some stairs and—"

"The wheelchair," Emmy whispered.

"The wheelchair."

"Good grief, Holden. That's…a lot." A lot for him to walk back through that door tonight. A lot for them to invite him to do the same. All those good people trying their best under truly trying circumstances. No wonder he'd needed her.

"It sounds like something out of a soap opera."

He looked to her then, a glint in his dark eyes, his laughter sudden and rough.

Emerson slapped a hand over her mouth. "That sounded so callous. I am so sorry."

"You're spot on. Imagine how it felt being caught up in the middle of it. It felt big and important and hyperreal. I never should have stayed. I never should have let it get that far. It took me far too long to remember that I was still the outsider, looking in."

Outliers in arms. She'd thought he was being flirty when he'd said those words at the wedding; now she understood what that had meant. That it was meaningful to him.

Emerson placed her hand gently over Holden's. "They were so happy to see you tonight. You might not be their son, but they do adore you. You were not an outsider then, and neither are you now. Not to them."

A muscle worked in Holden's cheek. He turned his hand beneath hers, till he cradled hers in his own. Then he slowly, *slowly* lifted it and placed a soft, sweet kiss upon her palm.

When his face turned to hers his eyes were deep and dark, unreadable, his jaw hard. Her hand remained tucked in his. "Thank you."

"For what?" she asked, her voice a husky whisper, her body now trembling despite the warmth of his jacket, of his body heat beside her.

His eyes roved between hers. "For saying yes when I asked."

Moonlight shone on half his face, leaving the other half in shadow. All angles and character and depth and dark male beauty. His thumb began tracing the inside of her palm, spreading warmth from the place he'd kissed up her arm and into her chest.

With some effort on her part, she took back her hand, ostensibly to adjust the jacket on her shoulders, mostly so that he didn't see how his touch affected her. "It was a hell of an evening. One I won't soon forget."

"I'll bet."

Emerson felt herself whipped back to the night of the wedding, when she'd said she wasn't sure if stars were happy or sad. What had Holden said? *The most beautiful things are often both.*

A few long, quiet moments later, Emerson said, "What happened to Chuck—it's not your fault."

Holden stilled. "I know that."

Did he? Emerson wasn't sure. The "ran away to Bermuda" slip made her think otherwise. Perhaps his lifestyle had less to do with having the means, and more to do with a need to keep moving. Not just around a park, and not just in the middle of a school term without stopping to say goodbye.

The revelation pressed against an ancient bruise that lived deep inside her. He was a runner, like her dad. No wonder that particular heartache had hit so hard.

Yet she kept her gaze direct, unflinching. While Holden did the same, his body wound tight, as if breathing too deep might unravel some long-held knot behind his ribs. But the longer he looked into her eyes, the more he seemed to loosen, his face easing, his eyes softening.

And that bruised place deep inside her began to pulse.

Emerson pressed herself to standing, Holden's jacket falling off her shoulder. He caught it, stood, and placed it back on her shoulders. Adjusting it, turning her gently to tug at the lapels, and not letting go as he looked into her eyes.

"Wanna get out of here?" she said, feigning a cool she did not feel.

He smiled. "And I thought I was hiding it so well."

She turned away from him then, releasing herself from the gravity in his eyes, hooking her hand through his arm, and said, "Last to arrive, first to leave. This might just be the perfect non-date date after all."

Holden kept hold of Emmy's hand as they said their goodbyes, finding her touch a comfort. An anchor. The shape of something he couldn't define but couldn't deny.

Chuck placed his hand over theirs, as if in some kind of benediction, while Bettina drew each into a long hug. And it all felt a zillion times lighter, easier, better than it had when they'd first arrived.

Then they were back in his car, heading through town, and pulling up outside her place far too soon.

As the engine cut, their breaths were loud in the sudden quiet. Moonlight fell on Emerson's quicksilver dress, her hands in her lap, her face remaining in darkness.

While Holden gripped the steering wheel, like a nervy teenager dropping off a pretty girl after the football game. If she lingered in the car, did it mean something? Would it be an invitation to tuck a hand into the heavy sweep of her hair and kiss her?

Or was it just that he *wanted* to kiss her? And had done since he'd seen her lift that glass of champagne in salute, not following anyone's rules but her own?

He'd imagined kissing her gently at first, getting a sense of her temperature, her texture, her taste. Taking his sweet time till his heart felt sluggish and thunderous all at once.

True, he'd also imagined hauling her into his lap and kissing her till he was wearing her lipstick and she was wearing none.

Either way, he might not be any good at spinning a line, but his moves were just fine.

The decision was taken out of his hands when she all but leapt from the car.

"Don't get out," she insisted, leaning back into the window. "It's been a big night, and I'm sure you want to get home."

Home? By that she must have meant the apartment he was staying in, a modern penthouse he'd bought off plan years back and had decorated by a friend of a friend when he'd heard his dad was sick. Made plans to come home, because that was what good sons did, if you could be a good son when you hadn't seen your father in years. Only to find out his father had died earlier that month and the funeral had gone ahead without him.

The walls were blinding white, the kitchen tiles and cupboards bright red, the dining chairs a mismatched array of rainbow colours—perfect for a hyperactive kindergarten teacher. And it made him think of his father. He was seriously considering selling it when he left.

He looked over Emerson's shoulder to her white picket fence, flowers spilling abundantly over the top, her quaint cottage, the porch light glowing warmly. Invitingly.

That was a home.

"What if there's a robber?" he said.

She reached down and took off a shoe with a mighty long heel. "I'll smack them with this."

She probably would too.

"And yet," he said, pausing till he'd hopped out of the car and shut the door, "I'm seeing you to your door. You would be just as gallant if you were dropping me home."

Her hand gripped her shoe as she watched him round the car. "I can't see that happening. Me dropping you home any time. Since this was a favour, and not a date."

"True," said Holden, even while it hadn't felt that way to him. In fact, he could have kicked himself for ever suggesting it.

Then it hit him—she was right. It was unlikely they'd even see one another again, now that his reason for being in Melbourne was done. Which felt… unacceptable.

They got on. They were attracted to one another. He remembered the way her hand had trembled when he'd brought it to his lips, remembered the sweet taste of her skin, and the shards of heat that had spread throughout his body.

Date or not, asking her to dinner had felt like one of the top five decisions of his life. And he wasn't ready for it to end.

"Then consider this," he said, following her as she

limped her way up her front path, shoe weapon still in hand, "me walking you to your door, at the ready to take down prowlers and peeping toms, that can be my favour returned."

"Ha," she said, shooting him a grin over her shoulder—a flash of white teeth, mischief in her eyes—as she hobbled up her front steps. "Not on your life. I am keeping that up my sleeve for when I need something huge."

"Aah. I get it." Holden stopped at the bottom of the stairs and rocked back on his heels. "You're not ready to be rid of me yet."

Something else glinted in her eyes then. A sense that she had been found out. Further proof he was *not* alone in this…curiosity.

As if she knew exactly what she'd just given away, she rolled her eyes and said, "Oh, shut up."

Holden laughed with the unexpectedness of her admission. And with that knowledge came another incremental shift in the ground beneath them both.

They weren't done here. Meaning he wasn't going anywhere. Not yet.

She shook her head side to side, as if she wasn't sure what she was going to do with him. If she'd asked, he'd have told her she could do *anything she liked*.

But she did not ask. She slid her other shoe from her foot, lowering her leg slowly to the ground, and said, "Don't go thinking I'd cry myself to sleep at the thought of never seeing you again, Holden Roarke."

Though far too late for it to have the impact it

might if he didn't know she'd be thinking of him all the same.

"I survived you leaving once, I can do it again. I'm holding on to my favour. For as long as it takes to find the perfect response."

With that she turned away from him, opened her front door and took a step inside.

"Thank you for walking me to my door," she said, innate politeness coming to the fore.

"Thank you for accompanying me to dinner," he said, gripping his hands behind him and bowing at the waist.

He thought about asking if he might, in fact, make a plan to see her again. That if she said yes he could stay in town another day or two.

Then he remembered, he owed her.

She'd be in touch. When she was ready. Meaning he might have to stick around just a little longer. At least until the ledger was square.

"Goodnight, Emmy."

"Goodnight, Holden," she said, surprise and maybe even disappointment flashing across her face, before she stepped inside and closed her door.

So much for his moves.

After a few moments the front lights turned off, and a light inside turned on. He heard a soft woof, a welcome home from her lovely old dog, and he felt a sharp twist of pain deep behind his solar plexus.

Once again he found himself back where he always seemed to end up—on the outside, looking in.

CHAPTER SIX

A HANDFUL OF days later Emerson, Camille and Phillip met up for the first time since the wedding at their favourite hang-out: a rustic little hole-in-the-wall café with moth-eaten velvet couches, and mismatched wooden chairs that was funky enough to boast "atmosphere" but not so busy they couldn't hear one another talk.

"It wasn't a load-bearing wall. I'm almost certain," said Phillip at the end of a long and rambling story about their first couple of weeks of home renovations.

Avoiding the spring that poked out at the back of her couch, Emerson took a hearty gulp of her super-strong double espresso. "Did you think to, you know, maybe, check? Before going at it with a mallet?"

"Turns out we're going with a more holistic, gut-based approach." Phillip glanced towards Camille, who was, if her dramatic hand movements were anything to go by, quite possibly telling the same story to the barista behind the counter.

"Enough about us," said Phillip. "Fill me in on the goings on in the life of Emmy Adler since the wedding. From what I heard, you and a certain gentleman rather hit it off that night." He waggled his eyebrows. "By that I mean Holden Roarke."

"Did you, now?"

"Ran into him yesterday, which was nice, because I was sure he'd planned to be long gone by now. Well, not so much *ran into,* as he called to thank me for the invitation, and then we met for a drink. And he had a lot of nice things to say about—"

"Phew! I'm famished!" Camille lolloped onto the couch beside her husband.

Leaving Emmy to wonder, *A lot of nice things to say about what? Or who?* Not that it mattered. Not a jot. For it was unlikely she'd ever see him again. Yes, he owed her a favour, but she'd never had any real sense it would happen. The man didn't even live in the same country she did, so she'd quietly planned to be magnanimous and let it go.

Only, now that he was unexpectedly still in town… Maybe she *could* call it in. Should she use his IT knowledge? Too easy. Could he build her a shed? A shed would be handy for storing gardening gear, in case she one day took up gardening. And the thought of him in her back yard, using a hammer, sweat dripping down his brow—

"Did he tell you about the water damage?" said Camille around the paper straw in her huge glass of Diet Coke.

"Not yet," said Phillip. "We were talking about the wedding night."

"Hey," said Camille, slapping him on the arm with the back of her hand. "She's my best friend. That's my story to tell!"

"Not *the* wedding night," Phillip muttered. "We were talking about Holden Roarke."

Camille's gaze snapped to Emerson's. "Yeah, so my husband and your Holden had drinks yesterday, did he tell you? Mere days into our homey-moon and he's already fleeing at the first chance to meet up with another man."

"I wasn't fleeing you," said Phillip, leaving Emerson to shift on her seat at Camille's casual use of "your Holden". "I needed a little space from the *house*, in order to see things from a different perspective. And he's such an interesting guy. Well-travelled. And the success he's had. At his age. Puts our efforts to shame."

"Speak for yourself," Emmy and Camille said at the same time, before leaning in for a high five.

"Anyway," said Phillip, "it seems our Emmy has a fan."

"Oh, really?" said Camille. "Who?"

Phillip blinked at her. "Holden."

Camille's gaze snapped to Emmy's again before her face broke into a grin. "Really?"

Emmy rolled her eyes. "Calm down. We chatted at the wedding, which you know. And a little more, again, after you left. And—"

"And he dropped her at her hotel that night," Phillip added, most helpfully, cutting off Emmy before she could try to explain about dinner with the Sandersons, and the favours.

Camille smacked Phillip on the arm. "First you invite *Heartache Number Four* to our wedding without checking with me, then you find out some truly excellent gossip, which my best friend was no doubt waiting to tell me in person, and you ruin it for her! Married five minutes and you've already forgotten the rules."

"It's a lot to remember," Phillip said. "I never did apologise, though, Em. About Holden and all."

"No," Emmy insisted. "I know you didn't know. And it was fine. He was fine. He was perfectly..." What was the word he'd used? "Gallant."

Even though, several times, she'd had an inkling, a feminine rush of knowledge, that he might have been *thinking* less than gallant thoughts. About her. Good chance she was projecting, for she'd definitely been guilty of thinking less than gallant thoughts about him.

"Doth the lady protest too much?" Camille asked, wide eyes now sparkling with patent interest.

"She does not," said Emmy. "Every encounter we've had has been totally PG."

"She rated it," Camille murmured, looking at Emmy as if she was seeing a whole new side of her.

"I heard," Phillip murmured back.

Emmy breathed deep, gathering her strength.

During which time Camille said to her husband, "Before you and Holden join a bowling league, don't forget Emmy was once utterly besotted with the guy. In fact, the List came about only after *he* broke her fertile, fecund fourteen-year-old heart."

Phillip winced. Then braced himself before saying, "I am glad he came, though. It's been nice getting to know him again. He'd never talk it up, but I know he didn't charge the uni for speaking the night I bumped into him. And he's helped out a few friends, on the quiet, over the years, when they've got themselves into trouble. He acts like he's this loose, jet-setting, I-am-an-island type, but at heart he's really a good guy."

"Maybe now," Camille interjected, glancing at Emmy, her best-friend-for-ever skills right up there with the best. "But back then…"

"He was a good guy back then too," Emmy assured them. Having found a couple of the corner pieces of the Holden Roarke puzzle, she knew a little more of who he was, and what he'd been going through.

His leaving in the middle of the night back then had felt…specific. And, yes, heartbreaking. But it hadn't been his fault. And if he hadn't been a good guy back then, Emmy wouldn't have liked him so much.

He just…hadn't liked her back.

Emmy came back around to find Camille playing with one of Phillip's shirt buttons and smiling into his eyes. And felt an overwhelming sense that she had her nose pressed up against the window, as she witnessed something private.

How had Holden described it? Like an outsider, looking in.

Emmy slowly rose from her chair. "Guys, it's been fab, but I really have to scoot."

"Aw," said Camille. "Housewarming, next week. Yes?"

"Of course. Let me know if you need any help leading up."

"Will do."

Hugs all round, then Emerson left.

Standing outside the café, she looked left, then right, not, in fact, having anywhere in particular to scoot to.

But with the messy mix of thoughts nipping at her heels—the realisation she hadn't told her best friend that she'd been to dinner with Holden, and that she was pretty sure she wanted to kiss the man, along with that bittersweet feeling of disconnection that had hit her so hard at the wedding—she went there fast.

Keys in the door of the apartment, Holden looked to his phone as it buzzed in his hand, hoping it might be a certain green-eyed brunette.

Instead, it was a blue-eyed blonde he'd been avoiding for days.

"Joel," Holden answered, holding the phone a smidge further from his ear in preparation for his business manager's voice to come booming down the line.

"Mate!" Joel replied, his attempt at an Australian accent less than convincing.

Holden threw his keys on the frog-green kidney-shaped hall table. When he perched on a canary-yellow kitchen stool, he was forced to move as the sun slanted right in his eyes. Not that sitting anywhere else in the crazy place felt much better.

"I was expecting you to land on my doorstep a week ago," said Joel. "Jenny even had the linen washed and ready, just in case."

Yes, he could stay anywhere in the world, but he still found himself sleeping on people's couches on occasion. An old habit, a safety net from his childhood, that he just couldn't break.

Holden looked around the apartment. While he knew he couldn't spend another night in this place, he was not yet ready to get on a plane. Not while Emmy, and her favour, were out there.

"Decided to stay on for a bit," Holden said.

"Clearly. Word is out. I'm fielding offers."

"What kind of offers?"

"Teaching engagements, speaking, consultancy, investments, product spokesmanship…" Joel paused, as if he'd run out of breath. As if he'd been waiting for Holden to cut him off far sooner. "Will you be home long enough to take something on?"

Home. There was that word again. Holden flopped back on the hard yellow leather couch and threw his arm over his eyes so that the colour didn't permanently burn his retinas.

"My youngest wants to start horse-riding lessons," Joel beseeched. "Do you know how expensive they are?"

Holden laughed despite himself. "I pay you a packet whether I take on any events or not."

"Yes, you do. For which my children are eternally grateful." A pause, then, "While the kids are hankering for some Uncle Holden time, I'm glad you've stuck it out a little longer. Make new memories. And while you're at it, make some local schools, or struggling businesspeople, or young entrepreneurs super-happy and talk to them. For money. It'll do you the world of good."

"Fine."

"Really? Brilliant! I'll swing the list over right away." With that, Joel rang off, sounding as if he couldn't believe his luck.

While Holden called up the app he'd built, the very one he'd gifted Chuck several iterations ago, and scrolled through a list of short-term rentals, focusing on places not too dissimilar from Emmy's cosy, comfortable, suburban spot.

Freya's cheeks were bright pink, her tablet in a death grip, as she swept into Emerson's office. "Phone call. Line one."

Freya could look like the sky was falling if someone was a minute late to work, so Emmy finished reading the contract page she was on before pressing the button to bring up the speakerphone, and said, "Emerson Adler."

"Emerson. Ah, that name of yours. It's like a song. Chuck Sanderson here."

Emerson flinched so hard the top few sheets of paper swept off her desk and landed on the floor.

Freya, as if expecting it, rushed in, her eyes preternaturally wide as she neatly plucked the pages off the floor and popped them back into order on the desk, before backing out of the room in a crouch and closing the door with a soft *snick*.

"Chuck! It was such an honour to meet you the other night."

Chuck laughed, entirely aware of his own power. "Well, you impressed me at dinner too. Even more importantly, you impressed my wife."

"That's so lovely," she said, sensing that Chuck Sanderson, CEO of the real estate and construction goliath the Sanderson Group, didn't make it a habit to call up house guests and personally thank them for attending a party. She picked up the sparkly paperweight on her desk, rubbed her thumb over the soft indent beneath, and said, "Is there something I can help you with today?"

"Well, Emerson, I find myself in need of some... key staff."

Emerson punched the air. Then reached for a notebook and pen so she didn't forget a word. "I thought I heard, at dinner the other night, that you were on the verge of retiring."

"Rumours. I'm as invigorated today as I've ever been. Now, human resources are your area of expertise, yes?"

"Very much. What are you after?"

"Temps. A few new bodies in middle management as we look towards expanding our development sector."

She jotted down a bullet list. "Temps. Middle management. Can do."

"I also have a very important position that needs filling. In the spirit of transparency, I have another couple of mobs on the case already, but they've yet to produce the goods, so I'd like you to have a go as well."

Normal business practice, at his level. "What position is that?"

"COO."

Chief Operating Officer for the Sanderson Group. A multimillion-dollar package, no doubt. With the kind of finder's fee that would pay her staff, her rent, and then some for some time. "My team and I are absolutely up to the task."

"So, you have someone in mind, then?"

She paused, mind ticking over several women and men she'd made relationships with over the years who would be ready and raring. "I just might."

"I can't tell you how glad I am to hear it. He's a stubborn fellow, but if anyone can swing him around to taking on the gig, you can."

And just like that Emerson's happy bubble popped.

Chuck Sanderson hadn't called because he'd been impressed with her. Not solely. He'd called because he thought she might be able to bring Holden on as COO of the Sanderson Group.

Emerson nibbled on the end of her pencil and thought it through.

Her own history with the guy aside, his relationship with the Sanderson family was staggeringly complicated. And he was very clearly *not* in need of a job, or looking for work, much less a high-pressure, high-investment, settle-in-one-place gig.

He was also, as far as she knew, still intending to fly off into the sunset whenever the urge took him. Because that was the kind of person he was. A man who walked into a room as easily as he left it.

And yet…

He *was* still in town, which went against his original plan. She knew because he'd begun texting her every day or so, asking if she wanted lunch. Asking after Pumpkin. Asking if she wanted help choosing her favour.

And he *had* worked for the company. He was beloved by the boss. They were all most definitely in a better place with one another than they had been before, thanks to that dinner.

If she was able to land Holden—even as a *candidate*—she had zero doubt the commission would be hers.

And Holden *did* owe her that huge favour.

No. *No.* She couldn't. She wouldn't. She didn't know the man that well, but, having heard his story, in his own words, in the silvery darkness in the Sandersons' own garden, she knew enough to know she would never ask it of him. Ever.

Holden may have given her the in, but he was not the answer.

"Chuck," she said, putting on her best I-am-the-expert-here-so-it-would-behove-you-to-listen voice, "in line with our spirit of transparency, I do not believe Holden is the right person for the job. He's brilliant, yes. He knows the business, yes. He adores you. He's in town. But as he said the other night, he's not keen on being tied down. And…"

Always better to be honest. Allowing someone to get their hopes up, knowing they'd be dashed, was, to Emerson, the cruellest thing in the world.

"I honestly believe your history together would make a partnership problematic." She paused. Let that sit. Then said, "There *is* someone else out there who is suited to the job. Someone just as brilliant, just as talented, just as charismatic—but keen. Eager. Excited by the prospect. And I am going to be the one to find them."

She would. She had to. For it would cement her position in the world of corporate HR like nothing else could.

She waited for Chuck to say something, hoping she hadn't just shot herself in the foot, but also knowing there was no way forward if he wanted her to be some kind of pawn in his get Holden game.

The man cleared his throat, and said, "I'll have my people contact your people to put the staffing contract in place. And I look forward to seeing these fantastic candidates you assure me are out there. Good day, Emerson."

"Good day—" she said, but he'd already hung up.

She stared into the middle distance, her mind whirring.

The Sanderson Group. *The Sanderson Group.*

As it truly sank in, she leaned back in her chair and let out a great, "Whoop!"

Emerson turned out the lights in her office late that same evening. Moonlight spilled through the huge windows, and the only sound was the hum of the exit signs.

Still buzzing with energy as she headed down in the lift, after hours spent with her teams working through the Sanderson Group portfolio, she pulled out her phone, thumb hovering over her contacts.

It was a Tuesday, so Camille would be at bingo with her dad. Phillip—if not painting something or ripping something up—would happily chat, and he'd make all the right noises, but it wasn't quite the same.

Strangely, though, neither was the "someone" she wanted to tell.

When the lift doors opened, she pressed call before she could change her mind.

"Emerson." Holden's voice came through the phone right as she pressed the door to let her out of the building. The night air was an icy rush against her body; in contrast, with the phone to her ear, his voice was warm and welcoming.

"Holden. Um, hi."

"Um, hi, right on back. What's up? What do you

need from me? Shall I rush out the door this instant, ready and raring to do your bidding?"

"There is nothing I need from you," she said, heels tapping on the footpath as she ducked around a group of young women heading out for a night on the town.

"I'm sure I could think of something."

She bet he could. "I called as I have news."

"And you thought of me. That's nice." No humour in his voice that time. Just easy acceptance. She imagined him saying so while lying back on a couch, head resting on his bent arm, bare feet on the opposite arm rest. He might have been wearing a shirt, he might not.

"The *only* reason I thought of you is because I have you to thank for said news. In a small, teeny-tiny, miniscule way."

"Now I'm really intrigued."

She reached the door leading to the car park and pulled out her key card. But held off, knowing the reception was patchy when she went underground.

There was no way she could hide her smile as she said, "I received a call from Chuck Sanderson this afternoon. Pitch Perfect is to be the Sanderson Group's new temp staffing *and* management recruitment firm."

In the beat that followed, the silence felt so loaded, she wondered if calling him had been the right thing to do at all. If she might be pressing on that ancient bruise of his after all. She opened her mouth to apologise, or take it back, or change the subject, when his voice tumbled into her ear.

"Why, Emerson Francesca Adler, that's damn fantastic news."

Emerson looked up at the dark sky and beamed, fizzy joy settling over her. "I know, right?"

Holden chuckled, enjoying her enjoyment. Which was nice. For all that the news was amazing, sharing it, with someone who understood, made it feel more real. While the sound of his laughter—deep and intimate—skittered down her arms, the sides of her torso, along her ticklish spots just above her hip bones.

"Hold up. How do you know my middle name?"

A beat. "Has it come up?"

"It has not."

"I can see it written down. Emerson Francesca Adler." His voice sounded a little faraway, as if he was tracing her name in the air. "I remember thinking it sounded like a character from an old movie. But when? It'll come to me." A moment, then, "Do you remember those mornings we both found ourselves stuck in the hall outside the guidance counsellor's office?"

Did she remember? Ha. Ha-ha-ha-ha-ha.

"Ancient Mrs Carmichael, on the front desk, had us check our medical histories constantly. One time she accidentally gave me yours."

Emerson remembered. She could feel the heat rushing into her cheeks as he'd leaned towards her, holding out the page, holding eye contact, with that gorgeous smile on his gorgeous face, as if it was happening in real time.

"I handed it straight over…after reading the first

few lines," said Holden, when Emerson remained unable to say words. "The big question is, did you do the same? Or did you take the chance to read about all my many stupid feats that led to many broken bones?"

"Of course not."

"Ah. So you were a good girl," he extrapolated.

Nope. She'd simply realised all too late what she'd held in her hand.

"I was always more curious than I was careful," Holden said. "Got me into trouble. But served me when it needed to. On that note, I'm taking you to dinner. News such as yours requires celebration."

Emerson's mouth popped open but no sounds came out. She'd avoided his lunch requests, blowing them off as a bit of a running joke. But dinner? Dinner leaned precariously close to a date-type encounter.

Maybe she could look at it as a business meeting. Maybe she could drill him for info. He had worked for the Sanderson family before, after all… No. She couldn't. *Wouldn't* ask it of him. Not even that little.

"You okay over there?" he asked, a smile in his voice. "I can hear the wheels cranking again. If you're concerned this is my way of chipping away at my favour owed, it's not. Heck, you can even pay if you'd like, just so you can be sure."

She couldn't help but laugh. "Magnanimous of you."

"Mmm. The celebration is a handy excuse, for the truth is, I would like to take you to dinner. I'd really like to see you again."

"Oh," she said on a sigh, then bit her lip to stop any more telling sounds from slipping out.

Holden Roarke wanted to see her again. And she wanted to see him too. Texting had given her a fix, but it wasn't enough. She'd started to miss that face. Miss how he looked at her, as if he liked what he saw. So much the thought of seeing him again made her feel light-headed.

Pumpkin had spent the day at home as the neighbour's university-aged daughter, Kerri, was using Emmy's sunny back sitting room to study. Kerri—who had grown up next door to Pumpkin, and house-sat if Emerson was away—had sent her usual babysitting proof-of-life picture, so Emerson didn't need to rush home.

But this couldn't be about convenience. What if she was wrong about Holden? Again? What if he was a flirty, enthusiastic, bored guy who enjoyed hanging out with her, but that was it? What if she was reliving the exact same arc as before?

Frantically swiping her card over the sensor and pulling the door open when she heard the latch unlock, she thought, *This is different*. But the only thing she could be sure of was that when he left this time, he'd say goodbye first.

"Emmy?"

"Thank you for the offer. But my mind is still spinning with ideas, and I want to get them all down before they fly off into the ether."

His outshot of breath made her wonder if his disappointment matched her own. "You've got this, Emmy. Remember, you're not the only one who's just made an excellent alliance. Chuck has too."

Emmy closed her eyes as she leaned her forehead on the cold metal door. "I'm at my parking garage and am about to lose reception, so… I'd better go."

She stepped through the door and into the dark. And just before the sensor lights flickered on, and she lost reception, Holden's voice washed over her, "Goodnight, Emmy."

She walked up the ramp to her car, their conversation playing over and over in her head. Until something he'd said snagged on something.

More careful than curious. That was how he'd described her, after a fashion.

When it came to clients, she was gung-ho, asking questions until she knew more about them—their motivations, their goals, their fears—than they did about themselves.

But when it came to her personal life she did hold back, having built big, strong firewalls around herself, and only giving a select few the password.

She pressed the remote to unlock her car as a flutter of melancholy overcame her. Somewhere along the way the young woman who had been hungry enough to start her own company had become so personally risk adverse she couldn't even allow herself to have dinner with a man she liked, just in case.

In case what? In case he didn't like her? In case he did? In case he stayed, and stuck by her, and she grew truly used to having him in her life, and *then* something bad happened? Because, according to the Heartache List, something bad always happened.

But if Holden didn't deserve his place on that list, after all, then his name wasn't a threat to that terrifying *Heartache Number Nine* slot that she so adamantly refused to fill.

The only person holding her back these days, was her.

CHAPTER SEVEN

THE NEXT MORNING, the second Emmy's eyes popped open she felt wide awake. Cleansed. Refreshed. As if she'd broken through some mental barrier.

This whole time she'd been telling herself that spending *any* time with Holden proved how much she'd grown beyond the Heartache List. For hadn't she survived a dinner, and a few cheeky texts, without a) accidentally falling in love with him, and b) having her heart broken?

So what? What did that prove? Only that *she was being too careful.*

She'd been half-hearted. If she really wanted to see where she stood, she needed to use her whole heart. So to speak.

Once at work, she waited till her teams were busy with the Sanderson brief, then, feeling tremendously determined while also slightly sick to the stomach, she punched Holden's number into her work phone and put it on speaker.

He answered, short of breath, "Hey."

"You're running," she said.

"That I am."

He's a runner, remember? Abort! Abort!

"Should I call back?" she asked.

"You can call me anytime you want. But I'm okay to talk now, so long as you don't mind me huffing and puffing in your ear."

Emerson lifted a finger to her mouth and nibbled on the end of her fingernail as she dealt with the image that put in her head. "Something you said last night has been playing on my mind."

"Which part?"

I really want to see you again. No, *not* that. Though it had been playing on her mind. On a loop. So much so she might have even considered going for a run herself so as to shake it off, till she remembered she didn't own running shoes.

"First things first, do you know how much longer you'll be in town?"

"I do not." A beat, then, "But I have no imminent plans to leave just yet."

"Great."

"I'm glad you think so."

Warmth fluttered in her belly, reminding her that she was dealing with a guy who didn't go for lines, or games. *No pretending required.* "What does your calendar look like at the moment?"

"Is that your way of asking *me* to dinner?"

"It's my way of finding out your movements before seeing if we might implement the next phase of our…deal."

"There's a next phase?"

"There could be."

"Intriguing. Sending it to you now."

Her phone pinged, with an invitation to add Holden Roarke's calendar to her own. A shimmer shot through her at the intimacy that suggested. The trust.

Rather than battening down the hatches, she followed her newly unleashed curiosity, opened his calendar, and found herself surprised to see that it was rather impressive. Especially for a guy who considered himself "retired". "Is this for real?"

He laughed. "Turns out I'm not just a pretty face. I have skills and people are keen to hear about those skills. And, since I am a generous soul, I am willing to share those skills, for the right price."

"So, you're a mercenary," she asked as she continued scrolling through his calendar, some in bold—booked—many more in italics—possibilities. Her heart stuttered when she saw their old school listed as a possibility. And she remembered Phillip's assertion that he picked and chose who he charged.

"East Kew High School is willing to pay you the big bucks to give a talk on… Youth Entrepreneurship?" she said.

"So many bucks."

Emmy sat back in her chair, distracted from her original plan. Something Holden was extremely adept at making happen. "I don't believe you."

"That's your prerogative."

"Does it bother you that people write you off as some sort of rich, easy-going, playboy type?"

"What people? Have you been reading up on me, Ms Adler?"

"I took a photo of you in case I went missing. I've introduced you to my dog. Yes, I've read up on you. It was the only safe thing to do."

He hummed into her ear, the sound doing things to her the huffing and puffing had not. "Good for you. As to your query, people hear 'retired in his twenties' and think I spend most of my days living on a beach somewhere being served pina coladas by nubile young women in bikinis."

She looked again at the list of groups he was speaking with, mostly small groups rather than corporate gigs. As if he really was an honestly generous soul. "Why don't you? No judgement, it sounds pretty fabulous."

"You are brimming with judgement, Emerson Adler."

Emerson rolled her neck. "A little bit."

"I imagine," Holden went on, "that when you go on a beach holiday, you book tours and naps and food stops down to the minute."

"That's what you imagine when you picture me on a beach holiday?" A slight pause, to let that sink in. Then, "I'm disappointed in you, Holden. I'd have thought you more imaginative."

She felt a wind of change, as if it swept over them both.

"I'm disappointed in myself," he said, his voice low,

confidential. "You said something I said has been playing on your mind?"

She had? "I did. Here's my thinking. Since you are sticking around a little longer than expected, and the chances of me coming up with a favour as huge, as mighty, as worthy as the one I did for you are slim, how do you feel about chipping away at it instead? A series of…mini favours, if you like?"

"Such as?"

"Nothing comes to mind, just yet. But it will."

"And if I have a small favour I need to add to the tally?"

It might take longer to redress the imbalance. "Bring it. Only fair."

"I'm liking the sound of this. And when the tally is finally even? What then? Phase Three?" Holden suggested.

"Sure. Let's go with that."

"Okay then. I await your next call with bated breath."

"Super. Enjoy your run, Holden."

Emerson reached out and pressed the button to end the call, her hands moving to cover her mouth. Then she started to laugh.

This was going to be fun. Or terrible. It was going to be something, which, after years of living within a very tight bandwidth, felt as if the lid had just opened on a box she hadn't known she'd been living in, letting in fresh air and sunshine.

And possibility.

* * *

"I need to get to work but I'm parked in," Emerson blurted, while standing by her car one morning to find a moving truck had parked halfway across her skinny driveway.

"Give me ten," Holden said, arriving in eight in a black convertible. With track pants and running top doing a terrible job of hiding a killer body beneath.

"What's with the new car?" she asked, trying not to stare at his arms. And the veins roping towards his wrists.

"I might take a run down the coast later. Better this than a sedan. Get in."

She did. Twisting like a pretzel in order to deal with the confined space.

Biting her tongue when Holden rested his hand on the gearstick, his little finger mere millimetres from the bare thigh showing beneath her pencil skirt.

Holding her breath when she glanced sideways right when he did the same, catching his eye, sharing smiles that seemed filled with some illicit promise. As if this was the beginning of something.

"Free for lunch?" he asked when he dropped her off, the engine still running while she slid from the car.

"I thought you were going for a drive down the coast."

He levelled her with a look. "Changed my mind. Lunch?"

"Sure," she said, feeling a sweeping sense of inevitability rock through her. “The place across the road. One o’clock. You’re paying.”

“You’re on.” He grinned and she felt it, like little spot fires all over her body.

Freya asked if she was feeling okay when she hopped out of the lift, ten minutes late, her cheeks still warm, the scent of him lingering on her clothes. “You look flushed. Feverish. Should I call a doctor?”

“I’m fine,” Emerson said, laughing. Before hotfooting it to her office, where she slumped in her chair and fanned herself with a stapler.

“I need a tie,” Holden said.

When Emerson showed up at his new digs—a town house not all that far from her place—it was to find him getting dressed for a keynote speech he was giving that night. Dark grey suit pants, beautifully cut, hugged his legs, his feet were bare and he was yet to put on a shirt.

“Really?” she said, trying to look anywhere bar the sculpted wonder that was his chest.

“What?”

She lifted the bag in her hand to cover the view.

Holden looked down and his abs flexed. “Please. You’d see more of me at the beach.”

The thought of seeing more of him had her swallowing. Hard.

He noticed. His grin widened.

Emerson chose to pretend it hadn’t happened, and said, “I think we’ve established I’m not a beach person.

More a laze-on-a-chair-by-the-pool person, while slathered in sunscreen, and wearing a big hat, under a huge umbrella."

"I'll remember that. If we ever find ourselves, at a beach, together." He said it as if it was a throwaway comment. But somehow it also felt like a promise. Like a plan. As if this wasn't some temporary deal they were seeing through before he went back to his real life.

"Hurry up," she said, shooing him away. "Put your shirt on, or you'll be late."

Trying not to stare at his gorgeous back, all muscle and warm skin and, *Oh, Mama*, she followed him down the hall. Then found herself in his bedroom. Where he kept his bed.

Expensive-looking sheets—no shock there—in shades of caramel and cream, lay tousled on the huge mattress. No blanket or comforter, for the man ran hot. A pair of pillows lay at one end, smushed and askew. As if he slept on one and hugged the other.

"What do you think?" he asked.

Emerson dragged her eyes from the bed, and the endearing yet aphrodisiacal story it told, to find him standing in front of a mirror holding up different shirts. Both snow-white.

She found the three ties she'd picked up at the boutique near work on her way over. Red, blue to match his eyes, and silver.

He chose the silver.

She rolled her eyes as she sat. "No ability to spin a line, and no sense of colour. Sigh."

He met her eyes in the mirror as he slowly did up the buttons on his shirt. Smiling eyes. Eyes that liked the fact that she was perched on the end of his bed. She popped up like a Jack in the box.

"Wanna come see me talk tonight?" he asked.

"I can see you talk anytime. Look at us now. Talking."

"'Tis true. But this is different. This will be me being erudite. And lauded. There may even be clapping afterwards. You never clap after I speak. It's quite the thing."

"Then, sure. That I have to see."

So she went to watch him speak to a room filled with IT types, after he made sure to snag her a seat at a table with friendly people. And he was brilliant and articulate, but also charming and warm, exactly the same man that he was when it was just the two of them.

No surprise, then, that, while a fair bit went over Emerson's head, the crowd lapped it up. She joined them in the standing ovation. And somehow, in the dark of the crowd, his eyes found hers. And he smiled. Smiled as he breathed out, a long, slow breath.

Oh, no, a voice inside her intoned, as the sense of sweeping that had been buffeting her for days swept over her so hard, so fast, it was a miracle she managed to keep her feet.

But by then, it was too late.

The next time Emmy had plans to see Camille, Holden finally took that drive down the coast road.

It was something he liked to do on occasion, just get in the car and go. Top of the car down, the wind in his hair, the engine rumbling beneath him. It satisfied the primal need to escape he'd never quite outgrown.

He'd been driving this very road when he'd had the idea for the app that had started it all. A virtual study app. Uni friends, Phillip included, had been his beta testers, before universities the world over had got wind of it and bought the app, making him a fortune. Ironic that its success had seen him never finish his degree, and not see those guys again for years.

He remembered the moment he'd realised that app might be something special. A magic trick that could yank him out of the state of impoverishment in which he'd grown up. He'd pictured himself finally having access to everything he'd wished he'd had as a kid—shelter, money, ease. And he'd been right.

What he'd not expected was the number of people who came begging, acquaintances, distant relatives, complete strangers—all after a hand-out, a leg-up, a crumb. The shine had worn off pretty quick, as soon he'd grown wary. His life was now littered with the detritus of those who'd pretended to be on his side, only to expect something in return.

Malaise set in. Loneliness. So he kept on moving, finding more out-of-the-way places, ends of the earth, depths of nowhere, as if standing still would be spitting in the face of his good fortune.

Until he built the next app. New levels of mania ensued. Bidding wars for his next app, unseen, undreamt. So was his new pattern. Build it up, then leave it behind. All the while chasing that feeling he'd felt while driving this road—dreaming what it might be like to get everything he'd ever wished for.

Till the day he'd woken up in Amsterdam, to a middle-of-the-night phone call, and realised he'd been chasing something that wasn't real. Something that would never satisfy him, even if it was.

An app functioned, or it didn't. It served a purpose, or it didn't. Success, on that score, was clear-cut. After the Sanderson debacle, he pared back, stopped wanting what it was clear he'd never have. And soon found balance that suited him.

Noisy Work—launching the occasional new app to applause and accolades and loud congratulations—which drowned out any interest in his Quiet Work—behind the scenes, sometimes anonymous, helping create frameworks for medical research, education reform, universal health care.

In order to protect that balance, his friendship groups, the people he trusted, had become restricted, or short-lived.

While unrecognisable from the life he'd dreamt of, the one people ironically thought he enjoyed, and the gruelling life he'd once known, he'd found it perfectly fulfilling.

Until Emerson Adler had come along and any feelings of fulfilment had gone out the window.

The woman confused the heck out of him.

She'd made it all too clear she wanted nothing from

him, which was unbelievably refreshing. Except those times she was outright demanding something of him. Where he'd found most people obscure to a fault, she was black and white. That he had to respect.

Then there was the attraction, a living, breathing thing that was becoming harder to contain. He could have kissed her a thousand times. And he knew, if he had, it wouldn't be the end of it. He'd still want to kiss her a thousand times more.

If Joel, his business manager, who knew enough about where he'd come from, had a single clue that he was here because of a woman, he'd have laughed till he split his spleen. His wife, Jenny, would likely burst into happy tears.

Infamously impervious Holden Roarke taken down by a bolshie brunette with a penchant for asking hard questions and sweet old dogs. And he had been taken down. Brought to his knees.

He wasn't sleeping. He had little room for ideas in his head that didn't involve ways to invent a favour he might ask or perform. And he had left behind a perfectly liveable penthouse so that he could rent a place, short-term, in the suburbs.

All so that he might be near to her.

Treading lightly all the while. His instincts assured him that was necessary. For all her big talk, there was something wildly delicate about Emerson Adler. Uncertain. Skittish.

Which was the only way he was able to stop himself from telling her how much he wanted to touch her, to hold her, to kiss her, to make love to her, to wake up beside her and do it all over again. This was the one time in his life where he had to be more careful than he was curious.

And so, rather than enjoying a delicious, torrid affair with a woman he found utterly captivating, before heading back to Stockholm or the Seychelles, or wherever the first plane he found might take him, he'd found himself in the midst of an old-fashioned courting.

And he couldn't get enough of it.

Yep. The woman confused the heck out of him.

Holden hung a left, leaving the beach huts behind and spinning up into the hills.

This he could measure. This he could enjoy without censure or self-recrimination. To be out here, mid-week, while others plugged away at their office jobs, he knew himself to be a very lucky man.

He would relish these spoils of his success, before the rubber band wrapped around his heart no doubt sent him thwacking all the way back to her.

At the same time, back in Melbourne, Emerson found Camille in the succulent section of Wild Willow Plant Nursery.

"Sorry I'm late!" said Emmy. "Heck of a morning. The family next door used their new barbecue and set off my smoke alarms. And you know how Pumpkin gets with smoke alarms. Then, would you believe I had a flat tyre?"

Camille looked at Emerson's white-on-white ensemble. "Not even slightly. You should have called me. Turns out I'm now amazing with a wrench!"

"Good to know," she said. "Anyway, I called Holden, but he's off on some joy ride, so I got onto the auto club, and here I am!"

Camille's eyes widened comically. "Back up. You called *Holden*? As in Holden Roarke? As in *Heartache Number Four*?"

Emerson blinked. "Um—"

"No," said Camille, turning away, holding up a dramatic shushing hand. "I get it. I've been replaced."

"What? No!" Emerson insisted, even while she felt prickly heat swoosh into her cheeks. "Holden is... Well, we've been doing these favours for one another, you see."

When Camille clearly didn't see, Emerson gave her a quick, awkward rundown of the past few weeks. Then added, "Serendipitous timing, really, as I can't keep relying on you because you're busy, you're on your homey-moon, Phillip is your person now—"

Camille reached out and took Emerson's hands. "Stop. Breathe. I get it. It's been weird, right? This new normal?"

Emerson nodded, and smiled, relieved to be talking this out rather than shoving it down deep inside. "But getting less weird. Don't you think?"

Camille nodded, eyes a little bright. Then pointed towards the outdoor plant section before ambling that way. "So, these favours of yours. You do realise this is basically how being a couple works. You drive him somewhere, he picks up your laundry. It's a relationship without the sex. Unless… Unless this is some long-term, stretch-things-out-until-you-feel-you-might-die mode of foreplay."

Emerson, who was sniffing the leaves of a velvety plant, stilled. A lightbulb, then a thousand more, like wild, out-of-control fairy lights, were springing to life inside her head. "Oh, my."

"I knew it!" Camille spun on the spot.

"Unless—"

"Here we go."

"Unless I'm right back where I was all those years ago, feeling all these feelings and he just thinks I'm his cute little hallway friend."

"You're not cute."

"That's what you took from that?"

"Honeybun, you're *va-va-voom*. So maybe he thinks of you as his *va-va-voom* little hallway friend."

Emerson shot Camille a look. "Not helping."

"Then *ask* him! Or better yet, jump him. Either way it's gotta be better than being wound so tight."

"I'm not wound tight."

"You know what? You actually don't look it, either. What's with that?"

"I have endeavoured to make sure I don't implode with all the pent-up, built-up, you know… Let's just say Holden Roarke is mighty good fantasy material."

Camille held up a hand for a high five, which Emerson duly gave up.

"Wow. This is some huge progress you've made. Like day-one-in-therapy-then-fast-forward-to-graduation-level progress."

Emerson agreed. This was *exactly* what she'd been hoping for when she'd allowed herself to enjoy being with Holden, rather than constantly waiting for the other shoe to drop. "I do feel like a stronger, more evolved version of myself. More…open to possibility."

"By possibility do you mean giving your vibrator a night off, dragging Holden Roarke into your bed for some good old-fashioned rumpy-pumpy?"

Emerson smiled at the grey-haired couple who gawped at them as they meandered by. "Maybe. Though without the old-fashioned bit."

Camille stopped in the middle of the aisle, sunlight dappling her face through the leaves of a row of potted palms. "Just so long as you don't forget, this is Holden Roarke."

"Meaning?"

"From what Phillip has told me—and he's told me a lot, because he is semi in love with the guy—Holden is not a stay-at-home-and-watch-true-crime-documentaries kind of man. He's a big deal. So, for all that you're having fun now, there's a really good chance he'll be heading back to his real life soon. And you… Well, you do know that people leaving you is your kryptonite. It's kind of a running theme in the… You Know List."

"I know," said Emerson.

And she did. She really did.

She still had his calendar linked to hers. Saw the eye-popping lists of people his business manager, an excitable-sounding guy named Joel, added to his "maybe" calendar—the majority of them overseas, in places like Geneva and Washington and Dubai. All of which had been crossed through, because Holden was here.

Still, hearing Camille say it sent little impacts all over her body. Like buckshot—not enough to take her down, but enough for it to sting.

Then Camille clicked her fingers. "Unless… Unless you're doing this because you *know* he'll leave. You're fooling around with him *because* there's an end point. That's genius!"

Emerson moved on, towards the fern section, Camille's theory running through her head. Maybe there was something to that too. A safety net to her experiment. Was that such a bad thing? "You make me sound so mercenary."

Camille shrugged. "You do you, boo. And, hey, when he does vamoose, after unlocking the wanton, voracious, cavalier side we all know is lurking beneath your pristine façade, I still have that list of Phillip's friends, who would ask you out in a heartbeat if only they weren't terrified of you."

"I'll keep that in mind," Emerson deadpanned. "So…plants!"

"Plants!"

While Camille talked up her idea of a wall of hanging plants in her tiny lounge, as inspired by some random Instagrammer with a much bigger house, Emmy nodded along, and tried not to think about Holden leaving, in actuality, and what that might feel like. Not having him at the end of the phone. Not being able to see him whenever the fancy took her.

And those thoughts set some small, dangerous thing alight deep inside her.

Not an ache. Nothing quite so blunt. More the sharp, painful constancy of an accidental burn.

That was the thing about burns, the small ones that travelled slowly through dry scrub. If not doused soon, a wind might whip up and soon the whole forest would burn to the ground.

"That's an A380." One eye open, Holden held his finger to the sky, tracing the underbelly of the plane as it lifted into the darkening dusk over their heads, heading to destinations unknown.

"How can you tell?" Emerson asked, while busy poking and prodding at the pile of soft blankets and cushions Holden had thrown in the back of the ute after trading it for his rental convertible.

"I know my planes," he said.

Giving up on perfection, she leaned back on her elbows, and squinted up at the plane as it lifted higher into the sky. "A man of hidden skills."

"Not so hidden, I hope. In fact, perhaps I ought to write them all down on a list, carry them on my person, so that any time people are in need of one of my many skills I can whip it out."

"Lists can be helpful." Her mouth twitched before her head turned his way. The dying rays of sunlight spilled over the dark waves of her hair, the delicate edge of her face, her shoulder. "Whip it out, you say?"

"At any time," he offered. "For the benefit of the community."

"For an ideas man, some of your ideas are whackadoo."

"The download numbers of my apps tell a different story."

"Over-confidence is not an attractive trait."

Holden's grin hit his face before he even felt it coming. "Not in my experience."

Emerson scoffed, but didn't argue the fact. Instead, she once more became preoccupied with getting comfortable.

For all that watching her wriggle about in a bed of blankets and cushions may not have been the smartest idea for a man who was struggling not to spook her by hauling her into his arms and kissing her senseless, he felt rather good about his decision to bring her.

Their arrival at their current location—an aircraft viewing spot in Greenvale—had come about due to his latest favour request.

Andy, another friend from uni, worked for Australian air traffic control. Nearing the end of a major software update, they were keen to get his input on how to make the interface less spartan, and more user-friendly.

Emerson had called the night before, asking for a

favour. One of her staff, an older, rather sophisticated gent, was having a birthday and could Holden recommend a unique gift? He'd agreed to pick something up—a signed Graham Greene book he'd spotted in a vintage store near hers—if she'd come along to a meeting as a second pair of eyes.

Partly because he had learned that spending time with her was better than not, and partly because the thought of spending any time in the bowels of the airport where his father had worked on and off his whole childhood did not entice.

Now—wriggling as if she had ants in the pants of the classy, black, all-in-one get-up that she had going on—she got her high heels caught in a blanket and it took her a good ten seconds to get free. Then she flapped a wild hand at some bug—real or imagined—that had wafted too close to her face. And huffed. Loudly.

"We can go," said Holden, not minding what they did, so long as he got to watch her do it. "If this isn't your thing."

"No! This is lovely. Really. It's…"

She looked at him a moment, her gaze a little hot, colour sweeping into her cheeks, and he felt the word *romantic* whisper on the breeze.

In the end, she went with, "Fine. If I wasn't here, I'd probably have taken Pumpkin into the office, as there is so much work to do on the Sanderson job, which is brilliant, but also a lot. My assistant, Freya—you'd have spoken to her on the phone a couple of times in the early days—sends me memes daily about ways to relax. If I tell her I lie out under the stars, on a pile of blankets, in the middle of nowhere, she'll be beside herself."

"Well, so long as you're excited to be here…"

Her grin was quick and intoxicating. The urge to stroke his thumb over that full bottom lip, to watch her eyes flash with surprise, then turn dark with longing, was a strong one. The certainty that it would change everything between them hovered on the air. Ripe and sweet.

The way her chest lifted and fell, he was sure she could feel it too. But then she lay back, and placed her hands over her chest like some kind of beatific painting. It was so damned endearing his chest hurt.

He was a goner. Truly.

With no planes in the sky, the great dome above having quickly turned dark, they watched in companionable silence as wispy clouds wafted by, blocking out the crescent moon, before wafting on again.

Emerson sighed, the sound warmed by a kind of contentment that Holden felt in his bones. "I've lived in Melbourne all my life and I never knew this was a thing."

"It's a favourite haunt of mine."

"You came here as a kid?"

"Mmm," he said. It hadn't been a thing to do, it had been a safe space, a lifesaver. "I grew up out this way."

"Really?" She lifted back to her elbows, and glanced

around, taking in the great tracts of farmland. "It's lovely."

"This is. Where we were was near enough to the airport for the plane noise to be a daily grind, not near enough to live on more than a postage stamp of land in dilapidated council housing."

"You and your dad?"

"Mmm. See that farm over there," he said, pointing over her shoulder to an undulating patch of shadowy forest green across the way. "It's a retirement home for ex-racehorses, including a few Melbourne Cup winners."

He knew she hadn't been fooled by his clumsy distraction. He only liked her more when she went with it. "Oh! That's wonderful. They get to live out their days frolicking through acres of lush pastures. Far better than the alternative."

"When they 'go to the farm', they actually go to the farm."

"Groan."

When he laughed, she lay back and smiled up into the sky. Now he wanted to trace the line of her nose, her chin, her collarbone. What was happening to him? It was like he was sixteen again, seeing a girl, liking a girl, not knowing what to do with a girl.

"So, if you grew up out this way, how did you end up in high school in Kew? And for such a brief stint?"

"You noticed that, did you?"

Her mouth twisted. "We had matching guidance

counsellor sessions every single week. When you didn't show up one week, or ever again, I noticed."

Holden squinted up into the sky. "Why don't you tell me more about the memes this assistant of yours sends—are they the types you find on inspirational calendars, all bordered in flowers? Or more along the black and white dirge line?"

She turned fully on her side, her hands tucked under her head. And said nothing. He knew it cost her—the girl with all the questions—but she held her tongue.

Holden breathed out hard. "I'd call you pushy, in the hopes of sending you spiralling off in another direction, but I get the feeling you'd take it as a compliment."

He tipped his head, and found himself looking into Emerson's curious eyes. Her lovely face, her warm body all curled up beside his. Happy to listen if he wanted to talk, or to simply be with him if he didn't. As if she wanted nothing from him bar what he was willing to give.

It cost her nothing to be that way, yet it didn't feel like nothing. In fact, it felt closer to a continental shift. If he hadn't been lying down, he might have had to reach out for something to grip.

"Change of subject," she said. "Your airport friend's proposal. It's a huge project. My advice? Don't say yes unless you see yourself surrendering to it for the next eighteen months to two years. Can you? Can you see yourself sticking to one thing for that long?"

The question was simple. And yet... That was the

second time she'd asked him how long he was sticking around. Which was not an accident. Did it indicate she had a vested interest in his answer?

The continental shift cracked open a fraction wider.

When he didn't answer she huffed out a breath. Of frustration? Then she reached out blindly, grabbed a fluffy cushion and brought it to her chest. "Where on earth did you find all this stuff?"

Finally, a question he could answer. "I may have called Camille last night to ask where I might find such frippery at short notice. After two of the longest minutes of my life, in which I was asked a barrage of questions far more brazen than even you dare ask, she sent me to some frou-frou boutique. Apparently 'the plan' is that she's happy to take it all off my hands for the new house when we're done here tonight."

"She is industrious," Emmy said, with a quick smile. Then he could feel her mulling over her next words. "So, you called Camille before I called you. Meaning you were already planning this before I agreed to come. I can either assume you always liked being surrounded by pretty cushions when watching planes, or—" She breathed in, breathed out, and said, "Or you did all this for me. Knowing, somehow, how very much I needed a break."

"Sprung," he said. He smiled, she smiled back, and he felt it like an arrow in his chest fired at close range. "When I was working on my first app, I turned into a madman, locked away in my dark tower, hunched over my work, squinting if I ever accidentally stumbled into the light."

"Like Quasimodo?"

"Ah, I think you mean Batman."

"He has a cave, not a tower."

"Can't you let a man dream?"

She lifted her fingers in submission. "Dream away."

Then she turned to face the sky as a plane began its descent up high over their heads, her eyes tracking the slow movement of the big, metallic beast.

While Holden's fingertips pressed into his chest.

Dream away, she'd said. When his wish was to reach out, and cup her cheek. Or sweep that rogue lock of hair behind her ear. Or tell her that if he didn't kiss her, soon, he might literally expire, and his disappearance would be on her hands.

Unfortunately, his talk of not being able to spin a line had not been a line. Meaning all he could do was tell her the truth.

"First time I came here I was fifteen," he said. "Too young for a licence, I stole my father's car. He'd just finished telling me how worthless I was, and passed out drunk. I drove and drove, with no destination in mind, only slowing when I saw a dozen-odd cars lined up in the field here, right as a plane flew low overhead. I pulled onto the hard shoulder, the noise of the thing filling my head. My panic slowly abated, as plane after plane headed off into the wild blue yonder. My dream, as it was, from that day on, was to one day be up there, heading far, far away from here."

He squinted at the first stars hovering above the horizon.

"A few weeks later, next time my dad passed out drunk, I packed up my stuff and left. My great-aunt lived in Kew—she let me stay with her so long as I kept going to school. Counselling meant I could attend without guardian approval. Then one day my dad turned up at his aunt's place with a cricket bat and a slur. I've been on the move pretty much ever since."

She was quiet for a few long beats, before she said, "Why do you think he was like that?"

"According to him, everything that went wrong in his life began the moment I was born. My mother died in childbirth, so there was some truth to it. Made it hard to disassociate that from his drinking, his anger, his self-pity."

"How does a man like that end up with a son like you?"

His chest squeezed, the hollowness that had lived behind his ribs for so long pressed so tight it nearly popped. "So, you're saying I'm *not* worthless," he said, turning his head and adding a smile to soften the joke.

She lay back on her side, watching him, her brow furrowed. As if, if the man was still alive today she'd take a swing.

He adored her for it. This beautiful, challenging, skittish, intense creature who made him work for every smile, every laugh, every drop of trust. Made him dig deep. And speak truth.

He *adored* her.

It was the only thing that made any sense. For the way he felt, had been feeling these past weeks, was nothing he'd ever felt before. It was as wholesome as it was raw. As comforting and gentle as it was a roar in the back of his head, thunder behind his ribs, a pressing and constant need that lived and roiled at his centre, all of which was held back by the barest thread of civility.

This woman he'd never even kissed.

It was past time he did something about that.

"Emmy," he said. "Emerson." Then he reached out for her. Slowly. So she knew what was coming. As if she couldn't hear it in the raw scrape of his voice. The clawing need.

Giving her time to make it clear if this wasn't what she wanted. But, gods, he hoped it was. Hoped more than he remembered hoping for anything since he'd last been here, hoping something up there might be the answer to making his life better down here.

His fingers slid through her hair, the strands falling over his hands like heavy silk. He exhaled with relief, as it felt as if he'd been waiting for this exact moment all his life.

He cradled her gently, his thumb tracing her cheekbone, as he moved in. Caught by the heat in her eyes. By the soft catch in her breath.

When he was close enough for their lips to almost touch, he paused. Took a moment to sink into the anticipation, grateful it was finally at an end. Or was this the beginning?

And then he kissed her.

When their lips met, she sighed, as if she'd been imagining this moment as long as he had. As if she too had been holding on for dear life and could finally let go.

When he tilted her face, so he could deepen the kiss, she opened to him, swept her tongue against his, and he was lost.

Lost to heat and need. And regret. Regret that they'd waited. And joy. Joy that they'd waited. That this moment had finally come, with the starlight raining down upon her face, as she scooted closer and wrapped herself around him, and met his kisses with her own, in this bed of blankets he'd built for her.

"Holden," she said, coming up for air. Looking into his eyes, searching.

Whatever she saw there, things soon turned frantic, desperate. As if they were trying to find a way into one another's skin.

She rolled on top of him, kissing him madly, even as her hands reached for his shirt, tugging it free of his jeans. When her hands found skin they slowed, tracing his sides with deliberation and pace, sending the painful prick of a million goosebumps racing all over his body. And it was a miracle it wasn't all over for him, then and there.

When his hands mirrored her pace, sliding slowly up her thighs, her whole body seemed to sing.

She rocked against him, setting off explosions behind his eyes, as she plied him with drugging kisses—

A car door slammed. And Holden remembered where they were.

"Emmy," he said, the word playing against her mouth.

She hummed, and rolled against him again.

With supernatural strength Holden rolled her over, till he was on top, his thigh between hers. He pressed down. Her eyes rolled back in her head, her front teeth bearing down on her bottom lip.

He gritted out, "We have company."

Her eyes flew open, her hands gripping his messed-up shirt as she lifted her head to look over his shoulder.

Glancing back, he saw a dad and three young kids pile out of a station wagon, holding apples and juice boxes, before piling into the boot when the dad opened the rear door, clearly about to set up for an evening of plane-watching at the popular spot.

Holden quickly sat up, fixed his shirt, tossed a blanket over his junk. The dad gave him a quick nod, and a wave, as if he remembered how it felt to be young and so caught up in another you forgot who you were.

Not *who* you were, where you were.

Holden was very aware of who he was—a guy whose dad would never have taken him on an "outing" such as this. Never packed him a juice box. Or told him to eat an apple. He'd offered cigarettes, drink, a kick in the backside as he shoved him out the door of a morning, telling him not to come back unless he had money in his pocket.

"Oh, my God," said Emerson, her hand flopping

over her eyes. "Can you imagine if they'd been a few minutes later?"

"Whatever do you mean?" he asked, moving gently, so as not to damage himself, even as his mind spun. "Explain it to me. In lurid detail."

She laughed, the sound bright and light. And gorgeous. A sound he could listen to for ever and never tire of it.

His earlier musings lurked, like a virus—who was he to think of forever? His first real attempt at such a life with the Sandersons had been disastrous. All these years later he still hadn't learned how to settle into a life that required a fixed address. He had no clue what *home* even meant.

"Why did it take us so damn long to do that?" Emerson asked.

"You tell me."

She tipped her head to face him, so utterly gorgeous it hurt. "Should I be asking you to forget that too? It was miles outside the boundaries of our agreement after all."

Holden's jaw twitched hard enough to crack a tooth. He said, "You can ask. But then, you'd also have to ask me to forget about how much you wanted to kiss me when I dropped you to your hotel room after the wedding."

Her mouth fell open.

"Or how much I wanted to kiss you on the garden bench after dinner at the Sandersons'. Then again when I dropped you home that night. And when you brought me those ties. I can go on."

"Mmm," she said, stretching like a cat who'd got the cream.

That was neither a yes nor a no, which, as far as Holden could see, was progress. Progressing towards what, he had no idea. All he knew was that it was going in a direction that felt right.

Then she shivered. For the night had turned cold.

"Come on," he said, climbing off the back of the tray, and holding out a hand. "Let's get you home."

Home he took her. And at home he left her. After a chaste kiss at her door. A press of his lips on hers that lasted a breath or two. A kiss that left her looking dreamy and soft as she floated inside her house, her voice already calling for her dog, as if she had a story to tell.

While Holden took the throws and cushions back to the town house he was renting.

He'd buy Camille a voucher to get her own.

CHAPTER EIGHT

Emerson hopped out of her ride share, juggling a large gift bag, a bottle of wine, and her phone. And looked, in marvel, at the changes her friends had made to their new home.

The garden bed was new, lined with little stones and boasting a string of tiny plants poking out of mounds of bark, much of which must have been done earlier that day by the team of friends and colleagues who'd turned up early for the Working Bee, Beer, and Barbecue extravaganza.

Emmy had been invited, of course, but Camille had followed up with:

do not show up before the after-party begins the rest of the day will be backbreaking love you!

With the new fence and Camille's beloved fairy lights strung along the front porch, it all looked so pretty. So very much theirs. Those bittersweet pickled feelings threatened to rise up inside Emmy again, only this time she was able to still them. For it was all okay. She was okay. They'd all be okay.

"Emmy!" cried Bernadette, Camille's lovely young cousin, when she opened the door. Dust in her hair, a scratch on her cheek, she wiped a hand down her old overalls before pulling Emmy in for a hug.

"Emmy's here!" she cried.

The crowd turned as one and called out, "Emmy!" before going back to their conversations, while Bernie took the gift bag from Emmy and popped it with the pile in the corner of the lounge.

"Did you hear?" Bernie asked, before flashing her left hand and showing off a tiny diamond on a band of gold.

"Oh. Wow! When?" *Who?*

"Barry," said Bernie, with a sigh. "We were high school sweethearts, you know. Fell apart, as you do at that age. Then reconnected at Camille and Phillip's wedding. It seems the bouquet worked after all."

Emmy's delighted laughter was genuine. "It seems so."

She wondered if Bernadette remembered trying to slip her room key into Holden's pocket. Then figured, by the lovestruck look in Bernie's eyes as she waved to Barry across the room, that she did not. Emmy decided then and there that it had never happened.

"Camille?" Emmy asked.

As if hearing her name, Camille appeared out of nowhere, looking glorious in a long green dress, her curls piled up on top of her head, making it clear she'd also managed to avoid the Working Bee part of the party.

Camille placed a glass of bubbly in Emmy's hand then gave her a quick tour. The place was still a mess, most rooms unfinished. But the pantry was huge, the light in the bedrooms gorgeous. It was on its way to being perfect.

"Do you love it?" Camille asked, as they ended up in the lounge.

"More than life itself."

"Good. Turns out we need a kettle. And a toaster. Remember we didn't put them on the wedding gift list?"

"Too bourgeois, I believe you said."

"Bit us on the backside, that did."

Emmy pointed to her gift bag. "Cream wrapping, rose-gold ribbon."

"I knew I loved you."

"These are great," said Emmy, running her fingers over the spring greens and dusty pinks of the cushions and throws draped over the couches in the lounge. Not at all like the greys and creams of the furnishings Holden had used in the ute the other night. She could still feel them under her head when he'd kissed her. Under her knees when she'd straddled him.

"New?" she asked, before clearing her throat.

"Yep! Holden gave us a very generous tab at a local boutique as a house-warming gift, so I went a little crazy."

"You came!"

Camille and Emmy both looked up at Phillip's enthusiastic outburst, only to find him looking to the front door. To Holden, standing there, holding a huge potted cactus.

Emmy's heart smacked against her ribs with such force she actually tripped forward.

They hadn't seen one another in person since the plane-watching night. They'd texted. They'd talked, sometimes late into the night. He'd called to ask for advice on a good house-warming present. Not a favour, *advice*. She'd gone with, "Something Camille can't kill." The promise of *next time* building between them like a dormant volcano.

Holden's smile when his eyes found hers was scorching. Emerson hid her own goofy smile behind her drink.

Then her view was blocked as a bunch of Phillip's friends saw who'd arrived and descended upon Holden with questions, app ideas, requests, before the guy had even made it over the threshold.

"Sit," said Camille, pressing Emmy into her old couch, when all she wanted to do was go to him, hold out a hand and tell everyone to back the hell away.

Knowing how crazy that was, Emmy sat with a whoosh of expelled air.

"Holden!" said Camille. "Lovely to see you. Drink?"

Emmy's heart thundered in her throat as she looked up to find he'd pushed his way through the crowd just fine. He'd done so to see her. "Iced water, please. With lime if you have it."

"Do I have lime? he asks. I'll be back." Camille left.

And Holden continued smiling down at Emmy, the heat in his eyes making her wonder which part of their recent kiss *he* was reliving. She was up to the part when his tongue had traced the edges of her top teeth, sending sparks rocketing through her entire body, as if she'd been hit by lightning.

She motioned for him to sit.

And he did. Close beside her. So close that, when he pressed his hand into the seat to make himself comfortable, his little finger stroked against hers.

Phillip plonked down on the tub chair near the couch, his cheeks pink from happiness. And beer.

Holden shifted so that his arm rubbed against hers.

Emmy may have shivered from top to toe, and Holden may have noticed.

Camille reappeared, handing Holden his drink before sitting on her husband's lap, bubbly sloshing over the edge of her glass, and looking as contented as Emmy had ever seen her. She waited for a flicker of the bittersweets, only this time it didn't come. No twinge, not even an echo, too swamped with happiness was she at seeing her friends so content.

"Look at us," said Phillip, beaming. "Camille and I, all grown up in our amazing new house. Then there's Holden with his apps and his world renown."

Holden laughed, rubbing a hand up the back of his head. And was that a little flush creeping up his neck? Emmy shifted so that her knee bumped his. The look he shot her was quick, but sizzling, and she tucked her knees together so as to hold herself in one piece.

"And then there's our Emmy," said Phillip, "the Heartache List now so far in her rear-view mirror she'd have to squint to see it."

"What's the Heartache List?" Holden asked.

Camille smacked Phillip on the arm.

"What?" Phillip asked. Then, "God, Emmy. I'm so sorry. It just slipped out. I figured he knew, considering…" Phillip waved a hand at them, motioning to how close they were sitting.

"Why do I get the sense Phillip just put his foot in it?" Holden asked, leaning into Emmy's side.

"It's nothing. Don't worry about it."

His hand moved to her knee, his eyes searching hers. "I'm not worried about it. What with all the stage-whispering and arm-hitting and the panic in your eyes, I am a little intrigued. And now that I think about it, you mentioned something about the List the night of the wedding."

"Do you forget nothing?"

"Big brain," he said, tapping the side of his head.

Emmy sucked her lips between her teeth, and glanced around the room, looking for an escape. Till Camille caught her eye and mouthed, *Tell him.*

Careful Emmy would never have considered giving up that part of herself to Holden Roarke. The evolved Emmy, the bold, brave, curious Emmy, pulled herself to standing. And motioned for Holden to follow.

Follow he did, through the lounge, the dining

room, the den. But everywhere they went there were people. Eventually they ended up in the kitchen.

The pantry! Grabbing Holden by the hand, Emmy dragged him into the huge walk-in cupboard. A light flickered on as the door opened, then off again after the door closed.

In the semi-darkness, lit only by a sliver of light coming under the door, she could feel Holden's warmth. Hear the shift of his clothes, the huff of his breath.

"It looked bigger from the outside," she muttered.

"Emerson."

"Hmm?"

"Was there a reason you brought me in here?"

Darkness was nice, but as her other senses heightened, forcing her to focus on his gorgeous scent, she started to feel a little woozy. She found her phone, switched on the light, and placed it on a shelf beside a bag of pasta.

The shaft of overbright light shone on one side of Holden's face, creating shadows and valleys in the most beautiful shapes.

The slide of his hands into the pockets of his jeans were the only sign he was holding his patience in check.

"Okay," she said. "I'm going to tell you something, but you have to promise not to freak out."

"Do I seem like someone prone to freaking out?"

"Fair enough. For a number of years, I kept a notebook in which I detailed the times I'd had my heart broken."

"The Heartache List."

"The very one. I only documented the big hurts. The ones I felt sure I would never get over. My third-grade teacher leaving mid-term, the rock star whose posters covered my walls marrying some other woman."

"Those were your big hurts?"

"They were big. To me."

"Of course," he said, his expression chagrined. "Go on."

"Yes, I had other knocks, disappointments, frustrations, and sorrows that did not end up on the list. Such as when a school friend 'washed' my favourite Barbie doll's hair in the toilet. When I missed making the Dean's List at university while the kid who never showed up to lectures who also had the same name as one of the college libraries made it." She paused. "Though, to be fair, I looked up that old Barbie when it came up in one of those 'you are this old if you remember this toy' things on social media. In pristine condition they're now worth a packet."

"Emmy, I am loving this insight into what makes you *you*, but I'm not sure you needed to drag me into a cupboard to tell me about it."

"Okay. Yes. Here goes. And I can't believe I'm about to say this out loud, but maybe it's all part of the great Heartache List therapy session I'm in the midst of—I had a crush on you. Back then. At school."

In the quiet that followed, the white noise of the party permeated, but it was a blur beneath the thumping rush of blood behind Emmy's ears.

"Yeah," Holden eventually said. "I kind of figured."

Emerson stared at him. Gobsmacked. "You kind of *figured*?"

"Well, you're not exactly the most subtle person on the planet," he said, reaching out to her as if he might cup her cheek before curling his fingers into his palm. "Back then, you'd look at me with those big eyes of yours and kind of..."

"Kind of what?"

"Sigh."

Kill her now.

"Hang on a second," he said, as he came full circle. "Are you suggesting I was on your Heartbreak List?"

"Heartache."

"Oh, good. I'd hate to think I'd broken you as opposed to making you ache."

His words, while flippant, hit deep. Aching, feeling broken, these were feelings she'd worked hard to keep out of her life. Something she still hoped to do, no matter how this "therapy" worked out.

"It wasn't your fault," she said. "You did nothing wrong." She knew that now.

"Then why—?"

"It all started with my dad." Emerson leaned back, needing space, only to rattle up against a shelf that was yet to be bolted to the wall.

Holden reached out, steadied her, and said, "Your dad."

"He left when I was ten. We… I…never saw it coming. And I… I don't think I've ever really got over it. My mum tried to help me understand, that marriage can be hard work, and some people aren't built for it, but the fact he could leave *me*, and never even get in touch… It broke my heart."

Yes, broke. Every other slight after that had been like pressing into a deep wound.

"During our sojourns in the hall outside Miss Kemp's office, you were so sweet to me. During a time when life felt sour. And when you left, and I didn't see it coming, again, it brought up things I'd been trying to pretend hadn't affected me as much as they had."

"Fathers, eh?" Holden said, moving in a little closer, his thumbs moving up and down her arms.

"Camille's dad is a gem. Phillip's too. And, from what you told me, Chuck was a pretty amazing stand-in."

"So, genetically we lucked out?" he asked, a dash of irony lighting his voice, even while it remained warm and kind and understanding.

"Ha. I guess we did."

Emerson looked up into Holden's eyes, and felt that flicker of familiarity he'd said he felt when he'd spotted her on the dance floor. Outsiders looking in. Only, here in this tight space, his hands on her, she didn't feel like an outsider. She felt as if she was inside something bigger than herself. Something magical.

Refusing to think, or overthink, or mentally play out any scenarios to their possible end games, she lifted onto her toes and kissed him.

His lips were cool and smooth, the taste of lime and ice sending a beautiful chill right through her. Already holding her, keeping her steady, Holden pulled her a little higher and kissed her back.

And while their first kiss—*their first kiss!*—in the back of the ute had been scorching hot—decades of pent-up frustration hot—a dam bursting—this…

This kiss was sweet. Slow. Lingering.

Tasting, testing, learning one another's shape and feel.

The whole thing felt as if it was happening in slow motion.

Pressed as high as she could go, Emerson slid her hands up Holden's chest, and around his neck, her fingers tingling at the touch of his hair. His hands slid slowly down her arms to circle her waist, pulling her close.

This beautiful man. This good, generous, gorgeous hulk of a man who knew what it was to hurt. To move beyond it. And to thrive.

Her limbs began to tremble as the kiss deepened. Incrementally. Unceasingly. Settling in her limbs like warm honey. Hands now roving. Touching, caressing. Finding tender spots. Finding skin.

Small sounds of pleasure backed up in her throat, keeping her breathless. Heat pooled in her centre, till her head spun. Until she was a molten puddle of gooey pleasure.

Aeons later, Emmy pulled back, needing breath. Needing to feel the ground beneath her feet.

She dropped slowly back to her heels. Rested her head against Holden's chest, her eyes filling when he wrapped his arms even tighter about her and dropped a kiss on the top of her head.

As her pulse thudded sluggishly through her body, she mused that until that moment it was entirely possible she hadn't known what heartache was.

For, like a foot that had fallen asleep, it seemed that her heart had been slumbering. And now, as it filled with blood, and warmth, and life, like pins and needles in her chest the pain was real.

This was no crush. A crush was tender, and warm. Distant.

The feelings rushing through her, the knowledge of how much she felt for this man, was wild, and raw, and out of control.

She felt as if she'd been sliced open, exposed.

His hands began sweeping over her back, calming her heart rate. Calming them both.

There was no chance he couldn't feel the thump of her heart, the tremble in her chest. No chance he didn't have some inkling that these feelings were overwhelming her. That this was not a test. That there was no going back.

"So, this Heartache List—"

"Forget about it. I have. Or, to be fair, I'm working on it."

"With the…great Heartache List therapy session that you're in the midst of."

"Mm-hmm."

"Am I a part of that?"

Emerson twisted to lay her cheek over his heart and said nothing. Not sure how he'd handle knowing he was all of that.

He lifted a hand to cradle her face, to turn it to him. "So long as you know that there is no point in asking me to forget about that kiss. It happened. And it's going to happen again."

He leaned down and kissed her once more. Pulled back to say, "And again."

Another kiss, this one rich with longing, turning her knees to jelly and her brain to mush.

He pulled back again just enough to hold eye contact as he said, "I'm done pretending this isn't happening, Emerson. I'm more than okay with you and me, if you are too."

She sucked in a slow breath, enough to gather her thoughts. "I'm more than okay with that, too." Adding, "For as long as you're in town."

His gaze intense, solid, true, he said, "I'm not going anywhere."

Then, before she could brace herself against the fresh onslaught of feelings *that* brought on, he took her by the hand and twirled her under his arm till she was tucked up against his side. With his spare hand he passed her her phone, and waited for her to turn off the light.

"Shall we?" he asked, his voice a rumble in the darkness.

She held his hand in place. And nodded.

With his arm around her he led her out into the fray.

A few wide-eyed looks from Phillip's friends, a few side-eyes from people who'd never have put "Emerson" and "public display of affection" in the same sentence. When Camille spied them her mouth dropped open, before she clapped her hands effusively, forcing everyone to look her way. "Everyone out back. Time for Strip Charades!"

Laughter and murmurs of dissent abounded before she said, "Fine. Normal charades."

Thus having provided the perfect distraction, Camille gave Emmy a quick wink and shuffled everyone outside. She gave Holden the two-fingered *I'm watching you* move. Then the party went on as if nothing had changed.

When, to Emerson's mind, it would never be the same again.

"I need a favour," Emerson blurted the moment the phone was answered. Then, "Aargh, I forgot to check your calendar. If you're busy—"

"Shoot," Holden said, no hesitation.

Emerson breathed out in relief. "It's Pumpkin."

"Is he okay?" Holden asked, his voice tight, as if he

wasn't merely asking. As if he truly cared about her patchy old pup.

Emerson had no hope of muffling the warm fuzzies that crept up her insides as she said, "Yes. Yes, he's fine. I left him home today as he was super-cute and sleepy this morning. It's just, I remembered he's run out of his special food. I usually pre-order it from the vet but they were changing brands last time we visited. I ran out this morning, the vet closes really early today, in about twenty minutes, and I have a pre-interview with an amazing Sanderson Group COO candidate in ten minutes, and Chuck is being very stubborn and I'm finding it harder and harder to even find anyone to talk to about the position much less suggest, so I won't make it in time, and I usually use Kerri, next door, who I pay to look after Pumpkin when I can't, but she's at uni this arvo, and—"

"Text me the details."

"Are you sure?"

"Emmy, I'm the one you call."

"Thank you."

"My pleasure," he said, in that voice of his that made her believe it really was. His pleasure. "Where's his bowl?"

"Don't worry about that. Kerri can feed him when she gets home."

"Emmy, just tell me where his bowl is?"

"If you're sure..." *Two favours to tick off the tally*, she thought. Then thought again. *Did any of that matter any more, now that things had shifted so considerably between them? And honestly, looking back, had it ever?* "Pumpkin's bowl is just inside the doggy door round the back, so if you reach a hand in you'll find it."

"Do I need a key?"

"For?"

"The side gate."

"No lock, so no key. It has been a while since you've lived here, hasn't it? His hearing isn't great but his sense of smell is top notch, so he'll come once you pour the food. And…thank you."

"You said that already."

"Well, I mean it."

"I appreciate the fact that you mean it."

To think, this man, this experiment to prove to herself she'd put the Heartache List to bed once and for all, had become top of her contacts list. He was the person she called.

When Emerson realised that she was leaning her elbow on her desk, head resting in her palm, thumb rubbing the paperweight, gaze looking dreamily into the middle distance while imagining what Holden might be doing, or wearing, or not wearing, she sat bolt upright, knocking over a pen caddy.

"I owe you one," she said.

He laughed, as if he too had been mulling over the fact that they'd moved way beyond favours into… something rather wonderful. "Don't mention it."

"I'm hanging up now. So I can call the vet."

"After you," he said. And waited for her to end the call, as if he believed she might not want to.

And he was right.

Emerson came home to find Holden's rental car—now a big, black, hulking all-wheel drive—outside her house.

Using the side gate, she followed the stepping stones around to the back of the house, past her mum's beloved lemon tree, to find the man himself sitting on her back porch. Fast asleep.

Emerson slowly made her way up the wide wooden back steps, to find Holden had taken a couple of cushions from her outdoor setting, sat on one and propped another behind his back. His left knee was cocked, his hand was resting on Pumpkin's sleeping back as the dog's head lay across the man's right leg.

Emerson crouched down, reaching out a hand to touch Holden's shoulder, to gently wake him. Only her hand stopped at the last second, and she took her chance to soak him in.

The sweep of tangled lashes against his cheek, the five o'clock shadow covering his sharp jaw, the smudges under his eyes as he'd spent the week working long hours with his friend Andy, at the airport, after all. The way his hair was mussed, as if he'd run a hand through it one too many times. The strength of his collarbone, the column of his throat, the veins that roped down his beautiful forearms…

Despite his "I'm not going anywhere" line at the

house-warming, convincing herself she'd be fine when he went back to his real life had become a daily mantra. And yet, seeing him in her space felt really good. It felt so right. It felt like a level of want she wasn't sure she was equipped to handle.

Pumpkin whimpered, having sensed her and woken.

Holden's eyes opened next, training instantly on hers.

Emerson stilled, like a hunter sighted by a deer, too slow, too helpless to shut down the thoughts that must be written all over her face.

"Hi," he said, his voice rough.

"Hi," she said, her voice barely a breath.

His smile was slow, and warm, and all too knowing.

But then he winced as some part of him that had been stuck in place too long pushed back.

Freed from the gravity of his gaze, Emerson quickly pressed herself to standing.

Then she clicked her fingers in front of Pumpkin's face, till the old dog groaned and eased himself away from Holden's lap to totter over to her hand for a pat. "Hey, boy, you like your new food?"

"Gobbled it down," said Holden, stretching out his long legs.

"You didn't have to stay," she said.

"Every time I tried to leave, he looked at me."

"Looked at you?"

"With sad eyes."

"Holden, he's a spaniel. Sad eyes are their superpower."

"Right." He ran a hand up the back of his neck. Boy, she loved it when he did that. "Either way, I figured it was best to settle him before I headed off."

"He looked plenty settled when I arrived."

Holden hauled his tall frame to standing. "I bet he did."

He wore old jeans, worn in all the best places, and an olive Henley T-shirt that had ridden up a fraction, revealing a flat stomach, more than one ab, and an arrow of dark hair pointing south. Not sure if she was allowed to look her fill now that they weren't "forgetting" about the attraction they both felt, she couldn't have looked away for all the world.

"Are you free now?" she asked.

He caught her eye. "As a bird."

"Do you want to come in?"

"Yes," he said, without equivocation. "I do."

"Great." She used the key to open the back door, hustled Pumpkin inside the kitchen, and watched till he found his way to his bed in the hall.

Then turned to find Holden right behind her. A wall of warmth. Of spice and cotton and fresh air. And a little bit like warm dog, which, when she imagined him sitting on her patio, his hand on Pumpkin's back, made for a very dangerous scent.

"You hungry?" she asked, then regretted it when his gaze dropped to her mouth.

"I'd love to wash up first. I feel like I'm sporting a layer of drool."

Emerson very deliberately did not offer to smell him

to make sure, knowing that kind of thing seemed to send her down mental rabbit holes she was finding it harder and harder to find her way out of.

She pointed the way to the guest bathroom, and watched him walk away. Allowing herself a quiet whistle of appreciation before she shook it off and quickly fixed herself.

Jacket off, bag away. Quick swipe of toothpaste from the spare tube in the kitchen. No particular reason—it had been a long day and it seemed rude to smell like the coffee she'd tossed back an hour before.

"So," she said, when Holden ambled back into the kitchen, stopping to lean in the doorway. All lanky legs and crossed arms, as if he was holding up the entire house by the sheer force of his presence. "Dinner."

She opened the freezer to find it fairly bare. Her fridge looked little better.

"Takeaway?" she asked, looking over her shoulder to find him watching her with a small smile on his face, heat flickering behind his eyes.

Holden pushed away from the doorframe, his pace unhurried, his gaze focused, stopping only when he was inside her personal space. Then he slowly swept her hair behind one ear, then the other, till his palms rested on her cheeks, his gaze coming to settle on hers.

"Is that a yes to takeaway?" she said.

"Thank you for inviting me in, Emmy."

His words seemed straightforward, but she couldn't help imagining he meant something deeper. Something big and wonderful and terrifying. It was the only excuse for her next words. "You sound like a vampire."

"Not a vampire. Vampires sparkle in sunlight, if I remember rightly."

Emerson snorted. "Not real vampires. They burn."

As she said the word, his fingers delved deeper into her hair, the band she'd used to loosely tie it off her face falling free.

Her nerves were so taut, her skin so sensitive, she shivered as her hair fell over her shoulders, skittering over her bare arms. While the heat from his body, so close to hers, seemed to infuse her, till she was the one in danger of burning.

"Either way," he said, his voice deepening, the colour disappearing from his eyes, "my blood is warm. My heart beats. And I'm not immortal. At least I don't think so. Only time will tell."

When he used his thumbs to tilt her chin, when she felt the sweep of his breath over her cheeks, her neck, her mouth, he could have been speaking Martian for all she knew as her head filled with clouds, her body nothing but sensation.

Her hands had curled into the front of his shirt. Was she pulling him in or holding him at bay? When her body seemed to roll into him with her next breath, she got her answer.

Her brain, the last bastion of defence, flickered one final time. "I'm not..." she managed to eke out.

"Not what?" he asked.

She licked her lips, and wild storm clouds overwhelmed the last of the deep blue in his eyes. "I know how much you've put your life on hold these past weeks. And I think… I think some of that is because of this, because of me. But I have no expectations."

"Isn't that meant to be my line?" he asked, his mouth lifting at one corner, his gaze sure and true.

"You don't do lines."

"You got me there." He breathed out through his nose. "I'm not asking for the world, Emmy. I'd just really like to kiss you again. And I think you'd really like to kiss me."

She opened her mouth to make some Smart Alec response when his thumb moved to the corner of her mouth, before bringing it into her eyeline. "Toothpaste? Was that for me?"

Sprung.

Hands already gripping his shirt, she gave him a tug, tipped up onto her toes, and said, "Of course it was for you. So what are you waiting for?"

That, apparently. A wolfish grin lit up his face before his eyes grew so dark there was no telling what he was thinking. Or feeling. Only what he wanted.

And while, by this point, Emmy was a quivering bundle of nerves, Holden's cool held strong. And he took his sweet time.

Starting at the corner of her mouth, where toothpaste, of all things, had given her away—a kiss, then a lick.

A nudge of his lips, as close to hers as they could be without actually touching.

Then he moved to her ear, a waft of warm breath, a tug of teeth. Before he buried his nose in her neck, breathing deep as he pulled her liquefied body up against his.

"Holden," she breathed.

"Mmm," he murmured against her mouth, the tightness in his voice, the rough burr, the want spilling into his touch. Roving hands. Hardening body. Need, barely contained.

While she was melting, melting, *melting*. "Do me a favour and kiss me already."

She didn't need to ask a third time. And once his hot mouth met hers, everything changed. Her warmth became heat, her pliancy need. Her arms reaching around his neck, she lifted so high on her toes they creaked, and then, pressing herself to him, she got as close as she could, so that she might kiss him right on back.

Only this wasn't a kiss. This was an undoing. An unravelling. A revelation.

She found herself reaching for the hem of his shirt, hands frantic, desperate to find skin. When she did, it was so worth it. Warm skin, rough hair, hard muscle beneath.

His muscles twitched at the sweep of her hands. His words no more than a growl.

Relishing the fact she could cause such a reaction in such a man, she kissed him hard, deep, her hips rolling against his, her fingernails trailing down his belly.

Tracing the edge of his jeans. Tugging at the button, snapping the thing free.

His moan, the hitch of his breath, the jerk of his body was like a drug. And she must have been high, as soon she was yanking his shirt up his body, her lips releasing his for a half second so she could whip the thing over his head.

Their eyes caught in that moment, their breathing rough and wild.

Her dress—black, frilly, with a deep V—was pulled off one shoulder, then the other, then tugged down her arms by strong, rough, sure hands, before it clung to her waist.

He stopped, breaths heaving in his big chest as his eyes roved over her. Her flushed skin. Her lace bra, her nipples pressing hard and painful against the fabric.

Eyes dropping, hungry eyes, he cupped her breast, his thumb sweeping over the peak.

Her head dropped back, her breath leaving her in a great long sigh.

"That's the sound," he said, his voice gruff. "That's how you used to sigh every time you saw me. I thought it was sweet. We were both too damn young to know what it meant."

Then he kissed her, his hands delving deep into her hair, before his arm tucked under her knees and she found herself lifted off the ground, literally swept off her feet. As he'd been doing to her since the beginning.

Not when they were kids. Not some foggy, long-ago era—aeons, ages, millennia before now—when she'd had no idea who she was, or what she wanted. When every turn, every decision, every comment slung her way had felt deeply personal. Deeply cutting.

Their true beginning was the moment he'd walked up to her, at that secluded bar, in that star-spangled marquee at her best friend's wedding, fairy lights dancing in his eyes, the most beautiful man she had ever seen, who had no clue how to spin a line.

She reached for him, holding his face between her hands, relishing the feel of his stubble against her sensitive palms, before she kissed him. Gently, deliciously, achingly.

"Where to?" he asked, when she pulled back to rest her forehead against his, unwilling to break the connection.

She cocked her head towards her bedroom.

His nostrils flared, his eyes a winter storm, before he all but sprinted for the bedroom, forcing Emerson to hold on for dear life, her laughter scattering behind her like sparks from a firecracker.

In her bedroom, her most private space, Emerson slid down Holden's big, strong body, took him by the hand and led him to her bed.

Where they took their time undressing one another with care. And curiosity. In equal measure.

Before tumbling onto the bed with abandon. And there they found their rhythms, their touchstones, gentle affirmations and slippery heat.

He kissed his way down her body, taking his time,

making it last, making it magic, while whirls and swirls of smoke rose inside her. She could taste the heat on her tongue, as he teased and tasted and tortured her till every thought, every fear, every last fragment of self-protection coalesced into a tiny sun bursting inside her.

And then she was lost. Dissolving, into a trillion tiny specks of light. When she came back into her body, slowly, she was all molten bones and trembling limbs.

And so it went on, savouring one another's bodies, one another's gasps, one another's sighs as the evening turned into night. And beyond.

As Emmy finally fell into a deep, boneless sleep, her head tucked into Holden's shoulder, her hand resting over his heart, her mind cresting and settling, adrift on the rise and fall of his chest, she could barely remember why she'd been so adamant as to deny herself this pleasure. This sweetness. This moment.

Her last thought was that perhaps *this* had been the way to put the Heartache List behind her for good, after all.

Emerson woke in the pre-dawn, the birds not yet chirping, Pumpkin not yet up and about, banging into walls as he tried to find his way to the doggy door. And a man's arm was slung heavily across her chest.

It was Holden Roarke's arm. For Holden Roarke was in her bed.

He'd stayed with her patchy old dog because he'd been given the sad eyes.

He'd stayed when all she'd been able to offer him for dinner was Vegemite on toast.

He'd stayed.

"Hello, gorgeous."

She blinked to find his eyes on hers. No storm within, just a clear summer blue.

She lifted a hand to the bird's nest atop her head. "That might be your worst attempt at a line yet. I'm a wreck. And it's all your fault. You wrecked me."

He ran his thumb down her cheek. "You're a gorgeous wreck."

Eyes locked onto hers, Holden shifted to cover her with his body. While she shifted to accommodate him, her breath catching in her throat as she felt exactly what she'd be accommodating.

Settled, for now, he twirled a lock of her hair around his finger, then leaned down to press a soft, sweet, place-marking kiss upon her mouth. She waited for some flutter of resistance, of instinct, reminding her that this—while lovely, and unexpected, and therapeutic—was temporary.

No expectations.

But her instincts remained quiet. Less than quiet. It was as if he'd wrecked them too.

She tipped her head so that her mouth brushed the underside of his thumb. Then, having distracted him, she rolled till she straddled his thighs.

The flimsy tank top she'd slipped into during the night twisted around her body. His big hands spanned her waist, before gently tugging the top back into place, his thumbs sweeping over the exposed sides of her breasts.

While she told herself she was in the power position, the look in Holden's eyes made her feel as if her whole world might go dark without him holding her there in place.

As if to prove it, he sat up, his arms going around her, holding her close as he buried his nose in her neck, one hand gliding into her hair, the other lining up along her spine.

Her hand went to the back of his head, the other wrapped around his shoulder till they were pressed together close. Entwined. Just breathing one another in.

Holden's lips moved to her neck, pressing, suckling, biting. Tracing her collarbone. His fingertips slipped the strap of her top over her shoulder and followed the move with his mouth till her breast was free, his mouth taking over.

By the time she was ready for him, her skin on fire, her soul stripped bare, he made quick work with a condom, waited for her to line up, then eased her down, his hard heat sliding into her.

Deeper. Deepest. Friction building, heat burning, sensation, feelings, sweeping through her, too much.

"Do me a favour," he murmured into her ear, creating sparks amongst the light.

"What?" she breathed.

"Come."

And she did. Boy, oh, boy, oh, boy, she did.

CHAPTER NINE

Striding down the busy city footpath on the way back to the office, after a fabulous first meeting with an excellent candidate for the Sanderson Group COO, Emerson let her mind wander to thoughts of Holden as it was wont to do. His smile when she caught him unawares. The deep notes of his voice when he'd pick up the book on her bedside table and read it to her. The sweep of his broad hand down her back as she fell asleep in his arms.

She slowed in front of a café-slash-bookshop boasting a bountiful display of classics in their beautiful front window. Her gaze picking out *Persuasion*, she imagined lying with her cheek against Holden's warm, bare chest as he read aloud Wentworth's final letter to Anne. Then she had to stop imagining it lest she expire on the street.

She looked over the artfully teetering piles till she found—there! *The Catcher in the Rye.* Way back when, she'd bought that book for Holden as a gift, as the hero had his name. She could still feel the press of it into her fingers as she'd clutched it to her chest while sitting outside Miss Kemp's office.

Before their previous session, they'd been stuck in the hallway a good half an hour, before Holden had turned to her, asking what her favourite movie was. He'd had to write a report in English and it had been so long since he'd seen a movie, he couldn't think of one.

"Field of Dreams," she'd blurted. "A movie about a guy who misses his dad, starring Kevin Costner? Come on!"

They'd moved onto favourite TV show, favourite breakfast, favourite song.

It had felt like fate, for favourites were *her* favourite. She kept copious lists of her favourite things, and always had—favourite actors, favourite cakes, favourite holidays. Hanging on tight to the things that brought her joy. And she and Holden had covered every topic, bar favourite books. Hence her gift.

That next week, Miss Kemp's door had bumped. Emmy had held the book tighter, her breath catching, her heart thundering in her ears.

But then some sullen grade twelve girl with long, greasy hair had left the counsellor's room before loping morosely by.

"Where's Holden?" Emmy had asked the counsellor as she'd approached the room, a sense of dread coming over her.

"He's gone, honey. To another school. Come on in and tell me about your week."

Emmy remembered nothing from that session, bar Miss Kemp telling her that Holden, the week before, had mentioned her love of lists. She'd told Emmy that writing things down could help some people and encouraged her to grab a notebook, start a journal, to see if it helped her let things go.

That afternoon, while Emmy had been laid out on her bed, awash with tears, Camille had arrived with notebook in hand. Sparkly cactus on the cover.

Only Emmy had never used her writings to let things go, only to hold on tight. How could letting things go be her intention when it was her actual nightmare? What Miss Kemp didn't know wouldn't hurt her.

Emmy blinked to find herself still in front of the bookshop.

In the window's reflection the sky looked ominous, meaning she should get back to the office. And yet she ducked inside, moving straight to the stationery section. No sparkles and cartoony motifs here, only high-end, leather-bound recycled paper. When she picked up a gorgeous cream notebook, with pages soft to the touch and thin black ribbon bookmarks attached, she felt a frisson of warmth run up her arm.

New notebook, and pen to match, in hand, Emmy ordered a double espresso and pointed to a table out the front. Once settled, she opened the notebook, the spine cracking just the way her Heartache List notebook had all those years ago. It too had started out clean and full of possibility, before it had become covered in her passionate scrawl, as a means to understanding why people disappointed her, why they left her behind.

The final entry?

Heartache Number Eight: twenty-five years old.

Losing Mum. That was all. No details. No questions. It had been enough. And too much.

She'd tossed that old notebook in the skip, along with so many memories from her childhood, before gutting the house and refurbishing it till it was unrecognisable. As if that put a great big underline beneath that part of her life.

All she'd kept was her mum's glass paperweight, the lovely old dog who'd marked time with her, and the façade of the house that quietly, secretly, she'd never changed in case her dad wanted to find his way home.

And, quite amazingly, since the day she'd thrown the Heartache List away, her life had been fine. Narrow, yes. Tightly controlled, sure. But *fine.*

Until Holden had strolled back in with his sexy smile, his quiet courtship, his constancy. And his favours.

Emmy popped the lid on her new pen, and the wind seemed to lift and bustle the leaves around her feet.

She let the pen hover over the page. Then, her penmanship not a lot better than it had been at fourteen, she wrote in bold capital letters atop the first page:

THE FAVOURS LIST. Turning the page, she ruled a line down the centre. Put an "E" at the top of one column, an "H" at the top of the other.

Then, as if she'd been taken over by some external force, she set to noting down every single favour she and Holden had done for one another since Camille and Phillip's wedding. Starting with him helping her with her shoe, and her helping him let Bernadette down gently, and ending with his command, *Do me a favour. Come.* Before she'd fallen apart in his arms.

Her hand shook a little as she wrote those last words. The power of them. The command. Her effortless acquiescence. As if her world was no longer so very narrow, as if she no longer had control of it at all.

A frown now tightening her brow, she went back to the beginning. Some favours were bigger than others. Meaning they ought to be given ratings. Which also meant she couldn't leave out the teeny, tiny favours they'd done, those that had occurred without asking, or any expectation of return.

When done, the list was pages long. Unwieldy. And with its scrawls and doodles and notes, and arrows, it resembled the Heartache List far more than she'd intended.

A drop of water hit the page, blurring the ink. Then another.

It had started to rain.

"Emerson?"

"What's up?"

So drenched had she been by the time she made it back to work, she'd changed into jeans and a blousy top she kept in her office in case of long late-night sessions where comfort won out over *va-va-voom*, but she hadn't thought to keep a hairdryer on hand. She added a note to her to-do list notebook on her desk and popped it under her mum's paperweight, along with her new Favour List notebook and an invitation to Bernadette's surprise wedding.

When Freya didn't answer, Emerson looked up to find her assistant in the doorway of her office, motioning over her shoulder with a pencil, to where Bettina Sanderson stood on the other side of Emerson's smoked windows, elegance personified in a drapey cream suit, hands gently clasped behind her back, gaze roving over the bright white office space beyond.

Emmy ran fingers through her damp hair, then under her eyes, hoping she didn't look like a crazed panda, as Bettina turned and caught her eye. She motioned for Bettina to come on in, moved around her desk, preparing for a handshake, but soon found herself enveloped in Bettina's warm hug.

"Thank you for seeing me at such short notice, Emerson."

"Of course. Sorry for the damp hug. I was outdoors when the rain bucketed down. In fact, I'd just had a wonderful meeting with a brilliant candidate for the COO job, which I hope balances out the fact I must look like a drowned rat."

Bettina smiled. "Not at all. Can we sit? Talk?"

Emerson motioned to the soft couches by the large triangular window at the end of her office, and quickly twirled her hair into a knot at her nape while Bettina made a happy sound as she took in all the details of the space, before choosing a chair warmed by a patch of muted sunshine.

Emerson was halfway to sitting when Bettina said, "How is Holden?"

A vision of the last time she'd seen him popped into her head, his clothes a little rumpled, shoes in hand as he'd grabbed her and kissed her as if his life depended on it, before jogging down her front steps. "He's fine. I think."

"Mmm. I'd thought we might see him again, after the dinner, but alas. Though he did send a lovely note, and a beautiful bouquet of wild flowers, to thank us for having the both of you along. A truly decent man, that one."

He really was, thought Emerson. Decent and wonderful. Solid and adventurous. Interested and interesting. A heartbreaker, yes, but only to those whose hearts were already damaged long before they'd given theirs to him.

"Now, enough about that," said Bettina. "I've come to ask a favour."

A bubble of laughter caught in Emerson's throat. Ah, the irony. She grabbed a pencil and notebook—she really did have a thing for notebooks—from the coffee table and settled them on her lap. "Tell me what you need."

"I need for you to convince Holden to consider the position of COO at the Sanderson Group."

The bubble burst, and with it came a wave of dread. "I'm sorry, Bettina. There must have been a misunderstanding. Firstly, I'm not sure anyone could convince Holden to do anything he does not wish to do. And secondly, as I told Chuck, I don't believe that would be in his best interests, or Holden's, considering their history—"

"I worked for the company—did you know that?"

Emerson blinked at Bettina's change of direction.

Bettina went on. "My name might not be on the letterhead, but the Sanderson Group is as much mine as it is Chuck's. I pulled back, a few years ago, when… family matters necessitated the move. Now that those family matters are no longer so pressing, I want my husband by my side for as long as I can have him. I'd all but convinced him, believing he might announce his retirement at his birthday dinner. Alas, seeing Holden sparked something inside him. And he's hanging on tight."

Something flashed behind Bettina's eyes—a mix of sorrow, and distress. As if, despite her elegant façade, it took an effort to be there. As if she knew what she was asking of Emmy was ill-advised, but she saw no other choice.

"I understand," said Emmy, leaning forward, her hand gripping the pencil as she madly tried to figure out a way around the request Bettina was about to reiterate. "Holden told me what you meant to one another. How you were so kind to him. How you took him in. About his wonderful friendship with Saul."

Bettina breathed out hard, her throat bobbing delicately, before she collected herself, pressing her shoulders back, lifting her chin. "Then you understand that my family has been through a lot. That I must do what I can to protect those I have left. My husband needs a reason to retire. Holden is it."

Emerson pressed her toes into her shoes, as she felt the ground tipping beneath her feet. "You are welcome to talk to Holden, Bettina, but I am certain he'll—in my opinion rightly—say no."

Bettina's smile was gentle, and painful, all at once. "I saw the way Holden deferred to you. I'd say you could convince that man of pretty much anything."

Emerson's world tipped just a little more, leaving her off kilter when Bettina steeled herself, and years of running a multimillion-dollar business came to the fore. "So here is what's going to happen. You will convince Holden to take the position, and the commission will be yours. In fact, I will double it. Personally."

Bettina's *favour* hung in the air between them. That kind of money, of prestige, was all that Emmy had dreamt of since the moment she'd opened Pitch Perfect's doors.

And yet Emerson desperately tried to come up with an alternative. Mind flitting over her best candidates, it landed on one she'd not yet considered. "Chuck clearly needs a little more time to transition into retirement. You want to spend more time with him.

Maybe…maybe it's time your name did end up on the letterhead. Then, together, we can find the right team to take over when the time is right for both of you."

Bettina held up a hand and shook her head, her gaze pained, but also stubborn, as she gracefully unfolded herself from the chair. "My mind is made up."

Emerson somehow managed to get to her feet, even while her legs felt shaky, her feet numb.

"And if I can't?" Emerson asked, when what she meant was, *If I won't.*

Bettina's quick, sorry smile showed she knew it too. "You are a capable young woman with a bright future. I have every faith that together we can make this happen."

Bettina held out a hand, not to shake, but to enclose Emerson's in hers. As if she knew what she was asking was impossible, but that, as far as she saw things, she had no other choice.

And then she was gone. Leaving Emerson in the very rottenest possible position after all.

Emerson made it back to her desk and plonked herself in her chair. She slung an arm over her face, as if an answer might come to her in the darkness.

What was she to do?

Write a pro/con list? Yeah, no. A list would not help her this time.

Emerson dragged herself upright and slumped over her desk, her eye catching on the new notebook under her mum's paperweight.

She'd made it clear to Bettina, *and* to Chuck, that

what they were asking was impossible. But the truth was, Bettina was right about one thing: all Emerson had to do was ask.

For, despite the many favours they had done for one another over the past weeks, officially Holden still owed her the Big One.

Could she actually do it? Would Holden understand? Was she making too big a deal of this? Holden and Chuck really did need to get in a room together and talk, so in instigating that she'd be doing him a favour!

And, a quiet yet hopeful voice piped up in the back of her head, *if, by some miracle, he accepted the job, even in the short term, he would have a reason to stay.*

He had told her, his voice earnest and deeply sexy, *I'm not going anywhere*, but he'd also swapped houses as if it was nothing and changed rental cars as though they were dirty socks.

Staying hadn't killed him so far. Staying so that they could continue their favour game. Staying as things had heated up between them. Staying, gifting her all the time she'd needed to get to know him, to trust him, to want him, to lean on him, to need him…

And to fall in love with him.

She had. She'd fallen in love with Holden Roarke. Utterly, hopelessly. Not with the shuttered gaze of a confused fourteen-year-old but the wide-open eyes of a woman who still never saw it coming.

And loving him meant she had her answer.

Asking him to go to that interview would be asking the man she loved to do something that would hurt *his* heart.

An end was coming either way. And endings, in her world, meant heartache.

Emmy picked up her phone with no plan in mind, only to find a missed call from Kerri from next door.

She called her back. "Hey, Kerri, everything okay?"

"It's Pumpkin." Kerri sniffed, as if she'd been crying.

And all the worries in Emerson's head fled, every thought coagulating into one singular fear. Ice-cold. And infinite. Her beautiful boy, her one constant through it all.

"What about Pumpkin, honey?"

"He's not moving. I fed him earlier today, but his bowl is still full. I came by to see if he wanted to go for a walk, and I can see him through the doggy door, that he's in his bed, but he won't come when I call."

"You have a key, honey. You can go in any time, you know that."

"I know. I just… I'm not sure I can."

"I'm sure he's fine," said Emmy, as she madly grabbed her keys, her jacket, and for some reason the damp notebook, and shoved them in her bag. "He's nearly deaf, remember, so maybe he just can't hear you. Is your mum home?"

"At work."

"Right. Well, I'll give her a quick buzz and let her know you're worried, then I'll be right there. You head on home and leave Pumpkin to me. Okay?"

"Okay."

Emerson rang off, then shot out the door. "I'm off for the day," she called to Freya as she ran past.

Freya, wonder that she was, sent Emmy a salute.

Running on instinct, as the lift doors opened, Emmy made one more call.

"It's Pumpkin," she said, the moment Holden answered.

Whatever he heard in her voice, all he said was, "I'm on my way."

Emerson somehow kept to the speed limit, even while adrenalin had her slightly out of sync with the world.

Pumpkin.

Her beautiful boy. Half deaf, mostly blind, fully sweet. He'd beaten kidney infections, a snake bite, a broken leg, near record old age. He'd run away. That would have been *Heartache Number Four,* except he'd come back, covered in detritus and matted fur that had taken two baths, a short clip, and a lot of gentle tugging to remove, but panting happily after his adventure.

He'd put her through the wringer, but she'd still loved him with her whole heart, all the same. Pumpkin, with his soft, sweet doggy fur, absorbing her tears when she knew for sure her dad was not coming back. Her last link to her big, funny, huggy, sad, shadowy dad, who'd left her with the words, "Life ebbs and flows, kiddo. When it feels hard, remember it'll be okay. It always gets better."

As if that might help.

As if she wouldn't use his desertion as an excuse to keep people at bay. As if she could ever again feel as if the foundations beneath her feet were truly stable. Leaving her preparing for the worst, and being happily surprised when things worked out, then believing that was a good thing.

Emmy shook her head, and blinked the tears from her eyes. Angry tears. Worried tears. Tears for Holden too. For what she might yet have to ask of him. And how he might look at her from that moment on.

There were too many feelings. She really wasn't *sensical* when faced with too many feelings.

She pulled into her driveway, the bump of the car over the old gutter rocking her from side to side.

Her hands shook as she opened the front door, her heart lodged in her throat.

She banged her feet on the floor, the reverberations in the floorboards often enough to rouse him. But no skitters of doggy claws met her ears.

"Pumpkin?" she called, as loud as her tight voice would allow.

Still he didn't appear.

Kicking off her shoes, she dumped her things on the floor and padded up the hall, her chest squeezing when she saw his sweet foot poking out over the edge of his soft bed, along with the white tip of his caramel tail.

Dropping to her hands and knees, she made her way to him slowly. "Pumpkin? Buddy?" she called, knowing he couldn't hear her.

She placed her hand on his back, her breath hitching when she felt him move, his chest rising and falling, gently, slowly. Then his eye opened, and he tried to sit up.

"Hey, boy," she said, keeping her hand on him as she leaned down to press her cheek against his. As tears slid down her cheeks, she kept whispering that she was there, that he was a good boy, the best boy. She told him how deeply and incessantly she loved him, how grateful she was to have known him, to have known that he loved her back.

Then, several minutes later, a long, slow breath left his body. And his chest did not rise again.

Tears flowing freely now, Emmy lifted the old boy gently out of his bed, his frail body lighter than it had been in years, as if he'd been slowly leaving her for a while now, but she'd been holding on so tight she'd refused to notice.

She held him in her lap, where he'd used to sleep when he was half the size, and stroked him. Breathed in his doggy scent. Committed the exact feel of his fur to memory.

A knock at the door had her heart leaping into her throat.

The door nudged open—she'd forgotten to close it.

Holden's big, broad body created a shadow in the doorway as he let himself in, his form taking shape, and colour, strength, warmth, and vigour as he padded down the hall. Such gentleness in his big body, as if he knew that was all she could take.

She felt his approach, a waft of warmth and fresh laundry, a flutter of sensation up the back of her neck, before his hand landed on her shoulder and he reached around for her chin, tipping it back, so he could plant an upside-down kiss upon her forehead. Setting off feelings inside her that at fourteen she'd never have been able to imagine, much less handle. Heck, she could barely handle them now, her heart squeezing and kicking, bucking against the constraints under which it had been imprisoned for so long.

His hair was mussed, his cheeks a little pink from the wind that had followed the rain, the rush to get to her. This big, beautiful man who'd carved such inroads into her life. The man who had set so many things in motion. The man whose simple existence might yet tear it all apart.

The person she called when she needed to make a call.

Her person.

Her person.

He dropped to his knees, then slid in behind her, wrapped his arms around her, and hauled her close.

Careful not to disrupt the bundle in her arms, he held her as she cried and cried and cried.

Emerson blinked up at the mottled grey sky above her house as she hopped out of the car. After what had felt like a lifetime at the vet's, her brain struggled to connect with the fact that it was still daylight.

She held Pumpkin's collar in her hand as she glanced

up at the façade of her childhood home, the paintwork dull despite the wash of recent rain. The home her father had left, the home her mother had gifted her, the home Pumpkin had shared with her on and off her whole life.

To think she was about to walk in there, on her own, truly alone, for the first time in her life. Legs rocky, she leaned back against her car, the warm metal a surprise against her sensitive nerves.

Holden came around the front of the car, keys in hand, and stood by her. He looked as wretched as she felt, his care for her etched into the lines and hollows of his beautiful face.

Every single atom in her being ached to reach for him. To have him envelop her in his strong arms. To lean on him. To breathe him in. So that he might absorb some of her pain. Which he would do, without question, without being asked. Not out of any favour nonsense, but just because it was who he was.

Yet when he reached out, she flinched. So thinly stretched did she feel. She'd not be surprised to look down and find herself translucent.

"Give me your house keys," he said, his voice gentle. "Let me take you inside."

It made sense. She could barely feel her feet.

But as she looked up at the house again, at the façade she'd never allowed her mum to change, even during the years she'd not lived at home, a kind of preternatural calm came over her. And she finally began to see things clearly.

"I've decided..." She swallowed against the dryness of her throat. "Decided what my favour will be."

"Favour?" Holden said, as if he'd forgotten that was ever a part of their story.

"The Big One. The one that you agreed that I could ask for any time I wished. So long as it wasn't illegal, or impossible, you could not refuse me. Remember?"

He cocked his head, the slightest smile easing across his lovely face. "You want to do this now?"

Did she? Not even slightly.

"Let's get you inside." Holden moved ever so slightly into the bubble of air surrounding her, his warmth like a balm. "I'll brew you a hot chocolate. Run you a bath. Make you dinner. And tuck you into bed, for real this time, then you can ask me any favour you want. As many as you want. As big as you want. For as long as you want."

He smiled, but his eyes were sad. Sad about Pumpkin. Sad for her. But also filled with tenderness, and steadiness, and truth. A decent man, he believed what he was promising. Even the "for as long as you want" bit. Only he had no idea that she wanted forever.

It was enough to give her a second wind, one last push of strength.

"Bettina came to see me yesterday." Or was it today?

"Did she, now?" he asked, his nostrils flaring, as if only now he sensed the fight in her and was grounding himself, ready to push back.

Emmy lifted her chin. "Chuck wants you for the COO position. He has done since the beginning. In fact, I'd go so far as to say that's why he took me on. Bettina came to my office to ask me to convince you of the same."

Time seemed to stretch and fold between them, before Holden said, "*That* is your favour? You are asking me to work for the man whose son I tried to replace, whose daughter left me, all of which put the same man into a wheelchair." He lifted his hand to the back of his neck and squeezed. "Why? For the commission? Chuck's respect? Hell, Emmy."

"No," Emerson said, her voice cracking. "That's not… I want you to refuse."

Holden's stormy blue eyes locked onto hers. "I'm not sure I understand."

"While I do think that it would do both you and Chuck the world of good to stop circling one another and actually talk, I want your authorisation to tell them no."

"My authorisation."

"Assuming that's your wish, of course. Say the word, and it's done. The Sandersons can move on and find the right person for the job. And you and I will owe one another no more favours. Decks cleared in one fell swoop."

Her declaration, such as it was, fell flat.

Especially when she saw the realisation wash across his face. For he knew her too well. He *saw* her. No wonder she'd accidentally fallen in love with him, after all.

He closed his eyes. Shook his head. "Sorry. It's been

a rough afternoon, I know. Not the time to be jumping to conclusions. Just…talk to me. Tell me what's going on in your head right now."

She glanced at her feet, unable to deal with the dislocation in his gaze, the dawning understanding. "It's been a lot, these last few weeks. The wedding, the insane workload, Pumpkin." *Falling in love with the last man I'd ever have expected could sweep me off my feet.* "I feel as if I hopped on one of your planes, thinking I was heading to a particular destination, then, mid-air, I jumped. And I've been free-falling ever since… weightless, and floaty, and still yet to land."

She glanced up to find him running a hand over his mouth, as if carefully considering his words.

"I hear that," he said. "I feel the same way."

If only…

Emmy breathed out hard. "The thing is, you're used to living like that. You feed off the adventure, the variety, the change of scenery." It was how he dealt with *his* past the same way she used lists to understand hers. "Me? I need to know I'm on solid ground. And with you… I don't. I never have."

His face, oh, his lovely face as he looked at her. As if he was the one who ached. "Emmy, I really thought—"

"You thought right," she said, not sure she'd be able to go through with this if he told her that he cared. And she knew he cared. Just as she knew that, eventually, it would no longer be enough to make him stay. "And it's been lovely. But I've seen your calendar. I know what you've given up to be here. This feels like the right time to... For us to..." She waved a hand between them.

"Say, it, Emmy. I need to hear you say the words."

Words. Like the words Miss Kemp had told her to write, so that she might let things go. When instead she'd used them to hold on tight.

The way she'd held on to dear old Pumpkin, not even allowing herself to imagine what choices she might have to make if his health had begun to fail him.

The way she'd held tight to her best friends, suffering a physical shock to the system when it had finally hit her that they were married.

The way she'd held on to the exterior of her childhood house, just in case her dad needed to find his way home...eighteen years after he left.

The very best thing she could do for Holden, and for herself, was to let him go.

"Holden, it's time for you to go home."

His expression didn't change, as if he'd been braced, expecting it. But his voice—rough, low, and grave—gave him away. "That's what you really want?"

Emmy nodded. Just the once.

Then Holden asked, "What about what I want?"

By that point Emmy felt as if she was being held upright by a single fraught nerve. Empathy spent, softness depleted, she said, "You are retired, then not retired. You move more often than I change my sheets. You flit from car to car depending on your whims. You don't want to be here, yet you don't leave. I don't think you know what you want."

Holden took a step back. A literal step back. Then he turned and leaned his hands against the bonnet of her car, his entire body taut.

He ran a hand over his face, the skin dragging at the last. As if he too was barely holding on. "If you weren't standing there, looking like a gust of wind might blow you over, I think I'd actually throw you over my shoulder, take you inside and demand you not to say another word till you'd eaten, drunk and slept."

In his eyes, the storm was real, confusion warring with the heat that simmered between them at all times. She squeezed the skin between her thumb and forefinger so as not to find herself swept up in him.

"This isn't about Pumpkin."

"Like hell it's not," he shot back. Energy no longer contained as it seemed to flicker about him, wild and wondrous. "I keep telling you I'm not going anywhere, even when I can see you don't believe me. Do you know how it feels, to be so easily dismissed? Hell, it's my father all over again."

The rush of emotion in his voice gave her strength. "Are you comparing me to your *father*?"

He threw his hands out to the side and paced away from the car. "I have absolutely no idea what I am doing. Clearly. In fact, I've been rudderless since I looked up and saw you standing on the edge of the dance floor. You were like this silent siren, grabbing me right through the middle and refusing to let go.

I've been stuck here, stuck in this place that gave me such grief for such a long time, because you… Because you…"

He reached out, fingers stretched as if he wanted to shake her. Or grab her and kiss her. Or hold her and rock her until whatever had taken over her had passed.

She licked her suddenly dry lips. "Lucky for you, then, you don't have to feel stuck any more. I'm letting you go, Holden. No more favours. Go, find work that engages you, rather than that which falls into your lap. Go, before that impressive restlessness of yours makes you regret staying. Before I—"

"Before you what?" he asked.

She bit her lip. Let it go when his eyes dropped to her mouth and stayed.

He looked up again, deep into her eyes. Soul deep. "You think I needed *interesting work* in order to have a reason to stay?"

You, his gaze said, *you were all the reason I needed.*

He moved to her then, slowly, reaching out to hold her gently by the upper arms. Then he leaned in, slowly, till his forehead touched hers.

Emerson's eyes drifted closed. Now it was only the thousand butterflies beating against the inside of her skin that held her upright.

"This is what you really want?" he asked. "What you really need?"

"Yes," she said, "it is."

He dropped a hand over his heart, his fingers curling over his collarbone. Then he lifted his head and stepped away. Then he placed her keys on top of her car and headed towards the street.

Only to stop, turn, look at the house, then look back at her. "I heard you, Emmy. I did. But if you need company, if you don't want to go in there alone, I'll stay. Just say the word."

"I'll be fine." And she would. Eventually. She always was.

Holden nodded, every angle of his body tight and hard as he strode towards his rental car, folded his long body inside, gunned the engine, and was gone.

Emerson somehow made it up the front steps and inside her house, where she folded up like a puppet whose strings had been cut.

Sitting against the wall, she waited for panic to set in. For she'd killed the biggest deal of her life and pushed away the only man she'd ever loved.

But, like a cat with nine lives, nine heartaches were all she had. And she'd just given that ninth to the sweetest pup who'd ever lived.

She had nothing left to give.

CHAPTER TEN

A FEW DAYS LATER, Holden sat in the reception area on the twelfth floor of the Sanderson Group building, pressing at his cuticles with his thumbnails, and frowning so hard his forehead hurt.

Despite the low grey clouds blanketing the city, a shaft of sunlight slanted into his eyes. But he didn't change seats. It kept him sharp. The only possible reason why he'd ended up in such a mess was that this damnable city had blunted him. Softening his edges. Turning him to putty.

No more.

When he'd told Emmy he'd heard her, given her "authorisation" to refuse a role he'd never asked for, on his behalf, he'd never promised he'd not have words with Bettina and Chuck himself.

He wasn't exactly sure what those words would be, only that they had to be said. There had to be some sort of closure, on all of this, once and for all. Or else the hot, heavy feeling that had taken up residence behind his ribs the moment he'd seen Emmy sitting on the floor, her lovely old dog on her lap, the knowledge that her happiness meant more to him than anything ever had, would haunt him for ever.

"Holden?"

Looking up to find Bettina Sanderson heading his way, Holden stood, wiped dry hands down the sides of his jacket, before leaning in to kiss her cheek.

"So lovely to see you, dear boy. I wish you'd called; I'd have put aside time for a coffee."

"I'm not here for coffee. I'm here to interview for the COO position."

He might have relished the shock on her face if he was actually there for some damn interview. But he was not. He was there to give Chuck—Bettina too, since fate seemed to have placed her there, right on time—a piece of his mind.

Lying in bed in the plush hotel room he'd moved to a couple of days back, right after leaving Emmy's for the last time, staring at a small crack in the ceiling, he'd come to the conclusion that there was no way around the fact Emmy's happiness had come to mean more to him than his own.

That alone meant he had to heed her wishes. What else could he do?

Yet, for all that Emmy had done his head in, and his heart, and most of his major organs if the ache inside him was anything to go by, and while he knew she could absolutely take care of herself, nobody messed with her on his watch.

He would walk away. Eventually. But not until he made sure she'd be okay.

"The COO position," said Bettina, her hands wringing, her expression riddled with guilt. Good. It meant she had some semblance of an idea of the mess she had wrought. "Might I ask why?"

Holden slowly dipped his hands into the pockets of his suit pants, his throat tight, his voice a little above a growl. "If you're asking if Emerson sent me here, after your...conversation the other day, she did not. In fact, she made it clear, it was her preference that I refuse to even consider the notion."

"Oh?" Bettina blinked. Then, strangely, her shoulders dropped, and she broke out in a smile. "Well, good for her. Bright, capable, *and* formidable. I knew I liked that one."

Holden opened his mouth but found he did not have the words. What the heck was he missing?

Bettina must have seen it on his face, as she reached out and squeezed his arm. "I know. I do believe Chuck and I have not handled this whole thing as best we might. Seeing you again, while wonderful, stirred up dust we thought had been brushed away. And, while I can't speak for my stubborn husband, I do love him. Which is why I had to do whatever it took to make sure he is taken care of. I hope the both of you can understand our hearts were in the right place, even if our efforts were inelegant. I hope you can forgive us."

"Always," Holden said, as, for all that his insides were a tangled mess in no small part due to Bettina's influence, he believed her. Considering her words very much mirrored his own recent reflections, he found that he understood her too.

"Oh," said Bettina, "and the COO position has been filled."

"By whom?"

"By me." Bettina held out both arms with a flourish. "Chuck is not ready to retire. I wish to spend more time with him in our twilight years. Then it seems about time I finally have my own name on the letterhead. It was your Emerson who gave me the idea."

"She's not—" Not his Emerson. He couldn't say the words. For, despite recent events, it still felt as if she was. His Emmy.

"Did she truly insist you not apply for the position?"

Holden nodded.

"Even while fully aware that would put her relationship with the Sanderson Group at risk. Bright, capable, formidable...and staggeringly selfless. Where you are concerned, at least."

Selfless. Holden grabbed onto that thought. He wasn't here for him. He was here for Emerson. "Back up a moment," he said, pinning Bettina with a glance. "If Emerson was the one who suggested you for the role, the commission is hers. Correct?"

Bettina's eyes widened for the briefest flash, the only sign that she'd been stymied. "Correct. And serendipitous, to have you on her side."

"Serendipity has nothing to do with it."

"No," said Bettina, "I can see that it does not. Now, dear boy, I have work to do. Was there anything else?"

Yes, there was. A good deal, in fact. "Dinner one night this week? You, me and the big guy. How about we put that dust to rest?"

Bettina's eyes misted over. "We'd like that very much."

Holden gave Bettina a quick hug, congratulated her, wished *her* luck, then headed outside where the clouds lurked low overhead, threatening to spill at any moment.

He'd done what he'd gone there to do—make sure Emerson would be okay. Which should have put a line under his time in Melbourne.

And yet…

Now he had dinner plans. And Bettina's words echoing in the back of his mind: *Your Emerson… Staggeringly selfless… Serendipitous, to have you on her side.*

He still wasn't going anywhere. Not yet.

Only now, his reasons why were shifting. Or maybe, just maybe, they were the same as they had been all along.

Thoughts now spiralling in a thousand different directions, Holden chose a number from his contacts list, and after it answered was aware of the irony as he said, "Mate. Can I ask a favour?"

Camille opened her door, eyes widening at the sight of her friend.

"Oh, honey," Camille said. "A little wet out?"

Emmy pushed her dripping hair out of her eyes. "A little."

More like a lot. It had been raining, on and off, ever since Emmy had let Holden go. Pushed him away. Told him to leave. *Semantics.*

"Wait there." Camille ran inside and came back with towels, one for Emmy to wrap around her hair, another on which to wipe her feet. Smiling apologetically, she said, "New floors."

After setting Emmy up on another huge towel on the new couch, Camille quickly made coffees before pulling her friend in for a long hug. "I'm so sorry about Pumpkin, hon."

"Thank you."

Camille pulled back, eyes fierce. "I know some would never understand, but if you need a proper funeral for the old boy, you know we'll be there."

Emmy hiccupped. It was not a laugh. It was far too soon for all that. "No funeral. I will scatter his ashes, though, beneath Mum's lemon tree."

"Well, that's far better." A pat on the knee, then, "So, did you hear Bernie's getting married?"

"Got my invitation."

"Super. We can car pool. Bernie mentioned something about my being Matron of Honour, but intimated it's all very casual. Show up, carry flowers, sit at the big table. Though I'm considering asking for a name change. Babe of Honour, perhaps? I'm working on it. So, how are things otherwise?"

Emmy tipped forward to grab her drink, only for

the towel on her head to slip over her face. Nerves a little tetchy, she quickly balled it up and hugged it to her chest.

"Super-well from the looks of things," Camille answered for her.

Emmy did laugh that time. Then reached inside her bag, pulled out the Favour List, and handed it over.

Camille—understanding the power of a good notebook—balanced it on her upturned palms. "May I?"

Emmy nodded.

Camille's eyes shifted from side to side as she read the title. "Ah. I didn't know you were still keeping track. I thought, perhaps, the two of you might have moved beyond that."

"I had. Until I hadn't."

"I see." Camille flicked through the pages. "The detail is impressive."

"Do you mean detective-impressive or the-psychopath-the-detective-is-investigating-impressive?"

"Oh, the latter, for sure." Then, "You really did all this for one another, in the past few weeks? This is more than Phillip and I would do for one another in a year. And we'd be all passive aggressive about it. Lots of huffing and puffing and muttering about being taken for granted. Does Holden mutter?"

"No muttering."

"Then the man is a saint. And clearly smitten." Camille's gaze hit a certain point in the notebook and her eyes grew wide. "Holy smokes. Did he really say that?"

"Which one?"

Camile turned the notebook and pointed, mouthing the word, *Come.*

Emmy nodded.

"That's…seriously. Wow. I mean… I'm feeling a little hot under the collar. And in need of my husband. But he's hiding in the bedroom." Camille shook herself so as to regain focus on the issue at hand. "Where is Mr Heartache, and why are you here rather than…" Camille's voice dropped an octave *"…doing one another favours?"*

Emmy held the balled-up towel closer to her chest. "He's gone."

"Gone where?"

"*Gone*, gone. Away. Elsewhere. Home."

Camille madly flicked to the last page, where Emmy had ruled a big angry line under the final favour. Adding squiggles. And crossing out all the space at the bottom of the page. Then, "Did he read the notebook?"

"No, he didn't read the notebook!"

"The bastard. I'll sic Phillip onto him. There's not much of him, but he's scrappy."

"No. It's fine. I'm fine."

It wasn't fine. *She* wasn't fine.

She couldn't sleep. She felt low, constantly. As if she had the flu. Yes, she'd lost her pup, and had screwed up her biggest contract to date, but she knew, *knew*, if she'd had Holden holding her through it all she'd be okay.

And yet…beneath the yuck was a sense of rightness

in making sure Holden was no longer marking time. That he was out there flourishing.

"That's not what I get from this crazy manifesto of yours."

"Ignore the crazy manifesto. We had simply...run our course. Our favours finally balanced out, and that..." She stopped to take a breath, though it did sound more like a sigh even to her ears.

Camille narrowed her eyes and tapped at the Favour List. "You know that man did not stick around to pick up your laundry because he felt morally indentured to some list. That's *your* kink. The man stuck around for you."

Emmy let the towel drop into her lap. "Maybe. Yes. Of course, I know that. But it doesn't matter. Because he's gone. For ever."

For someone so okay with *nothing* lasting for ever, saying it out loud felt raw. And unbearable.

Camille watched her face, before lifting her shoulders in a shrug and handing the notebook back. "He is gone. He is dead to me. Now, we can check out Bernie's gift list later, so we can pick something wonderful and whacky, but first give me your feet. Everything feels better when you have sparkly toenails."

Emmy slid down deeper into the chair, the notebook in her hand, and propped the towel behind her head as she leaned back against the couch. Eyes closed, she toyed with the notebook ribbon.

She'd decided not to tell Camille about the texts Holden had sent since she'd sent him packing, the ones checking that she was okay. No point Camille staying attached to the guy.

Attachment only led to ache. Bone-deep ache. Soul-deep ache. She knew as she was living it. Despite all her best efforts for that not to happen, it had happened anyway. Meaning, if she'd waited any longer to end things, his leaving would surely have cleaved her neatly in half.

"Salut," said Phillip later that evening, raising his near empty beer.

Holden shuffled on the barstool and clinked the bottle with his iced water and lime. "Thanks for getting away."

"All good. Camille's at home. In the middle of what might be days of girl talk with…you know who. I'm meant to be hiding in the bedroom till they're done."

Holden laughed, despite himself.

"I'm not kidding," said Phillip, looking over his shoulder. "If she knew I was here, no sex for a week. The woman's stubbornness knows no bounds. So, did you call me because you wanted to talk about it too?"

"*It* being Emerson?"

Phillip winced. "Spill, whinge, get it all out. I'll say *There, there* and pretend to be on your side, even though that can never happen. Or we can say nothing at all. Talk about football. Or stock prices. Or life on Mars. Whatever you need."

"I need a drink."

Phillip breathed out. "Thank God. Two beers!"

"Light," Holden added, holding out his phone to pay.

"So, what did happen?" Phillip asked. "If you don't mind me asking. Last time I saw Emmy she was all sparkly-eyed, and floating off the ground. And Emmy does not float. She's the most pragmatic person I have ever met."

A muscle twitched under Holden's left eye. Emmy had mentioned the floating thing to him too, in an accusatory way. The way Phillip put it made it sound nice. The woman still confused the heck out of him, even in absentia.

The thing was, he liked it. He fed off it. She'd charged him with feeding off adventure and variety and change of scene, as if she wasn't all of them combined.

The same woman who wore her hair twisted into a complicated mess at home, while eating peanut butter out of the jar, raged if a temp on her books was offered less than exemplary working conditions, and in the next breath listened, actively, intently, as he talked about the minutiae of his day.

She'd also accused him of playing house, when he hadn't played at anything when it came to her. Not for a single second.

He'd been all in from day dot.

Holding back, waiting for her to catch up, he'd had to keep reminding himself it might take her more time. Reminding himself she was softer than she thought she was. Trusted her own feelings tremulously. Determined, if she needed more time, to give her as much time as it took.

That was then. Before she'd told him to go home.

Phillip passed a beer to Holden and Holden took a slow sip. "You want to know what happened?"

"Sure."

"She told me not to take a job I didn't want."

"Right. Heartless of her. Terrible." Phillip paused. "I'm imagining, being Emmy, it was a really good job."

"COO of the Sanderson Group."

Phillip whistled long and high. "You really don't want it?"

"I really don't."

"Excellent. So, you're both on the same page. Yet here you sit. Oozing misery, like a barfly waiting to happen."

Holden glanced at his *light* beer. Then said, "I thought we were on the same page. Then she skipped right to the end when I was still very much enjoying the start. She told me, outright, to go home."

"Home?"

Exactly. When the only place he'd ever thought of as *home* was any place she was. What he said was, "By which she meant away. Back to where I came from."

"Ouch. Harsh. Makes sense though. Considering."

"Considering?" Holden repeated, letting his drink drop to the bar, and slanting a hard look Phillip's way.

Phillip leaned back in his chair, hands up, conciliatory. "I mean, you know…the Heartache List."

"She said that was all in the past."

"Well, yeah. But that doesn't mean it can't ever affect the here and now. What's her big bad wolf?"

"Her—?"

"The thing that scares her the most."

Holden didn't have to think about it. *Fathers, right?* "Her dad leaving."

"Her dad. Her favourite teacher. Her childhood best friend. As you said, all in the past. Then you came along. A guy who's infamous for never staying in one place long." Phillip took a swig of his beer.

While Holden blinked. And blinked again. "She didn't much talk about her mum passing, but when she did…it nearly killed me. And then poor Pumpkin." Hell. "I'm her big bad wolf."

"Not you, *per se*, but you—someone who has loomed large in her life—leaving her? For sure."

Holden's fingers slipped off the glass to run through his hair.

How had he not seen it? She'd pushed him away before he could leave, because in her mind that was what happened to those she loved. She'd pushed him away because she believed she was holding him back.

Meaning…

"She loves me."

"Yup," said Phillip. "Hell of a thing."

He'd been so busy giving her space, giving her time, he'd not seen it when it was right in front of his eyes.

She'd refused to put his name up for the COO gig,

knowing it would put her relationship with the Sanderson Group at risk. Knowing it would give him one less reason to stay. She'd protected him, and she'd faced her greatest fear, while torpedoing her own efforts in one fell swoop.

Because she loved him.

He'd felt so smacked by the "off you go" portion of her speech, as it had pressed into his own ancient wounds, he'd lost sight of the rest.

Phillip said, "If you don't want that job you mentioned, I'd take it. Do you think the renovation work we've done qualifies me for a gig in real estate?"

"Sorry, mate," said Holden, distractedly, his mind reeling. "It's already gone to someone else."

"Ah. Probably for the best. Camille wouldn't be keen on me working those kinds of hours."

Holden laughed despite himself. "Are you really as under the thumb as you make out?"

"Nah. And yeah, a bit. But I love her. She loves me. We have one another's backs no matter what. The rest we work out as we go along."

That, Holden was beginning to realise, might be the key to the whole thing.

There was no right way to be with a person, no balance sheet, or list you could tick off. No single set of qualities or interests or locations. A couple lived or died by how deeply they committed to whatever worked for them.

They both simply had to want it enough.

★ ★ ★

Later that same night, when Camille padded into the kitchen to swap coffee for wine, Emmy checked her phone to find a message from Freya.

Check the bank account!!!

The several smiley faces added to the end of the message took the edge off any concern as Emerson pulled up her bank details to see a staggering bump in the balance. Emmy typed:

What the heck?

It has to be the commission, for the COO position. Maybe one of your early suggestions impressed after all!

Maybe, thought Emmy. But surely the applicant would have let her know. The only other person it could possibly be…

"No," Emmy growled as she uncurled herself from the couch, her backside numbed from not having moved for hours. He couldn't have. He'd promised!

"Everything okay?" Camille called from the kitchen.

"Yep! Fine!" Emmy called, as she hobbled towards the bathroom. Door shut, she sat on the edge of the bath and stared at her phone. Knowing there was only one way to find out.

Yes, Holden had texted her. Several times. She'd answered him every time. But she'd yet to make the first move. She'd been the one to break things off, after all. Getting in contact, so that *she* might feel better for hearing from him, seemed cruel.

But this was different. This was insurrection! This made a mockery of the Favour List! And to Emmy such a list was sacred.

She swore, rather vociferously, as she jabbed at her phone.

Tell me you didn't!

Holden's message came back so fast it was almost as if he was waiting for it.

Didn't do what?

Take that stupid job you promised me you wouldn't take. If you did, tear up the stupid contract right now!

A few long, painful beats slunk by.

Not necessary.

She could almost hear his voice as he typed. Picture a small smile tugging at the corner of his beautiful, kissable mouth. It was agony.

So much agony, she pressed the call button before she had a hope of stopping herself.

He answered, but before he had the chance to draw breath, she stage-whispered, "Holden Roarke, you listen up and you listen good. I will not let you take that job. I will call the bank now and have them return the commission. And if Chuck or Bettina have a problem with that, they can go through me."

"You done?" he asked, the sound of glasses clinking and low-level chatter in the background of whatever fabulous faraway place he was enjoying fading as if he too was finding a quiet spot.

"So long as you do as I say."

"Ah, but that would be asking for a favour."

Emmy's heart was suddenly beating in her throat. A favour would mean they were no longer null and void. No. She couldn't keep doing this. She had to get over him.

"No. No favour."

"Right. Just wanted to make sure. After *the listen up and listen good* bit—"

At the tone of his voice, warm and intimate, a smile curled around her heart. She told it to calm down. The fact that she could sit here, talking to the man, missing him, aching for him, and smile—surely that was the kind of progress she'd have once believed she couldn't buy.

"For transparency's sake," he said, his voice low and lovely and just for her, "I did book in for an interview."

"Holden!"

"Only so that I could tell Chuck to back the hell off. You stood up to him, for me; I wanted to do the same for you. Not as a favour, so don't panic. It was something I had to do."

Wow. "And how did that go?"

"Bettina showed up instead. Turns out, she'd already taken the position herself. Said you'd given her the idea. Hence you get your commission."

"Oh, wow. Go, Bettina. But *boo* for putting us both through that." It was cutthroat stuff, playing with the big boys and girls.

Holden laughed, the sound of it spilling over her shoulders, and she held the phone tighter.

"We can hack it," he said, stressing the *we* in a way that had Emmy wriggling on the edge of the bath. "And she apologised, to us both. Explained that she was doing what she had to do to look after the person she loved."

"Right." Emmy closed her eyes tight and hoped her voice didn't sound as pained as it felt.

"Is Chuck okay, do you know?" she asked, showing her soft spot for the old guy. Even while what she really meant was, *Are you okay?*

"Well, we've made plans to have dinner. I took what you said on board. It's past time we cleared the air. Time I let go of all the old ghosts that kept me away, from here, from home, for far too long."

"Oh, that's...wonderful." It really was. "But hang on—how can you have dinner if—?" She swallowed her words, her hope.

"I'm far, far away? I'm still around, Emmy. Tying up loose ends. And I don't know if you remember, but I did promise you once that I wouldn't leave without saying goodbye."

Do me a favour, she'd said as he held her in his arms

at the hotel after the wedding. *Don't leave, this time, without saying goodbye.*

Emmy bit her lip and tipped forward to press her forehead against the cool of the sink. "I'm glad. About you and Chuck. You'll feel so much better for having let that go."

Like she did, having let Holden go? That was a laugh. But still, apart from the great, gaping hole that had taken up residence inside her chest, it worked out for everyone. She got her commission. Bettina and Chuck would be working side by side. Holden would be truly free to live his life however he saw fit.

"Look," she said, when her throat began to feel tight, "I'd better go."

"Right. Look, Emmy—"

When she realised her hand was clutching at her shirt, right over her heart, she said, "Good luck with your future endeavours."

She heard him say something, but her thumb was already pressing the button to cut the call.

When she came out of the bathroom, Camille was quickly hopping onto the couch.

Emmy said, "You were listening at the bathroom door, weren't you?"

"A little bit. I heard talking. Had to make sure you hadn't fallen and hit your head and started hallucinating."

"I was talking to Holden."

"Well, that's…whatever you think it is. I heard mention of favours. Figured I'd better walk away before they turned into a certain kind. Of a sexual nature—"

"Yes, I get it. Thank you." As she tucked herself back into the couch, Emmy glanced at the Favour List notebook which sat innocently closed on the coffee table. "When we started the Heartache List, what did we imagine the end game might be?"

"For you to not get your heart broken." Camille looked at her through the glass of wine. "If your next question is: did it work? From where I sit, I'd say it failed pretty spectacularly."

"A little bit," Emmy admitted, the heel of her hand now rubbing the spot where it ached most. "Thing is, this one was entirely my fault. I broke my own heart. Pre-emptively. Before Holden had the chance."

"Might be worth rethinking the efficacy of such a move in future."

Camille lifted her wine glass and Emmy grabbed hers to tap it in agreement.

They settled in to watch some horrid reality TV show, knowing that whatever was happening in their own lives they'd never be as screwed up as the contestants. But Emmy's mind wandered.

Once upon a time Holden had said, the *only way to find out if someone you like likes you back is to be a little brave.* Choosing to protect Holden's interests over her own had been pretty brave.

Was it possible he'd known that was why she'd done it, even before she'd known it? Was that why he was still messaging her? Why he'd stayed?

Emmy sat up, while Camille snorted before falling back to sleep.

Holden hadn't left. A man known for his inability to stay in one place for long, a man she'd accused of needing variety, adventure, and change of scene, more than he'd ever need her, Had Not Gone Anywhere.

He'd stood up for her against Chuck and Bettina, he'd looked out for her interests, he'd answered the phone the moment she'd called. As if nothing had changed at his end.

Was he trying to tell her something too?

Holden had stayed. Meaning, if she was very, very lucky, and the bravest she'd ever been, she might have one last chance to find out.

"Rain's meant to be good luck, right?" said Phillip, peering through the windscreen.

Raindrops slithered moodily down the car windows while Taylor Swift crooned softly through the speakers as they wound their way through the streets of east Melbourne.

It was the morning of Bernadette's wedding, and the perfect match for Emmy's mood, for, while she knew, in every bit of her banged-up heart, that aching for Holden while with him was far better than aching for him when not, she had no idea how to tell him. Or find him, for that matter.

She'd called Bettina, to thank her for the commission. Emmy had managed to leverage it into an even better deal for Pitch Perfect, but had not been able to trick the woman into giving away Holden's whereabouts.

She'd then bought a new notebook in which to write her "Find Holden and Tell Him How I Feel" ideas, but her list-building skills had deserted her right when she needed them most. She'd considered jotting down Phillip's idea—flashmob!—just to get things started.

Camille pulled down the sun visor to check her make-up and caught Emmy's eye. Emmy motioned for her to angle the mirror. Swiping a hand over the peacock-blue clip in her hair, then a finger along the edge of a red lip, she tried a smile on for size, only to be met with the faraway gaze of a woman who felt time slipping through her fingers.

"We're here!" Camille called as they pulled up a little way from Bernadette's parents' lovely house in Camberwell. "Look at that. Rain's stopped!"

When Emmy hopped out of the car, stepping up onto the verdant edge of the footpath, Phillip walked on tip toes to avoid the wet. While Emmy's heels sank into the wet grass. So deeply she couldn't move. Camille bit her lip before bursting into laughter.

Once Phillip and Camille had yanked Emmy out of the mire, they each took an elbow, and, arm in arm, just as they had been for so many years before this one, they made their way up the path, following the sound of laughter, and music and voices, until—

"Oh, my," Emmy gasped.

A big, round, red-and-white-striped marquee, with

a wilting roof and small red flags hanging limply from the gutters every few metres, sat plonked in the centre of the huge lawn.

"It's like a giant mushroom," Phillip said, awe tinging his voice.

"A giant circus mushroom," Camille added, clapping madly. "I love it so much I can barely blink."

"It's wonderful. It could not be more perfectly Bernadette," Emmy said, a true smile lighting her up for the first time in days.

"Now I have to go find the most easy-going bride that ever lived." Camille headed off towards the house, while Phillip led Emmy towards the opening at the back of the tent, where bunches of guests congregated, chatting happily, drinks already in hand.

Inside the circus theme continued, with flickering vintage circus videos playing across the walls of the tent like some magical dream. And up front, where the bride and groom would do their thing, a massive elephant statue looked over them all.

Emmy went to grab Phillip's sleeve to point out the monkey doll climbing a ladder to the trapeze set, when she turned to stone.

For there, just off stage, chatting to the groom…

Holden. Holden was here!

Emmy hiked up her skirt, and darted through the tightly packed crowd, her heels catching in the grass, eyes locked onto the beautiful man in the dark suit.

She had no idea what she'd say, only that she had to get to him. For after months of near constant contact, this was the first time she'd seen his face in days, and she could barely hold herself together.

She'd made it to the end of the aisle, right as Elvis started singing *Can't Help Falling in Love*.

The crowd all turned, right as a spotlight swung to land on Emmy, dress hitched, heels half sunken into the ground, heat creeping up her neck.

Holden, after giving Barry a nudge up onto the stage, was the last to turn. He stilled the moment he saw her, his hands dropping slowly to his sides. Then a smile stretched across his face. A slow, warm, charming, beautiful smile.

What could she do but smile back? A real smile. Not the kind she'd practised in the mirror in the car. One that started in her heart and spread out to her extremities, till she felt bathed in light and warmth and hope.

"Emmy! Move it!"

Emmy turned to see Camille heading up the aisle, a grinning Bernadette, giving her a thumbs-up, coming up behind. Camille spun Emmy to face the front and gave her a shove.

Emmy found the beat, and made her way up the aisle, ducking off to the side at the last second and finding a spot against the wall, which gave her the perfect view of Holden, who mirrored her position on the other side of the wedding party.

And there she spent the longest half an hour of her life staring into Holden's stormy blue eyes as Bernie and Barry promised to love, honour, and cherish one another for the rest of time.

* * *

Everything went a little wild after that, for the bride and groom were playing fast and loose with scheduling and had disappeared. The guests happily headed for the booze till they were told differently.

All bar Emmy, who'd lost track of Holden once the bridal party was swept away for photos, and began to worry that he had been a mirage.

After tables and chairs were brought in, and a huge dance floor set up by a swift staging team in red noses and clown wigs, Emmy found her seat. She kicked off her sodden shoes, tucked them under her chair, and stretched out her toes.

Then, adrenalin fading, she leaned forward, rested her chin on her hand, closed her eyes, and sighed.

When she opened her eyes again, it was to find a pair of long, strong male legs decked out in a beautifully tailored suit and shiny black shoes walking slowly towards her. She knew those legs. She knew that walk. Knew that unhurried confidence.

Feeling a little trembly, Emmy pressed herself to standing, and lifted her chin to face the man head-on. Only to remember her lack of shoes. And that he was well over six feet tall.

And so she sat, plonking back into her chair, her toes madly reaching for her shoes.

Holden, having played this game before, crouched down till his eyes were in line with hers. Tired eyes. Eyes that had seen some late nights and long days since she'd last seen them. But smiling eyes, all the same. Stormy blue and lovely. With those unfairly long lashes, and those endearing crinkles. Oh, how she'd missed that face.

"Emerson Adler," he said. "Fancy meeting you here."

"Holden Roarke," she shot back, trying to sound all confident and fine, but even she heard the note of yearning. "What are you doing here?"

"Always with the questions."

"Just one. I know Bernie didn't invite you. She doesn't even remember having met you."

His gaze hooked onto hers, as if he never wanted to let go. "Your calendar, it's still synced to mine."

"Ha!" She leaned in when she felt heads turn her way. Leaned in so close she could feel his warmth. "You totally crashed."

He leaned in a smidgeon himself, till their noses were mere inches from touching. "I don't look at it as 'crashing' so much as coming full circle. I feel somewhat involved in how those crazy kids came to fall madly in love."

Emmy shook her head. "How did you end up as Barry's leaning post?"

"Met him on the way in. Poor fellow looked ready to pass out. His best man didn't look much better. I offered my services until showtime. I can be pretty irresistible when I want to be."

"Oh, I know."

"You do?"

Emmy nodded. With no list to follow, she had to

follow her gut. And it was telling her to be honest. To leave her heart wide open for once and trust it to do its thing. To trust this man to do his.

When she let out a great big sigh, filled with hope and relief, Holden reached out and swept his thumb across her cheek. Gently. So gently. The same way he went about everything, with honour and kindness and thoughtfulness and decency.

"Holden."

"Mm-hmm."

"I should never have asked you to leave."

"You didn't. You told me to go home." His gaze roved over her face, as if it had been far too long since he'd seen it last. "And here I am, doing just as you asked."

Emerson swallowed.

"It did take me a little longer to figure out *why* you said it. That and a little advice from some folks with smarter hearts than mine. You want to know what we came up with?"

"I do," Emmy said, certain she was going to like his answer.

His eyes stopped roving and landed on hers. "You did it because you love me."

A smile bloomed in her chest before landing on her face, the warmth of it like a bubble around them, keeping out the damp, the past, the people milling around them.

"But how could I?" she asked, her voice growing

quiet, intimate, just for him. "We had a deal. *No* accidental falling in love."

"True," said Holden. "As I remember it, *you* promised not to fall for *me* while I made no such promise. So, while you failed miserably, I'm off the hook."

"You are?" she asked, her voice barely a whisper now. Enough that he dropped a knee, his suit fabric sinking into the squelch, so that he could be nearer her still.

"Completely and utterly," he said, his voice raw. "Deeply, shockingly, nauseatingly, incandescently. Off. The. Hook. In love, with you." He smiled a slow, easy smile at whatever he saw on her face. "You okay there?"

Emmy nodded. Then grinned as tears started flowing down her cheeks. Happy tears. Nauseatingly incandescent tears.

"Tell me," he said, his voice rough, as if he too was overwhelmed by emotion. "I want to hear you say the words. Tell me you knew how I felt about you, how I *feel*, all along. Because I can't stand the thought that a day went by when you didn't know that I am crazy about you."

Did she? Of course she did. How could she not? His love had filled up all the tender, yearning places inside her that had craved him, even before she'd found him.

She tucked her knees together, her bare feet crossed beneath her chair, and leaned forward till her forehead touched his. And she said, "I know it."

"Tell me you believe it."

She could feel the vibration of his voice through his hand at the back of her neck, through the point where their foreheads met. "I believe it."

"Tell me you feel it."

She slid off the chair until she was on her knees before him, her slinky peacock-blue dress meeting wet grass as she cupped his face and kissed him. A kiss that was half smile, half laugh, and half utter joy.

"Hey, folks," Phillip's voice boomed over the sound system, "Bernie and Barry have returned from wherever it is they've been, and, since this is their day, and they are doing things on their timetable, I've been told it's time for the bouquet toss. So all the singletons, please gather on the dance floor!"

Emmy lifted her head, but moved no further.

Holden did the same, a single eyebrow raising in question. "What do you say?"

She mirrored his cocked eyebrow. "I'm fine right here, thank you very much. Nice and invisible."

His eyes crinkled a moment before one side of his mouth lifted into a sexy half-smile. Their faces stayed close enough she could see an eyelash that had fallen to his cheek.

This time she lifted her hand, gently gathered it with her index finger and held it up to his lips. "Make a wish."

"You don't believe in the bouquet toss, but you do believe in eyelash wishes. You are an interesting woman, Emerson Adler." He took a hold of her wrist, pulling her finger to his lips, and blew, sending the eyelash spinning off into the ether.

Emerson grinned as she watched the eyelash flutter and disappear, and with the shift in focus came the realisation that many, many people were watching her. And Holden. On their knees in the grass. So much for invisible.

"Up," she whispered. "Up, up, up."

"Okay, okay, okay," he muttered. Pressing himself to standing, he reached down and lifted her to her feet and pulled her against him. As if, now he'd found her again, he was not about to let her go. "Much better."

"Mmm," she said, curling her hand into the front of his shirt and rather marvelling at the fact that she could do so with clear intent.

"Want to know what I wished for?" Holden asked, smiling down into her eyes.

"What if that means it won't come true?"

He seemed to think about it for a second, his mouth twisting, one eye narrowing, before saying, "I reckon it's worth the risk. I wished for you to enter the bouquet toss."

"You did not." Emmy glanced towards the makeshift dance floor, expecting to find the usual seething horde of glittery guests, only to find it was empty bar the bride, who was grinning at her like a loon. "What's happening right now?"

With a roll of her eyes, the bride all but skipped over to their table, stopped, sighed, and held out the bouquet.

“Ahh…” Emmy’s gaze moved to Holden for back-up, only to find him watching her, smiling, that face she loved so much full of questions.

Take the bouquet, or don’t take the bouquet.

As if one’s life really could hinge on a single moment.

The post-Heartache List Emmy would have fought that notion, found it terrifying. While the *post*-post-Heartache List Emmy knew it could happen and that it could be wonderful.

Emmy accepted the bouquet.

Bernie took her in a tight hug. Then gave the same to Holden, holding on a fraction longer, as Holden whispered something in her ear, after which she nodded enthusiastically.

When the wedding crowd hollered and whistled, Emmy couldn’t help but laugh. And curtsy. And offer up a little royal wave, the happiness rushing through her leaving her feeling as if she was floating an inch off the ground. In the best possible way.

At which point the bride headed to the dance floor, and her new husband, who met her there, right as the opening strains of *You Can Leave Your Hat On* burst from the speakers.

“Do me a favour.”

Emmy turned back to Holden, her nose buried in the sweetest spray of wild jasmine. “Depends on the favour.”

“I think it’s high time we move on to Phase Three.”

At the shift in Holden’s voice—deep, husky, and

compelling—her gaze skewed to his. "What's Phase Three?"

"We never did thrash that out. So, I guess it's whatever we want it to be." He took her by the hand, looked around, his expression highly focused. Then he looked back at her. "Why are you so short?"

"Took off my shoes."

Muttering under his breath about falling head over heels for a woman who couldn't keep her heels on her feet, Holden leaned around her, gathered her shoes from under her chair, then slipped an arm beneath her knees and lifted her off the ground. "First step of Phase Three," he said. "We're getting the heck out of here."

"We can't!" she said, holding on tight and brimming with breathless laughter.

Holden, holding all the cards as well as herself, ignored her, edging around tables. "The bride insisted. Just now. Said she hoped it made up for the key incident."

Emmy looked over her shoulder in search of the bride, only to find her dancing up a storm. "She *did* remember."

"Oh, yeah. Now let's go." Holden picked up the pace, a man on a mission.

Then Emmy caught Camille's eye. She gave her best friend a finger wave. Camille pretended to burst into tears, her hands clutched over her heart, before Phillip dragged her onto the dance floor.

Emmy sighed as Holden tucked her tighter against his chest and strode from the tent, just like Kevin

Costner and Whitney Houston in *The Bodyguard.* It was the single sexiest moment of her life. But, considering the intention in his stride as he made his way up the side of the house, she had a feeling it would soon be pipped.

Emmy lifted a hand to Holden's cheek. "How many points do I get for bagging a Back-Up Best Man Slash Wedding Crasher?"

He slowed, just a mite, as his gaze moved to hers. "Considering how rare a breed we are, it's gotta be up near seven hundred and fifty points. Maybe even a thousand."

"Wow," she said. "To think, I had no intention of playing the game, when it turns out I'm so very good at it."

With that, she reached up and grabbed her prize by the tie and dragged his mouth to hers. Or maybe she simply caught him on the way down.

Either way, if that kiss was anything to go by, Phase Three was going to be the very best of all.

EPILOGUE

EMMY FINISHED SMEARING Vegemite on her toast, tucked a corner between her teeth, and turned to find Holden ambling into the kitchen—suit pants unbuttoned, chest bare.

Her heart still kicked at the sight of him. "Nearly ready?"

Holden spun on the spot, arms out, showing off. "Thought I'd just go like this today."

"The investors will be thrilled."

He finished his spin, and moved in, his arm sliding around her waist before hauling her close. Then he tugged her a little closer still, till she was flush up against him, his smile growing when he felt her breath hitch.

Then he grabbed the slice of toast from her mouth, placed a slow, soft kiss upon her lips, followed by a quick swipe of his tongue that had her eyes all but rolling back in her head, before taking a bite of her toast and putting it back where he found it.

"Need a lift?" she asked, when he let her go, patting down her hair, tugging on her skirt, and generally trying to feel less discombobulated.

"No, but I'll take it. Lunch?"

"Not today. I can take off early if you want to try that new Italian place around the corner."

"Done."

"When do you head to Paris?" she asked. "This Thursday or next?"

Her hand went to her phone, to check their joint calendar, but his hand closed over hers, before spinning her back into his arms, then rocking her side to side, till they were slow dancing in the kitchen.

Dust motes fluttered through the shards of buttery sunlight pouring through her kitchen window. Her mother's lemon tree, nourished by Pumpkin's ashes, flourished just outside.

While Holden's eyes, gazing into hers, were such a sharp, clear blue in the morning light. No storm, no clouds, not any more. "I think you mean, when do *we* head to Paris?"

"We?"

"Why not? I *may* have had a sly chat to Freya, before confirming the dates, to make sure you could fit it in. Freya did consider coming with me to Paris, if you refused, but in the end she chose to stay behind, keep Pitch Perfect rolling along."

"A week in Paris," Emmy said out loud.

For this was the deal. A side effect of living with a man who was more curious than cautious, who had connections the world over, who *was*—it turned out—just as happy lazing on her couch watching her true crime documentaries, or building her a shed, as he was jet-setting all over the world to talk about his new app that people were already saying would lift the ability of small businesses to compete in the global space for ever.

Having been his wildly successful beta tester, Pitch Perfect could attest to the fact that business had never looked brighter.

"What do you say?"

"I say…yes. A week in Paris, with you, sounds perfect. Now, will you do me a favour?"

"Anything."

"When you finally decide to put some clothes on, wear the pale blue. Nobody will be able to say no to you in that shirt."

"Nobody says no to me anyway."

Emerson snorted. She sure had. For quite some time.

"Fine, I'll wear the shirt. And will you do me a favour?"

"Depends on the favour."

"Always so cautious," he said, a smile in his eyes as they roved over her face.

"Not always," she said, reaching around to run her hand over his backside, before pulling him a little closer.

"Fair enough. My request is that you go a little lighter on the Vegemite for our morning toast."

"This toast?" she said, holding out her half-eaten slice. "This toast that I made for myself?"

"Mm-hmm," he said, leaning down to nibble at her neck.

"Changing up my Vegemite-to-butter ratio is a far bigger favour than the shirt." Her eyes fluttered closed as he rained a trail of kisses over her cheek. "What do I get in return?"

"Rub your feet every night this week."

Gracious, that sounded good. "Fine. What else?"

He moved to her earlobe, nipping the lobe, before whispering in her ear what he was prepared to do, nightly, in vivid detail. And Emerson was mighty glad he was holding on to her as her knees gave way.

And soon the kitchen bench proved itself good for something other than making Vegemite on toast.

And, right before her mind turned to starbursts, and happiness and pleasure and heat and want, Emerson smiled. A smile so wide she was absolutely certain it would never, ever come to an end.

* * * * *

Bahamas Escape With The Best Man

Cara Colter

Cara Colter shares her life in beautiful British Columbia, Canada, with her husband, nine horses and one small Pomeranian with a large attitude. She loves to hear from readers, and you can learn more about her and contact her through Facebook.

Books by Cara Colter

A Fairytale Summer!

Cinderella's New York Fling

Cinderellas in the Palace

His Convenient Royal Bride
One Night with Her Brooding Bodyguard

A Crown by Christmas

Cinderella's Prince Under the Mistletoe

Matchmaker and the Manhattan Millionaire
His Cinderella Next Door
The Wedding Planner's Christmas Wish
Snowbound with the Prince

Visit the Author Profile page
at millsandboon.com.au for more titles.

Dear Reader,

My friends Bill and Rose are to gardens what I hope I am to writing. They transform empty—or even ugly—spaces into places of pure magic.

Thanks to them, my garden (I used to call it a yard!) has become the most inspiring of places. Uniquely beautiful, some of its spaces vibrate with ever-changing color and energy and light, and others—deeply shaded—offer room for tranquility and introspection.

This story really flowed from the solitude of early morning in the sanctuary that Bill and Rose created for me.

In that garden, I am reminded of how interconnected all our gifts are, and I am deeply grateful for that awareness.

My wish is that my gift brings you, the reader, moments of pure wonder, just like those I have received from Bill and Rose.

With best wishes,

Cara Colter

To Bill and Rose Pastorek, with deepest gratitude for how generously they have shared their gifts with me.

Praise for
Cara Colter

"Ms. Colter's writing style is one you will want to continue to read. Her descriptions place you there.... This story does have a HEA but leaves you wanting more."

—*Harlequin Junkie* on *His Convenient Royal Bride*

CHAPTER ONE

"SIR, WE'LL BE landing in a few minutes."

Matteo Keller opened his eyes. He wasn't sure if he'd been sleeping, or just drifting.

Either was unusual. Usually, he found the time on board his company's private jet to be perfect for catching up on work, uninterrupted.

He had a well-honed jet lag strategy where he used the flight time to start resetting his inner clock from the time in Zurich to the time zone he would be arriving in.

Definitely sleeping, he thought, bemused, as he looked at the business papers that had slid from his tabletop desk and now lay around him. So much for his jet lag strategy. The sun was setting out there, and now he was wide-awake.

Right on top of the scattered papers was a brochure, shiny and colorful. Matteo picked it up. It described his destination, one of the two thousand four hundred cays and seven hundred islands that formed the Bahamas.

Coconut Cay, the safest place on earth.

Glancing at the pictures of the boutique hotel, the white sands and the turquoise waters of the island, Matteo was not sure why safety had been picked as the main selling feature of the tropical paradise. If he was in charge of marketing…

You're not, he told himself firmly.

And maybe there *was* something to be said for the brochure's claim that doors could be left unlocked and your watch would be safe on the bedside table.

Well, maybe not *his* watch.

According to the brochure, the tiny island, which had several resorts and one village, had a zero crime rate, and each guest was carefully vetted.

He did vaguely remember his assistant asking him questions that had seemed, at the time, both mildly intrusive and slightly irritating.

Welcome to Sullivan's Island, he thought, calling it after a very old and very corny American sitcom about an unlikely group of people shipwrecked.

The island, as the jet descended, seemed idyllic, drowsy and gilded in gold. No doubt safe.

And yet he, of all people, knew that danger lurked in life itself. No matter how hard you tried, there would always be events out of your control, waiting to blow your world to smithereens.

Matteo was taken aback at himself.

That was what he got for dozing, instead of working, for not adhering to his rigid schedule to avert jet lag.

Those were unwanted thoughts, slipping outside of his customary discipline, his ability not to think of the world he had once had or lament how quickly it had slipped away.

He sincerely hoped *the safest place on earth* was not going to make a run at his carefully constructed barriers.

The plane touched down.

"It won't," Matteo told himself tersely, rising from his seat, "because I won't let it."

And yet here it was, nighttime, and he was wide-awake. And for some reason, when he disembarked the plane, he left the scattered business papers—his balm—behind.

Marlee Copeland decided she absolutely hated destination weddings. This was her third one in the past two years.

Admittedly, Coconut Cay was the most beautiful of the three. The small tropical island was extraordinary: gorgeous beaches, calm waters, rainbow-hued flowers the size of basketballs, mangoes, coconuts and banana clusters hanging in trees.

The resort was like something out of a dream. The color palette of the structures, inside and out, was creamy whites and soothing beiges, everything subdued and extraordinarily tasteful, in sharp and deliberate contrast to the vibrant backdrop of the island.

"So, what's to hate?" Marlee asked herself, the warm air—so different than the November dreariness she had left behind in Seattle—caressing her.

She was standing in darkness that felt somehow silky on her skin, on the pathway outside the private cabana she had wisely paid extra for instead of sharing accommodations with the other bridesmaids.

Night had fallen with the suddenness of a dark blanket being dropped over the sky, and she watched the stars wink out, one by one, and then a rising moon paint the caps of the gentle waves nearby in silver. She listened to them lap on shore. In the distance, she could hear laughter and voices at the pool.

The bridal side of the wedding party. Fiona, bride-to-be, had suggested they arrive a few days early, though not to unwind, as one might think after all the stress of planning a wedding three thousand miles from home.

No, the early arrival was to get rid of the "pasty" look. For the photos. Which had to be perfect, naturally. Marlee was fairly certain Fiona had cast her a glance when she made the "pasty look" comment.

Or maybe the bride's choice of a dress for her had just made her overly sensitive. Marlee sighed. She knew she should join them, of course. But she didn't want to. The fact she hated it all was just going to be too evident, no matter how hard she tried to hide it.

"What's to hate?" she asked herself again. A night bird chattered as palm fronds swayed in a faint breeze, the air faintly perfumed.

It was all so *romantic.*

And *perfect.*

And *that* was what Marlee hated. All the weddings she had been to lately—and there had been many as her friends were at that age where they were ready for the "next stage" in life—were like this. Romantic and perfect.

Admittedly, her cynicism had set in after her own wedding had fallen through, cancellation notices sent and her elaborate wedding gown boxed up and sent to the thrift store. Before that, at every wedding she'd attended, she had made notes, gleaned ideas and admired dresses.

This was the first wedding since her own matrimonial debacle. Now she felt weddings—including the one she hadn't had—were pure theater, where everyone played their part, especially the beautiful, joyous bride and the handsome, devoted groom, with eyes only for each other. It was pageantry, blind to the statistics that said it probably wasn't going to work out in quite the way the glowing bride and the besotted groom hoped.

Despite how justifiable Marlee's skepticism around weddings might have been, she knew in her heart that she was kidding herself. She still yearned for all that romance to be true.

"You're jealous," Marlee decided.

Was she? Of course! She was supposed to have had all this. Planning *her* day had consumed the better part of her life for over a year.

No destination wedding for her, because of her huge

extended family, but instead a gorgeous old church and a posh hotel…and then, the exit by her fiancé, Arthur, just six months ago, embarrassingly close to their spring wedding date.

Even with the help of sympathetic—make that pitying—family members and friends, canceling everything and letting people know there would be no wedding had been nearly as much work as putting it all together.

Add to that the humiliation…

Jilted at the altar.

"I'm *not* jealous," Marlee ordered herself. She was just tired. There was only a three-hour time difference between this tiny island and her home, but the crazy fifteen-hour travel schedule from Seattle to Florida, onward to Nassau, and then finally to Coconut Cay, had left Marlee exhausted and discombobulated. Really, she didn't know if it was time to get up or time to go to bed. Should she have supper now or breakfast?

The other destination weddings she had attended had not required quite so much effort to get there.

Now everything felt like too much. They had barely been whisked to the resort from the tiny airport when Fiona had rounded them all up and herded them into her luxurious suite for the big reveal: the bridesmaid's dresses.

They were Fiona's "surprise" to her girlfriends who were standing up with her, a gift intended to in some way assuage the huge financial and time commitment involved in saying yes to being a part of a destination wedding. She had collected all their measurements and refused to reveal any details of the custom-made dresses. Until now.

Until they were trapped here and couldn't say no, Marlee thought, perhaps unkindly.

There were three bridesmaids and the dresses were all the same color—hideous. Fiona called it sea foam, but Marlee thought it looked like the Spanish moss that hung in creepy fingers from cypress trees in the Southern parts of the United States.

Though the same color, each dress purported to reflect the personality of the person it had been bestowed upon.

So Kathy's had narrow straps and a form-hugging bodice. The short, full skirt flirted around her long legs and accentuated a subtle but undeniable sexiness. Kathy looked like she had been at the tanning booth for at least a month. Nothing pasty about her!

Brenda's dress was a sleek, strapless sheath that, even while hugging her curves, hinted at a woman in control, and indeed, Brenda was CEO of a huge cosmetics company. That company had made their name—and a considerable fortune—on a tanning product called Beach-in-a-Bottle, so Brenda looked sun-kissed and glowing at all times.

And then there was Marlee's. It was, sadly, the dress of the high-school-girl-trying-too-hard variety. In fact, the dress sang *future librarian gets invited to a prom*. Never mind that she *was* a librarian—and had the pasty complexion to prove it! The dress was high-collared and short-sleeved, and abounded with puff and ruffles.

And, as if the dress in and of itself was not like something out of a nightmare, Fiona had gushingly proclaimed, "It's *so* you, Marlee."

And the others had agreed!

After the great reveal, Fiona had ordered them all to their own rooms to change out of the precious garments, and then suggested meeting at the pool for drinks and hors d'oeuvres.

But Marlee was still here outside her cabana—not as luxurious as Fiona's suite, but still beachy and charming—not changed, and despite being starving, was not going to the pool. The highly orchestrated schedule was already giving her a headache.

Not to mention a niggling but growing sense of rebellion.

Her cabana had come with a complimentary travel-size bottle of rum and a cigar. Apparently, the island was famous for both.

Marlee had never smoked a cigar. Ever. And she had certainly never drunk rum straight, but no mix had been provided.

In defiance of how that horrible dress said she was perceived—by those who supposedly knew her best—she cracked the rum open and held the cigar between her fingertips, liking the way that felt—bold and glamourous in an old movie kind of way. If her friends were to see her now, they would get the message.

You don't know me at all.

She took a tentative sip of the rum. Her eyes watered. She choked. On her empty stomach, it was like swallowing fire.

Still, something warm and bold and lovely unfolded in her. She took another tentative sip of the rum and even looked at the cigar, considering whether she should light it.

That was when she became aware she was no longer alone.

The curving pathway that wound around the cabanas on its way to the beach was only faintly lit, solar lights twinkling in the deep, flower-threaded foliage on either side of it, but she could see a man was coming toward her.

In Seattle, alone outside on a dark night, she probably would have ducked back inside. But there was a light on in the cabana next door to hers, and through its open doors she could hear the faint sounds of people talking. Plus, she remembered the brochure's promise that this was the safest place on earth.

The hotel had even sent a pre-arrival questionnaire to make sure they were not inviting criminals or miscreants into their island paradise.

So, chances of the man coming down the walkway being an ax murderer were largely reduced.

Besides which, she felt holding the cigar and sipping rum straight from the bottle asked her to be a different person, not quite so timid, not quite so willing to play it safe.

So, instead of moving away, Marlee watched the

man approach. He was one of *those* men. You could tell by the way he moved. Not quite a swagger, but something smooth, confident and totally self-assured was in every step of that long stride.

The white towel draped around his neck was practically glowing against the darkness of the night.

He didn't have a shirt on, and as he got closer, the magnificence of him was fully revealed to her.

He was like a poster boy for *perfect.* Wide shoulders, a broad chest, faint lines of ribs under taut skin, a flat, hard belly that dipped into boldly colored swim shorts, the bareness of his legs showing off how long and sculpted with muscle they were. He was barefoot.

Really, Marley told herself sternly, there was nothing sexy about that. Barefoot went with the beach. He was obviously on his way for a swim.

In the ocean. Not the pool. In the darkness. By himself.

Okay. There was something a little sexy about that. Or maybe a lot.

Or maybe not. He'd probably heard all that feminine giggling at the pool and made a fast detour toward the ocean.

Some instinct stopped him in his tracks then and he squinted up the walkway in her direction. The moon painted silver tips in his dark hair and gilded his face, which was as perfect as the rest of him.

He seemed unfairly handsome, exactly the kind of man who never paid any kind of attention to a woman like her.

Marlee resisted, again, the impulse to slide back toward her open, French-paned door. Wasn't it exactly that shrinking librarian attitude that had earned her this dress?

CHAPTER TWO

AT THAT EXACT MOMENT, the man spotted her in the shadows. He hesitated, then moved forward cautiously, as if he knew a shrinking librarian when he saw one.

"I'm sorry," he said. "I didn't mean to startle you."

Since Marlee was trying very hard not to look startled, his apology was annoying. Still, if she was going to be startled, eyes like his would do it. In the faint illumination of the pathway lights and the moon, they seemed as turquoise as the sea had been before darkness fell.

"According to the resort map, I think this is the only way to the beach."

Now he was practically apologizing for using a public path. Exactly how buttoned-up did she look? Well, there was the dress, which she had not taken off, despite Fiona's orders. Perhaps she thought a few swigs of rum could improve it.

She was counting on the the cigar and the rum bottle, now to be contradicting the message of the dress!

His voice was rich and deep and reassuring in some way. She heard a faint and intriguing accent. The old Marlee—the one she had been just minutes ago, before being presented with this dress—would have just nodded, smiled politely and watched him move away, resigned to being dismissed.

"It seems like an odd time to indulge in a swim," she said, not quite flirting, but not retiring, either. *Engaging* him. She took a defiant swig of the rum.

Both the rum and engaging him felt deliciously dangerous in how terribly out of character they were for her.

He tilted his head toward her, faint surprise crinkling around his astounding eyes, making her notice they were fringed in lusciously abundant lashes.

"I've been working all day," he said. "There were some unexpected challenges. I need to clear my mind."

So he worked here. At Coconut Cay. She wondered what he did. Management of some sort, no doubt. There was something in the way he carried himself that suggested he dealt with people, and he was good at it. She wondered if those unexpected challenges he'd dealt with today had anything to do with Fiona's arrival, and was practically certain that they did.

"Well, I'm sure a midnight swim is good for that," Marlee said, though she wasn't sure at all. What did she know about midnight swims? She felt a sudden, sharp and somewhat shocking yearning for worlds unexplored.

Now that he was stopped, he was apparently quite

happy to *engage.* His eyes trailed to the unlit cigar in her right hand. A smile twitched, drawing her attention to white, straight teeth, the fullness of his bottom lip.

Something happened to the air. It went from soft, and faintly perfumed, to charged, a before-the-storm intensity humming through it.

Marlee found herself entranced by him, and either emboldened by the rum—or by the persona she had indulged by holding the cigar as if she knew what to do with it—she took a long, leisurely look at him. It felt like a drink of cold water on a hot day.

More perfection.

His hair was a little long, tucked behind his ears, the feathered tips riding his shoulders. It was very straight, dark and milk chocolate strands sewn together. He had high cheekbones, a straight nose and full, sensual lips.

There was a scent coming off him, as if his golden-toned skin had absorbed sunshine all day and was now emitting that tantalizing smell.

She was suddenly way too aware that she likely smelled of a day's travel overlaid with rum, but it didn't stop her from wondering if his skin would feel as warm as it smelled. Her fingertips had this funny little itch in them.

To touch him. A complete stranger. Ridiculous! She was not that kind of girl.

Though, for the first time in her life, Marlee was aware of maybe wanting to be.

She noted again that his eyes were—impossibly—as turquoise as the waters of the bay.

"Speaking of odd indulgences..." he said. "Cigars and rum at midnight?"

Marlee noticed that thread of humor that totally confident men always had in their tone in his voice.

"Actually, I don't think it is midnight," she said.

The stranger did not seem the least insulted by Marlee's tone, which may have been faintly querulous in the face of his sheer attraction, his easy confidence, and a whole different world his mere presence was letting her know she missed.

He lifted a shoulder. "You suggested it first. *Midnight* swim?" he reminded her.

"It's just a turn of phrase."

"Ah," he said, utterly composed. Of course, he no doubt spent his days dealing with cranky, demanding tourists, and soothing them with his deep, accented voice and his lovely eyes. In fact, his smile deepened. "It's midnight somewhere."

He'd know that, too, dealing as he did, with guests from all over the world.

He had a dimple, just on one side.

"Are you going to smoke that?" he asked, nodding to the cigar in her hand.

Apparently she *was* diverting attention from the sheer ugliness of the dress as he appeared not to have noticed it yet.

"I'm thinking of it," she lied, as if she was sophisticated and mysterious and smoked cigars all the time.

Unfortunately, that made her feel as if she had to prove something. She put it to her nose and sniffed it, something she was fairly sure an expert would do before lighting it.

He lifted a wicked slash of a dark eyebrow at her. "First time?"

So much for sophisticated and mysterious. He wasn't fooled. She wasn't sure how he managed to make those two words—first time?—sound quite so naughty.

She could pretend it wasn't her first time, but there seemed no point.

"What gave me away?"

"You're holding it as if you thought you had picked up a friendly neighborhood cat, but you've just realized it was a skunk, instead."

Marlee felt an unusual tickle. It wasn't the cigar. It was a giggle, and it shocked her, because she was not a giggler.

At all.

Could she chock that up to two or three mouthfuls of rum? Doubtful, no matter how strong the island rum was. It was him, teasing something girlish to the surface in her. So he was charming as well as handsome. He should come with a flashing neon sign.

Danger.

Again, though, if he dealt with people all day every day, this would be his skill set. Charming. Setting people at ease.

"I might smoke it," she said.

"Ah. And what would be the occasion for your first cigar?"

Was he just being conversational, or did he find her interesting? The possibility nearly tied knots in her tongue.

"People should try new things."

He cocked his head at her. "Forgive me for being presumptuous, but you don't look like the kind of woman who would voluntarily try anything that comes with a health warning on it."

Well, that either meant she looked healthy. Or like a nerd.

"It's the dress," she admitted reluctantly.

Why had she said that? First cigars were about celebrations: babies, job promotions… Instead, she had directed his attention to the full horror of her attire. The dress practically screamed wedding, and Marlee didn't actually want him to know she was a member of the demanding wedding party that was driving him into the sea in the darkness in hopes of clearing his head.

He regarded her attire solemnly and at length. She experienced the full, mesmerizing enchantment of the amazing color of his eyes and their framing in a decadent abundance of sooty lash.

She refused to squirm under a gaze that might be called stripping.

"That dress inspired the loss of cigar virginity?" he finally asked.

The word *virginity* coming from his mouth felt as if he had said something naughty and personal, especially since his thorough inspection had left her feeling as if something was tingling along her skin.

He didn't seem to recognize it as a bridesmaid's dress.

"It's vugly," she said.

He tilted his head. "I'm sorry. English is my second language. I'm rarely caught out, but I don't know that word."

"My own creation: vugly. A combination of very and ugly."

Her creativity was rewarded with a smile tickling the luscious sensuality of those lips.

"Vugly," he said, and gave a pleased chortle. "I'll have to file that one away for future use."

Yes, Marlee thought, it might be a useful addition to his vocabulary. He could use it to describe a bride having a temper tantrum over some tiny detail not quite right.

"Besides the fact it's vugly," Marlee went on, "it's frilly and fussy and it scratches."

"Where?" he asked, softly.

He managed to make that sound naughty, too, as if he could aid her in some way.

"Everywhere!"

"Ah," he said. He took a step back from her and studied the dress even more carefully. Those dark slashes of brows lowered in a thoughtful frown.

"It doesn't seem *you*, somehow," he decided.

At his proclamation, Marlee was sure she felt the

ground shift under her feet, like rock crumbling in warning right before a cliff.

A complete stranger had *seen* her, when her own girlfriends had not. It made him even more compelling than he had been before. And he had already been plenty compelling.

Well, it wasn't as if she hadn't seen the danger sign.

But Marlee decided, right then and there, she was giving up on her lifelong tendency toward caution.

She would *embrace* the cliff. She wouldn't fall. She would jump! Not her, precisely, but the woman drinking rum and contemplating the smoking of a cigar.

"This dress makes me want to get on a horse, pull a bandanna over my face and rob trains," she told him.

The smile that had been tickling the wickedly attractive curve of his mouth formed fully, revealing the full straightness of his teeth, as white as the towel around his neck.

Then he threw back his head and laughed. The column of his throat looked strong and touchable. The sound of his laughter was more intoxicating than the rum.

She, Marlee Copeland, had just made a very attractive man laugh. That felt like a cigar-worthy reason for celebration!

"The cigar matches your start on your career as a criminal. People sometimes lick them before they light them."

"What?"

"They're usually wine-dipped."

She flicked the cigar with her tongue.

"Here," he said, gently. "Let me take that."

And just like that, his hand brushed hers, and a few more rocks crumbled from that cliff.

He took the cigar.

His eyes lingered on her lips.

A fire leaped to life within her.

"I wonder if there's really a wild, train-robbing outlaw under all that green fluffy stuff."

"It's not green." Her voice was hoarse, a choked whisper. "It's sea foam. Chiffon."

He held up the cigar and his tongue slipped out and licked it, exactly where her own tongue had been. His eyes were steady on hers. It was shockingly sensual.

"I need to get out of this scratchy dress," she said. What had made her say *that*? It was totally inappropriate. Did it sound as if she wanted to get out of the dress *with him*? Did it sound like an invitation?

Why did she always have to be so socially inept, blurting things out awkwardly?

Why did men like this always make her feel like a tongue-tied teenager?

Fiona had been right. This dress *did* suit her.

On the other hand, what would a train-robbing, cigar-loving, rum-drinking outlaw do? She could be that. For just a few minutes in time, she could. Maybe just for one night.

She took a deep breath. She felt as if she was on the edge of a cliff, trying to build up her nerve to jump.

"Want some company for your swim?" she asked.

This was complete insanity. She was not a very good swimmer.

He tilted his head and regarded her, no doubt as surprised as she herself was.

Marlee's breath stopped in her chest. That was what you got for trying to break out of your mold, she thought, a little nervously.

A one-way trip off a cliff. The cigar, the rum, the remarks had made her feel as if she could be bold.

One thing she should remember about cliff jumps: as exhilarating as the ride down was, the landing was going to be bumpy. Painful.

He was going to think of a way to squirm out of it.

He needed to be alone. He'd had a hard day at work.

"Of course, I'd love for you to join me," he said.

A man like him—just like a dress like this—made her reconsider the kind of girl she had always been.

She was on a tropical island with a complete stranger. Why not let loose? Why not let down her hair? Did she really want to be the person that was looked at in a dress like this and heard the proclamation, *It's you.*

Marlee was not the kind of girl who went for moonlit swims with strange men. But what had she ever gotten out of life by being the kind of girl she was?

"Are you allowed to?" she blurted, realizing she was scrabbling for an exit.

He raised a questioning eyebrow at her.

"You know. Um, fraternizing with the guests. It's usually against the rules. Of a resort."

Sheesh. As if she was any kind of expert in resorts.

"You're right," he said, after a moment. "It usually is. But there's something about a cigar-holding woman that just brings out the outlaw in me, too."

She shivered. He was so sexy it felt as if she was swan-diving off that cliff, her arms flung open wide to a terrifying and exhilarating adventure where there was absolutely no way of predicting how or where she would fall.

CHAPTER THREE

SHE DIDN'T EVEN know his name and there was something thrilling and electrical leaping in the air between them.

Marlee was aware she was playing with the proverbial fire.

Still, she was on this island for five days for a wedding. Only three whole days if you took out the travel days. It felt as if the clock was ticking.

She could remake herself into anything she wanted to be.

Couldn't she?

She suddenly couldn't wait to rid herself of the dress and any remnant of the person she had always expected herself to be.

"I'll babysit the cigar while you go change." He put it to his lips again and took a leisurely taste of it. Even though it was not lit, the air was filled with sweet, smoky sensuality.

Unfortunately, there weren't many ways that could

draw a woman's attention to a man's mouth more than that.

"Almost as good as a kiss," he decided, his voice sultry and hot like the tropical night. "I can taste you on it."

As if this wasn't dangerous enough without kisses entering the discussion! She felt a deep sense of wanting to taste him.

And not through a shared, unlit cigar, either.

"I don't even know you name."

"Matteo," he offered. "And yours?"

"Marlee."

He bowed slightly. "The pleasure is mine."

Good grief! It was? *Matteo.* What a gorgeous, exotic name.

"I'll just be a sec," she croaked, and slipped through the open door of her cabana. Her heart was beating as hard as if she had just run a hundred-meter dash with a gold medal at stake.

Now what? She hoped good sense—something she was known for, which meant she probably deserved this dress—would return. But it did not.

Her cheeks felt hot. She hoped the darkness had hidden that from him.

Or did he suspect she was a little naive and not very worldly?

Still, here was the truth. She, Marlee Copeland, librarian from Seattle, was going to go for a midnight swim with a gorgeous, exotic man named Matteo. Was it midnight?

Who cared? It was just as he said. It was midnight somewhere. It was dark. It was completely against her nature to be so spontaneous, so throwing-caution-to-the-wind. Maybe that was why it felt so absolutely exhilarating.

Marlee went through the darkened space of her tiny cabana, not wanting to turn on a light. What was that about? She was afraid the dreamlike quality of this experience could not hold up to having a light shined on it, that's what.

That should have given her pause, but it didn't. Instead, she found her suitcase, open on the bed, and rummaged through it in the dark until her hands found the slippery fabric of her swimsuit.

She ducked into the bathroom. Again, she was reluctant to turn on the light, as if the fairy tale would come to an end if exposed to light. Plus, of course, she'd have to look at herself in her swimsuit.

That would be enough to make her lose her nerve.

Somehow, she got out of the dress and left it in a rumpled pile on the floor. She wriggled into the swimsuit. It was a one piece. It felt as if it was binding. She knew she had gained a bit of weight since her jilted-at-the-altar fiasco. Five pounds. Maybe ten.

That's why she had been earmarked for the hideous dress. To artfully hide a few pounds so she wouldn't wreck the wedding photos.

Okay, so she wasn't sexy in a swimsuit. She did not need any more sexiness than his presence already provided. And despite the cigar and the rum and saying yes to the invitation, she didn't want him to get the wrong idea.

Or did she?

Suddenly wrong and right and who decided these things seemed like terrible constraints to adventure and boldness and living life one hundred percent.

Was she really going to go for a swim with a stranger?

She came to her senses, just like that. She threw on the light. As she had suspected, the bathing suit did absolutely nothing for her. She looked like she had been stuffed into a sausage casing.

She looked extraordinarily plain, with her mousy, shoulder-length hair still travel-crumpled. Her green eyes had tired smudges under them. The bathing suit revealed way too much skin that had a certain lard-like shade to it. No wonder Fiona had suggested a few extra days in the sun!

In fact, Marlee thought she looked exactly like a person who spent their days in a library, carefully selecting wonderful books for the highlight of her week—story time!

She was the kind of person *that* dress was made for. The kind of person abandoned a week before their wedding because her fiancé had suddenly discovered the painful truth.

It was all too dull and unexciting for him.

Which she translated to mean *she* was too dull and unexciting for him.

For Arthur. Who had not exactly been a ball of fire himself.

She quickly gathered the dress off the floor and hung it over the shower bar. She took a deep breath, mourning the moment that almost had been. Then, Marlee wrapped a towel around herself, marched across the floor and poked her head out the door.

She could see him standing out there, his wide, naked back to the cabana. Matteo. What was that, exactly? Italian? They liked their women more on the voluptuous side, didn't they?

The words she was going to speak—*I've changed my mind, I've come to my senses*—froze inside her. She took a deep breath. They still didn't come out.

A voice inside her begged her to prove Arthur wrong.

Live.

For once, just live.

Marlee backed away from the door and returned to the suitcase. Tucked into a corner of it was the lingerie she had chosen for her own wedding night.

When she had packed it, she had told herself she was being practical. Why let it go to waste? The underwear—which had promised to be seamless—had been beautiful underneath her wedding gown. Why not use it with her bridesmaid's dress? Wouldn't those same seamless qualities be great for a day where she would be somewhat in the spotlight? Where she would be posing for pictures?

The reveal of the bridesmaid's dress really rendered all those reasons to use the underwear unnecessary.

There were so many frills that an extra underwear line or two would hardly be noticeable!

Her hidden self, she thought, as she touched the exquisite lace on the matching white bra and panties.

Of course, when she had purchased them, she had done so in anticipation that someday her hidden self was going to be revealed to her delighted groom.

The saleslady had even shown her a quick release on the bra, saying, "To minimize the, er, awkward moments of your wedding night."

Marlee was so tired of being the good girl. She was so tired of living by the rules.

Yes. She would go for a midnight swim. With a sexy stranger. In her underwear, instead of her frumpy bathing suit. These days, and in the dark, who could possibly tell the difference?

Matteo waited on the darkened path in front of Marlee's cabana. The night was unbelievably beautiful: stars studding an inky dark sky, the air so soft and moist it felt like a touch, the waves whispering a timeless song. A nearby bird screeched loudly, and he caught sight of bright feathers through the waxy green foliage of palm trees.

He had not been to the tropics before, and standing here, in the utter enchantment of it, he wondered why.

Of course, how much of the enchantment was his chance encounter with her?

Marlee.

He was, he thought, misrepresenting himself just

a bit. For some reason the cigar-wielding vision that had materialized on the pathway thought he worked at the resort.

She had been a surprise, tucked in among the foliage, fondling the cigar and drinking rum.

She said it was because of the dress, but it wasn't until she mentioned it that he had even noticed it.

Not when he was entranced by her eyes. They were as green and lustrous as jade. They were so compelling, now that he thought about it, he couldn't recall the color of her hair.

But he could imagine her lips: wide, plump, unglossed, and not in need of any kind of improvement, either.

There was something about her both understated and overstated, which made her an intriguing contradiction that begged exploring. She had the clear eyes of an angel, but she was debating corrupting those luscious lips by smoking a cigar and dreaming of robbing trains!

He increasingly lived in a highly predictable world. Everything was highly scheduled. Managed. Controlled.

He liked it that way.

But if he liked it so much, why was he so susceptible to the intrigues of a spontaneous encounter?

Maybe, Matteo admitted reluctantly, it was a distraction from that troubling thought he'd had looking at the brochure, which claimed Coconut Cay was the safest place on earth. His painful experience was that danger rarely came from outside sources.

He didn't want to think about that, revisit the pain of his mother's long illness and his brokenhearted father's terrible slide…

He deliberately avoided relationships deepening into the zone where they could cause that kind of cataclysmic destruction of a world.

He was a numbers man, and he had done the cost-benefit analysis. He had seen, firsthand, the terrible cost that could be extracted at the altar of love.

So, given all that, this distraction itself had the potential for danger, didn't it?

Not really. He was here for a few days. Tonight was his only free evening. There was, thankfully, no time for developments of the complicated romantic kind.

He was going for a swim. Period.

Because of the meteoric rise of the family business he had saved from near ruin, Matteo was a public figure now. He could not risk being politically incorrect, letting his guard down, not even for one playful moment.

As was so much these days, this forever being on guard was part of what made living life in the spotlight so tiresome.

He'd told Marlee he'd been working all day. That there had been some unexpected challenges. She had jumped to the conclusion that he'd been working *here.*

The truth was he'd been thirty thousand feet above

the earth, in his private jet, working on a business issue so complicated and dull it had put him to sleep.

To be honest, he found it hard to envision what kind of unexpected challenges might arise in a place like Coconut Cay.

Still, he had not rushed to correct her, to assure her he would in no way be fraternizing with her.

The truth was he had *enjoyed* her not having a clue about who he was. Increasingly, and distressingly, in Europe he was recognized as the CEO of Monte Rosa Alpen. He'd recently been stopped, in downtown Zurich, by a French tourist who had wanted his autograph and a photo together!

But success wasn't just making him highly—and uncomfortably—recognizable by strangers.

It was changing the way people around him interacted with him.

Women, in particular, seemed besotted with what his success could mean to *them*.

And for all that the attention was flattering initially, Matteo found he had quickly become quite jaded. When was the last time he had been liked for himself, instead of being seen as an opportunity, an important connection, someone who could be *used?*

He was grateful for old friendships, the ones he had had since long before he had achieved such success.

Which was how he found himself on Coconut Cay when he really didn't have the time right now to be here, and when this, despite its exotic beauty, wasn't his kind of place.

Or at least he had thought it wasn't. But now that he was here, he wasn't so sure.

He hadn't allowed himself the gift of downtime for as long as he could remember. He sometimes dreamed of the high and rugged places of his youth, far away from the pressures of his electronics and his life, but he did not indulge.

He was driven, absolutely and utterly. He had been consumed by a single mission. Saving the business that had been in his family for four hundred years.

No, there was no time for frivolities in Matteo's life. Even now, there was a sense that he could not let his guard down, that it all could slip away, as it had done for his father.

But when an old university friend—a friend who knew Matteo inside and out, and was unmoved by the fact he had graced the covers of business magazines or that he had been listed as one of the one hundred wealthiest people in the world—asked a favor, the answer was simply yes.

Because you knew that friend would do the same for you. And would do the same for you regardless of whether you were one of the richest men in the world, or down-and-out on a street corner somewhere.

The door whispered open behind him, and he turned.

Marlee appeared, and it seemed as if she might be dressed in only a towel!

CHAPTER FOUR

Matteo's mouth went dry.

Though, now that he looked more carefully, he could see—thank goodness—narrow white bathing suit straps over her shoulders.

For some reason, the realization she had something on under the towel did not take away the dryness from his mouth.

He was not sure he had ever seen eyes as green as hers. In an environment that shimmered with a thousand enchanting shades of that color, her eyes put all else to shame.

They invited something in him to let go.

It felt as if his barriers dissolved completely. Instead of feeling terrifying, it felt freeing. For this one moment in time, he would accept the reprieve he had been granted from all his responsibilities and obligations.

Marlee's hair—the hair Matteo hadn't remembered because he was so entranced with her eyes—was light brown, and the moonlight played with that, spinning it into shades of gold.

Her feet and shoulders were bare, the skin of her shoulders milky white, but the moon played with that, too, and her skin seemed to be shimmering with silver.

Were those straps over her shoulders bathing suit straps, or was she in her underwear?

Matteo gulped. What, exactly, had he allowed into his well-ordered life? He set down the unsmoked cigar on a rock wall as if it was the problem, the reason he was in this predicament.

He, of all people, should know what a terrible path giving in to these kinds of temptations could take a man down.

They walked, in silence, to the beach. He was aware the scent of her was clean, fresh, unperfumed.

He had seen the beach from the plane earlier, but nothing could have prepared him for the astounding beauty of it at night. It was a crescent of pure white sand, surrounded by gently swaying palms. The foamy waves caressing the shore were, like her skin, spun to silver.

He hesitated. He recognized this as a jumping-off point. A choice to turn away from the organized life he had made for himself.

This encounter was ripe with opportunities for what Matteo liked least: the unexpected. Could he say to her he had made a mistake? Or that he didn't feel like swimming after all? Could he alter the course, right now, of what was about to happen? Did he want to?

He could feel her hesitation, too.

He turned and looked at her.

Her eyes captivated him, again. So many contradictions. How could she seem both bold and shy?

How could she seem both strong and fragile?

If he said, right now, he had changed his mind, he felt, intuitively, he would hurt her in some way and he could not do it.

He took the towel from his shoulders and dropped it to the sand. He was aware that his senses were intensely engaged: he could smell the sea, and Marlee. It felt as if he could feel each individual grain of sand beneath his feet.

And so, when the towel dropped from her, it was but a whisper, and yet, with his senses so heightened, it sounded like thunder in the distance.

He was afraid to look.

And he could not have stopped himself from looking. Not if his entire future and his entire fortune were on the line.

She was not dressed in a bathing suit.

She was dressed in a bra and panties, brilliantly white against the night darkness. They were heart-stoppingly skimpy and appeared to be constructed of mist and cobwebs. Marlee was a goddess of sensuality. Her creamy white skin—perfect—pebbled as the night air touched it.

Matteo thought of all his control, and how, even with all that, he could not have predicted the day ending like this, in a moment that shimmered and sizzled with her pure allure. Her femininity, the sweet curves of her, made him feel masculine. And strong.

And completely powerless at the same time.

As Matteo took her in, Marlee felt the air turn electric around them, as if a power line had broken and was whipping back and forth, snapping and cracking.

Her skin shivered with awareness as she contemplated the fact that she—Marlee Copeland, librarian—was on a beautiful beach, nearly naked in her wedding night lingerie, with a man she did not know.

It had to be a dream.

And if it was, she was making the most of it. The new her—the one that was surprisingly embracing this bold persona—laughed out loud and relished how Matteo's eyes darkened from turquoise to navy blue.

She broke the intensity and dashed by him.

"Race you to the water," she called over her shoulder.

They raced across the creamy, fine sand. Despite her lead, he surged ahead of her, but they reached the edge of the water together, and the shocking chilliness of the ocean would have stopped her dead, except he continued forward. When he realized she had lost momentum, he reached back, grabbed her hand and flung himself into water the color of black ink, drawing her in with him.

The water closed over her head. Choking, she found the sandy bottom with her feet, and she rose out of the water. It occurred to her she wasn't sure how transparent her underwear was when wet, so she ducked back down, squatting in the water, the sea lapping at her chin.

He was not so self-conscious. Well, why would he be? Marlee watched the water sluice off the beautiful lines of Matteo's sculpted chest. He looked just a little too pleased with himself, though, because he was such a fine male specimen, or because he had managed to duck her, she wasn't sure.

"Hey!" she scolded him. "I wanted to get in slowly."

He made chicken sounds. Because she wanted to get in slowly, or because she was up to her chin in water?

"I'm not a very good swimmer," she said.

He looked immediately contrite, and she took advantage and splashed him mightily. He laughed and darted away from her before she could wind up and get him again. And the game was on. Soon, as they chased each other through the dark water, she lost all sense of self-consciousness. They ran and played until they were utterly breathless with laughter and exertion.

The resistance of the sea pulling on their thighs made it feel as if they were slogging through quicksand.

He was way stronger than her. Way faster. He could have easily outstripped her, but he was deliberately slowing down, teasing her, making her think he was within arm's reach, before putting on another burst of speed.

When he slowed again, with a mischievous, you-can't-catch-me glance over his broad shoulder, Marlee threw herself in his direction. She connected! Gleefully, she wrapped her arms around his waist and clung there. His skin was warm and slick, alive somehow, beneath her fingertips.

With a shout, he toppled, and as he splashed into the ocean, she let go of him, not feeling nearly as cautious of the water as she usually did. When Matteo rose out of the water, she was already running away from him.

She was laughing so hard she could not gain traction. She could feel him gaining on her, his breath hot on her neck. She tumbled down under a wave. He sliced in behind her, grabbed her foot and held while she came to the surface, stood on one leg and tried to kick free.

The water didn't feel cold anymore. It was now as warm and sensuous as his touch.

"I'm going to drown," she warned him, bouncing on one leg and splashing him. "From laughing."

"Ah," he said, not releasing her foot. "But what a way to go."

It would be a great way to go, Marlee decided. It felt as if she could drown on laughter. And joy. Freedom. When had she ever felt this free?

And then he took the captive foot and, his eyes locked on her face, he lifted it to his lips.

It still felt, again, as if she was going to drown, but suddenly not from laughing. Her laughter died. His lips touched her big toe, and then, shockingly, his tongue darted between her big toe and the next one.

The sensation was so strong it felt as if it could not

be borne by something as inconsequential as a human being. Time stood still. Her every sense rippled and her every nerve tingled. She could see each drop of water as it slid through his hair, down his neck, caressed his bare, wet chest.

He let go of her foot, apparently as stunned with himself as she was.

She stared at his lips. She wanted desperately to taste him.

It occurred to Marlee that she had nearly married a man who had never once made her feel anything like what she was feeling now.

The earth shifting beneath her feet, the stars swirling in the inky night above her.

Earthquake.

Or maybe tsunami.

The playfulness seemed to be gone from the moment, but it had felt so much safer that she tried to restore what they had been seconds ago. She splashed him, hoping to somehow recapture their earlier mood. But the water caught at her legs and she went down. She swallowed water and floundered. She felt panic set in.

Then strong arms caught her, lifted her to her feet. She leaned into him and sputtered as he pounded her back.

Finally, she got her breath and took a step away from him.

"I think I might live," she croaked.

"Uh," he said, "Marlee?"

She nodded, licked her lips. How could her mouth feel so dry with all this water around them?

"You seem to have, um, lost something."

She tilted her head toward him. She was aware she had indeed lost something. Her sanity. And it was the most blissful loss of her life.

"Your bathing suit top," he said, his voice a hoarse whisper.

She dropped her head and felt the absolute shock of it. Obviously her quick-release wedding night bra was not made for strenuous water play. The magic drained from the moment like air from a needle-pricked balloon.

She squealed, folded her arms around herself and sank down in the water to her neck.

"Don't look!" she ordered him.

"Um, okay."

But he was still looking!

"Stop it!"

"Okay," he said. He held up his hands in surrender and turned away from her.

Not trusting him at all, Marlee duckwalked toward shore, and when she was close enough, she rose and sprinted. Utterly mortified, she practically catapulted from the water and up the beach to where her towel was. She grabbed it, wrapped it around herself and raced for the safety of her cabana.

That had been just a little too *free.*

She did not look back. She did not want to see his

embarrassed expression. In fact, Marlee hoped with all her heart that she would never see Matteo again.

This was a lesson for her: she was not the carefree kind of girl.

She was not the woman who could let go of control and experience no consequences. She was not the bandanna-wearing-bandit type.

It had been an experiment and it had failed. She should never have let go of who she really was.

And she never would again.

Never.

Considering how humiliating the experience had been, she expected embarrassment might keep her up all night. Instead, she slept deeply and dreamlessly and woke up ravenous. When she looked at herself in the mirror in the morning, she expected to look as if she had a hangover.

But even though her hair was a mess from sleeping on it wet, her eyes had a shocking glow to them. Her appearance really suggested more had happened than chasing each other through the sea and losing her top.

Marlee tossed on a sweat suit and a pair of dark glasses, and pulled a ball cap low over her eyes. Although satisfied that her disguise would keep her from being recognized for the underwear-clad nymph who had played in the water, or for a cigar-holding, rum-swilling bandito, she kept a wary eye out for a certain hotel employee in case she had to duck behind a palm tree to avoid an encounter.

Marlee made her way to the resort restaurant, marveling at how the early-morning sun made the sweat suit seem as if she was overdressed already.

The resort had a different feel in the bright morning light. The thick foliage lining the curving paths rioted with kaleidoscopes of flowers whose scents tickled her nostrils and perfumed the air. Sparkling white villas and cabanas were nearly completely hidden by thick greenery, even if they were only steps from the path.

The path opened to the pool, blue waters mirrorlike. Navy-striped lounge chairs underneath huge, taupe-colored umbrellas were scattered around it. Off to one side of the pool was the main dining center and a cluster of quaint, partially open-air shops that specialized in resort must-haves: everything from books to snorkels to swimsuits. A bright yellow sundress caught the breeze in front of one of them and danced, flirting with her.

Ignoring its temptations, she entered the restaurant. Marlee lifted her sunglasses and let her eyes adjust to the sudden dimness. The dining facility was utterly gorgeous, displaying an eclectic mix of antique cane furniture and amazing portraits of local island people.

Still, she mustn't let her curiosity and her love of such things get her guard down. She took a furtive look around and settled her sunglasses on the brim of her ball cap. She quickly filled a plate at the buffet, intending to take it back to her room. She was starving. She hadn't eaten at all last night.

"Marlee! There you are!" Fiona came through the doors and sailed over to her, a battleship on a mission.

"You didn't come to the pool last night," she said accusingly.

"I'm sorry. I was exhausted. I fell asleep."

Marlee was a little shocked by how easily the lie tripped off her lips. However, the truth—that she had been playing in the sea with a handsome stranger—was more likely to seem like a fib to the woman who had chosen *that* dress for her.

Fiona regarded her with very real concern. "You're not sick, are you?"

"I hope not."

"Because that would throw a real wrench into the wedding."

Marlee looked at her friend and felt as if she was seeing something she had never seen before.

Not about her friend. Fiona was just Fiona.

But about herself. And what she had accepted in life, from a fiancé who would abandon her at the altar, to a friend who was more concerned about appearances than her friend's well-being.

That was the problem with experiencing life the way Marlee had experienced it last night.

Yes, it had been brief.

But she had been so on fire with life. So engaged. So joyous. So uncontrolled. So free.

A person was changed by that.

No matter how badly the unfortunate consequences made them want to leave it behind them.

"Look," Fiona said. "I want to show you something."

She pulled her phone out of her pocket and held it up to Marlee. A woman in a beautiful bridal gown was kissing the nose of a wide-eyed foal.

"Isn't that the best wedding picture ever?" Fiona asked dreamily.

"Um..." Marlee said. She was aware yesterday she would have just demurred. Sure. Best wedding photo ever.

But she could feel a shift in her. "I guess I don't really see the relevance."

Fiona tsked. "*You* wouldn't. Anyway, eat up." She took a sudden interest in Marlee's plate. "Goodness, all those carbs!"

And the carb addict had been cavorting in the sea with the world's most attractive man last night. Perhaps losing her top hadn't even been the most embarrassing part of the evening. Her wedding lingerie! And the extra bulges from mourning her canceled wedding. Madness.

Marlee thought of Matteo's lips on her foot and shivered, felt again some shift inside.

This time she was annoyed with herself. She and Fiona had been friends since the fifth grade. You didn't start looking at your friends with a critical eye because a strange man had kissed your foot!

"Please don't be sick!" Fiona instructed her. "I've made spa appointments for this afternoon. Pedicures. Matching toenails for all of us! Won't that make a great wedding photo? Not as good as the baby horse, of course, but still."

Despite her desire not to be critical of her friend, Marlee bit her tongue to prevent herself from asking if Fiona planned to have Mike, the groom, in any of her wedding photos.

The door to the restaurant swung open.

Oh no! Marlee felt panicked. It was Matteo. He looked even more gorgeous in the light of day then he had last night. She felt paralyzed.

He wasn't in the tidy gray uniform the hotel staff wore. In fact, he looked exceedingly casual in a patterned button-down shirt, pressed khaki shorts, and sandals.

His hair was wet. He must have just showered.

He looked effortlessly sexy.

Move, she ordered herself while Fiona was distracted by him. Well, what woman wouldn't be?

The man had seen her bare breasts! She certainly didn't want him to see her crumpled, pale pink sweat suit or her plate full of carbs!

She yanked the sunglasses down and pulled the cap low over her eyes. She set down her food on the nearest table, never mind the looks of the astonished people dining there.

Marlee looked desperately for an exit that would not take her anywhere near him. She saw one and slunk toward it.

CHAPTER FIVE

ALMOST THERE. MARLEE just had to squeeze behind that warming tray full of scrambled eggs and then—

"Oh my!" Fiona squealed. "Matt!"

Marlee froze and watched in horror as Fiona raced across the room and enveloped Matteo in a hug as if he were her long-lost friend. Then, the bride-to-be turned and scanned the room.

Marlee's hand was on the door. She hoped it wasn't one of those exits that was for emergency use only.

She pressed down on the lever and allowed relief to sweep her when no alarm went off as the door swung open a crack. The relief was short-lived.

"Marlee," Fiona cried, "come here! You must meet our best man."

What? No! Matteo was *not* their best man. Their best man's name was Matt. It was somebody Mike had gone to college with. They'd been roommates.

Still, she lost that precious opportunity to make

good her escape as she grappled with the fact that Fiona knew Matteo.

Fiona was gesturing her over.

Run, Marlee ordered herself.

She let the door close with herself still on the inside of it. If they were all in the same wedding party—and apparently they were—why put off this horrible reunion?

With one last forlorn look at the exit, Marlee reluctantly shuffled across the room.

"Marlee, this is Matt Keller, our best man," Fiona gushed. "Marlee is one of my bridesmaids. I've been telling her all about you, haven't I, Marlee?"

Yes, indeed she had.

Mike's best man, his friend from college, had gone on to become some kind of international tycoon who regularly front-covered all the European business magazines. Fiona seemed to regard someone of his reputation and fame being part of the wedding party as a personal coup.

"We've met," Marlee said awkwardly. She glanced into those turquoise eyes. She was pretty sure they were dancing with mirth. She took interest in the buffet. She didn't offer her hand.

"You have?" Fiona stammered. "But how is that—"

"Barely," Matteo said smoothly, and Marlee shot him a look. A little smile was tickling the gorgeous line of those lips. Those lips that had touched her toes ever so briefly.

Marlee could feel a blush rising in her cheeks. Still,

she tilted her chin bravely and gave him a narrow-eyed look of warning.

"I found the suit you left me," Matteo said to Fiona without looking at Fiona at all. His eyes, brimming with laughter, were intense on Marlee's face. "Double-breasted."

Her face felt incredibly hot, like it might catch fire. She prayed Fiona would not notice.

"What?" Fiona said. "It was not! Double-breasted? That would be a disaster."

"Not at all," Matteo said smoothly. "I quite liked it."

Marlee felt as if she would like to kick his shin to wipe that smug look off his face.

Fiona's voice rose shrilly. "Please tell me they didn't deliver the wrong suit. I'm not sure it could be fixed at this point. I'm finding out it's very hard to get things here."

"Come to think of it, I don't think it was double-breasted," Matteo said, apparently taking pity on the misery he was causing poor Fiona by having a laugh at Marlee's expense. "I'm just preoccupied."

If his eyes dropped to what he was preoccupied with, Marlee thought she would probably die. But they didn't. They remained steadfast on hers.

"Of course you are, Matt," Fiona cooed. "Such a large company! But if you could check the suit as soon as possible. I'm panicking!"

"I will. No need to panic." He still did not take his eyes off Marlee. She tilted her chin a little higher at him.

Fiona shot a look between Matteo and Marlee. She frowned suspiciously. Marlee could see Fiona didn't really like it that Matteo was focused on Marlee and not her. She whipped out her phone.

"I was just showing Marlee this picture. What do you think?"

Marlee caught a glimpse of the bride-with-foal shot before Matteo took the phone and squinted thoughtfully at it.

"Interesting," he said, his attention turned briefly to Fiona's phone.

"It won the bride photo of the year."

Matteo turned his attention back to Marlee. He lifted an eyebrow. He might as well have spoken, their thoughts were so close.

Who knew there was a bride photo of the year?

Fiona drew in a breath. "There must be horses here on Coconut Cay. There must be! I bet if I can find a horse, the photographer could replicate this shot."

Marlee didn't want to lengthen this encounter by pointing out to Fiona that replicated shots probably had little chance of becoming a bride photo of the year.

"Isn't that odd?" Matteo said smoothly. "I know someone else who was looking for a horse. And a bandanna, and a train to rob."

Fiona looked at him, bewildered.

"Well," Marlee said brightly. "I was just leaving—"

"How hard could it be to find a horse?" Fiona asked. "Matteo, could you do it?"

He lifted a shoulder. "I doubt it. I'm not familiar with this place."

Now it was Marlee's turn to feel her mouth quirking upward. "Of course he could find a horse," Marlee said. "How hard could it be?"

He scowled at her. "I barely found the beach last night."

"Mike says you're totally a genius," Fiona said. "That you can do anything."

"Finding a photogenic horse will be child's play for you," Marlee could not resist adding.

His look darkened. He looked exceedingly sexy with that sinister look on his face.

"So that's settled," Fiona said with relief. "Thank you, Matt."

He looked slightly stunned. Marlee smirked.

"This morning? Please?"

Marlee's satisfied grin turned into a snicker, which she tried to suffocate. A mistake, as it drew Fiona's attention to her.

"Marlee, you go with him."

"What? No. I—"

"I mean, he's a businessman. The artistic aspects of it would probably be totally lost on him."

"The artistic aspects of finding a horse?" Matteo muttered.

"Exactly the problem," Fiona said. "It's not *any* horse. It's a baby horse. Not a white one, though, I don't want it to disappear in my dress."

"Now, *that* would make a photo," Matteo said, deadpan.

Marlee stifled another giggle.

"I meant the horse needs to contrast with my dress," Fiona clarified, annoyed. She looked between them. "That's the part I'm trusting you with, Marlee. You're very artistic. Remember the time you turned the library into a medieval castle for—"

"The library?" Matteo asked, arching one surprised eyebrow upward.

"Marlee's a librarian."

"A librarian," Matteo said, and the eyebrow went up even further.

"Actually, I can't remember why you turned the library into a castle," Fiona said, tapping her lip thoughtfully with one finger.

"King Arthur Days," Marlee said, a bit tightly. There. She was completely unmasked. Though after her quick exit from the water last night, Matteo had probably already figured out she wasn't really any kind of a wild outlaw.

She was a nerdy girl.

"I'm not asking too much, am I?" Fiona asked with a soft flutter of her lashes at Matteo.

Yes, Marlee thought, *she is.*

"Of course not," Matteo said evenly, seeming to have put away his reluctance for the task. He winked at Marlee. "We will make it our sacred mission."

We?

Marlee was not sure it was safe to think about sacred missions with a man like this.

"Won't we?" he prodded her. "Get abreast of this request, immediately?"

"I had something to do this morning," Marlee said.

"Nonsense," Fiona said dismissively. "Matteo, just make sure Marlee's back in time for pedicures."

He looked pointedly at Marlee's sandal-clad feet. She remembered the feel of his mouth on her toes.

This was the problem with giving up your customary inhibitions. Now, when she should have been shaking his hand and saying, *Nice to meet you*, she was thinking of his mouth on her toes.

"Two o'clock, for the pedicures," Fiona said, "And Matt, please check the suit. Can you take a picture of it and send it to me?"

"I will," Matteo promised.

"I'd love to stay and chat," Fiona said, "but I can't. I'm just going to grab a fruit plate—"

Did she send Marlee a look? Had she shoved them together on this sacred mission on purpose? Was Fiona matchmaking?

It seemed unlikely, since she was so preoccupied with her wedding.

"—and go to my meeting with the floral arranger. She doesn't think she can get gardenias!"

And then Fiona was gone and they stood looking at each other.

"A librarian," he said, tilting his head at her, obviously seeing her in a new light. "I suspected, from your reaction to a little wardrobe malfunction, you were not a rum-swigging, cigar-loving outlaw after all."

"I never said I was. I said that dress made me *want* to be."

"A librarian exploring her wilder side," he said softly, "Ooh-la-la. Take off your glasses for me."

She realized he was teasing her and that she was still wearing her sunglasses.

She took them off.

"Oh, my heart," he said, and placed his hands over it and staggered backward.

Did he have to be so effortlessly irresistible?

She leveled him a look.

"You should have also told me who you were last night," she said.

"I did!" He moved past her to the buffet and took a plate. He was, she noted, a protein guy. Lots of eggs and bacon.

"You let me believe you were an Italian hotel employee," she said, picking her plate off the table where she had left it. She followed him as he took a seat. She sank into the one across from him.

"I never said I was a hotel employee."

"I assumed. Since you said you had been working all day. You could have fessed up when I asked you if it was against the rules for you to fraternize."

"I had been working all day. On my jet."

His jet? She was sitting across the table from a man with a jet. A man with a jet had tasted her toes last night.

"Plus, I never said I was Italian."

"The name sounded Italian to me."

"We do border Italy," he pointed out mildly.

"You had a million opportunities to tell me who you really were, and did not," she said primly.

"Maybe not a million."

She leveled a look at him.

"Uh-oh," he said, "is that the quiet-in-the-library look?"

"No, it's the I-don't-believe-your-dog-ate-your-homework look."

He laughed. She shouldn't have found it nearly as satisfying as she did. Then, he was suddenly solemn.

"I did play along with your misconception," he confessed. "Sometimes it's exhausting being me. You don't have any idea how precious privacy is until people start recognizing you. I was so relieved that you didn't know who I was."

So now she felt ever so slightly sympathetic to one of the richest men in the world.

"Huh," she said, her sympathy feeling like a weakness, "if you want to be liked for who you are, maybe you shouldn't announce you have your own jet so soon after meeting someone."

His lips twitched. She couldn't tell if he was amused or annoyed.

"I can see there will be no winning with you, since you're equally irritated by me not telling you who I am *and* me telling you who I am. And meanwhile, you harbor a few contradictions of your own. Librarian or outlaw?"

"I'm all done exploring my wild side," she told him firmly. "Look at how that turned out."

CHAPTER SIX

MATTEO SMILED AT HER, a smile that was bone-meltingly sexy. "I thought it turned out rather amazingly," he said.

"It was mortifying. And it's particularly insensitive of you to not see that and to continue making jokes about it."

There! Exactly what an uptight librarian would say.

"Don't be embarrassed about last night," he said quietly, suddenly serious. "Please."

"Does that mean you've run out of puns?"

"Oh, no, I could come up with dozens more of those."

"Please don't! They aren't funny."

"And that's the naked truth."

She wanted to remain uptight. Prim. For the first time in her life, Marlee wondered if that was a persona she hid behind.

Hid what? she asked herself, appalled. She thought

of his lips on her toes. She frowned at him to hide the shiver that went up and down her spine.

"Okay, okay," Matteo said, holding up his hands, as if in surrender. "I'll try to be sensitive. Why are Americans so uptight, anyway? Most of the people in the world enjoy beaches without their tops on."

And he would probably know, because he, sophisticated, star businessman that he was, had probably visited all kinds of beaches like that!

"Speaking of which, I have something that belongs to you."

He took a crumpled wisp out of his front pant pocket and dangled it in front of her.

"Is this your idea of sensitive, waving my underwear around in public?" Marlee hissed at him in an undertone.

"I'm not waving it. But I could."

He gave her a mischievous look. She grabbed her bra—still damp—from him and stuffed it in her own pocket.

"I'll work on sensitivity," he promised. "I'll work on it the whole time we go in search of the horse."

Save your dignity, Marlee told herself. *Wriggle out of this.*

But he was being so charming. How could anyone resist that playful expression?

And really, logically, wasn't the damage already done? It was not as if it could get any more embarrassing.

And they were going to run into each other.

They were both members of the same wedding party. They might as well get along, develop some comfort with each other.

It would make for better wedding photos if she wasn't glaring at him.

That was the logical explanation. The illogical part was that she *wanted* to be with him. Why? It could go nowhere.

They were obviously from different stratospheres.

But there was also an appeal in that. It could go nowhere. She was only going to be on this island for a few days.

She was newly single, and definitely sworn off the complexities of relationships, anyway. There didn't have to be an agenda all the time. She didn't always have to be the uptight librarian, weighing every option, considering the future. It was marvelously freeing, if you thought about it.

Why not enjoy her time here on Coconut Cay, and by extension, Matteo? He was smart and funny, not to mention attractive. She could have fun. She could! People were always talking about being in the moment.

Last night she had experienced that. It was an elixir that made you want more.

Matteo sat outside the resort gate waiting for Marlee and enjoying the warmth of the sun, so different than the Zurich experience at this time of year.

He had come from the airport by limo last night,

through a different entrance, and was now surprised to see the pedestrian access to the resort actually opened onto a chaotic main street of the village of Charlee.

The narrow, cobblestoned street was swarming with morning activity. Buildings, plastered in pastel shades and filled with crowded shops, seemed to lean in toward it. The noise, colors and scents were in such sharp contrast to his own villa that it seemed almost as if the resort was tucked behind a cloister wall.

His observations stopped as Marlee came out the gate. His focus narrowed to just her.

She was carrying a large purse and had on a yellow sundress, the antithesis of that dress she'd had on last night and the horrible velour number she'd had on at breakfast.

While the dress wasn't quite as sexy as her bathing attire, it was decidedly daring, with its spaghetti straps and short, swirly skirt.

She looked darned uncomfortable about it, too, and for some reason her discomfort was endearing.

A breeze chose that moment to lift the hem, showing off the long length of her legs. She tried, unsuccessfully, to pin the dress in place with her arms.

She glared at him when she saw him grinning at her. Arms still holding the dress down, she shuffled over to where he was parked at the curb.

"What the heck is this?" Marlee asked.

"It's a scooter," Matteo said, straddling the two-wheeler he'd rented.

"Clearly it's a scooter," she said, annoyed. She looked down at herself.

She wasn't dressed for a scooter.

It was truly refreshing that she had no idea she was the goddess she had revealed to him last night.

"Sorry," he said. "It turns out transportation options are limited on the island. There are two cabs, both taken. I went online and found the name of a stable, but it's not within walking distance."

"Oh."

"Did you want to go change?" he asked sympathetically.

She considered this, and him. She took a deep breath, like someone about to leap off a cliff.

"No, I'll be fine," she said.

"Okay." He patted the seat behind him, and she slid onto it. Amazingly, given how small the seat was, he could have inserted a travel trunk between the two of them. She put her purse in the space.

"What do I hang on to?" she asked. "There doesn't seem to be any handles back here."

His mouth felt quite dry. The exact same way it had felt when her bathing suit had surrendered itself to the sea.

"Scooters don't come with handles. You hang on to me," he said. "You might want to move your purse."

There was a long silence. Her purse was moved over her shoulder and her hands crept to his sides, and rested there lightly, tentatively. How could that possibly feel so sexy? And it was about to get worse.

"Uh, I think you might have to hold on tighter than that."

"Now, that sounds like some kind of Italian playboy scheme," she said suspiciously.

"I am not a playboy."

"You have a jet. I'm not sure you need many qualifications beyond that."

"And I told you I'm not Italian. Anyway, suit yourself."

"I will."

He gave the scooter some gas. It spurted forward, and Marlee squealed and wrapped her arms around him.

"You did that on purpose," she accused him.

"I didn't. That wouldn't be sensitive. It's been years since I was on a motorbike."

"Jets will do that to a man," she said. "Make them give up their cheaper forms of transport. Don't go too fast."

Which, naturally, made him want to go faster. The next little spurt to get them into traffic might have been on purpose, but he was the one who suffered for it. Her arms wrapped tighter around him, snugging her right up against his back. Those long legs formed a warm V around him.

What kind of strange turn in his well-ordered life was this? Sharing a scooter with an unbelievably sexy woman in search of a horse?

This had not been his plan for this morning at all.

In case he ran into the mystery woman from last night he had intended to be cool.

To let her know he wasn't usually the type of man who cavorted in the sea with strangers.

To not let her know that a mere glimpse of her moon-gilded breasts had kept him awake most of the night thinking of how cool he would be next time he saw her!

But he might as well accept it.

Nothing on Coconut Cay was going to go according to his plan.

This morning being a prime example. He hadn't expected to see her, and he hadn't expected to feel so protective of her when she was so clearly embarrassed about what had happened. How could you be cool in the face of that?

How could you express regret when you had no regrets?

So maybe it was her—Marlee, librarian-slash-outlaw—who threw a wrench into a man's carefully planned life.

Because here he was, going in search of a horse, of all things, and sharing a scooter with the goddess from the sea in a way he couldn't ignore how she stirred him physically.

He should have said no to Fiona. He should be working.

There was always work to do and it was always the antidote to any kind of uncomfortable feeling.

He glanced back at Marlee again, felt her physical closeness to him. Something unfolded in his gut.

"Keep your eyes on the road," she snapped. Then a squeal and "Watch out!"

"I saw her," he said, screeching to a halt that threw Marlee, impossibly, even harder against him.

A ruffled hen glared at him, clucked indignantly and guided her brood of chicks across the road in front of them.

Marlee giggled. Her breath was warm in his ear and he realized how glad he was that he wasn't working.

"I'm going to relax now," she told him firmly.

"Would you?"

With lots of stops and starts—and with near collision with a donkey cart—they finally made it out of the twisted, cobbled streets of the colorful town center.

The main road—it wasn't quite a highway—curved in and out of jumbled neighborhoods of humble but cheery houses with bright, painted doors and shutters and overflowing, flower-filled window boxes. Those districts gave way to ritzy residential areas built onto steep, green hills to capitalize on stunning views. The road meandered through dense vegetation, wound up steeply, hugged the edges of cliffs and then plummeted back down toward the sea.

It was all quite hair-raising, and after having to swerve around a pig napping in the middle of the road, Matteo declared it was time for a break. He pulled over at a roadside café that claimed to make the most famous iced coffee on the island.

They ordered coffee and sat at an outdoor table, chickens pecking around their feet as they admired the view that looked out over the Atlantic. Several other islands were visible in the distance. Matteo consulted his phone for a map to the stables.

"I think we should have been there by now," he said. He couldn't get a signal. He didn't want to tell Marlee, but he was pretty sure they were lost. How did you get lost on an island with one main road?

Marlee looked beautiful, her hair tangled, her face glowing from wind and sun. She did, indeed, look relaxed. She lifted a bare shoulder. "We'll find it. How hard can it be?"

He took a sip of the coffee. His eyes crossed. He pushed it away. "I think the famous coffee might be laced with the famous rum," he said.

She tasted hers. "Oh, yum," she said, and took a generous sip.

"I think your shoulders are getting burned," he said.

"That will never do! Think of the wedding photos." And then she snickered. Could the rum work that fast? He didn't think so.

In between sips of coffee—she had finished hers and started on his—she rummaged around in that big bag and found a tube of sunscreen. He glared down at his phone rather than watch her apply sunscreen to her shoulders. Maybe the rum was working that fast, because unless he was mistaken, she was being deliberately tantalizing about it.

"Can you check my back?"

He could hardly refuse, could he? He took the tube from her hand and got up from the table. He went behind her.

She lifted her hair off her neck, and he looked at the slender column of it and wanted to taste it. What was it about her that made him want to taste her?

He thought of how he'd lifted her toes to his mouth last night.

Stop it, Matteo ordered himself. Her skin, so delicate, was already starting to burn. Steeling himself to be a first aid man only, he slathered the cream onto her skin.

The minx closed her eyes, tilted her face to the sun and leaned into his fingertips.

He capped the tube, tossed it back at her and headed for the scooter. "Let's go," he called.

If he had hoped for a distraction from the sensation of her skin beneath his fingertips, he'd hoped in vain. She melted against him and he could feel her cheek on his back.

"Let's pretend," she suggested gleefully. "You're an Italian beach bum, and I'm an outlaw pretending to be a librarian."

He was going to say, *Let's not*, but he glanced over his shoulder. Her face had a light on in it—playful, invigorated, alive—that would take a man much stronger than him to put out.

He had the awful feeling she wasn't drunk on rum, but on life, and it was unbelievably appealing.

"I've never been on a motorbike before," she called.

"Calling it a motorbike is a bit of a stretch," he called back to her. "It's a scooter."

"Whatever it is, it's awesome. Go faster!"

He thought they were probably at about maximum speed already—in every single way—but if he could squeeze a little more power out of the machine, did that mean she would cling harder? He couldn't help himself. He had to find out.

And just like that, it *was* awesome: the wind, the sun, the charms of the island, a beautiful woman clinging to him. Matteo did something he rarely did.

He surrendered to the day.

He was pretty sure he was lost in more ways than one.

CHAPTER SEVEN

MARLEE WAS WELL aware she was flirting with a wilder side. It had started with the impulse buy of the bright yellow sundress this morning.

It was not the type of thing she *ever* bought. Loudly colored. Sexy. Flirty. Way too short.

But then again, she was not the type who swam in the sea with a stranger, either.

Or rode scooters.

Or invited men to apply sunscreen on her.

But something about breaking all these rules—doing what she had never even pictured herself doing, ever—was making her feel as if joy was shimmering inside her.

Okay, maybe the coffee *had* had rum in it, but Marlee felt intoxicated on life. It probably spoke to a life not well lived that this day, so far, felt like one of the highlights of her entire existence.

She was actually sorry when Matteo doubled back

and found a worn sign that pointed down a rutted road to the stable.

The "stable" turned out to be a rickety lean-to with a palm frond roof.

And there was not a horse in sight.

Three tiny donkeys were saddled, and their owner introduced himself as Mackay and welcomed them with gregarious hopefulness.

Matteo explained their mission. Mackay's face fell.

"There are no horses on Coconut Cay," he said. "It's all donkeys."

"Not a single horse on the whole island?" Marlee asked.

"They eat too much," Mackay said. "The donkeys are better here."

Marlee considered this in terms of Fiona's request.

"They are cute," she said, moving over to one of the donkeys and rubbing his head. His friend, jealous, brayed loudly. She laughed and went to scratch his head, too.

"Do you think Fiona would be flexible?" she asked Matteo.

"On our short acquaintance I would guess, no, but you know her better than me."

"Hmm, I guess I'd say no."

"On the other hand," Matteo pointed out, "They are equines, aren't they? Same family?"

She felt doubtful. "It's a bit like calling a scooter a motorbike. A stretch."

"Here's to stretching," Matteo said.

She turned to Mackay. "I don't suppose you have a baby one?"

Mackay sadly shook his head no.

"They look like babies, even though they aren't," Matteo said, "And they aren't white, they're gray. And that one has black ears. That's three out of three checked on Fiona's list—equine, kind of a baby, not white."

"I think that's why I was sent along. For a guy, it's just a checklist. I'm in charge of the esthetics of the thing. But it's true," Marlee said, "the cute factor is off the scale."

"I think we have to make an executive decision. We've been given an assignment. We have a time crunch. Today's Thursday. The wedding is Saturday. Why don't we book one, and then we've got our bases covered? I'll take a picture and if Fiona vetoes it, that's okay. We did our best. Mackay, would one of the donkeys be available for a wedding on the weekend?"

Mackay puffed up as if one of his children had just won first prize at the spelling bee. "It would be my honor."

They worked out delivery details and gave him instructions to arrive shortly after the wedding for the photos.

"Which one would you like?" Mackay asked giving each donkey an affectionate rub on the head as he introduced them. "Henri, Harvey, Calamity."

"Let's eliminate Calamity just for the name," Marlee suggested.

Matteo inspected the two remaining donkeys with such a pretense of seriousness that she could not help laughing. “This one has the best ears,” he decided.

“But look how hopeful that one looks!” she said, the laughter still bubbling.

“Okay,” Matteo agreed. “This one.”

“Henri, a fine choice,” Mackay said with approval as if they had picked a great wine.

Matteo looked at his watch. “Our wedding assignment is completed. And before lunch! Which brings me to the topic of lunch. Are you hungry?”

“Starving,” she said, and it was true, despite her carb-loaded breakfast.

“Can you recommend a place for lunch?” Matteo asked.

Mackay preened. “I have a lunch special today! I will take you to a secret beach. Very romantic.”

“Oh.” Marlee could feel herself blushing. She looked everywhere but at Matteo. “We’re not, um, romantically involved.”

Mackay looked between them, clearly disappointed. “Maybe by after lunch!” he said.

Matteo wagged wicked eyebrows at her, clearly enjoying her discomfort. “Here’s to stretching,” he said.

“Here’s to sensitivity,” she said.

He laughed.

“I don’t think we have time,” Marlee said. There was, thankfully, no time for *stretching.* Certainly not for romance.

Thank God.

"I have an appointment at two," she said.

"Only an hour!" Mackay promised. "Delicious lunch. Island cuisine, made by my mother."

"Made by his mother," Matteo said persuasively.

How could she resist this?

"It's only just gone noon," Matteo told her. "What do you say?"

And so she found herself perched in a sundress on the donkey named Henri, following Matteo, who was mounted on Calamity. Matteo should have looked hilarious, his long legs nearly on the ground, but instead Marlee found herself loving how he had embraced what the moment offered them. Not to mention loving the view of his broad back.

They rode a rutted trail with a lime grove on one side and a cliff on the other. The views out to the sea were spectacular, as was the scent of the limes. The sun kissed her face and a faint breeze lifted her hair.

It was bliss. No other description would do.

Mackay led the way on Harvey, down a steep, cliff-hugging trail. The stones that they knocked off the path seemed to clatter for a very long time before they hit the ground far below.

She would normally be a nervous wreck, but somehow she wasn't. The sense of bliss continued. It must be that rum-laced coffee!

The trail leveled out, and twisted through mangroves, opening up to the most beautiful beach Marlee had ever seen, the fine sand a pink as subtle as a young girl's blush.

Mackay spread a blanket on the sand and unpacked lunch from huge baskets. The cuisine was unbelievably good. It consisted of a jerk chicken, an amazing salad and a selection of island-grown fruits. Mackay produced a bottle of the local wine. Matteo refused because he was driving, but Marlee had some. It was foolish—she'd already had the rum-laced coffee—but what the heck? She'd never really been foolish before. She was quite enjoying it!

"Swim," Mackay insisted as he put lunch away. "The water is beautiful."

"I don't have a—"

"Not required here. I won't look," Mackay promised with a wink. "Henri might, though."

He shot Matteo a look that was loaded with male kinship. Their host was determined to get a romance going.

It was Matteo's turn to look uncomfortable. Considering he was familiar with sophisticated beaches around the world, he had a deer-caught-in-the-headlights look.

"I'd love to have a swim," Marlee decided. When had she ever felt this relaxed, this go-with-the-flow, this spontaneous?

She'd only had two glasses of wine. It wasn't that.

Matteo looked at her, then looked at his watch and yelped. "It's after one. We can't today."

Did she hear just a bit of relief in his voice at the

time constraint? Marlee felt the sharpness of regret. On the other hand, if they got back in the water together, who was to say what could unfold between them? She thought of his lips on her toes. The look in his eyes when she had risen out of the water topless.

Maybe they would end up lovers!

That had to be the wine whispering to her, and still the possibility shivered up and down her spine. She was getting into deep water. She needed to remember she barely knew how to swim!

Matteo seemed suddenly extraordinarily eager to go, and helped Mackay pack up the baskets. In moments, the donkeys plodded their sure-footed way back up the cliff and to the stable. They got off and said goodbye to their host.

Matteo paid Mackay and gave him a tip that made him grin from ear to ear. Marlee kissed Henri right on the tip of his soft, beautiful nose.

And then they turned to where they had left the scooter. Matteo looked in shocked disbelief at the now empty space.

"It appears we've had a theft," he said.

"No, no," Mackay assured him. "Not stolen. Not on Coconut Cay."

"It's missing," Matteo pointed out. "I parked it right here."

"Borrowed, maybe," Mackay conceded.

"Borrowed, certainly," Matteo said. "The result is the same. We are left without a means to get back to the resort."

"I am without a vehicle today," Mackay said, but then brightened. "We can ride the donkeys to the main road, and from there you'll be able to make your way back to the resort."

"Make our way how?" Matteo asked skeptically.

"There's a bus," Mackay told them, "twice a day."

"I don't suppose I'm going to be back at the resort by two, am I?"

"Just stick out your thumb if you don't want to wait for the bus," Mackay said. "Someone will give you a ride."

"Hitchhike?" Marlee asked.

"Very safe here," Mackay promised.

"Uh-huh," Matteo said. "Safest place on earth. That's what I plan to tell the scooter rental place."

Marlee knew it was the wrong thing to do, but she giggled.

Matteo cast her a look and shook his head.

"It's just such a day of firsts," Marlee said. "Scooter ride, donkey train, and now hitchhiking. It feels kind of amazing when you just surrender to what's happening, instead of fighting it. I don't even really care if I make the pedicure or not."

"Surrender," Mackay said brightly. "The place where the adventure begins."

Matteo contemplated that word. *Surrender.* He was riding in the bed of a truck on top of corn husks bundled together. The breeze from the open-air ride made the temperature feel perfect.

The family who owned the truck were crowded into the cab singing, their joy drifting back to him, and Marlee was nestled under his arm, fast asleep, her head on his chest, her breath causing puddles of warmth on his skin. Her scent—lemony—was mingled with the scent of the sun on the corn husks.

He was not sure when, if ever, he had felt so content.

It pressed at the edges of his contentment that to feel this way was dangerous. It made a person open, vulnerable to being hurt.

Matteo had enjoyed the day.

More than enjoyed it, really. He had been exhilarated by it.

By every second of it, even the loss of the scooter. He had not been this spontaneous for a long time.

If ever.

He had enjoyed Marlee.

No, more. Been exhilarated by her.

She was beautiful. And she was interesting and smart. He wasn't sure if she made him laugh, or if being with her opened him, in some way, to the delights of life that he had been closed off from before.

Whichever, she was just the type of woman who could make a man forget the inherent dangers of caring about someone.

He gave in to the temptation to touch her hair. It would be so easy to care about her.

Deeply.

To take it one step further…

She stirred, and that dress hitched up a few inches

further on the shapely length of her leg. He thought of her in the water last night, goddess rising, and snatched his hand away from the sun-warmed silk of her hair.

He needed to get this situation back into control.

His control.

And he needed to do it fast.

The truck lurched to a stop in front of the resort, and Marlee's eyes snapped open. She struggled to sitting, and he noticed the linen pattern of his shirt was traced in the softness of the skin on her cheek.

She took him in, those gorgeous green eyes bewildered. She looked at the bed of corn husks around her. Drowsy confusion gave way to a smile that tickled her lips.

Beautiful lips. Wide and generous.

Lips that begged to be kissed. He remembered the faint taste of them that had lingered on that cigar they had shared a taste of.

She touched his shirt. "Look," she said, her voice husky—and sexy—with sleep. "I drooled on you."

Matteo had a shocking thought of what a life could be like waking up to her.

He leaped up and scrambled off the back of the truck. Unfortunately, chivalry demanded he help her down. He turned back for her.

Marlee had stood and was navigating the corn husks. Her dress was rumpled. There was a smudge—donkey spit?—across the front of it. There was also a corn husk tangled in her hair.

He was not sure a woman had ever looked so beautiful.

He held out his hand to her, and when hers closed around his, it felt right and good.

And terrible and wrong.

And as if that control he longed for could be taken by such a simple thing as her hand in his.

She let go of his hand and put her arms around his neck, instead, and of their own accord his hands closed around her waist and he lifted her down off the truck bed.

There was something about the small gesture that made him feel strong. Masculine. Possessive. Protective.

The chatter of the happy family they had shared the truck with died. So did the street noises: cars, horns, vendors calling, children laughing, chickens cackling.

His whole world felt as if it was this: her corn-husk-tangled hair, her eyes, the plumpness of her bottom lip, the sweet sensation of her body pressed into the length of his.

Surrender.

CHAPTER EIGHT

SURRENDER. MATTEO HAD not said the word out loud, and yet it was as if Marlee had heard it. Her body relaxed against his, and she tilted her head upward, her gaze sleepy, unconsciously sensual.

And then her gaze drifted to his lips. Hungry. Curious.

He knew, when her tongue flicked out and wetted her own lips, what was coming. He commanded himself to go into full retreat. But something stronger within him commanded something else.

Surrender.

Pressed full against him, she stood on her tiptoes and her lips touched his lips.

Her kiss was a study in contradiction: sweet and sexy, sharp and soft, questing and fulfilled.

She tasted of salt and wine and of a bottomless womanly mystery.

Everything in him cried to go deeper, to tangle yet further, to know her more, to explore her secrets.

Thankfully, before he totally lost his mind—forgot they were on a public street and tangled his hands in her hair to pull her closer and claim her lips more thoroughly—she pulled away.

Her blush rose above the sun-kissed glow the day had given her cheeks. She laughed, self-conscious.

"Thank you for an incredible day," she said so sweetly awkward that he wanted to kiss her again.

Surrender.

Was it really where the adventure began?

Or was it where life as you knew it ended?

Matteo realized he did not want to find out. He needed to get a hold of himself. He needed to do it now.

It would be easy, wouldn't it?

Their mission was completed. He didn't have to see her again until the wedding. No, that wasn't quite right. There was the rehearsal dinner tomorrow night. That would give him a time to reconstruct his battered barriers.

"Yes," Matteo said, "It's been an interesting day."

It was a deliberate understatement. His tone was formal, and he could see the bewildered hurt in her eyes. He moved past her before his resolve was slayed by that. He opened the gate to the resort and held it for her.

They walked in silence along the pathway to her cabana where he had first encountered her.

It seemed impossible that that was less than twenty-four hours ago. He already felt as if he knew her, deeply.

Which was the dangerous part. Wasn't it better to hurt her now, than later?

This was what he knew: the more you cared about someone, the deeper the hurt you could cause them.

There was no sense following the intrigue that beckoned to him from those jade green eyes. There was no sense following that trail of laughter they had been on all day. Thinking of her laughter made him look again at her lips.

No, there was no sense following *that* desire any further.

One of them had to be the sensible one. He felt vaguely resentful that it didn't appear it was going to be her.

If you couldn't count on a librarian to be sensible, what exactly could you count on?

"I'll leave it to you to brief Fiona," he suggested.

"Sure," she said, uncertainly.

"And I'll see you at the rehearsal dinner."

"But—I thought we might… I thought we had—" She stopped herself. The injured look gave way to one of pride. She knew he was brushing her off.

She apparently had no appreciation whatsoever for all the pain he was saving them both.

"Yes," she said, her voice tight and wounded. "That's fine. All right."

"I have to report the stolen scooter," he said, trying a little too late, to soften the blow. "As the only crime that's ever occurred on Coconut Cay, it'll probably be complicated. I don't want to drag you into it. You know, in case it involves jail time."

His attempt to lighten things fell flat, which made him want to try even harder to coax a smile out of her.

"Not that that would bother a hardened outlaw such as yourself."

No smile. Marlee gave him a long, level look that let him know she was not fooled, and then, head high and chin up, she turned away from him.

"Plus," he said weakly, knowing the damage was done, "according to the schedule, I'm supposed to golf with the guys tomorrow."

"Oh," she said, trying for breeziness and failing, "Of course. The schedule! Golf."

Her tone made him feel like a complete ass.

Which, come to think of it, he was.

Neither of them had noticed Fiona barreling toward them until it was too late and she was standing, hands on hips, right in front of them.

"There you are! You missed the pedicures," Fiona snapped at Marlee, without greeting either of them. "Everything is going wrong. Everything."

Matteo shot Marlee a look and gave her a slight shake of his head letting her know that now didn't seem to be the time to break it to the harried bride she might have to substitute a donkey for the horse in her photos.

"Let me see what color you got," Marlee said soothingly. "I'm sure I can get a pedicure tomorrow, so that we all have matching toes, just like you wanted."

"As a matter of fact, you can't," Fiona said. "She only comes one day a week, so it's a little late to be thinking about what I wanted."

Still, she wiggled a toe at them, and he caught a glimpse of glittery gold.

"I'll figure it out," Marlee promised.

"I hope so," Fiona said petulantly, and then eyed Marlee. "You must have found a horse."

"Um..."

Fiona leaned a little closer to her and sniffed. "You did!" she said, "I can smell horses!"

She brightened. For a moment Matteo could almost see what Mike saw in her. Almost.

"There are a number of good options," Marlee said carefully.

Fiona visibly relaxed, but instead of acting grateful, she shot Marlee a look. "Good grief! Did you get right in the corral with them? You have something in your hair. And on your dress. You look like you lost a fight with a cat."

So much for glimpsing what Mike saw in her! Her tone was so acid that Matteo felt a need to put his body between Marlee and Fiona.

"You don't," he said firmly to Marlee when he saw she was clearly calculating if that was why he had turned cool toward her.

Fiona glared at him as if she was actually thinking of arguing about it, and then with a miffed sigh turned and left.

He stood there feeling the shock of the encounter.

"Good God," he said. "Is she always like this? She was downright vugly."

"She looked like she'd been crying," Marlee said.

"She did?"

"She just wants everything to be perfect."

He made a note to remember Fiona when he was thinking control was the be-all and end-all of life.

"I'm not sure why you would come to her defense," he said.

"Fiona didn't have the best childhood," Marlee confided in him. "We've known each other since fifth grade. That's when she moved in down the street from me. Her house was always so chaotic. I think that's why she's so intent on perfection with the wedding. From the moment she met Mike it was as if she felt she could finally have what she thought everyone else had."

Matteo looked at her and saw yet another side to Marlee—a deep well of kindness and compassion.

"If getting my toes painted gold will help her feel better, even a little bit, I'll do it," she said.

And somehow, after seeing how her friend had treated her, and how she had responded, he couldn't just abandon her because he needed to be in control.

Fiona had just managed to shatter his beliefs about control, anyway.

"Do you want to have dinner together tonight?" he asked her.

He was shocked at himself.

Because ten minutes ago he had promised to pull back from the temptations of Marlee. And now, he seemed to be entangling himself further than ever.

She stood stock-still and searched his face.

It occurred to him she was going to say no.

"No," Marlee said, injecting far more firmness into her tone than she felt. How did anyone say no to spending more time with him?

It had been one of the best days of her life, sun-kissed and sizzling with connection, fun and adventure.

Of course, then she had to go wreck it all by kissing him. No wonder he was trying to run away from her.

She'd had too much to drink. She'd slobbered on his shirt. She looked—and smelled, according to Fiona—as if she'd been mucking out stalls.

While she'd been thinking *best day ever*, who knew what he had been thinking? He came from a different world, no doubt filled with glamorous novelties that made scooter rides and donkeys and traveling in a truck full of corn husks seem, well, corny to him.

Marlee had known from the outset he was way out of her league, and when he'd dismissed her—said he would see her again at the rehearsal dinner—she had realized he was reminding her of that.

Now he was changing his mind.

She hadn't missed how he had inserted himself protectively between her and Fiona. It had felt rather nice, but on the other hand, she wasn't going to spend more time with him because he felt sorry for her.

The heart that had blossomed at his gesture of protectiveness whined that she could take whatever she could get, even if it was motivated by pity!

Her heart wanted her to let him be in charge: he'd decide when he'd have enough, when they were going to spend time together and when they weren't.

Even though she'd been abjectly disappointed when he'd pulled the plug after their wonderful day, Marlee was so aware something was shifting in her.

You could not have a day like today and not be changed by it, not have a stronger sense of yourself and what you wanted.

She realized she had always felt that with her ex—as if she was begging for his time, for little crumbs of his affection. She realized now she had not required nearly enough. Not of Arthur, who was just Arthur, in the same way Fiona was just Fiona. She had not required enough of herself. She had not set her standards high enough.

Maybe it was the story of her life.

And it was never too late to change that story, so even as a part of her said, *Yes, please, let's have dinner together*, another part of her held proudly firm.

"No," she repeated. "I'm not hungry. I'm eager to wash off the donkey dust. You need to go make your stolen scooter report. Call me if you need bail, otherwise I'll see you at the rehearsal dinner. Enjoy your golf game!"

Matteo looked utterly shocked. Marlee was willing to bet it was the first time he'd ever had a woman call the shots on his charming self. Particularly refusing his invitation in preference to washing off donkey dust!

As she turned away, went into the cabana and shut the door on his stunned face, Marlee found herself smiling.

She was *glad* she had kissed him. Shaken him out of his stuffy world enough to make him take a startled step back from her.

It felt good to take her power back, even if there was a price to pay. And so when the temptation was to retreat from all her discoveries—stay in her room with a book that evening—she didn't. Using the very rudimentary seamstress kit she always traveled with—librarians ferreted out every potential disaster, after all—she took the bra she had worn last night off the shower bar where she had flung it after its return this morning and sewed the breakaway clasp firmly and permanently shut. She wouldn't be needing that feature anytime soon.

Then she stripped, exchanged the bra she was wearing for the repaired one and slipped a swim cover-up on. She then went to the resort store and bought some chicken being kept warm under a burner.

Then, she took the pathway past her cabana. The

cigar was still sitting on the wall where he had left it last night and she picked it up.

Because it was litter, not because he had tasted it!

Then she went down to the beach she had shared with Matteo.

She watched the sun go down in a brief but glorious display of color. For one suspended moment, the ocean turned to fire and every grain of sand on the beach glittered gold.

It was, she told herself firmly, the perfect ending to the best day ever. She didn't need a man to make it all lovelier. It couldn't be any lovelier than it already was.

But then, just as she was on the brink of convincing herself that was true, a shiver up and down her spine let her know she was no longer alone on the beach.

She turned her head to see Matteo coming across the sand. She switched her attention quickly back to the orb of the sun, disappearing on the horizon as if it was plunging into the sea. For a woman discovering her own power, the mere sight of him coming toward her in the soft golden light was doing things to her heartbeat. She felt weak instead of strong.

"Hey," he said, quietly. "Beautiful night."

"It is," she agreed. "Probably looks even better after your close brush with jail time."

The question was, what was he doing here after his close brush with her lips?

"I don't think there is a jail. I reported the missing scooter at the rental place. Same response as Mackay.

No, no, not stolen. Borrowed. They seemed to have every confidence it will just show up."

"So what brings you here? Extra time now that you've been freed of potential legal wrangling?"

I couldn't get your ravishing kiss out of my mind. Ha ha.

"Fiona saw me. She told me to find you and give you this." He dropped a tiny brown bag on her lap. "When you weren't at your place, I thought you might be here."

So he hadn't sought her out of his own accord. It was an *errand.* He was here because he had been *instructed.*

He was probably thinking, *Pathetic thing. Reliving memories of last night and very ordinary, workaday kisses that she thought were ravishing.*

Reminder: girls like her were not even on the radar of men like him.

Marlee told herself sternly that she was rethinking the kind of girl she was. Her hand found the cigar she had picked up, and she clamped it between her lips.

"Those are habit-forming," he warned her mildly.

"Only if you light them." *Or taste another person's lips on them.*

He nodded solemnly. "An outlaw prop."

Without invitation he dropped down in the sand beside her.

"I thought you said you weren't hungry," he said, eyeing the chicken.

Good. He understood her refusal had been about him, not about hunger. She shrugged.

"How is it?"

"After Mackay's mother's? Barely edible." She took the unlit cigar from her lips and held it between her fingers, as if she intended to light it at any time.

CHAPTER NINE

"Can I have a piece?"

Matteo's errand was done. Why was he hanging around? Marlee thought.

"Have a piece of chicken at your own risk. But don't feel you have to sit in the sand with me. You've achieved your mission."

She put down the cigar—who was she kidding? She was no outlaw. He was right. It was just a prop. She had no hope—ever—of being the real thing. She dug in the bag he had dropped on her lap and drew out the items one by one.

Sheesh. It was pedicure in a bag. The last item she took out was a bottle of glittering gold nail polish.

"See? Matteo, you've saved the world. Or at least the wedding. Donkey acquisition and pedicure rescue all in one day. You must be exhausted. It will probably affect your golf game. That's a shame."

"You're being sarcastic," he said, his voice low. "I've hurt your feelings."

Marlee did not want to be that transparent!

"Is this part of your intention to be more sensitive? It's completely unnecessary. You haven't hurt my feelings."

Matteo regarded her intently. He said nothing. It felt as if he saw straight through her—right to her soul. It was very discomforting.

"I get it. Entirely. You move in different circles than me. No sense the plain-Jane librarian from Seattle getting romantic notions. Not that I was. But I don't blame you for thinking I was. I mean, who wouldn't? I kissed you. It was an impulse. A bad one. But you're pretty easy on the eyes. You have a jet. You're kind of funny and entertaining. But just for your information, I've had a recent breakup. The last thing I'm looking for—"

He cut off the flow of words—good grief, she was babbling—by laying a gentle finger against her lips.

After all she had just said, how could she possibly be having a temptation to nibble that finger?

She should want to bite it! It was insulting. He was silencing her.

"You thought I didn't want to see you until the rehearsal dinner because I found you a—what did you say—plain Jane? You think I found you unattractive?"

His voice was a low growl that felt like a touch shivering along her spine.

She nodded, which had the unfortunate effect of moving her lips on his finger, creating a sensational feeling.

"Marlee," Matteo said, his voice low and pained, those color-of-the-sea eyes intent on her face, "the exact opposite is true."

She tried to let that sink in, but she couldn't comprehend what he was saying.

"What do you mean," she asked, "the exact opposite is true?"

Matteo looked suddenly uncomfortable.

"It might all be a moot point, anyway," he said. "I don't know if there's going to be a rehearsal dinner."

"What?"

"The lovely bride-to-be is up there throwing a fit at Mike right now."

"About what?"

"Who knows? Gardenias. A delayed champagne delivery. The flower girl's hair. Maybe she wanted Mike to get a pedicure for barefoot pictures in the sand and he missed his appointment. Just like you."

"You're making her sound very unreasonable."

Matteo cast Marlee a look but didn't say anything.

"Okay, she's being a bit of a bridezilla."

"A bit?"

"After what she grew up with, Fiona just wants it all to be so perfect. That's why she has to have control."

"What did she grow up with?"

Marlee felt as if she had to make a choice. On one hand, she didn't want to reveal personal information about her friend. On the other hand, she didn't want Matteo to think Fiona was purely horrible, with no redeeming characteristics.

"Her mom and dad both drank too much. Her house was crazy. Nothing—and I mean nothing—was predictable, except for the fighting and chaos. I think part of the destination wedding decision was because her mom's terrified of flying. Fiona didn't want them here for her big day. She knew they'd wreck everything."

Matteo was silent. "Thank you for telling me that. It puts things in a different light. She's very lucky to have you for a friend. Actually, anyone would be lucky to have you for a friend."

There was something about the look in his eyes that a woman could fall toward. But Marlee was pretty sure there was a not-so-subtle message in there.

That maybe they could be *friends*.

Friends didn't kiss each other at the end of the day!

She looked at the bottle of nail polish. "I'm going to put it on and go show her. Maybe it'll be a distraction for her. A 'See? Everything is going to be fine' moment."

His lips twitched.

"It's a lot to ask of toenail polish."

"I don't know. It's an interesting color. It looks like it's been mixed with dreams and fairy dust."

He pretended to inspect the bottle. "A little magic mixed in there."

"Here's to magic," she said, and kicked off her sandals and regarded her toes.

"You don't know any more about nail polish than you do about cigars, do you?"

"And you do?"

"Older sisters," he said. "You don't put it on surrounded by sand. I know that much."

"Oh," she said. "Of course!"

"And if you wanted to swim, we should do that first."

We.

"Because I don't think you can get your toes wet for a while after you've painted them."

She noticed the stars winked on in an inky dark sky.

She noticed the air smelled of the sea.

She noticed her breath inside her chest, its simple rise and fall feeling like a celebration of life.

In all its glory, and all its surprises.

You think I don't find you attractive? The exact opposite is true.

It was as good as hearing he'd been dazzled by her kiss.

Still, Matteo was giving her mixed messages. He wanted to be just friends? Or he wanted more?

Maybe it was time for her to make some choices!

And her choice, right now, was just to embrace the moment.

She stood up, peeled off the swimsuit cover-up and let it drift to the sand beside her. She stood there before him in her underwear again, feeling bold.

He had never clarified exactly what he meant by *the exact opposite is true* but Marlee could see the obvious truth in his eyes.

He found her beautiful.

It allowed her to do what she had never done—to see herself as beautiful, too. She liked the way his eyes had darkened to midnight as he took in her moon-painted body.

"You're going to try that, um outfit, again?" he asked, his voice hoarse. "You do like to live dangerously."

"Only recently. Allowing my inner outlaw free rein. I fixed it, anyway. No wardrobe malfunctions tonight."

"More the shame, that," he said.

And then he rose to his feet, and with a shout of laughter, chased her into the water.

Finally, exhausted from playing in the ocean like children, they went and threw themselves on her blanket on the sand. She shivered.

"We should go in," he said. "It's warm here, but it's still chilly at night if you're wet."

We?

What did that mean? She should offer him a nightcap?

"We still have to paint your toenails."

This time she said it out loud, with a lifted eyebrow. *"We?"* She didn't actually think it would be safe to let him touch her feet.

"I know lots about pedicures."

She remembered his lips on her toes last night and shivered.

"I told you, I have sisters."

That took some of the white heat out of her mental meanderings.

"Time to go," he said, getting up. "You're freezing."

Actually, she felt as if she was melting. He waited for her to gather up her things, then shook the sand out of her blanket and put it over her shoulders.

It was a small gesture. It felt so nice.

Inside her cabana, he shooed her into the shower. She debated what to bring in there to change into.

What exactly did one wear when the world's most gorgeous man had offered to help with your pedicure?

She wanted it to be super sexy without giving the appearance she was trying to be sexy. Finally, she chose an oversize pajama top that came to her midthigh. She usually would have worn the top with pajama bottoms. Tonight, she left those off.

She looked at herself in the full-length mirror before she went out into the main room. Her hair was damp and curling. Her face glowed from her day out in the sun. Her eyes were luminous. She had what some might have called a come-hither look.

She wondered what she was playing at. What were *they* playing at? How was this all going to unfold?

That, she told herself firmly, was the librarian talking.

That was not how outlaws talked to themselves at all! A proper outlaw didn't think of consequences, or the future.

A proper outlaw embraced the dangerous thrills of the moment.

She went out into the main room. Matteo glanced up at her, then looked quickly back at his phone.

His phone, she thought, disappointed about her wasted come-hither look. Arthur had always seemed to find his phone more interesting than her, too.

"You caught me," Matteo said, and flashed the phone at her.

She burst out laughing.

The screen read: *How to do a pedicure like a pro.*

"You said you'd done this with your sisters."

"Well, a hundred years ago."

"You look much younger than you are," she said, giving him a wide-eyed look. "How many sisters?"

"Two. Mia and Emma."

"Are you close?"

"Oh, yeah. We run the family business together. I also have two nieces and two nephews. They're incorrigible brats."

"You adore them."

His easy grin gave her the answer.

She liked it that he was close to his sisters and his family.

"Okay, enough chitchat," he said sternly. "Come over here and sit down."

She went and sat at the sofa, while he sat on a stool facing it. Really? A pinch-me moment. The most gorgeous man in the world was at her feet.

"This is serious business," he told her, so seriously that she wanted to laugh. "I don't want to be distracted and chop off your toe. A large, bandaged appendage would wreck the wedding pictures."

"I don't think you could chop off my toe with those," she said, pointing at the clippers. Then she frowned. "You don't think you're going to use those, do you?"

"It's step four: trim and shape toenails."

He took her foot. His hand slid along it as he eyed her toenails. Considering he was only touching her foot, Marlee felt ripples through every cell of her body!

"Just put the nail polish on!"

"Uh-uh. I'm a follow-the-instructions kind of guy."

He did something with his fingertips to her instep that she was pretty sure was not in the instructions.

"That's a long way from my toes," she said, through gritted teeth.

"I know," he said and tilted his head to smile at her.

Marlee wondered how she was going to survive this.

CHAPTER TEN

MATTEO LET HIS hand slide along her instep one more time. Then, with a let's-get-to-work sigh, he picked up the toenail clippers that had come in the kit.

"Give me those," Marlee said. "You are *not* cutting my toenails."

"Wait!" He held them out of her reach when she grabbed for them. "I missed steps. We're nowhere near the part where we argue about toenail cutting."

"Humph."

"Step one," he read, his officiousness coaxing an inward smile out of her, if not an outward one. "Soak your toes and feet. Have you got a basin I can fill?"

"I think the shower and ocean probably looked after that."

"Okay, moving along, then. Step two: get rid of any dead skin."

"That's gross. Let's just skip to the painting the nails part."

"Then we're at step three: remove old polish."

"There is none," she snapped. At this moment, she *hated* it that there was none. It made her feel unglamorous and downright dull.

He had already moved on. "Step four: trimming and shaping your toenails. Now we're at the arguing part."

"They are fine the way they are," Marlee insisted.

He gave her a look, took her foot firmly and inspected it. He was probably deciding they were librarian toenails, nothing elegant about them at all.

"I cut them straight across the top like that because it's recommended to prevent ingrown toenails."

Who said that to a man like him? Sheesh! Worst conversation ever. Still, she shivered at the way her feet looked in his hands, pale against his darker flesh, delicate against his obvious strength.

"Are you still cold?" Matteo asked, glancing up at her.

"No, you're tickling me."

"Oh," he said, pleased. "Ticklish feet. I'll file that away for future reference."

Future?

There was no future, that was what she had to remember about him. They had been thrown together for a few days. After the wedding they would never see each other again.

Which should have given her pause about what was happening between them right now, some exciting and dangerous awareness sizzling in the air between them.

But Marlee was already not who she had been twenty-four hours ago.

Because instead of the fact she would never see him again giving her pause, it felt as if it was giving her license.

Still holding her instep, he studied her toes intently. He leaned very close to them. She could feel his breath tickling them. If he kissed them, as he had done last night, she was pretty sure any hope of a friendship would be lost, and she was going to exercise the liberty that came with never seeing him again.

His mouth on her toes would unleash something in her. She would not be responsible for what happened next. It felt as if a secret side of her was crying to get out, and that side was totally uninhibited.

Shockingly wild. Unabashedly sexy.

He did not kiss her toes, and Marlee was not at all sure if she was disappointed or relieved.

She was aware, too, that she was quite literally leaving it all in his hands.

"I think you're right," he decided. "They're already pretty short. No trim required."

She did something she would not have done twenty-four hours ago. She reached out and touched the silk of his hair with her fingertips.

"What did you mean when you said the exact opposite was true?" she asked him.

Matteo felt her hand in his hair. He glanced up at Marlee.

He was aware he had placed himself in this position, even knowing the dangers inherent to it.

For him, it was delightful that she had no idea how beautiful she was.

In the short time he had known her, he already knew that her beauty not just on the outside of her, but on the inside of her, too.

He had to fight the temptations of her. And he had to let her know why, even if it meant doing what he least liked to do.

Exposing his own fears and insecurities.

It felt as though if ever there was a person he could trust with his deepest secrets, it was her. How could he feel that way?

He barely knew her.

On the other hand, you couldn't spend a day with someone like Marlee and not feel as if you knew her.

He had seen her laugh and fall in love with donkeys and embrace adventures and roll with the punches.

But it was her gentle compassion toward a friend who might not have deserved it that made Matteo feel, not just as if he knew her, but as if he knew her deeply.

To her heart. To her soul.

His trust in her felt extraordinary.

He focused on the array of items that had come from the pedicure kit. Her hand was still tickling his hair.

"Step five," he said, avoiding her question about what he'd really meant, "toe separators. Never mind that we missed the first four steps."

She laughed, low in her throat. It was a sound that could make a man forget he had a history that warned him away from women like this one.

Gently, he inserted the toe separators. Her hand went very still in his hair.

"Step six: base coat." He waggled the bottle at her. "Crucial, apparently."

Carefully, he took out the brush and began to apply a thin layer of the base coat. He began to speak, knowing he had to warn her off, now, before it was too late.

"My mother and my father had a grand passion for each other," Matteo said. He could hear the roughness of pain in the slight hoarseness of his own voice. "They could not be together enough. They could not keep their hands off each other. The romance never died—the little gifts, the love notes, the exchanged looks, the heat between them. We didn't have a family so much as the two of them, my mother and father, being the sun, and the rest of us orbiting around their light."

He finished the toes of her right foot and moved on to the left. There was a stillness in the room that reminded him of a cathedral.

"And then my mother got sick," Matteo said. "And then she got sicker. And then she died. My father, this man who had been so powerful, and so in control of everything, except his love for her, could not change it. When she died, she took part of his soul with her."

He swallowed hard, capped the base coat, and blew on her toes to dry them. He opened the bottle of gold.

"He never got it back."

Matteo stared at Marlee's toes. Were they blurry?

No, of course not! He was a man in control of his emotions.

If she had said anything, he was not sure he could have continued. He dared not look at her. If he saw softness in her eyes, he felt as if it would finish everything he believed about his own strength.

He dabbed the gold onto her nails, took a deep breath and finished what he had to say just as he put the last stroke of the polish on.

"His grief ignored the fact he had children to live for, and it almost destroyed a business that had been in our family four hundred years."

Finally, Matteo got to *the* question.

"I didn't say I didn't want to see you again until the dinner because I don't find you attractive, Marlee. Maybe you see yourself as a plain-Jane librarian, but I don't. I feel something. Don't you?"

Marlee didn't say anything, and he didn't dare look at her for her answer.

"I feel it," he continued, his voice a ragged whisper, "shivering in the air between us. A terrifying potential. I'm not sure I'm brave enough to know what you could be to me."

He set down her feet abruptly. He looked everywhere but at her.

"I feel foolish saying that." He glanced at his watch. "I've known you all of twenty-four hours. But that's what I wanted you to know. That the exact opposite is true. You may be the most beautiful woman I have ever encountered."

And then finally, Matteo looked at her.

He saw the stillness he had experienced in the room reflected in her face. The greenness of her eyes reminded him of a cool pond on a hot day, a place a man could dive into and find relief from everything that troubled him.

Did he throw himself into such a promise of sanctuary as Marlee offered, or did he flee from it?

What was in the air between them felt as impossible to fight as a tsunami would be if it swept up that beach.

"I've burdened you with my difficulties," he said, and heard the stiffness in his voice. "I'm sorry. I don't usually have jet lag, but I may be suffering from it now. It has—"

Weakened me. Made me less a man.

"—been extraordinarily inappropriate."

With what small remnants of his strength that remained, Matteo made the decision to find higher ground. Without another word, he carefully lined up the things left over from the pedicure kit, got to his feet and walked out of the cabana.

Wiggling her freshly painted toes, Marlee sat there, stunned by the abruptness of Matteo's departure. She felt abandoned. And let down.

Who told someone they might be the most beautiful woman they had ever encountered and then forsook them?

Confusingly, the sting of desertion warred with the incredible gift of Matteo's trust.

"Which he is now sorry he bestowed," she reminded herself sternly. "Jet lag–inspired confidences!"

Besides, she shared his terror of the forces that were drawing them together, didn't she? Though there were much larger forces drawing them apart if she thought about it. Their fears and past experiences formed quite a wedge.

And so did time.

The wedding was on Saturday. She had to see him at the rehearsal dinner tomorrow night, and at the wedding, of course. She could avoid encounters of the truly scary kind. That was what he wanted to do. He was being very sensible.

It would be dumb to put her already battered heart at risk! Matteo had exited in the nick of time, and she would respect that.

The decision for self-preservation made, Marlee got up and, mindful of the fragility of freshly painted nails, tiptoed cautiously into the bathroom. She used the hair dryer to finish drying her toes, then glanced at the clock. It was late, but chances of her going to sleep were nil.

Her family had always taught her the remedy for discomfort was to stop thinking about yourself and do something for someone in need.

Marlee thought that Fiona might be up and in need of comfort. That was why she had done her toenails in the first place, she reminded herself.

She changed out of her pajamas and into that horrible but exceedingly comfy pink sweat suit, then made her way across the darkened resort to Fiona's suite.

As she had suspected, the light was on inside. She knocked lightly on the door. After a long pause, Fiona flung it open.

Her face fell when she saw it was Marlee.

"I hoped you were Mike," she said, glancing over Marlee's shoulder as if she might have hidden Mike somewhere behind her.

"I just came to show you my toenails," Marlee said, hoping to lighten Fiona's mood. She lifted one leg and wiggled her toes.

Fiona bent over and looked at them. "Oh," she said, with an exasperated sigh of long-suffering. "Didn't you get my text?"

Marlee put her leg down. "What?"

"I sent you a picture of what I wanted. I'll show you."

Fiona went and grabbed her phone. "It was bridesmaid photo of the year."

Marlee looked at the picture. Four perfect feet were photographed against a backdrop of powdered sugar sand. Each one's toenails were painted gold, but each had a tiny white flower on it.

"You're supposed to have the flower on your fourth toe. I have one on my big toe, Kathy has one on her second toe, Brenda on her third."

"Well, I'll just have to be plain gold," Marlee said, stung by the criticism.

"You're wrecking everything," Fiona said.

"*I'm* wrecking everything?"

Marlee contemplated catching the next flight home. Three birds with one stone: she wouldn't have to steel herself against meeting Matteo again; she wouldn't have to put up with Fiona; and she wouldn't have to *really* wreck everything by admitting she'd found a donkey instead of a horse.

"I could tell by your face you hate the dress I picked for you. You missed the welcome party by the pool. You missed the pedicures. You're acting like you hate it all."

And here she thought she had been hiding that so well! Marlee was very aware that there was something about having spent the day with Matteo that had brought out this more forthright side of her. She took a deep breath.

"Fiona, I have gone to a great deal of trouble, time and expense to be here for you. I spent the whole day trying to find you, um, an equine. I did miss the pool get-together, and I wasn't here for the spa thing, but I've done my best to give you what you wanted. And instead of being grateful, instead of acting as if you want me here, you're just being self-centered and mean."

How much of having a man at her feet admitting he thought she was beautiful and that he found himself terribly attracted to her had given her the courage to say this?

Fiona's mouth fell open.

"And I *do* hate the dress," Marlee said, while she

was getting things off her chest and being courageous. "I'm not wearing it."

"Well, you won't have to," Fiona said, and burst into tears, "because there is not going to be a wedding!"

Marlee took her friend by the elbow and guided her to the couch.

"What's going on, Fiona?" She sank onto the couch beside her.

"Mike said the same things to me as you. Only he wasn't as nice about it. He called me the B-word."

"I'm sorry," Marlee said, and she genuinely was.

"The B-word! My dad used to call my mom that when they were fighting. I screamed at Mike that I wouldn't marry him now if he was the last man on earth.

"How can this be happening to me?" she whimpered. "I knew my parents wouldn't come if I had it here, but it doesn't matter. It's the very same as if they were here. Fighting. Chaos. Name-calling… Marlee, I'm going to end up just like you," she whispered as if that was the worst thing on earth. "Abandoned at the altar."

Marlee considered that for a moment, and the truth unfolded in her like a flag unfurling.

"It was the best thing that ever happened to me."

CHAPTER ELEVEN

IT WAS THE best thing that ever happened to me.

"What?" Fiona said. "You're devastated! You've looked sad for six months."

Either Fiona was actually capable of seeing how others felt, or she was worried about *that* look for the photos. Marlee decided to give her the benefit of the doubt.

"I was sad. But I'm not now."

Marlee could probably pinpoint just about the precise moment when that had happened, and it had been when she had embraced a bolder side, and been drinking rum and contemplating smoking a cigar. The moment when she had met the man who would change it all.

It was as if from that point a new world had opened to her. A world full of wonder.

"You and Arthur were so perfect for each other," Fiona said dejectedly. "When it didn't work, it kind of shook my sense of safety. It made me aware that anything could happen to anybody at any time."

"Why do you say we were perfect for each other?"

"You were just so *stable.* That's what made the breakup so shocking. You were like your mom and dad."

Marlee smiled. "Yes, we were. Arthur actually brought that up when he called it off. He said we were much too young to be so settled. He used the word *comfy.*"

"Like your mom and dad! That's what I've yearned for my whole life."

"He said we were like two worn recliners in front of the TV set."

Fiona giggled through her tears. "Okay. Maybe that's a little *too* comfy."

"If I had married him," Marlee said softly, arriving at the realization herself for the first time, "I would have missed so much. Boldness. Adventure. Spontaneity."

"Oh! As if *you* are going to embrace those things now!"

"I might surprise you," Marlee said.

"I'm sorry. I didn't mean that to sound as if you're dull and boring. It's just, I rely on you to be the stable one." Fiona sighed. "I've been totally awful, haven't I?"

"Look, I get it. I know what you come from."

"You're the only one here who actually knows. I mean, I've told Mike I didn't have the best family life, and he's seen it for himself when he's met my parents, but I've always controlled everything about him meeting them. Dinner in a nice restaurant with strict timelines. Like, I'd book a show right after, so that they didn't have time to…well, you know, do what they do.

"I've never even had him to their house. It's such an embarrassment to me. Who knows what you'd find this week? A window somebody has thrown something through? A wrecked car in the yard? I wanted this whole wedding to be like the opposite of that. I wanted it to be classy and romantic and beautiful."

"As if you were leaving all that behind."

"Exactly," Fiona said sadly.

"Fiona, you can't leave parts of yourself behind. Believe it or not, some of the things that are best about you come from that."

She contemplated that for a moment. "You think so?"

"You need to go talk to Mike and tell him exactly what you told me just now. You need to let him know why being in control is so important to you. And you need to let him know you believe in the power of love, above all else."

Fiona looked at her hopefully, through wet eyes. "Okay," she said. "Am I a total mess?"

"You are."

"I need to—"

"You need to go to him exactly as you are, Fiona. Exactly."

Fiona stared at her.

"No makeup?" she whispered. "He's never seen me without makeup."

"You wear your makeup to bed?" Marlee asked, astonished.

"Just a little bit."

"Doesn't it end up on the pillowcase?"

"I look horrible without any makeup on."

"I'm sure he doesn't love you because of your makeup."

"I'm not even sure he does love me."

"Go find out. Be brave. Fiona—" she said the next part carefully "—think about what *he* needs. Not what you need."

"Okay," Fiona finally said, as if she was a child who had been given a reprehensible task to fulfill.

Marlee made her way back to her own cabana. She thought she might lie awake for a while but found she was pleasantly exhausted from her day of sunshine and unexpected adventure. She fell asleep thinking about those words.

Be brave.

When her cell phone rang beside her bed, she glanced at her bedside clock. It was one in the morning. She had the crazy hope it was Matteo, even though they had never had a reason to exchange phone numbers.

But it wasn't. It was Fiona.

"The wedding is on!" she cried.

"That's great," Marlee said, sleepy but genuinely happy for her friend.

"Mike hadn't seen me without makeup before and he said I looked *adorbs.*"

"That's true love," Marlee said.

"Isn't it? And my face was all blotchy and tear-stained and he didn't even care."

"That guy is a gem. I've always thought so."

"He thinks the same of you. You were part of what we fought about."

"Me?"

"I was, er, complaining about you missing the warm-up party at the pool and the pedicure, and he said I was being insensitive. He said maybe all this wedding stuff made you sad."

Marlee contemplated that. It made her uncomfortable that she was being talked about, especially in the context of Mike pitying her.

"He seemed very relieved when I told him just now that you decided your wedding cancellation was a good thing. He never liked Arthur for you. He didn't think you should just go for the first guy who paid attention to you."

Again, Marlee did not like the sensation of being talked about, her life and choices dissected. She didn't like it at all that she was seen as some kind of fading wallflower, so pleased at any kind of male attention that her marriage had been seen as an act of desperation instead of love. How much of that was true? She was silent.

"Now that we're on," Fiona said, moving right

along, "do you think you could do something about that flower?"

She was confused since she had just been thinking of wallflowers. "What? What flower?"

"The white flower on the fourth toe."

"Um—" Marlee suddenly wasn't sure Fiona had learned anything at all from her wedding nearly not happening.

"I'm not sure painting a white flower on my toe is in my skill set." She was pretty sure it was not in Matteo's, either. Not that she planned to ask him!

"I know you'll figure it out," Fiona said cheerfully. "Thank you for being there for me tonight. Best friend ever!"

And then the phone went dead.

That left Marlee to lie awake, thinking about people pitying her. But her thoughts soon drifted to contemplation of Matteo's abrupt departure last night. She understood why he had gone. He was terrified of love.

He'd made that clear. He had watched it destroy his father, and he was, understandably, steering away from it.

Lying in the darkness of her room, Marlee thought about the words she had said to Fiona.

Think about what he needs.

She had meant it in the context of Mike, but she found herself thinking about Matteo. He appeared to be the man who had everything, and yet he had revealed a damaged heart to her.

It struck her as sad that a man who had accomplished

so much materially had condemned himself to such a lonely existence.

Really, what he had confided in her was that he wasn't going to care about anyone, because caring hurt too much.

Of course he had his sisters, his nieces and nephews, but she wondered how much he held back, even from them.

"You can't fix this," she whispered to herself.

But suddenly she was ashamed that she had made the decision to avoid Matteo, to follow his lead, for self-preservation.

That was not the set of values she had grown up with. Maybe it was even the kind of safe decision that inspired pity for her from people like Mike.

It was two more days.

They didn't have to fall in love.

She shivered as that thought entered her mind.

They just had to believe it was okay to care about each other. It was okay to let their guard down. It was okay to have fun and believe that life had natural checks and balances.

It held sorrow and joy.

It was okay to be curious and open to what happened next. Why not ask him to expand his skill set a little bit?

The next morning, in the safest place on earth, Marlee had absolutely no problem getting his room number out of the front desk clerk. She probably could have gotten the key if she'd asked for it!

Her heart beating unreasonably, she found her way to his room.

Except it wasn't exactly a room. Matteo's villa made her tiny cabana look like a shoebox. She suddenly didn't feel at all as confident that she knew what anybody needed. She had deliberately dressed casually—shorts, sandals, a white shirt—but now she wished she'd given in to the temptation to buy a second sundress from the resort boutique.

Too late for doubts! She took a deep breath.

She knocked on the door. Again, Marlee gave herself the same advice she'd given Fiona.

Be brave.

Think about what he needed, not what she needed.

The door swung open and Matteo stood there.

A towel was wrapped around his waist.

She totally forgot about what he needed, or what she needed.

"Do you open your door like that in Switzerland?" she croaked.

"Like what?"

"With no clothes on."

He glanced down at himself. He looked at her, and a small smile tickled his lips at her discomfort.

"You've seen me in my swim shorts," he said. "I don't think this is any less modest."

"Um…"

"Unless," he said wickedly, "there was a wardrobe malfunction."

She gulped.

He laughed. "What gives me the pleasure this morning?"

A reminder that last night he had been *sorry* about the confidences he had shared with her, sorry he had shown her his poor, bruised heart.

It came back to her why she was here.

To rescue him, the man who had everything, from his self-imposed prison of loneliness.

She waved a bottle of white nail polish at him. "Fiona wants some modification to the design. Can I come in? I have a picture."

He hesitated, and then with a slight bow, he held the door open to her.

Surrender.

Marlee stepped by him and his shower-fresh scent tickled her nostrils. She was aware of the perfect, deep carve of his chest and how utterly and beautifully masculine he was. She remembered the accidental touches of her fingers on his naked skin when they had swum together.

They were alone in his villa. The potential for danger—of the most delicious kind—seemed high.

But then she came to a full stop. Her mouth fell open as her eyes adjusted from the bright light outside to the dimmer interior of the villa.

The ceilings soared. The couches were white leather.

If she sat on one in her white shirt, she would disappear!

The rest of the furniture was rich, subdued and sophisticated. The huge abstract art pieces were gorgeous. The rugs were, no doubt, priceless. A bouquet of island-bright fresh flowers was in a huge vase in the center of a coffee table.

In her cabana, she had gotten a free cigar and a travel-size bottle of rum. The rich and famous got baby-elephant-size bouquets of flowers.

A whole wall was covered in windows that looked out to a pool. A waterfall cascaded off one end of it. Its marble decks were scattered with huge wicker furniture baskets—giant eggs—with bright pillows inside them. Concrete pots held flowering trees and shrubs. There was a bar at the opposite end of the pool from the waterfall.

"Is that a pool?" she asked, though it was obvious it was.

"Yes."

"Just for this unit?" Marlee was aware her voice was slightly strangled.

Matteo wagged a wicked eyebrow at her. "Privacy has its perks."

She glanced down at the towel and blushed. She had assumed he was in the shower, but maybe he'd been in the pool.

In his altogether!

"Why were you going to the ocean to swim that

night if you had this at your disposal?" Including, of course, all that privacy!

The danger she had felt a moment ago felt as if it was diluting, like pouring a glass of red wine into the ocean. He was from a different world than her.

A faster world. A more sophisticated world.

He swam in the nude!

Still, now was not the time to lose courage. She had made it past the first barrier, the front door. The second, if she included him being dressed only in a towel, which a few days ago would have been enough to make her turn tail and run.

"It's a palace," she said. *Who did she think she was?* He was not only from a different world, he was also one of the richest men in that world.

The third barrier appeared to be her own sense of inadequacy, and she was not so certain she could overcome that one.

She had convinced herself he needed rescuing.

It was laughable.

Was it just an excuse to give in to her desire to be with him? There it was—just sharing the same space with him, she became so aware of a deep and all-consuming hunger.

To know him.

To share air with him.

To make him laugh.

To touch him.

To be touched by him.

"What's wrong?" Matteo said, frowning at her.

Marlee reminded herself firmly of the life she had almost had. As comfortable as two old recliners in front of the television set.

She remembered suddenly a part she had not shared with Fiona.

Rump-sprung.

Arthur had called the recliners that he thought represented their future together rump-sprung.

If she wanted a rump-sprung life, she could leave right now. Holding that thought firm, Marlee held her ground.

CHAPTER TWELVE

MATTEO WATCHED MARLEE take in her surroundings. She looked as if she was contemplating bolting.

"Is something wrong?" he asked her, again.

But then she relaxed, and he knew she would stay. He felt inordinately pleased.

He thought about her question. With a pool at his disposal, why had he gone to the ocean to swim that night?

He was not a whimsical man. Not even a little bit.

And yet, it felt as if destiny had drawn him to the ocean, to his path crossing hers, literally.

Last night, after he had opened his heart to her, he had made a decision. No more being weak when he wanted to be strong.

And yet, when he had opened the door to her standing there, clutching that silly bottle of nail polish, something in him had sighed.

With welcome.

And maybe the most dangerous thing of all, hope.

"Nothing's wrong, exactly," she said, looking about, "but it's all just very glamourous, like the set of a movie."

"Is it?" He looked around, seeing it through her eyes. To him it looked just like a thousand other high-end hotel rooms he had stayed in.

"You don't even know it's out of the ordinary, do you? I mean the bathroom is probably bigger than my whole apartment in Seattle."

"It's not like it's mine," he pointed out.

She didn't look convinced. Her insecurity had a funny effect on him. He wanted to be the one who made her feel secure.

"It's just a rental. I call this decor style 'generic posh.' I mean, look at that painting over there. Would anybody actually hang it in their house?"

"Nobody has a twelve-foot wall in their house!"

"Besides how huge it is, it has no meaning. Big black looping lines."

She cocked her head thoughtfully at it, and he saw, pleased, just a tiny bit of the tension leave her.

"Maybe it's like an inkblot test," she suggested.

"What do you see in it?"

"The LA freeway," she decided, and they both laughed, and Matteo was grateful something eased even further in her. "What about you?"

"Tangled yarn," he decided. "My grandmother used to knit."

He turned back to her and caught a look on her face. Unless he missed his guess, she also knitted. It endeared her to him, and the fact she was embarrassed about it endeared her more.

"I was just having coffee by the pool," he said. "Come join me, and then we'll discuss the latest in bridal demands. Let me guess. It has something to do with photos."

He was satisfied when he coaxed a little laugh from Marlee. "How did you know?"

He lifted a shoulder and led her through to the patio. He settled her at the table and went and got another cup. He poured her a coffee from the carafe on the table, then sank into his chair across from her. She helped herself to cream and sugar and took a sip.

"So good," she said.

The quality of light on Coconut Cay was magnificent. It danced in her hair and lit her eyes.

She was wearing a crisp white shirt today, button-down. She had on a pair of khaki shorts with it.

So good.

How was she making the quintessential tourist outfit look so sexy?

"Are you, um, going to put on some pants?"

"Am I making you uncomfortable?"

"Yes!"

He grinned. "Good."

He deliberately stretched out his legs. She glanced at the length of them, gave him a warning look, then took out her phone and showed him the picture.

"You're kidding, right?" he asked, contemplating

the feet in the picture with the tiny flowers painted on the toenails.

"No, I'm afraid not."

"There are people who specialize in painting miniatures. I'm not one of them."

"But you'll try, at least?"

He looked at the picture again. Dangerous to get into this! To be touching her feet, again, the way he had been last night.

When all his barriers had come tumbling down!

So no one was more shocked than he was, to hear himself saying, "Oh, why not? How difficult could it be?"

Actually, it was quite difficult. After they had finished their coffee, Matteo got Marlee settled among the bright, deep cushions of one of those big, egg-shaped wicker things around the pool.

He took her foot in his hand and bent over it, fighting a ridiculous impulse to kiss her instep. Carefully, tongue between his teeth, he took the brush out of the bottle.

"Is your house in Switzerland as palatial as this?" she asked him. "The house of a man who flies around in his own jet?"

"Do you want to know a secret about me?"

Now he was going to tell her *more* secrets? She leaned up from where she was reclining among the pillows and it weakened him in some delightful way that she *did* want to know a secret about him.

It was just to make her comfortable, he told himself.

"I still live in the same room I had as a boy. To be honest, not much has changed about it. The model airplane my father and I made together still hangs from a fishing line in one corner."

She leaned back against the pillows, relaxed.

He was not sure he wanted her quite that relaxed. He thought about running his thumb down the side of her instep that he already knew was so tender, but resisted.

"My house in Zurich is old. Just as our business, it's been in my family for generations. When my father died, neither of my sisters wanted it. Mia said it was haunted, and Emma was worried about her children destroying the antiques. I couldn't bring myself to move into the bedroom my mother and father had shared, so there I am, in my boyhood room.

"I'm planning a complete renovation, eventually, but I haven't gotten to it yet."

It occurred to him that the space called *home* was a low priority to him, linked in some way to the dangers he had revealed to Marlee last night.

The dangers of caring.

"Tell me about your family business," she invited.

Matteo found it so easy to talk to her.

"Family legend has it that it started hundreds of years ago on my mother's side, when my great-great-great-grandmother sold a handmade winter coat. And then another and another. Her name was Rosa, which coincidentally is also the name of Switzerland's highest peak.

"Over many generations, Monte Rosa Alpen Wear became a company that was known for extremely high-quality winter clothing, and a contract to supply an army with wool jackets moved it to the next level. And then it expanded into mountaineering and outdoor supplies and survival equipment.

"By the time my father took it over, the reputation of the company was cemented. But after the death of my mother, he took his hands off the reins. I think that though she stayed in the background, she was the detail person. Maybe even the driving force behind the company. Anyway, after her death, he wasn't watching the quality control. He wasn't interested in trends or how to stay current in an increasingly competitive market.

"My sisters and I watched helplessly as his indifference nearly drove the family business into the ground. Our four-hundred-year-old reputation was badly tarnished. We were getting reviews and complaints, and many of them said we were overpriced, old-fashioned, and skating on our name.

"I took marketing in university—that's where I met Mike. And by the time I was done, I knew exactly what needed to happen with Monte Rosa. I wanted my sisters involved. It seemed to me it had always been a women-driven company, even when men took the credit. So my sister Emma applied her brilliant design ideas to bring the clothing lines into this century, and

Mia took over the quality control for the mountaineering and survival equipment lines. We dropped the *Wear* from the name and surged forward."

Matteo was aware he did not usually talk this much. It was very comfortable to talk to her. That was what he had wanted, wasn't it? Her comfort? But now it felt as if maybe it was too comfortable. The spell he'd tried to weave around her had spun back and caught him.

Because the next words out of his mouth shocked Matteo.

"I sometimes wonder, though I've never admitted it, if saving the family business made me feel as if I could save all that we were before my mother died."

"And did it?" Marlee asked softly.

"Not really," he admitted. "My father died before we began to enjoy the enormous success we have today."

He felt suddenly wildly uncomfortable with his confidences. He renewed his interest in the job at hand.

Matteo dabbed at Marlee's toenail. He frowned. It didn't really look like a flower. He tried to repair it. The brush slipped and a blob of white nail polish nearly obliterated her whole toe. He jumped up, relieved to be away from the intensity, and went in search of something to clean it off.

"I should have thought of this in advance," he muttered, feeling more composed when he came back. He wiped the botched nail polish.

"Toilet paper?" she said, the outlaw dancing in her eyes, and yet there was something right beneath that, too. Compassion. Concern. “I thought this was a classy joint.”

He was grateful that she understood his need to move past what he had just said, to keep it light.

The nail polish was a perfect distraction. It had dried ever so slightly and his clumsy attempt to wipe it had left a cloudy smear on her toenail.

“So classy they hid the damned tissue. The nail polish brush is too big. I need something smaller. Aha!”

This was what got him through everything: razor focus, an ability to prioritize. And keep things—especially untidy things like feelings—in compartments.

He went into the suite and came back with a pen. He dipped the tip in the polish. And carefully put a single drop on her toe. Still a blob!

He scowled, wiped it off, dabbed again.

“Quit laughing,” he told her sternly, “it makes your toe shake.”

“I can’t help it. I feel like Cleopatra.”

Again, he felt grateful to her for moving on, for keeping it light between them, and shifting the topic away from his confession.

“And to think yesterday you were just an outlaw,” Matteo said, in the same vein as her.

“I know. Quite a promotion in one day. Not only am I Cleopatra, but I have a slave.”

“Ah,” he said. “My queen, your wish is my command.”

For a moment, she was very silent. He glanced up at her. His mouth went dry.

"I wish," she said softly, "that you could find what you're looking for."

He stared at her.

"I wish you could have your sense of family back. And safety."

He felt as if what he was looking for—the thing he had been searching for without knowing that he searched—was in her eyes, like a promise.

He looked away from her. He concentrated on the job in front of him. His hand didn't feel steady.

"There," he said, putting her foot away from him, and with it, hopefully, the sense of weakness and wanting that seemed to be enveloping him.

She pulled up her knees and inspected his work. Her suppressed mirth gave way. She gave a shout of laughter.

"I don't get what's so funny," he said gravely.

"It doesn't look like a flower. It looks like an octopus."

He retrieved her toe and studied it. "You might have something there, Queen Cleo. Call Fiona. Change the theme."

"Egyptian?" she suggested.

"Or Down by the Sea."

"Which theme will Henri fit into better?"

"Oh, Henri! Have you told her yet, about Henri?"

"Not yet. The time hasn't seemed right. She's a nervous wreck."

After all the hoops Fiona was making her jump

through, Marlee was still able to think what Fiona was going through?

He was not at all sure he had ever met anyone this big-hearted before.

It was a warning. She was too soft. Too tender.

A person like Marlee would be so easily hurt.

And yet, the impulse to kiss her foot was so great that he sprang to his feet.

"Well," he said, "our work here is done."

Her eyes went very wide.

He felt the sudden breeze on his bare skin.

He looked down, already knowing what he would see. The towel must have caught on the edge of the basket chair. It lay in a white puddle at his feet.

Matteo looked at Marlee, expecting to see her laughing now that the tables were turned and the embarrassing wardrobe malfunction moment was his.

But she was not laughing.

Matteo turned and dove in the pool.

CHAPTER THIRTEEN

MARLEE WATCHED THE faint splash as Matteo dove cleanly into the water and disappeared under its tranquil blue surface. She was unabashedly appreciative of him. He was quite gorgeous with no clothes on. He would make the perfect male specimen to carve in marble.

She found herself continually shocked by the surprises life held after she'd made that decision to be bold, and by the fact a different side of herself was being revealed.

For instance, if she was still the woman she had been when she arrived at Coconut Cay, she would get up now, go inside the villa and give Matteo an opportunity to exit the water and retrieve his towel and his dignity.

Instead, she got up and wandered to the water's edge. She stuck her toe in, just as he resurfaced, treading water. He shook droplets of water from his hair, scowling at her.

"Don't get your feet wet," he ordered her.

"I can if I want."

"You'll spoil the nail polish."

She smiled at him. "As if that's our biggest problem," she said sweetly.

His scowl deepened. "If you could just put my towel where I can reach it and turn your back for a moment, I'd be most grateful."

She leaned over and picked up his towel. She made a grave show of contemplating it thoughtfully. Then she tossed it behind her, well out of his reach.

"Hey! That isn't funny!"

"It is," she said. "Barely."

"Marlee, be reasonable."

"You thought it was hilarious when it happened to me."

"I didn't really."

"Where is all your European sophistication now?" she asked him. Slowly, deliberately, she moved her hand to the top button of her shirt. She flicked it open.

His eyes went wide.

She flicked open the next one.

He licked his lips. "Marlee, just pass me the towel. Before we—you—do something you regret."

"What would I regret?" she egged him on softly.

"Wrecking the nail polish!" he said, and she heard something desperate in his tone.

"It didn't look like a flower, anyway."

"If you'll just be reasonable, I'll try again. I'm sure I can master a flower—"

"I'm all done being reasonable," she interrupted him.

"No, you're not," he insisted.

She laughed. She was not sure she had ever felt her full feminine power quite so delightfully as when she slowly removed her top and let it slide from her hand to the pool deck.

Ever so slowly, she trailed her hand down over her belly to the button on her shorts. She undid them and stepped out of them.

If she expected sanity to hit her as the sultry tropical air caressed her skin, she was completely wrong.

She didn't feel shy at all. The woman who had run from the ocean trying to hide herself was gone forever. Wallflowers who inspired pity were banished from within herself!

Matteo had done this to her.

He was doing it to her now. The look in his eyes—desperation, hunger, appreciation—emboldened her. She was not who she had been before.

"What are you doing?" he croaked.

"I'm going skinny-dipping."

"No, you're not!"

"But you're doing it."

"By accident!"

"I bet it feels wonderful."

"It doesn't."

"The water right up against your skin, no barriers. I'm curious."

"You've experienced that every single time you've taken a bath."

"I don't think it's the same."

"It is."

She smiled at him, then she reached behind her own back and flicked open the clasp on her bra. It fell away. Nothing awkward about it at all. She stretched up and enjoyed the sensation of sun on her naked skin.

Matteo groaned, an almost animal sound of suffering.

"Imagine that," she said. "I'm twenty-six years old, and I've never felt the sun on my breasts before. I could get used to it, I think."

"Marlee," he said hoarsely, "you are killing me."

She smiled more deeply at him. "But what a way to go, right?"

She stepped out of her panties and then jumped off the edge of the deck way out into the pool. She felt the water close over her head.

For a split second, she enjoyed the sensation of warm water, silky, against her naked skin. It was just as she had hoped. Utterly freeing. Unbelievably sensual.

But then her feet did not find the bottom of the pool. She had not thought she was going in the deep end. A little too late, she remembered she was not a very good swimmer.

Marlee realized, panic beginning, that she was in way over her head, in every possible way.

Her feet finally found the bottom of the pool. She hated opening her eyes underwater, but she did.

It seemed as if the light was a long way away. She pushed against the floor of the pool and rocketed to the surface. She drew in a single, strangled breath, and managed one distressed yelp. She flapped her arms frantically and struck out for the safety of the side.

But gravity was winning. Panic made her limbs heavy.

And then safety found her.

If it could be called that.

Matteo's arms closed around her, and she twined her arms around his neck.

"Hang on," he said. "I've got you."

Had more beautiful words ever been spoken?

"Relax," he told her, his voice deep and calm and soothing in her ear. Effortlessly, he moved them to shallower water.

"You can stand now," he said.

But somehow, she could not let go. And somehow, they were not safe.

Probably the farthest thing from it.

She looked up into his face, so familiar to her already. And in some way that was beyond explanation, given the shortness of their acquaintance, beloved.

Maybe that was what happened when someone saved your life.

She traced the wet surface of his face with her fingertips, hungry to know his brow, his eyelids, the straight line of his nose, the cleft of his chin. He moved his head until his lips found her questing fingers.

One by one, as he tasted them, she gloried in the larger sensation of their bodies touching, wet skin slippery as silk connecting them both.

His hand moved to the back of her head, and he drew her face to his. His mouth found her mouth.

There was no tentativeness in either of them. No hesitation.

This kiss had none of the innocence of the kiss she had bestowed on him yesterday after their adventure.

Though it was everything that kiss had hinted it could be. There was savagery and sweetness combined as Marlee was engulfed by sensation.

Every cell in her awakened to Matteo's quest, Matteo's call. Every part of her, from the tips of her toes to the tips of her hair, tingled and sparked. It was as if her desire had been a dying ember at her core and was now flickering to life, after a breath of air had found it.

The breath intensified. A breeze. And the ember of desire within Marlee flared, glowing red hot. Just when it seemed it could not become any more intense, as if the heat could consume her, Matteo dropped his head to her breast.

That fire within took hold, roared to life.

It felt as if the water should boil around them.

He lifted her easily and carried her from the water. The sensation in the pit of her stomach was deeply primal, as if she was the woman a warrior had come home to. He kicked open the door of the villa with his foot and took her through to the coolness to the master suite, his easy strength stealing her breath.

He laid her on the center of the bed, and she felt herself sinking into the deep comfort of its snowy whiteness.

Matteo stood above her, looking down. He waited, his eyes drinking her in, for a signal from her. She noticed everything: the water droplets on his lashes, the plump line of his bottom lip, the broadness of his shoulders, the deepness of his chest, his ribs marching down his sides to the narrowness of his waist.

The woman she used to be—yesterday, though it felt as if it was a hundred years ago—put up a faint fight.

Think, the old Marlee implored her.

About what? the new Marlee asked.

Consequences. Tomorrow.

But none of that mattered. There was no tomorrow, and the consequence of not following her heart seemed as if it would be the worst one of all.

A form of death.

The kind of nonlife—dull as a rump-sprung recliner in front of a TV—that she had accepted for far too long.

She opened her arms to him.

And everything within Marlee sang.

Live.

And so she lived.

Matteo was an exquisite lover. He wanted her pleasure. He teased. He tantalized. He found each of her ticklish secrets—particularly that delicate instep—and tormented her with them.

And he coaxed her to open a thus unexplored side of herself. She experimented. She indulged. She risked.

Much later, they lay in a tangle of sheets and the glow of utter fulfillment, splashes of sunshine striping them in light filtered green from the thick foliage outside his window.

Then they showered together, learning the textures and secrets of each other's bodies all over again. He shampooed her hair, something in the tenderness of his touch exquisitely possessive.

You belong to me.

And then they dried each other off, kisses following the path of the towel.

And then reality knocked.

Literally.

Someone was hammering on the villa door.

They both froze, silent.

"Hey, Matt," Mike called through the closed door. "What's up? You coming golfing?"

Marlee stifled a giggle. Matteo put a hand on her arm. As if that was necessary. She was hardly going to go throw open the door!

Mike knocked again, and then they heard other male voices join his, jovial. And then they moved on, their voices drifting away.

"Go golfing," Marlee told him, casually, as if it didn't matter to her one little bit. As if she was suave and sophisticated and did things like this all the time.

Not once in a lifetime.

But she was holding her breath and Matteo was not the least fooled.

"You think I would go golfing after that?" He laughed, and his laughter filled her to the brim.

"Come on," he said, "Let's get dressed. I am not

wasting one minute that I could spend with you. What do you want to do?"

She started breathing again.

Be with you. That was it. All of it.

"What I don't want to do," she said carefully, "is risk running into Fiona." She shuddered inwardly at the thought of the grilling that could ensue if the bride saw them together.

"Or Mike," he agreed.

What had happened between them felt raw and real and as if a neon sign was blinking above them announcing their newfound intimacy: *lovers.*

Marlee could not bear the thought of sideways looks, smiles, conjecture, interrogation. For a while longer, she wanted this just to belong to her and Matteo. She wasn't ready to share it with their circle of friends.

Especially her friends.

Who saw her as prim and controlled, always the stable one, always the responsible one. They would be utterly shocked to see her now.

How would she and Matteo get through the rehearsal dinner?

But that was tonight and that seemed a long way away. Only this moment seemed to exist, glittering, sparkling, infused with their newfound awareness of each other.

So much so that it was hard to keep their hands off each other as they made their way to the resort gate, both of them stealing furtive looks about, not ready just yet to have their togetherness spotted. Confronted. *Challenged.*

Outside the gates of the resort, Marlee heaved a huge sigh of relief.

She felt gloriously free. The street—vegetable stands and trinket booths and chickens and cars and children in school uniforms—shone with a spectacular light.

And then she saw the donkey cart, parked at the curb, waiting sleepily for passengers. It felt as if even the universe was on their side, providing a perfect getaway plan for them, two outlaws of love on the run.

CHAPTER FOURTEEN

"Look," Marlee said to Matteo, taking his arm and tugging him toward the ancient and colorful cart, "It's Mackay with Henri and Calamity."

"It's obviously Mackay, but how do you know which donkeys those are? He could have a whole herd of donkeys, for all you know."

"Are you skeptical of my ass expertise?" Marlee asked. She let her hand graze ever so lightly—possessively—over the back of Matteo's shorts.

She relished the unexpected direction of her life: she was teasing her lover on the colorful main street of an exotic island.

"I consider myself something of an expert now, on ass…ets. Having been exposed, so to speak." She leveled him a look and wagged her eyebrows at him.

He rewarded her with his laughter, that rich deep sound that she could live the rest of her life trying to coax from him. Even more precious was the slight blush.

"Right, Mackay? Henri and Calamity?"

"That's right." Mackay tipped his hat to them as if he had been waiting for them to appear. His glance went between them and he grinned, as if he *knew*—probably from Matteo's blush—that the romance he had predicted for *maybe after lunch* yesterday had unfolded.

To Marlee, his knowing look confirmed the wisdom of them leaving the resort.

"I knew it was Henri immediately because of his cute ears," Marlee told Matteo. "Calamity is sporting a pink feather headdress to let the world know she's a girl."

She went and bestowed each of the donkeys a kiss on their furry, soft noses.

"Miss Marlee. Mr. Matteo. Where can Mackay take you?"

"Where to?" Matteo asked her.

"Anywhere. No plan is a good plan."

Matteo snapped his fingers and turned to Mackay. "We need somebody who can do a pedicure."

"Really?" Marlee said, wiggling her toes and gazing at them. "I kind of like the octopus. It's growing on me."

"It's not faring well after the pool. And the other activities."

It was her turn to blush. And then he was laughing again and her laugher joined his.

"I'm not willing to spoil a perfect day by risking the wrath of Fiona," Matteo decided. "I've already missed the scheduled golf event, so let's make sure we pass pedicure inspection."

Marlee felt a little disappointed. She had hoped for something a bit more romantic.

But then he leaned close to her and said in her ear, "I'm going to watch very closely so I get it just right next time."

Next time.

"I think you got it just right last time," she said huskily.

"I'm talking about the pedicure," he said.

"Oh, *that.*"

And there it was between them: that sizzling connection.

"You know someone, Mackay?" Matteo asked. "Who can paint Marlee's toenails?"

"Yes, yes, my cousin." He regarded them sagely for a moment. "There are all kinds of hunger."

Evidence they were practically telegraphing what had just happened between them.

"But perhaps some food first?"

"Absolutely," Matteo said.

And so they found themselves at the kind of place Marlee would *never* have gone to. It was an off-the-beaten-track establishment that tourists did not find. It was part roadside stand and part house. A picnic area, packed with locals, had been cordoned off on the street and cars steered cheerfully around it. As soon as they sat down, three men appeared on a makeshift stage.

The joyous shouts and sounds of calypso filled the

air as Marlee and Matteo fed each other spicy local food off their fingertips.

"I think this may be the most delicious food I've ever eaten," Marlee said with a satisfied sigh when the plates in front of them were empty.

"Or your senses might be heightened," Matteo said in her ear.

Might be?

She hadn't had a single thing to drink beyond water and yet she felt intoxicated. Marlee could feel all of life tingling against her skin. As if she was breathing in the colors and sounds of Coconut Cay until they were part of her.

Her eyes fell on him.

Matteo.

Part of her.

And no matter what happened next, part of her forever.

Not that she was going to spoil one second of this by asking herself what could possibly happen next.

But what happened next was astonishing.

Mackay bowed before her. "Would you dance with me, Miss Marlee?"

She cast a look over his shoulder. A space had been cleared and people were up on the makeshift dance floor.

The music had become even more lively. People clapped and sang along. A spontaneous party had erupted.

"I don't—"

She was about to say she didn't dance. And she particularly didn't dance like *that.*

But that was the old Marlee. The wallflower. The object of people's pity.

The new Marlee was open to all the invitations life threw at her. After just a moment's hesitation, she kicked off her sandals, took Mackay's extended hand and allowed him to lead her out onto the now quite crowded dance area.

The lyrics of the song were unabashedly sexual.

I want you,
I want you moving against me,
I want your heart to beat against mine,
I want you, I want you, I want you.
I want to intertwine.

Marlee stood frozen to the spot. She looked at the people around her. So free. So uninhibited. Celebrating the sensual part of themselves and life.

She closed her eyes. She felt the primal beat of the music stir within her.

She lifted her hands over her head and swayed. Almost of their own accord, her hips did a slow circle. The music caught her and carried her.

Marlee was aware that she felt more fully a woman than she had ever felt in her life. She danced in recognition of her softness. She danced in celebration of her curves. She danced in honor of her rightful place in the cycle of life.

She realized she might be dancing *with* Mackay, but she was dancing *for* Matteo.

Matteo watched Marlee dancing.

She delighted him. From teasing him about asses, to kissing donkeys, to this.

Something in her had been unleashed since they had made love, and all of it was extraordinarily beautiful to watch.

But now, as she danced, he could see the changes in her were remarkable. This was not the same woman who had stood outside in that fluffy dress defiantly contemplating smoking a cigar, as if by doing that she could erase what she so obviously was.

A little shy.

A little uptight.

And yet, even then, he had known something lurked beneath the surface.

And Marlee had unveiled that something for him in the last few hours. She was on fire with life.

It didn't feel as if she was becoming someone else. Not at all. It felt as if she was peeling away layers of reserve, and underneath, with a light that outshone the sun, was the real Marlee.

Everyone seemed to see it. It was as if all the other dancers were orbiting around her brilliant light.

These, he decided, had been the best hours of his entire life.

As he watched her dance, Matteo became aware that

something had stolen up on him and come to reside right in the region of his heart.

It had been so long.

Could it possibly be?

Yes.

Happiness.

In its purest and simplest form.

Not the flush of success, not the satisfaction of filling hours with production, not the rush of saving his family business. It was something more intrinsic than that.

The song stopped, and Matteo got to his feet. He was not a dancer. Had two left feet. And yet the dance was within him, calling him, insisting that, like Marlee, he acknowledge the ancient rhythms of life and his part in those rhythms.

And nothing could have stopped him from sharing his just-discovered happiness with Marlee, who was, after all, the source of it all.

Marlee and Matteo danced. They became part of a joyous conga line that stopped traffic and snaked in and out of local yards and stores. They participated in a spirited game of limbo, which, as it turned out, Marlee had a real gift for.

Matteo, not so much.

Finally, they had to acknowledge the time. With Marlee clutching her limbo trophy—a carved coconut—they waved goodbye to all their newfound friends and boarded the donkey cart. Mackay serenaded them as he drove.

Leaning against each other and hands intertwined, they enjoyed the clip-clop of the donkeys' hooves and Mackay's song. He brought them eventually to a tiny salon on a narrow back street, where children were playing with a ball and sticks.

The children stopped and thronged Mackay. Finally managing to put them aside, Mackay took Marlee and Matteo into the shop and introduced them to his cousin, Margaret. Marlee showed her the picture of the painted toenails on her phone, and Margaret indicated it would not be a problem to achieve that result.

"I'll watch." Matteo swept his hand toward Marlee's feet. "I made that mess. Next time I can do better."

Next time.

Tomorrow was the wedding.

And on Sunday they would all begin to go their separate ways. He had an important meeting in Zurich on Monday.

Marlee was watching him, and he could see it in her eyes, too. The questions about next time.

How could there not be a next time?

Margaret was frowning at Marlee's feet. She guided her to a row of rather elaborate-looking chairs, sat her down and slipped her sandals off. She shook her head at Matteo's handiwork and moved Marlee's feet into what seemed to be an ancient, but spotlessly clean, basin. She turned a switch and the basin bubbled to life.

"Oh, it's lovely," Marlee said, leaning back in the chair, relaxing.

"I told you feet soaking was a necessary step," Matteo reminded Marlee.

"Customers only," Margaret said sternly, pointing to a sign. The look on her face clearly said she didn't intend to make an exception.

Instead of leaving, he went and took the spa seat beside Marlee. He kicked off his shoes.

"Okay," he said. "I'll be a customer, too, then."

Margaret, obviously calculating the extra fee, looked quite pleased with this development. She turned on the basin at the foot of his chair and he lowered his feet in. Marlee was right. It was lovely.

Matteo looked around. The shop was very clean, but everything, including Margaret's dress, was faded and worn, and the basin his feet were soaking in was making a whining noise.

What he saw was how poor Margaret was. But it was evident in the set of her chin and shoulders and in the meticulous tidiness of the shop that she was extremely proud.

"I'd like the donkey done, too. Not the girl one."

Margaret's mouth fell open.

So did Marlee's.

"He's to be in the wedding photos," Matteo explained. "It's important we all look our best."

Marlee's mouth closed and she regarded him thoughtfully. It was apparent she could see right through him. To be honest, Matteo wasn't sure that if having someone read you so accurately was a good thing or a bad thing.

Still, Marlee was smiling at him with a look that could make him want to get up in the morning and decide, every single day, how to be a better man.

Her hand came across the space between the two chairs and closed over his. When had life ever felt so right?

Margaret considered him for a moment, trying to decide if he was a crazy tourist pulling her leg.

"Dead serious," he told her, squeezing Marlee's hand. She squeezed back, a secret language between them.

"Expensive," Margaret warned him.

He nodded, and she went to a drawer and began pulling jars and jars of gold nail polish. At the door she shouted at the children, handed over the polish and pointed to the donkey.

"Don't forget the flowers," he called to her. Soon the sound of children laughing drifted in and filled the space of the tiny shop.

"I love that sound," Marlee said, settling back in her chair, a smile tickling the delicious curve of her lips. "It's better than music."

Matteo considered that. Marlee didn't just love that sound. She loved children. It felt like a warning trying to pierce the bubble of happiness around him. What was he doing, exactly?

CHAPTER FIFTEEN

THE QUESTION BUZZED around Matteo—what was he doing, exactly?—like a bothersome fly intent on ruining a perfect picnic.

"So," he said, carefully, "are you planning on having children someday?"

"Oh, yes," Marlee said. "I've even recently picked names."

Something like panic reared up in him. He'd thought—well, he wasn't sure what he'd thought—but certainly not about naming children!

And then she hooted at the look he could not keep from crossing his face.

"Henri and Calamity," she told him mirthfully.

She was letting him know that it was okay to keep it light. That it was okay not to think about the future.

But was it?

"Do you like it?" she asked. "Calamity for a little girl?"

"That's a terrible name for a child," he told her

sternly, and yet it felt as if he could see a little girl—all curls and mischief and green eyes—who could live up to that name.

A shy assistant appeared and began working alongside Margaret, and it was easy to follow Marlee's lead, to dismiss pressing questions, to just be here enjoying the sensations and the novelty of it all.

It was easy to press Mute on the warning bells that wanted to spoil everything.

Matteo and Marlee's feet were removed from the basins and carefully dried. Matteo then watched in fascinated horror as the two women plugged in apparatuses that looked for all the world like miniature circular saws with cement-cutting blades in them.

"What are those?" he asked in an undertone to Marlee.

"I'm not expert on pedicures but I think it's some kind of defoliating device."

"If they pull down welding helmets, we'll run," he said.

"I think we're at step two," Marlee decided. "Remember from last night? Get rid of dead skin."

"Last night you thought it was gross," he reminded her.

"These are professionals," she told him.

"Those look suspiciously like grinders," he said.

"Grinders?" Marlee asked.

"You know. They can grind paint off buildings with them. Destroy concrete. Cut nails in two, that kind of thing."

"Cut toenails in two?"

"Nail nails!"

"Don't worry," Marlee said, "they are not going to grind off your feet."

He wasn't so sure about that. The grinding apparatuses were coaxed to life. He discovered Marlee wasn't the only one with a ticklish instep.

"She's having her wicked way with my foot!" he said to Marlee.

"Is that trepidation I detect in your oh-so-fearless self?" Marlee teased him.

It felt wonderful to be teased by her, to leave the warning bells on silent, to enjoy her hand finding his and tightening on it.

"Be brave," she told him.

And somehow it didn't feel as if her instruction had anything to do with what was happening to his feet.

At all.

Marlee knew the exact moment she recognized the true danger of her fling with Matteo.

And it wasn't when she swam in the ocean with him, or rode behind him on a scooter, or let him paint her toenails. It wasn't when she'd decided to skinny-dip with him. Or when they had made wild, impetuous love together.

All that had deepened the attraction.

Inflamed her infatuation.

But when Matteo asked Margaret to paint the donkey's feet, too, the quiver that had been within her grew to a tremor that felt dangerous, like the pre-earthquake kind.

Because she knew exactly what he was doing.

It was more than apparent to her he was finding a way to be generous that still allowed Margaret her dignity.

Looking at him after he requested a pedicure for Henri, Marlee felt as if she could see him all the way to his soul.

And what she saw was innate kindness.

Decency.

A lovely kind of honor.

But then, because she could see those things, she saw the moment it turned on her.

So, are you planning on having children someday?

As if he could clearly see, despite everything she had become in the last few hours and days, that under all that boldness lurked a traditional girl with traditional dreams of family and forever.

Trapping dreams, if the expression on his face when she said she had already named the children, was any indication.

For once in her life, Marlee didn't want to think about the future. Or forever. She didn't want to complicate things with imagining repercussions or making moral judgments about right or wrong.

She didn't want her world to be predictable or rule-bound.

She just wanted to immerse herself in the delightful surprises that were being handed to her, moment after moment.

She would deal with the fallout, the inevitable devastation of the earthquake, later.

And who said there had to be fallout? Couldn't she just have a lovely fling like all the rest of the world was doing?

Of course she could.

An hour later, they were laughing together as they walked gingerly out to the donkey cart. They had been provided with cheap flip-flops and the toe separators were still in.

She had a perfect white flower on the fourth toenail of each foot.

He had opted for an octopus.

To the delight of the waiting children, they made a huge fuss over Henri's beautifully painted hooves.

And then, aware they had not left themselves enough time, they urged Mackay to make haste back to the resort.

It was a wild ride as the donkeys clattered through the narrow streets, bouncing Marlee and Matteo into each other and making them hang on for dear life.

At the resort they quickly went their separate ways to get ready for the rehearsal. Thankfully, it wasn't a dress rehearsal!

The yellow sundress had been picked up off her floor, sent to the cleaners, and was now hanging, refreshed, off the shower bar in her bathroom.

Totally wrong, of course, for the rehearsal dinner. It drew too much attention. It was too loud. It was the bride's time to shine.

"That's tomorrow," Marlee told herself and slipped the dress over her head.

She arrived a few minutes late, breathless, and took her place beside Fiona, who threw her—and the dress—a faintly disapproving look.

In response she wagged her newly painted toes and actually earned a nod of approval.

"Love that color on you," Brenda said. It seemed perhaps a defiant reaction to Fiona's look. "You should wear bright colors more often."

"The length is very daring," Kathy chimed in. "I love it! You carry it perfectly. You look hot!"

And she obviously did not mean the melting-from-the-heat kind of hot.

The approval of her friends was really confirmation that Arthur had been right. Somewhere along the way she had become too muted, too comfortable and dull in the way she approached the ultra-predictable life that had made her feel safe, yes, but had also shut down parts of her.

She felt the moment of Matteo's arrival, the air shifting as he joined the wedding party on the beach. She looked everywhere but at him.

How could she look at him without their intimacy being obvious to every single person there?

Especially with the new dress, people might start arriving at conclusions!

Even knowing that, she could not stop herself. She slid a look at him.

He had put on shoes. He was dressed in a light pair of slacks and a shirt so hastily buttoned he had missed the top one.

Her eyes fastened on the part of his chest that she could see.

She remembered her hands on his naked flesh. He glanced at her. Some white-hot memory darkened the turquoise of his eyes to navy blue. They both looked away at exactly the same moment.

The rehearsal was a tense nightmare of trying not to look at him.

Trying not to touch him!

Thankfully, in the wedding party, he was coupled with Kathy, not her. They endlessly practiced gliding down the aisle, to Fiona's instructions.

"Kathy, just a little slower."

"Brenda, hold the flowers up a bit higher."

"Marlee, a little less swish."

Swish. She had become a hot girl in a yellow sundress who swished. She shot Matteo a look.

He was looking deliberately off into the distance. His lips were twitching.

"I think we should practice how we're lining up for the register signing one more time and we'll have it perfect," Fiona decided.

"Forget perfect," Mike said. "I'm famished. Let's eat!"

"But we need to talk about photos. That will happen in between the ceremony and the dinner."

Photos.

Marlee suddenly realized she had not broken it to Fiona yet about a donkey instead of a horse.

"I'm trying to decide if I'll wreck the dress or not. It's a hard decision. Such a nice dress to jump in the ocean with!"

"Decide over dinner," Mike said firmly. "Or maybe don't even decide. You could just be spontaneous."

It felt as if he was speaking to Marlee about the donkey decision, not to Fiona about the photo decisions.

The very idea of being spontaneous seemed to appall Fiona.

No matter what happened next, Marlee thought, she would always be grateful for this: that Matteo had broken her away from her own rigid need for control.

And then, to Fiona's horror, the whole wedding party mutinied and stampeded toward the dinner that had been set up for them at the wedding venue, a private grotto just off the area marked for the beach ceremony.

It was stunningly beautiful, with a waterfall at one end, the deep greens of thick foliage forming walls of privacy around it. Cables of outdoor lights hung above tables already set up for tomorrow.

As waiters brought out dinner, other staff came and lit tiki torches that illuminated the dining area as well as the dance floor and bar.

Again, they rehearsed. The order of the toasts. The

timing. Who would stand where, who would say what, what would make the best photos?

Matteo, appearing neither bored nor as if he had other plans, rose from the table when Fiona finally stopped to catch a breath.

"It's been a long day," he said casually. "And I seem to have jet lag. In the interest of being nice and fresh for the wedding tomorrow, I'm going to head off."

After a suitable amount of time had passed, Marlee also got up.

"I seem to have a tiny headache." This was a bald-faced lie, but not being the woman she had been when she'd arrived at Coconut Cay, Marlee didn't feel even a little bit guilty. "I think, also in the interest of being at my best tomorrow, I'll turn in."

"But we haven't rehearsed cutting the cake yet. Or the first dances."

Once, Marlee would have sat back down.

But not now.

"You can fill me in tomorrow," Marlee said.

Once, Fiona would have argued with her. But now she scanned her face, and must have seen something different there, too.

On the other hand, maybe she thought all the wedding planning was making Marlee sad about her own missed day. Did Mike nudge Fiona?

"All right. But you have to be at my suite really early. There's so much to do."

"I promise I will be." There was so much to do. She had a dress that needed complete altering! But first things first. Marlee set off to find Matteo. His place? Hers? Their beach?

Before she could decide, a hand shot out of the darkened shrubbery and pulled her in. Her surprised cry was silenced by a very familiar hand.

"I thought you'd never leave," he whispered in her ear.

And then he kissed her. Thoroughly. Until she wondered if you could die from kisses. Or, more accurately, from wanting what the kisses promised.

Hand in hand, breathless with anticipation, neither of them acknowledging the end was near, they went to his villa.

And they didn't walk.

They ran.

CHAPTER SIXTEEN

MARLEE WOKE UP in a nest of sparkling white sheets, to the sounds of birds. They were loud as they celebrated the first rays of light that heralded the coming of the new day.

She was beside Matteo, sleeping on her side, one knee up, her hand splayed possessively across his beautiful chest.

It was the wedding day.

And she didn't feel sad at all. There was no longing for her own canceled day. In fact, it seemed like a perfect day to celebrate the glories of love.

She was aware she should feel exhausted. They had barely slept. They had so much to say to each other. It felt as if they needed to squeeze it all into one more day.

He had told her about his carefree days as a young boy, exploring the Alps with his father.

She had told him about her large, traditional family.

And then about Arthur, and the fact that her longing for the traditions of her family was so strong that she might have read qualities into his character that he didn't have, and accepted things in the relationship she should have never accepted.

She had told Matteo about practically being dumped at the altar.

Not as if she was telling him of a terrible tragedy, but as if it was a wonderful story about how something that seemed bad could turn into something good.

"My niece Amey likes gaming," Matteo had said to her. "She told me that in a game as soon as you hit trouble, or more bad guys, you know you're going the right way."

As she looked at his sleeping face now—so extraordinarily handsome, so beautifully familiar to her—Marlee had never been more certain that every single thing she had once judged as bad had just been a way of getting her life on the right path.

Still, as much as she would have liked to linger, taking in his face and the texture of his skin and the gorgeous male aroma of him, she had a great deal to do, and that was before factoring in Fiona's inevitable last-minute errands.

She left Matteo quietly, so as to not wake him. Then, bathed in the first pink stains of dawn, she made her way across the resort to her own cabana.

The morning seemed to shimmer with the same brilliant light that was shining within her.

She took the bridesmaid's dress down from where it was still hanging in the bathroom. She laid it out carefully. And then, using her handy sewing kit, she began to take the dress apart.

Finally done, she put on the dress.

Marlee looked at herself in the full-length mirror behind the bathroom door. She smiled.

Matteo's first waking thought was that Marlee wasn't there. He could feel her absence deeply, as if something essential was gone from his world.

He buried his nose in her pillow and let her fragrance fill him.

He thought of all the confidences they had exchanged last night. And the other things, too.

He was aware he could not wait to see her again, as if his life would not be complete until the moment he laid eyes on her.

As it turned out, that was at the wedding.

For the first time, as he gathered with Mike and the other members of the groom's party on the beach, he saw the payoff of all of Fiona's persnickety pursuit of perfection.

Because that was exactly what she had achieved. Perfection.

Framed by an arbor arch threaded through with gardenias was perfect white sand and an endless blue sea.

The guests were beginning to arrive and take their seats on the white chairs, a pink silk bow on the back of each.

Mike took his place under the arbor, and just as they

had rehearsed—who would have ever thought Matteo would be grateful for that endless rehearsal, but he was—they lined up beside him.

For a panicked moment, Matteo thought he might have been so besotted with Marlee that he'd forgotten the ring. He felt in his pocket and drew in a deep breath. No, there it was.

The notes of a piano filled the air. It wasn't a recording. He noticed the real piano and he had to give kudos to Fiona. The music rising to join the lap of waves and the call of birds could not be more beautiful.

Kathy, the maid of honor, came through a break in the hedge and walked—glided—through the sand and up the aisle between the chairs. He recognized the color of that dress.

Behind her came Brenda, and again, the color triggered his memory of the first time he had seen Marlee.

And then—his mouth dropped, and he quickly slammed it shut—came Marlee.

She was wearing the same dress that he had first met her in. Except that it wasn't the same dress at all. The neckline had been altered, and the sleeves removed. Every puff and every ruffle had been stripped from it.

It clung to her like mist, and Marlee carried herself like a queen. Matteo was not sure he had ever seen a dress that so perfectly revealed the beauty and the boldness of the person who was wearing it.

Her hair was piled up on top of her head, and her makeup showed off everything about her, the height of those cheekbones, the bow of her mouth, and especially the depth and mystery held in those green eyes.

He felt as if everything faded, except her.

But then the subdued gasp of the crowd made him draw his eyes away from her. Fiona had entered the pathway.

Her dress and veil were extraordinary, but it was the light in her face that kept everyone's gaze on her.

Matteo glanced at Mike.

And felt pure envy for the look on his best friend's face.

Matteo was shocked by what he felt next.

A kind of devastation. *This* was what Marlee deserved. A man prepared to commit to her. A man ready to devote his life to making her dreams come true. A man who wanted a future that held only her.

Last night, lying in the circle of his arms, she had told him who she really was and what she really needed.

Instead, what had Matteo given Marlee?

An affair.

A surrender, not to all the things she deserved, all the things that she had revealed to him last night she longed for—like tradition and family—but to base impulses.

He knew now what he didn't know then. She'd been betrayed by love. And still, she had come to him with hope.

She had never said that. That she *hoped*.

But he knew her now, and he knew she hoped for all

the things a woman like her would hope for: a fairytale ending. Something with the word *forever* in it.

What he had given her, he thought, shocked, was a place that did not honor her.

Or himself.

Look at how they had been the day they had first made love. Hiding from their friends, as if they had something to be ashamed of.

Marlee arrived at the arbor. She looked at him. A smile, with their every intimacy in it, was directed at him.

Apparently she was not going to hide anymore. The dress said that.

And neither was he.

It was never too late to be a better man, Matteo decided then and there. Or even the best man, just like he was at this wedding.

He could become worthy of all that they had shared.

He could become worthy of this remarkable woman who had trusted him—of all people—with her broken self.

Fiona arrived at the altar and handed off her bouquet. She and Mike joined hands and faced each other.

The ceremony went off as practiced. It was flawless and without a hitch. They kissed to thunderous approval from those gathered to witness the miracle of love.

Her bouquet was handed back to her, and the bride and groom moved off to the side where a white cane desk had been set up on the beach. They signed the register, and then Fiona gathered her bouquet and stood to one side.

As the piano played on, each member of the wedding party took their turn signing the documents.

But then, just as that was finishing, the air was split with an ear-piercing bray.

Down the same path that the bridal party had walked down, came Mackay leading Henri.

The donkey was obviously angry. He was kicking his nicely painted back hooves to the side, nearly hitting the chairs. The guests were diving out of their seats to get out of his way.

Matteo abandoned the wedding party and raced down the aisle to help Mackay. "What's wrong?"

"He's missing Calamity," Mackay told him tightly. "They've never been apart. I couldn't even load him in the trailer without her. Listen."

Matteo cocked his head.

He could hear a smashing sound from the resort parking lot, located right above this entrance to the beach.

"It's Calamity," Mackay said. "In the trailer. By herself. Love-stricken."

Matteo listened to one final smashing sound. And then, not even his strength and Mackay's combined could hold the love-maddened Henri, who broke free of them, turned and stampeded up the aisle, back the way he had come.

But now, Calamity burst in through the hedge.

The donkeys raced toward each other. They skidded to a halt. They rubbed noses. They kicked up their heels, turned and ran down the path through the arbor, which was not wide enough for both of them to be side by side. It toppled. The minister sprang out of the way. The wedding party scattered. Mike threw himself on top of Fiona to protect her from the rampaging donkeys.

CHAPTER SEVENTEEN

HENRI AND CALAMITY cavorted up and down the beach braying loudly and kicking up their heels.

And then, suddenly, they were done.

As if they had created no mischief at all, they clomped back to Mackay, and sending him looks that could be interpreted as faintly apologetic, began to feast on the bridesmaids' bouquets that had been abandoned on the cane registration table.

Mike helped Fiona up out of the sand.

The decision to wreck the dress seemed as if it might have been made for her. It was crushed and had sand ground into it.

It felt as if the whole world had gone still, every single person focused on her.

Matteo, like everyone else, held his breath.

Waiting.

For tears.

For a tantrum.

For the bride to express the inevitable frustration at the moment she had built to for so long being ruined.

Instead, as Fiona stared up at Mike, her expression softened with tenderness. She looked at her new husband with an expression of pure wonder on her face.

"You saved me," she said, brushing at his suit jacket. "You put my life ahead of your own."

"That might be overstating it a bit," Mike said. Matteo could see how his friend's pragmatic nature was the perfect foil for Fiona's more dramatic one.

"What on earth is going on here?" Mike asked, running a hand through his hair. "Donkeys? Seriously?"

They all watched as Henri and Calamity contentedly finished off the bridesmaids' bouquets, flower stems dripping from their mouths.

"Um," Marlee offered, "the one on the right is Henri. He's here for the photos."

"But he's not a horse," Fiona said, a frown creasing her brow. Matteo wondered if perhaps they were going to have their bride meltdown moment, after all.

"Don't tell him," Marlee suggested in a stage whisper, and then, as a distraction, "Look at his hooves!"

Fiona crept a little closer to the donkey and looked.

And then, the best thing of all happened.

She beamed. And then Fiona laughed. Henri noticed her—or more accurately her bouquet—and shuffled over. She held it out to him.

Now the perfect gentleman, Henri bobbed his head and nibbled his acceptance of the bride's offering.

"Best wedding moment *ever*," one of the guests said.

And the beach reverberated with sounds of applause that rivaled the enthusiastic approbation that had been given to the first kiss.

One thing about getting disaster out of the way early, Marlee decided, was that everyone relaxed after that.

The worst had already happened.

Except it wasn't really the worst.

It was just one of those obstacles that showed you that you were probably on the right path.

Marlee thought if she lived to be a hundred she would never forget the look on Fiona's face when she had gazed at her groom after he had thrown his body over her to protect her from perceived harm.

The donkeys also broke the ice as the guests swarmed them, making a fuss and taking pictures. Laughter filled the gathering and everyone was engaged with each other.

Marlee had a feeling the wedding photos—both the spontaneous ones and the official ones—were going to be the best ever. Award-worthy, no doubt.

Or maybe it was just that her own feelings were painting everything around her in shades of joy.

Because something had shifted between her and Matteo, too. How they felt about each other didn't feel as if it should be kept a secret anymore.

It didn't feel as if it *could* be kept a secret anymore.

It was spilling out of them. In the way they looked at each other. In the way they found excuses to touch each other. In the way they laughed together.

By the time the meal was done and the toasts completed and the dancing began, it felt as if they had sent out announcement cards.

Lovers.

Marlee danced with him the way she had danced to the sounds of calypso at the street restaurant.

She came into herself.

He had eyes only for her. He acted as though he were enchanted.

And he was so darned sexy! She could not wait to claim him as her own again tonight. And then, they would talk about the future. What they would do after they left Coconut Cay. How they would work out the challenges and logistics of meeting.

He had a *jet.* That should make everything easier.

The laughter nearly bubbled out of her.

Marlee Copeland was in love with a man with a jet.

Love.

Despite the party going in full swing around her, everything in her went still. It was way too soon for that. Wasn't it? But she had never felt this way before.

Not ever.

Not even when she'd been planning on marrying another man.

Who had, she reminded herself, walked away from her. If she felt this way about Matteo after just a few days, how was it going to feel when he came to his senses? When the magic they had experienced here was but a distant memory?

This wasn't the real world.

Not one single thing they had experienced here had anything to do with their real lives. He was the man with the jet, the international business tycoon.

She was the unexciting librarian from Seattle.

The thoughts threatened to crush the joy that was bubbling in her.

You didn't go from Arthur Drabeck to Matteo Keller. In the real world a woman like her didn't have a hope with a guy like this. Who did she think she was?

Love? Matteo had never mentioned the word *love*. Why would he? She, hopelessly naive, had fallen for a man who was enjoying a tryst with a willing partner. He knew the rules. He moved in a superfast world that included a jet and topless beaches. A world that she probably couldn't even imagine.

It was she who was breaking the rules by falling for him. By wanting more than he had ever offered.

The devastating fact was, once they stepped out of this bubble, it was over.

But she was not going to be devastated. Not just yet. In the days and weeks ahead, there would be plenty of time for that.

But now, Marlee decided, *this* was her moment. It felt as much like it was her moment as it was Fiona's.

This was the pinnacle of her whole life.

Right now.

This time she would be the one to walk away, before reality set in and Matteo realized the humiliating truth. It had been a fairy tale few days. She had become something she wasn't really. It was inevitable that he would come to realize that.

How much better to leave it like this? On a high note? Everything about them shimmering and untarnished? His memory of her of someone far bolder and more exciting than she really was or could ever hope to be.

She allowed the music back into that moment of utter stillness. She danced, immersed in the intensity of the experience. She knew they were counting down to midnight.

And then, the princess he had made her became an ordinary woman again.

The coach became a pumpkin.

The frills would probably magically reappear on her dress!

But regardless, it would be over. She had to make certain of that. She had to leave with her dignity intact, not as a woman who had lost her heart.

She danced as she wanted Matteo to remember her. She was uninhibited, sexy, sure of herself.

She danced as a woman who was memorizing every single thing about him. The way his eyes held hers, the curve of his lips, the flop of his hair over his brow, the utter sexiness of the way he moved.

The feeling of bliss, with its counterpoint of loss, was exhilarating and excruciating at the same time.

Be brave, she ordered herself, when the sense of loss would try to overwhelm her. *Just for a little while longer.*

She intended to make the next moments the best of her life. Given what the last few days had held, she was aware that was quite the challenge she had set for herself.

As if the universe understood the momentous occasion of a goodbye, the music slowed and the love song that played was heartbreaking and romantic.

His arms closed around her. He pulled her against himself.

She felt the heat of his body and the beat of his heart. She felt his breath on her hair, and his hand on the small of her back.

She breathed in his scent, hoping to take it in deeply enough that it became part of her, so she could remember it forever.

The music ended.

She reached up and took his lips with her own.

She tasted him as deeply as one human being could taste another. She savored him. She memorized him. She drew his essence deep into herself, an ember to warm her on the cold days of winter ahead.

A chime rang.

Smiling—the tears would come later—she took a step back from him.

"It's midnight," she said. "And I'm Cinderella. The ball is over."

And then she turned. She forced herself not to run, but to walk away from him slowly, not looking back. Unlike the fairy tale, there was no glass slipper to leave as a clue for him to follow.

Because life was not, after all, anything like the fairy tales.

CHAPTER EIGHTEEN

STUNNED, MATTEO WATCHED as Marlee walked regally past the staff carrying in trays of food for the midnight snack. The darkness of the tropical night folded around her, and she was gone.

What the hell had just happened?

The taste of her was still on his lips, and it felt as if the imprint of her body was seared into his own.

He went to follow her, and then he stopped himself.

Obviously, she was being the sensible one. They needed a cooling-off period. *He* needed a cooling-off period.

Just hours ago, he'd been thinking he'd done it all wrong. That he had dishonored her. That he had needed to do things differently. That he *would* do things differently. What did he think he should do instead? Ask her to marry him?

Insanity.

She'd been right to walk away.

They'd known each other *days*.

But it really bothered him that while he had, apparently, completely lost his mind, she still had good sense about her.

So, no, he was not going to chase her.

Marlee was right. It had been a fairy tale, but she was wrong if she thought she was the one under the spell! This island, from the moment he had walked down that path and found her on it, had put him under an enchantment.

It felt urgent to get away from here, to be restored to the person he had been a few short days ago. Then, maybe he'd be able to do what he did best. What people counted on him to do. What he was famous for, really.

Make a rational decision.

Not be swept along by the powerful currents of attraction and emotion.

Mike appeared in front of him. The look on his face warned Matteo he was not the only one whose magical evening had just come crashing to an end.

"Fiona's just had devastating news," Mike said quietly. "Her mother's had a heart attack. It's serious. Our flight isn't scheduled until late tomorrow afternoon. Even with extenuating circumstances, I'm pretty sure there's only the one flight out every day."

Matteo gave one final look at where Marlee had disappeared, and he drew in a deep breath. There.

Who was he kidding?

He couldn't have resisted the temptation of going to her if she was only steps away from him.

He probably would have ended up *begging.*

The thought was repulsive to him. It was an *attraction.* He was not powerless over it. And he especially wouldn't be powerless over it if he put some distance—physical distance and lots of it—between them.

Selfishly, he realized Fiona and Mike's crisis had just become his perfect escape.

"I'll take you," Matteo said to Mike. "We can use the jet."

Mike tilted his head at him. "You know, I still think of you as my college roommate, that guy who could figure out how to suspend a car from the bottom of a bridge with a budget of zero. I totally forgot there was a jet."

This was what Matteo loved about being with old friends.

His college buddies, in particular, rarely saw the trappings he'd accumulated. Instead, they saw just him.

And oddly, even though she knew of the trappings, it felt as if Marlee had never seen them, either. Just him.

And yet there she was, walking away.

What did that say?

"Thank you," Mike said. "We can be ready right away. We'll just grab passports and essentials. I'll ask the other members of the wedding party to pack up the rest of our stuff and get it home."

As he and Mike gathered a nearly hysterical Fiona and shepherded her toward the plane, Matteo knew it was better this way. Marlee had referenced a fairy tale. They had been on their own cloud, out of touch with reality, for days. Time for the landing, painful as that promised to be.

For one of the world's most respected businessmen, he did not think he had made a rational decision almost since his arrival on this tiny cay.

Except maybe one. This one. To be of service to his friends in their time of need.

Was he being of service? Or was he escaping the enchantment that had held him captive?

In less than an hour, Matteo had tossed his few items into a bag, a flight plan had been filed and they were onboard. Fiona sat in a forward seat. Mike snapped the belt for her. She was still in her wedding gown, covered in a blanket, shivering despite the warmth still seeping through the open cabin door.

"Who doesn't invite their own mother to their wedding?" she whispered. "I was worried she'd wreck it. I deserve this."

Mike made a shushing sound like one might use to comfort a child. "It's lucky she wasn't here. A hotel isn't the best place to have a heart attack."

Fiona seemed to consider it, and it seemed to bring her comfort.

Mike put his arms around her and she sighed into his chest.

But her pain reminded Matteo of the loss of his own mother.

It reminded him, starkly, of the danger of loss always lurking in the corridors, waiting to strike at the most unexpected moments.

As Matteo looked out the window, the lights of Coconut Cay, the safest place on earth, winked off one by one, until the island was lost in a sea of darkness.

He was aware of the irony. It was not, for him, the safest place on earth. The most dangerous thing of all had happened to him here.

The protective layer he had built around his heart had fallen away.

And love had crept past those broken barriers.

Matteo contemplated that word.

Love.

He looked over at the sobbing Fiona and remembered his father.

His father had been one man before the loss of his mother, and another after. His father had fallen on the sword that was hiding in love's cloak.

He couldn't possibly love Marlee, Matteo told himself sternly. They barely knew each other.

And yet that did not feel like the truth, at all.

Which made this quick exit a blessing in disguise. What would knowing her longer do to him?

And then his memory dredged up this: his family picnicking on a wildflower-strewn hillside in the Alps.

His mother was chasing his sisters through the meadow, and shrieks of laughter filled the air.

He and his father were on the picnic blanket, and his father's eyes followed his mother as if he was unable to look away.

People said we were foolish. We got married within weeks of meeting. But you just know.

You just know, Matteo thought, like a fatal flaw that ran through the family. And then he reached for his headphones. To shut out the sounds of Fiona weeping softly.

And the weeping of his own heart as it broke in two.

So, Marlee thought as she packed up Fiona's belongings, she'd been wrong.

Because she had thought the donkey debacle had meant that a wedding disaster had been gotten out of the way early.

Of course, that was based on a thoroughly naive assumption that life was fair.

The truth was that disaster was random. There was no catastrophe roster, where some benign being checked his list and said, *Oh, I see they've already had their run of bad luck. No more for them. Their quota is used up.*

Now Matteo was flying Fiona and Mike home. They were already gone. Marlee had heard the roar of the jet engine split the quiet of the night.

It meant there were no second chances. Maybe part of her had hoped he would follow her and return the symbolic slipper, after all.

But there were fairy tales, and then there was reality, and reality had returned with a vengeance.

Brenda came into the room. "I just heard from

Fiona. Her mother survived the night. I guess it's still touch and go, though."

"I'm glad they got there in time."

"Thanks to your dreamboat."

Marlee shot her a look. Was there just the slightest sarcastic emphasis on *your*? Or were her insecurities making her read things that weren't meant?

And yet, just beneath those insecurities, was there a new strength, too?

Marlee might have been kidding herself about Matteo, but something felt real and true about the woman she had become.

She intended to find out what was true about herself, and those few days with Matteo were what had given her the courage to do that.

To be what she had never been before this time on Coconut Cay.

Brave.

And that was the one ingredient that she had come to know was absolutely required to live a life fully.

Seattle, in November, was probably the dreariest city in the world. Weather roiled up and off the Pacific. The rain fell in ice-cold sheets. Clouds, gray and ominous, shrouded the nearby mountains. After the warmth and colors of Coconut Cay, the November nastiness should have seemed even worse than it normally did.

But the strange thing for Marlee was that it did not seem nasty.

Seattle—maybe her whole life—felt as if she had sleep-walked through it, and now she was wide-awake.

She had expected she might return from her romantic rendezvous on Coconut Cay to find herself more reserved, more fade-into-the-background, more insecure, more rigid in the habits that made her feel safe and secure in the world.

Instead, she was seeing the whole world with different eyes.

Marlee was well aware that she could have felt broken.

But that she didn't.

Some might say she made a choice to be brave instead of broken, but she didn't feel she was making choices so much as acknowledging she was changed in some fundamental way that made her embrace *everything.*

She found herself chatting with neighbors she had ignored in the past. She walked in the rain with no umbrella, loving how it soaked her hair. She said yes to a kayak lesson at a local pool from an expert who had presented at the library.

Fiona's mom, Mary, was released from the hospital, and Marlee dropped by and enjoyed reminiscing with her about the old neighborhood.

Marlee deepened other friendships with women at work and in her book club. And Fiona's rocky relationship with her family—and her close call with her mother—made Marlee appreciate her own family more.

She spent time with her mom and dad, appreciative of the solidness of their relationship, even as she realized the safety of it no longer appealed to her.

She made a full stop at a colorful poster that appeared in the library foyer one morning. It was advertising dance classes, and Marlee pulled off one of the tabs with a phone number on it.

And then she actually called it!

And then she actually signed up for dance classes. And loved them!

She thought missing Matteo would go away. They had only known each other for a few days.

But it didn't. She ached for him: to share these stories with him, to make new stories with him at her side.

One day, she was straightening a closet when the suitcase she had taken to the wedding on Coconut Cay fell off the top rack. After she put it back, she noticed something on the floor.

She picked it up.

It was the cigar. She held it to her nose, then ever so tentatively touched it to her tongue. Had she hoped she would taste Matteo on it?

She did not. Only the sweet, smoky taste of the wine the cigar had been dipped in. She thought of the woman she had been that night, and it was almost like looking at a stranger, and a childlike one, at that.

Had she really believed that sipping rum and toying with a cigar could change everything about you? She tucked the cigar into her bedside table.

As the dreary days of November turned to December, she still wished, every single day, that he would get in touch.

And when he didn't, she celebrated what he had given her: a verve for life that was like nothing she had ever felt before.

Fiona called and asked her to attend her and Mike's Christmas party.

Marlee's heart nearly stopped.

Would Matteo be there?

Of course he wouldn't! Not even international jet-setters flew to another country just for a Christmas party, did they?

"I know why you're hesitating," Fiona said.

"You do?" Marlee thought of how she had kissed Matteo at midnight and felt her cheeks burn.

But she wasn't sure it was with embarrassment. Maybe passion.

"I was awful," Fiona said. "A horrible person. Mike says he's surprised I have any friends left, and I'm darned lucky he married me. But he's forgiven me, because I have the best excuse ever. Can you guess?"

"Oh! Are you—"

"Yes! Pregnant. A complete surprise! I had no idea. No wonder I was such a wreck. And you were so patient with me. And you found the donkey! I can't wait to show you the photos. I just got them this week. Please come."

Marlee couldn't think of a way to ask if Matteo would be there, so she just accepted the invitation and decided to act as if he would be there even though she knew it was a one-in-a-million chance.

She bought the most gorgeous dress she had ever owned. It was red, in keeping with the holiday spirit, but other than that, there was nothing Christmassy about it.

It was predawn mist, made into fabric. The neckline was daring, and the length was bold. She bought amazing heels to go with it.

She curled her hair and put on makeup. As she looked at herself in the mirror, Marlee was so aware of who she was.

Strong and confident.

And very, very beautiful.

Fiona and Mike were hosting the party at their new condo. It was already packed when Marlee arrived, and it took nearly half an hour to sort through all the people and figure out Matteo was not among them.

Still, all that mingling in search of him had brought her in contact with a lot of people.

After her initial disappointment that Matteo wasn't there, she relaxed. She was shocked by how much men liked her. She was shocked by how good she was at flirting!

And dancing. The lessons had helped her confidence, but she also carried something within herself from that wild street party and the fairy-tale wedding on Coconut Cay. She didn't feel in any way inhibited.

She relished the attention. It egged her on. And she found it so easy to let go, have fun.

"Here she is," Fiona called. "Marlee. Look who I've got on Boom-Boom."

What the heck was Boom-Boom?

Marlee did a whirling turn in the crush of people on the dance floor to find Fiona with her phone pointed at her.

She realized there was something on the screen of the phone. And then she went stock-still as she realized.

Boom-Boom was that new video app.

Matteo.

"Marlee," he said.

He was thousands of miles away. He was talking to her through a screen. His voice felt as if it touched her.

"Matteo."

She was shocked by how he looked. His hair was too long. He looked gaunt. There was something haunted in his eyes when he looked at her.

And hungry.

And yet his tone was cool. "It's good to see you," he said. "I'm sorry. I seem to have a bad—"

And then the picture died.

And so did all the fun she had been having.

CHAPTER NINETEEN

MATTEO STARED AT the blank screen of his phone. Breaking that connection had been the hardest thing he had ever done.

Marlee had been so beautiful. So radiant.

As Fiona moved through the crowds with her phone, he had spotted Marlee well before she knew he was watching. He had seen her dancing. If it was possible, she had come even more into herself than she had on the cay.

Marlee's movements were totally sensual, made even more so by her confidence and her comfort with herself.

Matteo had seen the look on the man's face that she was dancing with.

He was enraptured with her.

And then she had turned, and there had been that moment's hesitation before she knew it was him.

Sometimes a man came face-to-face with his own weakness.

Because the look on her face made him want to beg, just as he had known he would have if he had stayed on Coconut Cay the night of the wedding.

She had been shocked to see him, and then the shock had melted to a pure welcome, which had made him feel weak.

Be with me.

He was changed since he had come back from Coconut Cay, and not in a good way. Marlee, it seemed obvious, had changed in good ways. She radiated confidence.

He, on the other hand, did not miss the fact his sisters were exchanging worried glances behind his back.

But here was the terrifying truth: if three days with Marlee had made him feel this empty, this bereft for a life without her in it, what would following these feelings do?

Because if he was to give in to the temptation to see what a life with Marlee held, one day, no matter how hard they tried to hold it off, they would say goodbye to each other.

And if he had known her a lifetime, instead of a few days, he would be like his father. It would not be survivable.

And what if he went first? What if he went first and left her to live in a world they had made bright together, and now there was nothing but darkness remaining?

Not, Matteo reminded himself, that Marlee had looked like she was suffering in the world without him in it. Not in the way he was suffering in the world without her.

Still, he'd done the right thing. To shut off the phone. To not feed his hunger to drink her in, to look at her, to let that unexpected glimpse of her feed his spirit.

He was aware he was not as strong as he wanted to be.

Because he went to his computer. He went to the photos that Fiona had just sent him. And he knew another sleepless night lay ahead of him as he drank his fill of the wedding pictures.

The bride and groom interested him only slightly.

It was her, Marlee, that he went to, again and again. One picture in particular made him look at it endlessly, trying unsuccessfully to grasp some secret it held.

"But we haven't looked at the photos yet," Fiona protested when Marlee announced, as soon as she could do so without being too obvious the call with Matteo had upset her, that she had to go.

"Let's do it another time," Marlee said with fake brightness. "There's so much going on here tonight. We have a bit of catching up to do. We haven't had a chance to talk about the baby, even."

"Let me see you to the door."

They stepped outside the noise of the party. Rain pattered on the porch roof.

"Thanks for going to see my mom," Fiona said. "I love that about you. You really care about people."

She *did* really care about people, and the look on Matteo's face was making her feel distressed.

"Did you notice?" Fiona said. "She's sober. And so excited about being a grandmother. She wasn't even mad at me about having a wedding she couldn't come to because she's scared to fly. She said she knew I did it on purpose. That it was the wake-up call that she needed."

"I'm glad for you. Things tend to work out, don't they?"

Did they? She wished she believed that just a little more strongly. After seeing Matteo, she suddenly wasn't that sure.

"I have something for you." Fiona handed Marlee a gift.

It was wrapped but obviously one of the wedding photos. Marlee decided to wait until she got home to open it.

"You look so gorgeous," Fiona said. "I've always known you had that hiding in you."

Not that your choice of dress had been a clue, Marlee thought dryly.

They hugged and promised to get together again soon. And then Marlee went home to her troubled thoughts.

Sitting alone in her living room, she opened Fiona's gift.

She had expected a framed picture of the bride and groom. But instead, it was a picture of herself and

Henri. She was nose to nose with the adorable troublemaker, bestowing a kiss.

She radiated light.

A woman in love. And not with a donkey, either.

And Matteo, slightly out of focus, was in the background. But even out of focus, there was a particular look on his face as he watched her.

It was so clear he was a man who cherished her.

The truth was evident in the gaze that rested on her—possessive, protective, utterly entranced.

It was not a look that said—in any way—that she wasn't good enough. And it wasn't a look that suggested that their worlds were stratospheres apart, separated by chasms that could not be crossed.

Matteo looked so beautiful in this picture. As light-filled as she herself looked. Confident. *Sure.*

And yet, tonight he had looked so *awful.*

There was no other way to describe the brief glimpse she had caught of his face before the connection died. She went to bed thinking about it, distressed by it, trying to decipher it.

It could be anything. A bad day on the markets. A poor business decision. Expensive problems with the jet! There were a thousand things that could have been troubling Matteo, and she had no hope of guessing what it was.

But when Marlee woke suddenly, in the middle of the night, she *knew.*

She knew what was troubling Matteo. The look on his face had been the look of a man who had touched a dream he knew he would not ever allow himself to have.

And Marlee was pretty sure that dream was her.

And that every single thing she had done since she got back to Seattle—her embracing of life—had been in preparation for the biggest challenge of all. It was as if she had been in training.

She had to be more confident of herself than she had ever been.

She had to know her strength.

She had to be braver than she had ever been.

She had to rescue Matteo from the lonely life he had set himself up for. With her blankets wrapped around her against the damp chill in her apartment, she went and found her computer.

It occurred to her that the third barrier—her own sense of inadequacy—had already been overcome.

That left only the physical barrier of distance.

It seemed paltry in comparison. She looked up flights to Switzerland. The closer you got to Christmas, the less choice there was and the more expensive they became.

There was one on Monday.

Three days away.

She hadn't gotten that brave. She could not be that spontaneous. She could not just travel halfway around the world because she thought a photo had revealed a secret to her.

She told herself it was crazy. Worse than crazy. Absolute insanity.

She had never been to Zurich.

That's what map apps are for, an inner voice told her with shocking confidence.

She didn't have a clue where he lived.

You know the name of his company, though.

He had an international lifestyle. She didn't even know if he would be there when she arrived.

Could there be anything better than chasing true love around the globe?

Stop it, Marlee told her inner voice. *We have to be practical.*

Fiona and Mike's wedding had already nearly emptied her meager savings account.

Plus, she couldn't just not show up for work. She wasn't that kind of person. People counted on her to be dependable.

And the days before Christmas were so busy at the library. In fact, on Monday they were having a special guest—a wildlife refuge was going to bring a real live reindeer to story time. How could she not be there to supervise that?

But not one rational thought could stop her.

When the button popped up saying "Purchase seat", she pointed her mouse at it, lined it up, took a deep breath and clicked.

It felt, for all the world, as if she was a warrior who had just let loose an arrow.

She snapped the computer shut and waited for the fear and doubt to set in. She went back to bed. She lay there with her eyes open.

She hoped she could get her money back.

But when morning came, Marlee was shocked to find she was no more interested in getting her money back, no more willing to back down, than she had been when she had clicked on that purchase button.

She didn't really lose her nerve until she was in the back of a cab in a foreign country. In her other life, a reindeer would be entering the library right about now!

Everything she saw reminded Marlee she was not in her own world. The cab driver had greeted her in three languages before settling on English. There was snow on the ground, which was rare in rainy Seattle. To her American eyes, Zurich had a fairy-tale-like atmosphere, with its old castle-like structures, cobbled roads, twisting streets.

She was dropped off in front of a very old building. There was a beautifully carved sign hanging over the street on a wrought iron arm—Monte Rosa Alpen.

So she was in the right place. There was a storefront and offices above it. She went to the display window and looked in.

There was an array of outdoor items: cross-country skis, snowshoes, what might have been a survival stove of some sort.

But what caught her eye was a beautiful, belted, woven jacket.

Oddly, that was what gave her courage. She wasn't a stranger here. She knew about this company. She knew about the great-great-great-grandmother who had started it.

What a courageous woman that long-ago Rosa must have been, striking out in a man's world.

As she opened the door, Marlee felt as if she might be channeling some of that long-ago courage.

The entry to the store was on her left and a narrow staircase went up to the right. She followed it and came to a glass door with the company name emblazoned on it.

What was she going to say?

No doubt some snooty secretary would send her on her way. Matteo probably worked in an impenetrable fortress. He was rich. He was powerful. Even if you had traversed the globe to do it, seeing him wasn't as easy as just waltzing into his office. Was it?

Taking a deep breath, she opened the door and stepped in.

The office space was soothing. The old bricks were exposed, and there was deep, inviting, leather furniture. There was a striking photo on the wall of the sun rising over a mountain, and Marlee assumed it must be Monte Rosa.

There was a counter and a woman behind it.

She looked up, startled, obviously not expecting anyone so early.

"Yes?" she called.

Marlee found herself frozen. She didn't know what to say. She debated turning and running. Her heart was beating so hard.

He could be anywhere, but Marlee could *feel* it. Matteo was here. Somewhere. Possibly, just feet from her.

The woman's face softened. "You're her," she said softly.

"Wh-who?" Marlee managed to stammer.

"The woman in the photo. I'm Emma."

"His sister. What photo?"

"You know who I am," Emma said approvingly. "He's spoken to you about his family. Go. Second door on the right. Don't knock."

Marlee went down the hallway. She felt as if she was in a dream, floating. She opened the door and stepped inside it. She closed it behind her.

Matteo was behind a desk.

He glanced up.

There were shadows in his face that had not been there before. His hair was too long, and he had not shaved.

Beloved, she thought.

His expression was stunned, and in that moment, Marlee saw everything she needed to see. She saw the reason she had come.

His expression quickly shut down.

"This is a surprise," he said, as if it wasn't a good one.

"Isn't it?"

She came toward the desk, paused in front of it, and then changed course. She scooted behind it. He got up from his chair, backing away from her. He shoved a framed photo facedown first.

"What are you doing here?"

She picked up the photo. She smiled. It was the same one Fiona had given her.

"This really is a good picture," she said.

"It's okay."

"Why do you have it on your desk?"

He was silent.

"Is it because you love me madly?" she asked him softly.

"Don't be ridiculous. We barely know each other."

"Barely," she said. "That reminds me of swimming in your pool."

He actually blushed. He looked flustered.

"Why do you have a picture of someone you *barely* know on your desk, Matteo?"

"I like the composition," he said. "The donkey."

"Uh-huh." That could be insulting, but she was not insulted. The truth felt as if it shimmered in the air between them.

"Do you miss me?" she asked softly.

Silence.

"Do memories of being in each other's arms keep you awake at night?"

Silence.

"Do you dream of my lips on your eyes and your ears, on your chest and your—"

"Stop it!" he said, his voice a croak. "This is all so wrong."

CHAPTER TWENTY

"WRONG?" MARLEE ASKED MATTEO, stunned.

"It's not what you deserve. An affair? You? The world's most decent girl?"

"I was trying out being an outlaw," she reminded him.

"Well, it was a poor fit. It became more than evident that you are not that kind of woman."

"I've realized that. In fact, it seems almost funny that once upon a time I believed a cigar and a sip of rum could change something fundamental about me."

He nodded. "You're decent to the core," he said. "It's obvious."

"Was it when we were swimming in your pool that it became that obvious to you?" Marlee goaded him a bit.

"That was no more who you are than the rum and the cigar."

She smiled. "I disagree. You see, smoking and drinking are just outside things. They could never change what's inside a person. But that day in the pool—"

He interrupted her, obviously not wanting to think about the skinny-dip in his pool!

"I knew," he said firmly, stubbornly, "as soon as I saw Fiona in her wedding dress how wrong it all was. That's what you deserve. Underneath it all, you're an old-fashioned girl. You deserve forever. Commitment. I thought you had realized it, too. I thought that's why you did your Cinderella exit from the reception."

"No. Some old insecurities reared their ugly heads. They said I was making a fool of myself over you."

Matteo looked stricken. "You weren't," he said, making an effort to wipe the distressed look off his face. "In fact, you looked as if you'd embraced that part of yourself quite nicely when I saw you at Mike and Fiona's Christmas party."

"I think I have embraced lots of parts of myself quite nicely. That's what I'm trying to tell you, Matteo. When I got home, I realized it wasn't about changing myself with silly things like cigars and rum. It wasn't really about changing myself at all. It was about uncovering who I really was, inside, not outside. You gave me the courage to take that journey. To learn how to live."

He was silent.

"Can we talk about forever?" Marlee asked softly. "Since you brought it up?"

"Yes," he said harshly. "Let's talk about it. There's no such thing. Look at the marriage statistics. Abysmal."

He grabbed his phone out of his pocket, tapped away furiously. "Fifty percent end in separation or divorce." He held up the screen so she could see the cold, hard evidence. It felt as if he was holding up a shield.

"That means fifty percent don't," Marlee pointed out mildly. "My parents have been happily married for thirty years. That's my model for being married."

"You're thinking about being married?" he said. "Who said anything about being married?"

"Uh, I think you might have mentioned it."

"Not in the context of *us*," he said. "Like you and me. Married."

"I wasn't suggesting tomorrow. I thought we could have a courtship first. You know, nice and old-fashioned. Exactly what you've decided I deserve."

He was silent. But she thought she saw a faint flicker of hope in his eyes.

"Your parents would have been married forever, too," she said softly. "If your mom had made it."

"Well, she didn't!" he said.

And just like that, they were at the heart of the issue.

"Those few days with you, Matteo, gave me courage I've never had before to embrace life completely. To really live. To find out who I really was, and then to be that. That was your gift to me."

Still, he was silent.

"Do you know why I'm here?"

He shook his head, mute.

"To return that gift to you. To give you the courage to embrace life completely, to really live. To ask you to take the biggest risk of all. To risk loving me, even though there might be pain involved."

"The pain might be yours," he warned her.

Which, he seemed to realize, was not an out-and-out no. He glared at her.

"It might be," she agreed. "You'd like to protect me from that, wouldn't you?"

"I saw what happened to my father."

"Yes, you did. You're not just trying to protect yourself, are you? You're trying to protect me?"

After a long time, he nodded, accepting that he had been unmasked.

"If we can feel this strongly after such a short time," he said, his voice with rough edges to it, "what would it be like to lose each other? After a year? After ten years? After a lifetime?"

"We can't look at all the things that could happen. It would make it impossible to live life, let alone fall in love."

"It's part of what I do," he said stubbornly. "I'm a businessman. I do the cost-benefit analysis. I ferret out all the things that could go wrong."

"And where does choice figure into your calculations, my darling?"

He could have flinched at the use of the endearment. Instead, she watched as he softened toward her.

"Your father made a choice, Matteo, to let his pain break him instead of make him stronger. He made a choice not to see he had three beautiful children carrying the legacy of his and your mother's love into the future."

He was leaning toward her as she crossed what remained of the small distance between them.

She laid her forehead against his forehead and took both his hands in her own. The sensation of his skin against her skin was like a homecoming.

"I think," she said, ever so softly, "a bigger risk than not loving someone because they might die is dying a slow, painful death inside each and every day because you have not loved someone. Be brave, Matteo. We can write our own ending. Say yes."

His voice was a whisper, but it was enough.

"Yes."

She took his lips with her own, with welcome and hunger. At first, he answered, but then he pulled away.

"No," he said. "If we're going to have a happy ending, I must prove to myself I can be a better man—"

"I like the man you are now just fine," she assured him.

But he shook his head, vehement. "I can be everything you deserve. I want to treat you with complete respect and honor."

"I never felt disrespected or dishonored," she said.

"If I can't keep my hands off you, it clouds everything."

"But in the best possible way."

"No," he said. "It's going to be an old-fashioned courtship, worthy of you, or nothing at all."

"If those are your terms, I accept," she said and held out her hand.

When he took it, she pulled him to her and kissed him soundly on the mouth.

Finally, he pulled away from her. "You don't intend to make this easy, do you?"

"Absolutely not," she warned him. And then she took his lips again.

And he answered, and they explored peaks higher than Monte Rosa. Finally, he broke away.

Flustered, he glared at her.

"If you can keep your lips off me for a few minutes—"

"Nearly impossible, but I'll try."

"I can make a plan. For our courtship. How long can you stay?"

"If I combine my Christmas holidays with a few days of annual leave, I could stay until just after the New Year. But don't make a plan. Let's just be spontaneous."

"That's not a good idea," he decided. "That's what got us into trouble in the first place."

"Outlaws like me love a little trouble," she told him.

"Behave yourself. I'm going to introduce you to my sister."

That night, after being thoroughly wooed over the best dinner she had ever eaten, Marlee was dropped off by Matteo at the hotel room he'd insisted on booking.

His good-night kiss was disappointingly gentlemanly, despite her efforts to tempt him. Now, alone, which was also disappointing, she took in her accommodations.

The room was like a room in a palace. And she felt as if the prince had found her slipper after all.

And there was something quite adorable about him having to try so hard to keep his hands off her!

She called home.

"Um, Mom, I'm in Switzerland."

"What? Where? Have you lost your mind?"

"Maybe. I don't think I'm going to be home for Christmas."

"Not home for Christmas?" In her family this was akin to saying you would be playing a tambourine in an airport with a money collection basket at your feet.

"Mom, I've met someone."

"In Switzerland," her mother said, flatly.

"No, I met him at Fiona's wedding."

"The man from the picture!" her mother said, her whole tone changing entirely.

"What? What picture?"

"Fiona has some posted online on Chatter or whatever that app is called."

"You have the Chatter app?" Marlee asked, astounded.

"You're not the only one full of surprises," her mother said dryly, and then added, with relief in her voice, "That's totally different. You know him. He's friends with Fiona and Mike. You know what your father said when he saw the picture of you and that man and the donkey?"

"No, what did he say?"

"He said, there's the man who is going to marry our daughter."

Was her mother crying? "He did not," Marlee said.

"Do you want to ask him? James, it's Marlee. She's in Switzerland with that man from the picture."

"The news is on. Tell her hello."

That was more like it! Chatty Cathy, indeed.

"He never did like Arthur," her mother confided.

"Did you?"

Her mother hesitated. "I just wanted whatever would make you happy."

In the next few days, it felt as if Marlee discovered an even deeper well of happiness than she had found on Coconut Cay.

Because if there was one thing better than Switzerland at Christmastime, it was being in in Switzerland at Christmastime and being madly in love.

Matteo wanted to show her *everything*. They explored the Christmas markets in Zurich's old town and admired the fifty-foot Christmas tree at the train station. They went to Château de Chillon and Rhine Falls, and they took a dinner cruise on Lake Zurich.

They spent Christmas with his family and Marlee loved his sisters and his brothers-in-law and his two nieces and his two nephews instantly.

And they loved her.

"We've been waiting for you," Mia told her as they did dishes together after Christmas dinner. "I've never seen him so happy. You could not have given us a better gift."

One of the best parts of it all was the wonderful game they were playing, where he tried to resist the temptations she offered him—he still clung to the ridiculous notion that he must now be a perfect gentleman—and she played outlaw to his gentleman by trying to seduce him.

She was winning, and she found it so endearing that he felt guilty about that, as if by finding her totally irresistible he was failing her in some way!

The ten days went by in the blink of an eye.

But then, just as she thought the ball was over, and they were going to have to navigate the lonely days of a long-distance relationship, Matteo granted reprieve.

The day before she was supposed to fly home on the commercial flight she had booked, he informed her he'd cleared his schedule.

"I'm going to fly you home," he said.

She widened her eyes at him. "Does this mean we're going to join the mile-high club?"

She loved it when she did this to him. He was shocked. He sputtered.

"I'm going to meet your family. Have mercy, Marlee."

But she didn't.

Once they arrived, he insisted on staying in a hotel, and even though Marlee felt like that particular horse had already fled the barn, she could tell her father approved mightily of the arrangement.

His approval just made Matteo even more convinced that their courtship should remain unclouded by passion.

And made her more determined to test him at every turn.

It made the most delicious of tensions build between them as they explored her hometown together.

She kissed him madly at the top of the Space Needle, and again in the middle of the crowded Pike Place Market. She didn't work at the Central Library, but she took him to it anyway, because it was the flagship of the Seattle Public Library system and an architectural wonder. It felt particularly naughty dragging him behind the bookcases for an extended kiss!

They spent time at her apartment, but only if she promised to keep her hands off him. So they did ordinary things. Who knew that baking cookies and playing Scrabble and watching movies could make anticipation build to a place that was so painful you just had to give in to it?

It rained and it rained and it rained.

And her life had never felt so light-filled.

The day came when he had to leave. But the light did not go out. In fact, impossibly, beautifully, their relationship intensified.

He sent flowers.

She sent love notes.

They video-chatted deep into the night. He read

her poems. She read him a funny story. They used an app that allowed them to watch movies together.

He sent his jet and they spent a wonderful weekend in Venice. After they'd been apart, his resolve was absurdly easy to overcome. They never even got to ride a gondola! The next time he sent the jet, they went to Paris. She was sure the Eiffel Tower and the Louvre couldn't compare to drinking hot chocolate in bed, anyway.

Saying yes instead of no was really an affirmation that the whole universe seemed to turn its ear to, Matteo had discovered.

Of course, he was saying yes to some activities he had promised himself he would say no to, but no man was perfect, after all. There were temptations no one could be expected to resist, and Marlee made sure he knew that.

He did penance for his weakness by pulling out all the stops in his courtship of Marlee. He made sure every single thing about them falling more and more in love was worthy of the fairy-tale ending.

Now, Matteo had never been so nervous in his life. Marlee didn't even know he was back in Seattle. In what he considered a proper culmination to their romance, he was meeting Marlee's father for lunch. He wished he could be meeting him with a clearer conscience.

And if the meeting with her father went well, he

already had a ring, purchased from the best jeweler in Switzerland.

"Mr. Copeland—"

"What? Jimmy."

"Uh…okay, Jim. As you might have noticed, Marlee and I have been spending quite a bit of time together. It's become quite serious. I mean, I've been honorable. Tried to be honorable… What should I order?" he asked, panicking and switching tack.

Mr. Copeland—Jimmy—was looking at him, clearly baffled. "We're in Seattle," he said, as if Matteo needed reminding, and maybe he did. "Seafood is always a good bet."

Matteo stared at the menu. Seafood. Where was he? Speaking of "fish," he wanted to fish in his pocket and have a quick glance at his talking points.

Treated her with honor.

Wooed her.

Old-fashioned respect.

Well, for the most part.

"Spit it out, man," Marlee's father said, not unkindly.

"I love your daughter. I can't even think straight for it anymore. I want your permission to marry her."

Jim Copeland was smiling broadly at him. "It's about time, son. Of course you have my permission. But who asks the dad's permission in this day and age, anyway?"

Matteo could tell he was pleased despite his protest.

And this old-fashioned request felt as if it confirmed

what he had been working toward all this time: to be worthy of being not just Marlee's lover—for where was the worth in that?—but worthy of being her husband.

It was pouring rain—did it do anything else here?—an hour later when Matteo knocked on her apartment door.

The look on her face when she opened it said it all.

Surprise became delight.

Delight melted into heat.

She threw herself into his arms.

And he could not wait one minute longer. He slipped the box from his pocket and held it out to her.

"A cigar box?" she asked, puzzled.

"Open it."

She did. Still puzzled, she reached for the cigar. And then she saw what encircled it. The ring flashed bright against the brown paper of the cigar.

"Yes!" she squealed.

"I haven't asked you yet. Stop it. I'm getting down on one knee and—"

"You stop it! Yes, you have asked me. You've asked me a million different ways on a hundred different days."

"Marlee!"

"Okay, okay," she said. She was quivering with excitement.

He sank to one knee and gazed up at her.

"I love you madly," he said. "I cannot picture a life without you in it. You have made me a better man.

Braver than I ever imagined I could be. Wide-open to the adventure of life in a way I never was before. I want you to marry me. I want you to be my wife. I want to walk all the rest of my days with you at my side. I cannot imagine a life without you in it."

She reached for his hand. She drew him to his feet. She handed him back the cigar, and he took the ring from it and slid it onto her finger.

She didn't even glance at it. She really didn't care if it was a million-dollar ring from the best jeweler in Switzerland, or if it was a dime-store ring from the corner confectionery by her apartment.

"Yes," she whispered.

The cigar fell to the floor between them.

EPILOGUE

MATTEO SAT ON the beach alone, his arms wrapped around his knees, his feet dug deep into the sand. He was waiting for the sun to come up, and it was one of the rarest of moments on Coconut Cay. Except for the gentle lap of the waves, it was absolutely quiet.

The beach was not yet transformed. In a few hours, the arbor would be going up, the gardenias woven through it. A piano would be brought down, along with a registry table. There would be chairs—one hundred and fifty of them, at last count—set up on the sand, facing the arbor and the sea.

Matteo sighed.

This was *not* what he and Marlee had planned.

No, they had planned to celebrate their meeting on Coconut Cay with a quiet exchange of vows. They had wanted to ride donkeys down to the private pink sand beach Mackay had shown them over a year ago. They had wanted to say "I do" as a tropical sun set and gilded the entire island in gold.

Then, they had thought they would have one reception in Zurich for his family and friends, and one in Seattle for hers.

The problems had really started when his sisters had caught wind of the plan.

They had been appalled.

Because they thought his and Marlee's wedding plans separated them into two families.

"We're one family now," Emma had informed him sternly.

Never mind the logistics of several thousand miles and an ocean between them. Never mind the logistics of figuring out which of the great-aunts and old friends and second cousins and work colleagues could be asked to make this incredible journey.

Meanwhile, Fiona, high off the success of her own wedding, had started a wedding planning business. Before Matteo and Marlee quite knew what had happened, they were being swept up in Fiona's plans for them.

Fiona was not even slightly slowed down by that adorable baby she now had on her hip most of the time.

Matteo had never considered himself a "baby" guy. In the past, he had found the charm others found in the little creatures quite baffling. When his nieces and nephews had been babies, he had found them to be shockingly boneless little bundles filled with puke and poo. He would do the obligatory uncle-holds-the-baby-and-gets-rid-of-it-as-soon-as-possible.

But that little girl of Fiona's absolutely melted him. She had a smile Matteo was convinced she reserved only for him. He even held her sometimes and was always taken aback by the deep longing he felt when that baby nestled into him.

For the love he shared with Marlee to be made manifest in a child. A little girl or a little boy that he would call Calamity when he teased and chased him or her around wildflower-strewn meadows in the Alps.

Matteo would have thought Marlee would have wanted more say in her own wedding plans, but she laughed at the very suggestion.

"I planned a wedding once," she reminded him. "Devoted myself to it. Every little detail *mattered*. And yet somehow, I was missing what mattered most of all."

How grateful he was that that event had never happened, a reminder to both him and Marlee of silver linings in the clouds of life.

"Planning a wedding was nerve-racking," Marlee continued. "Not to mention time-consuming. Truly? I'm nothing but relieved to have someone else looking after all those endless and pesky details. It leaves me more time to, well, you know."

He did know.

She grinned that wicked outlaw grin that she reserved just for him.

And so now, really, their wedding was completely out of control. The budget was shot, the guest list was bloated, the whole island was bursting at the seams, and the logistics of bringing everything together in just a few hours was mind-blowing.

His wedding, Matteo mused, had a bit of a three-ring-circus feel to it.

Tomorrow, post-wedding, Fiona's mother, once so terrified of flying she had taken a miss on her daughter's own wedding, was going to celebrate one year of sobriety by organizing a skydiving excursion involving a frighteningly decrepit Coconut Cay airplane.

Naturally, the bride, not being the least sensitive of Matteo's fear of the death of the woman he had chosen to be his life partner, had been first to sign up!

Fiona had egged Marlee on, even suggesting she wear her dress. Ever since Fiona had been nominated for that bride photo of the year for that picture of her feeding her bouquet to Henri, she looked for photo opportunities everywhere.

It seemed to always be in the back of her mind as she organized flower girls and a ring bearer, caterers, florists, donkeys, musicians, special arrangements for Great-Aunt Hetta.

Matteo's wedding: the three-ring circus.

As he thought about it, the birds began to wake. They acted as if it was their job to sing the sun out of the sea, and the quiet air was soon split with a cacophony of sound as each bird tried to outdo the other in welcoming the new day.

Really, Matteo reflected, wasn't this exactly what he'd been missing since his mother died? Family was a three-ring circus: joyous, loud, colorful, a million different things unfolding at all times.

Then, a feather, pure and white—maybe a gift from one of those birds—drifted out of the sky and touched his cheek, feeling for all the world like the gentlest of kisses.

He took the feather and held it. For one stunning, beautiful moment, Matteo knew his mother was with him, and had always been with him, guiding him to this day.

To saying yes to love.

To realizing it was the one thing worth risking everything for.

He knew, of course, that he and Marlee were not promised a life without challenges. Hardships. Losses.

Just as he knew this was the message from his mother: that it was the power of love that sustained the human spirit, even through unfathomable sorrow.

In the face of it all, love was the only real power.

That sense was confirmed a few hours later, as he was standing under the arbor. He was wearing a simple white linen shirt and dark slacks, and he was barefoot. Mike was at his side. Waiting.

They came first: family, his giggling nieces tossing flower petals, his nephews solemnly leading Henri and Calamity. The donkeys had bright pink hooves and each carried a ring on the matching pink pillow on their backs.

His nephews, Matteo noticed with enjoyment, had

looks of pure terror on their faces, not from the donkeys or from the responsibility they'd been entrusted with, but undoubtedly from the fear of incurring Fiona's wrath if they blew this.

And here came Fiona, now in a hideous dress that she and Marlee had shrieked with laughter over as they chose it.

"My mother isn't the only one who knows how to make amends," Fiona had declared, admiring herself and twirling in the fluffy dress in the glorious shades of a three-day-old bruise.

And then, Matteo's whole world stopped as Marlee appeared.

Her mother was on one side of her and her father on the other, not so much giving their daughter to him as joining them all together in that ancient circle of love that was family.

He was only peripherally aware of her parents.

All he could see was her.

Marlee.

She was not wearing a wedding gown. She had put her foot down with Fiona over that.

"In the heat?" she had said. "Forget it."

And he was so glad she had *forgotten* it. She came toward him in a white sheath that was exactly like her. Simple, unpretentious, natural. The dress sang of the summer that Marlee carried within her, even on the rainiest of days.

The most unnatural thing about her would be her toenails, which he had snuck into her room last night to painstakingly paint bright pink, to match Henri's and Calamity's. She had something Henri didn't have, though. There was an octopus on the fourth toe of each of her feet.

Marlee's smile put the sun to shame.

The look in her eyes as she gazed at him filled him to the top.

In Marlee's unfaltering stride, he could see everything that she had become, loving and being loved, unveiling her innate beauty layer by gorgeous layer.

And he could see his whole future walking toward him.

And it was brilliant.

★★★★★

Keep reading for an excerpt of
McKettrick's Choice
by Linda Lael Miller.
Find it in the
The McKettricks: Past & Present anthology,
out now!

CHAPTER ONE

Arizona Territory, August 12, 1888

HOLT MCKETTRICK HOOKED a finger under his fancy collar in a vain effort to loosen it a little. Wedding guests milled on the wide, grassy stretch of ground alongside the Triple M ranch house, their finery dappled by shivering patches of shade from the young oaks thriving there. Two fiddlers played a mournful rendition of "Lorena," and there was a whole hog roasting in the pit Holt's three half brothers had dug in the ground and lined with flat rocks from the creek. The wedding cake, baked by Holt's sisters-in-law, was the size of a buckboard, and a long table—an improvised arrangement of planks supported by half a dozen fifty-gallon barrels—wobbled under the weight of a week's worth of fancy grub.

The old man and the rest of the McKettrick outfit had spared no effort or expense to make the gathering memorable. Holt reckoned he might have enjoyed it as much as the next fellow—if he hadn't been the bridegroom.

A hand struck his back in jovial greeting, and Holt nearly spilled his cup of fruit punch, generously laced with whiskey from his brother Rafe's flask, down the front of his dandy suit.

"I reckon that's the preacher, yonder," said Holt's father, Angus McKettrick, nodding toward an approaching rider splashing across the sun-dazzled creek, driving his horse hard. "'Bout time he showed up. I was beginning to think we'd have to send somebody out to the mission to fetch that crippled-up padre."

Holt swallowed, squinted. Heat prickled the back of his neck. Something stirred in him, a sweet, aching feeling like he got on hot summer nights, when a high-country breeze curled around his brain like a voice calling him back to Texas.

"I reckon," he muttered. Holt wondered where Rafe had gotten to with that flask, though he didn't look away from the rider to search the crowd.

The newcomer, his features hidden in the glare of midafternoon light, spurred his horse up the creek bank on the near side, man and mount flinging off diamonds of water as they came.

"Margaret is a fine woman," Angus said. He had a way of cutting a statement loose without laying any groundwork first.

"Who?" Holt asked, distracted. The skin between his shoulder blades itched, and his chest felt wet beneath the starched cotton of his shirtfront.

"Your bride," Angus answered, with a note of exasperation. Out of the corner of his eye, Holt saw his father tug at the knot in his string tie. Like as not, his wife, Concepcion, had cinched it tight as a corset ribbon.

The rider gained the edge of the yard and dismounted with the hasty grace of a seasoned cowpuncher, leaving the reins to dangle. He came straight for Holt.

"That ain't the preacher," Angus remarked unnecessarily, and with concern. Though he had almost no formal education, the old man read till his eyes gave out, and when he let his grammar slip, it meant he was agitated.

Holt glanced toward the house, where Miss Margaret Tarquin, his bride-to-be, was shut away in an upstairs bedroom getting herself gussied up for the wedding, then went to meet the messenger. The fiddle-playing ground to a shrill halt, and a silence settled over the crowd. Even the kids and the dogs were quiet.

"I'm lookin' for Holt Cavanagh," the newly arrived young man announced. His denim trousers were wet with creek water, and he shivered, despite the shimmering heat of that August afternoon. "You'd be him, I reckon?"

Holt nodded in brusque acknowledgment. It didn't occur to him to explain that he'd set aside the name Cavanagh, once he and the old man had made their blustery peace, and went by McKettrick these days.

Angus stuck close, bristly brows lowered, and Rafe, Kade and Jeb, elusive until then, seemed to materialize out of the rippling mirages haunting the grounds like ghosts. Holt and his brothers had had their differences in the three years they'd been acquainted—still did—but blood was blood. If the rider brought good news, they'd celebrate. If it was bad, they'd do what they could to help. And if there was trouble in the offing, they'd wade right into the fray and ask for the particulars later.

Holt's affection for them, though sometimes grudging, was in his marrow.

The visitor handed over a slip of paper. "Frank Corrales told me to give you this. He sent you a telegram, and when you didn't answer, he figured it didn't go through and told me to hit the trail. I carried that there letter all the way from Texas."

A shock of alarm surged through Holt, like venom from an invisible snake. He hesitated slightly, then snatched the soggy sheet of brown paper and unfolded it with a snap of his wrist. He felt his father and brothers move a stride closer.

He took in the words in a glance, absorbed the implications, and read them again to make sure he had the right of the situation.

JOHN CAVANAGH ABOUT TO BE
DRIVEN OFF HIS LAND.
GABE TO HANG FOR A HORSE THIEF
AND A MURDERER ON THE
FIRST OF OCTOBER. COME QUICK.
FRANK CORRALES

Holt was still digesting the news when a feminine voice jarred him out of his stupor, and a slender hand came to rest on his coat sleeve. "Holt? Is something wrong?"

Holt started slightly, turned his head to look down into the upturned face of his bride-to-be, resplendent in her lacy finery and gossamer veil. She was a pretty woman, with fair hair and expressive blue eyes, a sent-for wife, imported all the way from Boston. Holt never looked at her without a stab of guilt; Margaret deserved a man who loved her, not one who wanted a mother for his young daughter, a bed companion for himself and not much else.

"I've got to go back to Texas," he said. The words had been shambling along the far borders of his mind for a long while, but this was the first time he'd let them come to the fore, let alone find their way out of his mouth.

Angus cleared his throat, and the whole party started up again, like it was some sort of signal. Reluctantly, Rafe, Kade and Jeb moved off, and Angus handed the rider a five-dollar gold piece, then steered him toward the food table.

One of the ranch hands took care of the exhausted horse.

Margaret's smile faltered a little as she gazed up at Holt, waiting.

"Maybe when I get back…" he began awkwardly, but then his voice just fell away.

She sighed, shook her head. "I don't believe I want to wait, Holt," she said. "If that's what you're asking me to do, I mean."

He touched her face, let his hand fall back to his side. "I'm sorry," he rasped, and he was, truly, though he doubted it would count for much in the grand scheme of things. At his brothers' urging, he'd brought this woman out from the east, and now here she was, all got up in a bridal gown, with half the territory in attendance, and there wasn't going to be a wedding.

"I'll go ahead and marry you anyhow," he said, against his every instinct, because he was Angus McKettrick's son and a deal was a deal. But he couldn't make himself sound like that was what he wanted, and Margaret was no fool. "I've still got to leave, though, either way."

A tear shimmered on her cheek, but Margaret held her chin high, shook her head again. "No," she said, with sad pride. "If you really wanted me for a wife, you'd have gone ahead with the ceremony, put a ring on my finger so everybody would know I was taken, maybe even asked me to come along."

"It'll be a hard trip," Holt said. From a verbal standpoint, he felt like a lame cow, turning in fruitless circles, trying to find its way out of a narrow place in the trail. Nonetheless, he kept right on struggling. "Hard things to attend to, too, once I get there."

She worked up another smile. "Godspeed, Holt McKettrick," she said. Then, to his profound chagrin, she turned to face the gathering.

All attempts at merriment ceased, and a hush fell.

"There will be no wedding today," Margaret announced, in a clear voice, while everyone stared back at her in bleak sympathy. Her spine, Holt noted, with admiration, was straight as a new fence post. "But there *will* be a party. I'm going upstairs right now and change out of this silly dress, and when I come back down again, I expect to find every last one of you making merry."

With that, Margaret started for the house. Holt's sisters-in-law, Emmeline, Mandy and Chloe, all flung poisonous glances in his direction and hurried after his retreating almost-bride.

Only Lizzie, Holt's twelve-year-old daughter, had the temerity to approach him, and her cheeks glowed pink with indignation.

"Papa," she demanded, coming to a stop directly in front of him, "how *could* you?"

Holt loved his child, though he hadn't known she'd existed until last year, and except for Margaret herself, Lizzie was the hardest person in the crowd to face just then. "I've got business in Texas," he said, because that was the stark truth and he had nothing else to offer. "It can't wait."

Lizzie stiffened, blinked her large hazel eyes, and bit her lower lip. "You're leaving?"

He reached out to lay a hand on her shoulder, but she shrank from him.

"Lizzie," he whispered.

She turned on her heel, fled to her grandfather. Angus put an arm around the child and glowered at Holt. The old man looked like Zeus himself, shooting thunderbolts from his eyes.

"Hell," Holt muttered, and started for the barn.

His brothers fell in beside him, their faces hard. Holt lengthened his stride, but they stuck to his heels like barn muck. Stubborn cusses, cut from the same itchy cloth as their pa, every one of them.

"What the hell is going on here?" Rafe snarled. The firstborn of Angus's three younger sons, Rafe was a bull of a man, and always the first to demand an accounting. He and Kade and Jeb formed a semicircle in front of Holt, barring his way into the barn, where his horse was stabled, blissfully unaware of the long, arduous ride ahead.

Holt might have shoved his way through, if he hadn't figured that would lead to a fight. He wasn't afraid of tangling, but a brawl would mean a delay, and the need to get where he was going made an urgent clench in the pit of his belly.

He pulled out the crumpled letter, thrust into his vest pocket earlier, and shoved it at Kade, who happened to be the one standing directly in front of him. "See for yourself," he said.

Kade scanned the page, while Jeb and Rafe peered at it from either side.

"I'll saddle your horse," Kade said, handing it back. He was the middle brother, the thoughtful, practical one. "Best pack yourself some of that wedding grub, too, for the trail."

"Have a word with Lizzie before you go, Holt," Rafe interjected. "She doesn't look like she's taking this real well."

"I could ride along," Jeb put in, with typical eagerness. The youngest of the brood, he was also the fastest gun, and hands-down the best rider. Jeb was handy to have around in a tight place, for those reasons and a few others, but the plain and simple truth was that Holt didn't want to have to look out for him. He wasn't fool enough to say so, though.

He might have grinned, if he hadn't just humiliated a fine woman and learned that two of the best friends he'd ever had were in trouble. Jeb had a wife to look after, and a baby daughter, barely walking. Rafe and Kade were in the same situation, since all three of their brides had managed to come a-crop with babies a year ago last Independence Day.

"This is my fight," Holt said. "I'll handle it."

Rafe looked thoughtful. "John Cavanagh. That's the man who raised you, isn't it?"

Holt nodded, though Rafe's assessment didn't begin to cover what Cavanagh meant to him. "He's got a spread outside San Antonio."

"And this Gabe yahoo…?" Jeb fished. "Who's he?"

"We were Rangers together," Holt explained. Gabe Navarro was a wild man—part Comanche, part Mexican, part devil—but he was neither a murderer nor a horse thief. Holt had known him too long and too well ever to believe either accusation.

Apparently satisfied, Kade headed into the barn to get Holt's horse, Traveler, ready.

Rafe and Jeb went to the feast table and commenced gathering food for the journey. Holt looked for Lizzie and found her still in Angus's arms, her head resting against the old man's broad shoulder.

"Here, now," Angus murmured, giving his eldest son an unfriendly but resigned glance as Holt approached. "You talk to your papa, Lizzie-beth. It's no good parting without saying what needs to be said."

Lizzie sniffled, raised her head, and met Holt's gaze.

Angus squeezed her upper arm, then favoring Holt with a withering glare, he walked away.

"Are you coming back?" Lizzie wanted to know.

"Yes," Holt said, with certainty. He wasn't through with Texas—he'd left too many things undone there—but in the deepest part of his heart, he knew the Arizona Territory and the Triple M were home. He belonged on this stretch of red, rocky dirt, with his impossible father, his rowdy brothers and his spirited daughter.

She dashed at her face with the back of one hand. "You promise?"

"You have my word."

"What if you *can't* come home? What if somebody shoots you?"

"I *will* come back, Lizzie."

"I guess I have to believe you."

He chuckled, extended an arm. Lizzie hesitated, then curled against his chest, clinging a little. "You be a good girl," he said, resting his chin on top of her dark head, wishing he didn't have to leave her behind. "Mind Concepcion and your grandfather."

She trembled, tugged a cherished blue ribbon from her hair and tucked it into Holt's vest pocket. "A remembrance," she said softly, and Holt's heart ached. Before he could find words to assure his daughter that forgetting her would be impossible, she went on, "Are you going to visit Mama's grave? She's buried in San Antonio, in the cemetery behind Saint Ambrose's."

He nodded, still choked up. Lizzie's mother, Olivia, was part of the unfinished business waiting for him in Texas. He needed to say a proper goodbye to her, put her to rest in his mind and his heart, even though it was too late for her to hear the words.

"Will you take her flowers—the best you can find—for me?"

Holt's throat still wouldn't open. He nodded again.

Lizzie stared into his face, looking, perhaps, for the half-truths people tell to children, or even a bold-faced lie. Finding only truth, she straightened her shoulders and hoisted her chin.

"All right, then," she said. "I guess you'd better ride while there's still enough daylight to see the trail."

He smiled, cupped her chin in one hand. "Don't eat too much cake," he said.

Her eyes glistened with tears. "Don't get yourself shot," she countered.

And that was their farewell.

Lizzie was a woman-child, with the run of one of the biggest ranches in the Arizona Territory. She could already ride like a pony soldier, and Kade's wife, Mandy, a sharpshooter, had taught her niece to handle a shotgun as well as a side arm. Lizzie had lost her mother to a fever and seen her aunt murdered in cold blood alongside a stagecoach. She knew only too well that life was fragile, the world was a dangerous place and that some partings were permanent.

This one wouldn't be, Holt promised himself as he rode out, Lizzie's ribbon in his pocket.